SIDURI

SIDURI

J J VASON

T

Troubador Publishing Ltd
Unit E2 Airfield Business Park,
Harrison Road, Market Harborough,
Leicestershire. LE16 7UL
Tel: 0116 2792299
Email: books@troubador.co.uk
Web: www.troubador.co.uk

ISBN 978 1805143 727

British Library Cataloguing in Publication Data.
A catalogue record for this book is available from the British Library.

Printed and bound by CPI Group (UK) Ltd, Croydon, CR0 4YY
Typeset in 11pt Minion Pro by Troubador Publishing Ltd, Leicester, UK

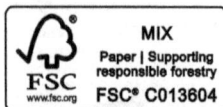

To Pollyanna, my K and the girl that never was. Without you, Siduri would still be waiting for that train.

Chapter One

The Path Less Travelled

On a bleached and crumbling wooden bench, I sat alone. Marhasyow station was past its prime. The ticket office walls were cracked and chipped, with mortar so loose in places that several bricks had fallen. The posts supporting a white picket fence were rotten, and only the wrought-iron gate that separated the fence from the building kept it vertical. No doubt the gate's countless layers of paint would let it see out the sun.

The chilly ocean breeze tugged at my skirt. Whatever happened to summer? I wondered. Once, I'd thought it would never end. At its start, I met a boy and, on a hot and sweaty night, fell in love.

A season can be so very long if there is a dying in it, even if that death is just your heart.

If this is now autumn, then it too will be lengthy. While summer stole my heart, autumn took everything else. Iresh, my mother, died three days ago.

It is Wednesday. It is 8am, and I will leave.

It took an age to find Iresh's suitcase. Despite knowing

its likely location, I'd first tried everywhere else. In the end, though, I found it where I always knew it would be.

Under her bed.

The case was empty except for an ornate wooden box. Inside the box was a letter that was sealed and old and certainly not intended for me. I might have torn it open anyway if I hadn't seen the piece of parchment below. In the middle of the parchment were the words:

So, if there is an end, what is the loss? To those who see, he was a failed possibility. To the rest that cannot, he was only a dream.

The words seemed to be a fragment of something longer.

I looked at the name on the letter. Unlike the parchment, the typeface was neat, clear, and meticulously capitalised. I honestly believed Iresh put money in a swear box every time she used cursive.

EANNA AGADE.

My aunt.

I don't remember Eanna. She'd left soon after I was born. What I do know, however, was that whenever I failed to meet some arbitrary expectation, Iresh would, at length, scold me with some parable involving my aunt. I had my doubts that Eanna had ever been that wild, but what was certain was that she had left and was never heard from again.

Or so I thought.

The strange thing was that Iresh had addressed the letter to a house in Sulis. Sulis was famously conservative, famously funless, and famously filled with the old. It seemed odd that a young Eanna had made that place her home.

I decided to deliver the letter. In Marhasyow, I had no

income, no prospects, and in a town filled with empty houses, a dilapidated home no one would buy. I was already leaving, but until I saw the letter, I had nowhere to go. While that antique scrap of paper was a poor excuse, surely my aunt would welcome the visit?

She might even let me stay.

If Eanna did, then she might also be willing to tell me the things Iresh would not. Little things. Things like how Iresh met my father or why he left before I was born.

She might even know where I might find him now.

I folded the parchment and put it and the letter into my jacket pocket. As I did so, I glanced again into the box and saw one more thing – a small metal key. I'd never seen it before, but I knew that key. It opened the door in a dream that I'd had since childhood.

A dream that turned out not to be a dream.

I could say what I did after finding the key was an act of instinct, but that would make it worse. Instinct is what you are. It defines you. If you instinctively do something wrong, you are a bad person in a way that brooks no argument – especially from yourself.

I am a bad person, but I am one that wants to forget. It's a kind of forgiveness if you can forget.

⤳

I grimaced as the breeze picked up. My favourite skirt had been a terrible choice for the day. For the sake of modesty, I pushed the thin material further between my knees. Despite the station being deserted, I could feel eyes watching me from behind.

And... it would seem... from in front.

Over the railroad tracks, beyond a line of maple trees, someone walked towards me. A woman? It was too far to see their face. I watched them for a while. A woman, yes. Men move so clumsily, this woman flowed.

A puff of smoke rose from the rail tracks to my left. In response, the woman broke into a run.

She glided through the trees as a leopard might while hunting its prey. As she drew closer, I realised she was darker than I thought. Perhaps a panther, then. One of the deepest black.

Suddenly, a loud *thud* behind me made me jump and turn. While the gate lay flat on the ground, the picket fence remained defiantly vertical. Bemused, I shook my head in disbelief before glancing at the ticket office wall beyond.

The poster had been plastered to that brickwork for years. Indeed, there were similar posters all around Marhasyow. The face was pleasant enough, but I never liked the eyes. They consumed my very soul.

The reward underneath the name on the posters hadn't changed and wouldn't. After all this time, there was little point.

I turned back. The woman had vanished. I couldn't see her on the platform or the track, and she certainly wouldn't stop to hide behind a tree – not when there was a train to catch.

And miss, it would appear.

There are racehorses and warhorses. I've heard of proud stallions challenging the range and Arabians that punch through hot desert sands. In comparison, the train that approached was a donkey, and a whiny one at that, as it squealed to a halt.

I gathered myself and stood, wincing at the welts on my thighs. Never sit too long on a slatted seat, or at least not in a short skirt.

Beside me lay Iresh's suitcase. If the letter failed to gain sympathy, then Eanna might take pity at the sight of this impractical curio of baggage. It looked old enough to be remembered fondly – or at least remembered.

I lifted the heavy case onto the rear coach and followed, slamming the door behind me. Almost as it clicked shut, the train lurched forward. Sliding open the internal glass door, I stepped into the carriage proper. Ahead of me lay a relative mass of humanity. After pushing the case into the luggage rack, I looked for a seat. The only one free was at the far end.

When I got there, I found a handbag placed possessively in its middle. It was an expensive bag, all pink and leather and frosted with yellow flowers. A bag owned by someone confident in their fashion sense – and their right to occupy more than was theirs. I looked expectantly at the owner: mid-forties, plump but pretty, with straight auburn hair washing down a rosy-cheeked face. My eyes drifted lower. Beneath a salmon-pink jacket, she wore salmon-pink slacks.

'Excuse me,' I muttered. I admired her hair. I even liked the jacket.

The slacks? Not so much.

Plump-Face's hand shot out, grabbed the handbag, and thrust it to her feet.

Slacks are the domain of mothers and the old – and I would never be that old.

'Thank you,' I said before sitting down.

Or anything like Iresh.

When I set out for Sulis, I'd kept my expectations of those I might encounter on the way pretty low. As I looked around, few came close to challenging them.

To my left was the plump-faced woman. In virtually every

other seat in view sat the "family". Across the aisle but facing me were two women who looked and spoke like sisters – surely only the familiar can make such a racket. Opposite them in the aisle seat sat a bewildered old man trying to stay relevant to the pink-clothed infant squirming in his lap. Judging by the stern glances from one of the two women opposite, the old man had already failed.

Sitting opposite me were a younger man and an older boy. The younger man, whom I assumed to be the boy's father, gazed at the view. The boy stared fretfully across at the sister by the window. With snotty tears running down his face, it seemed some apron strings remained to be cut.

When Eanna left, she'd likely sat among a similar group. Yet this family was surely different from any she might have encountered. Here, the women wore scarves on their heads to hide their nakedness.

I did not.

Here, the mothers clucked words of faith.

I most certainly did not.

Completing the table with the old man and the two women was an exotic. As I label them, an exotic is someone of a different race, colour or even dress sense that is so unusual there's a need to stare. It wasn't prejudice, or not consciously so, but there's always that constant itch to look longer than allowed by etiquette. This exotic was female with skin the colour of jet. Her age was on the younger side of indeterminate. Her head, also uncovered, had hair so short she seemed almost bald. With a face that was a template of symmetry, she looked quite beautiful. The cynic in me made me look again. No, I concluded, she wasn't perfect after all. Her legs were too long, at least for the cramped seating. Now, when I looked, I could only think of a grasshopper unable to spring.

Plump-Face tapped my left elbow.

'That was Marhasyow?' she asked.

I turned and nodded, already knowing the next question.

'*The* Marhasyow? It still has a station?'

Or perhaps not. 'Well… yes.'

'But… after the storm?'

I gave her my best blank stare. 'Which one? Marhasyow is a coastal town. It has a lot of storms.'

'Er… the one eighteen years ago?'

'Ah,' I said, nodding sagely.

'So, it was just the harbour then… and the governor's castle… do you know what happened to him?'

And there it was.

'No,' I said icily. Transforming a port into kindling deserves more than a "just". However, all anyone not local seemed interested in was Stephen Izdubar. Stephen Izdubar, the unloved but ironically not unmissed Governor of Marhasyow.

The one thing known was that the governor hadn't drowned. That night, a farmer saw Izdubar on a wagon heading inland. It was only the next day the townsfolk wondered what else might be in the wagon.

The gold missing from the Treasury, for example.

Plump-Face saw the scowl on my face. Giving up, she shook her head, rummaged around in her bag, and pulled out a trashy gossip rag. There may or may not have been a subvocalised "cow" somewhere in that sequence.

Tough.

Anyway, I could hardly tell her that Izdubar, a man whose wanted poster still adorned many a wall, was my father. It's just not the sort of thing you share, at least with a stranger, particularly when you've only recently found out yourself.

While the scale of Izdubar's theft may have thrilled Plump-Face, those who survived the storm were far less happy. Many were destitute. Some, like Eanna, abandoned Marhasyow altogether. There were others, though, that arrived. That stayed. Cloaked in black, they wore their religion on their robes and in their eyes. These "Fedhyow" brought manna to the needy.

And their dogma.

I glanced at the mother in the aisle seat – a Fedhyow wannabe who'd obviously been listening.

'Whore!' she hissed, staring at my naked head.

The Fedhyow also had a thing about hair.

Of course, Plump-Face and the exotic also exposed their heads, but they were at least ignorant. A girl from Marhasyow should appreciate the need for modesty. To the aisle mother, calling me "whore" was only appropriate.

I'd got used to it.

Outside the window, the scenery had changed, with the houses and fields replaced by yellow-flowered gorse and purple heather. Even in summer, the peat bogs of Marhasyow remained cold and wet. Their contents, and I testify from experience, are a pain to dig out of your toenails. While I never covered my head, I always wore boots.

Except when sitting down.

Slipping my hands below the table, I undid the laces and slid my boots off. To my surprise, the stench of something rank overwhelmed my nose. Surely not? I'd only washed my feet that morning. The putrid taint made my throat cramp as I fought the urge to cough. Embarrassed, I turned towards the aisle to discharge my croup.

I failed. The hack literally stuck in my throat.

The exotic was staring at me. Caught, she didn't look away. Instead, she watched and waited, her deep-brown eyes sprinkled with flecks of bright orange.

My panther was on the train.

I coughed, no longer able to hold it back.

The exotic let her eyes drift away. Before even a quarter turn, though, she stopped abruptly and blinked. The exotic seemed undecided – but then she chose. The exotic gazed hard at the child.

Although I was no longer the victim, her stare was still unsettling. It appeared the pink-clothed infant agreed, since it flushed. Soured by the heat of the exotic's glare and, I dumbly realised, the acrid damp patch growing underneath, the child screamed.

The aisle mother turned away from her sister, looked across, and caught the exotic staring at her child in a way akin to hunger.

I coughed once more. The frog refused to leap.

The aisle mother's expression changed quickly from one of mild concern to that of total hate. Unsettled, I decided what was in my throat was only a tadpole. I swallowed hard and lowered my head, desperate to avoid being noticed.

I heard the aisle mother stir. Indeed, I think she growled. I glanced back. The woman, now standing, ripped the pink-clothed infant from the old man's arms and shuffled off down the corridor. The window mother seemed more confused than concerned at what had happened. Staring blankly at the exotic, she edged out of the seat and trailed her sister down the corridor.

The exotic sighed, slumped back, and puffed.

I looked away and out of the nearby window, the intrigue hopefully over. What had once been a flat blue sky had broken into smaller segments, each separated by white cirrus clouds. Even while I watched, the sky grew milkier.

'Miss?' the snot-faced boy squeaked.

Oh, for… what now!

I turned my head and faked a smile. 'Yes?'

'Miss? Why is your hair blue?'

The boy's father was staring out the window. Had he noticed I was there? Had he heard his son's question? I had my doubts.

I looked into the boy's eyes. The reflection revealed a girl with black hair almost touching her shoulders. A girl with a flick of colour above her left ear. It was likely this use of colour the aisle mother despised the most.

'It's not blue,' I said. 'It's ultramarine, and it's only a tuft.' I fingered the thing that hung around my neck. A thing also blue, a thing so recently found.

'Miss? What is ulta – ultramarine?'

My smile fell into a frown. 'Ultramarine is a blue pigment occurring in nature as a proximate component of lapis lazuli. Basically, it's ground-up stone made into a dye.' Boys of this age were the bane of all existence.

Well, my existence.

'Da?' the snot-faced boy said. The man shushed him without turning his head.

I returned to the window.

In the short time that had passed, the sky had turned muddy green. The train fell silent as the carriage lights clicked on. Everyone, even Plump-Face, gazed at the scene beyond. The only sound heard was that of the wheels on the track.

Clickity-click.

Unexpectedly, beads of sweat formed on my brow, throat and chest, causing my top to cling uncomfortably. My lower back, inner thighs and even the backs of my knees felt clammy. I looked at my table companions. Plump-Face's jacket was open, and her cleavage appeared almost ridiculously exposed. While the faces of the snot-faced boy and the younger man had turned bright pink, they continued to stare out of the window.

Clickity-click.

The sky grew darker. Aside from the walls of a railway cutting, nothing else was in sight.

Clickity-click.

The cutting disappeared as the train rounded a bend. Beyond the engine, I saw a bridge.

Clickity-click.

The squat bridges of Marhasyow snaked across eight miles of moorland, placed on patches of firm ground where they could set their feet. A blanket of fog stretched out from beneath this one, as far as my eyes could see. The mist, the colour of feculent milk, straddled the moor, obscuring the streams, rivers and stagnant pools beneath.

Clickity-click.

The train launched itself upon the riot of corroded metal, stone and pockmarked wood that made up our crossing.

Clickity-click.

I heard a gasp and looked across the aisle. The old man had fainted. The exotic? The exotic sat composed and returned my gaze, quite unconcerned about the health of the man she sat beside.

Pop!

The weight of humid air vanished in an instant. My ears

screamed at the release of pressure. The coach shuddered and lifted off the rails as a wave of wind and rain hit an exposed flank. Then... then, like drawing breath, the wind pulled back, and the coach regained its traction.

We ploughed on.

The younger man opposite must have bitten his tongue as we landed. Blood ran freely from the corner of his mouth. The snot-faced boy sobbed. Plump-Face sat... actually, she sat still; her face an unmoving mask of terror.

Just like mine.

I was frightened, literally petrified. My pupils pulsed in time with a heartbeat louder than anything beyond my ears. I couldn't hear. I could hardly see. Like Plump-Face, my eyes darted around, taking in everything and understanding almost none of it.

Lightning sparked across the sky. To thunderous applause, it danced a jig from cloud to cloud. I looked down beyond the bridge. The fog was gone. The water of the river below churned and thrashed, buffeted by the sudden squall.

Then lightning struck.

A shaft of incandescence transfixed our donkey, burning through its metal skin like a torch through gossamer. The engine shuddered, caught fire and plunged into the morass below.

And...

Blackness closed in like an apologetic shroud.

∽

When I awoke, my forehead was flat against the table, my stomach pivoting on its edge. My knees, now skinned, had saved me from a fall. Beneath my right eye, my cheekbone was cut. Strangely, though, the blood from the wound seeped upwards.

I turned my head, which hurt even more than expected, and stared at Plump-Face. Superficially, the poor woman's predicament was like mine. She must also have hit the table hard. Still dazed, we remained eye to eye for quite some time, or at least I hope we did. It should take that long before you realise the person you faced, that you were almost kissing, was actually dead.

My throat filled with bile. I screamed incoherently within – before repeating it aloud.

Loud wasn't any better. It came out as one shriek among many. It was also pointless. Swallowing the sick and drawing in a breath, I forced my heartbeat to slow a little. Rather than shout, I should be asking questions.

How to get out? was a question.

Actually, it was a good question and one I could answer.

The blood had flowed upwards. The carriage stood on its end. Being at the back of the train, it hadn't fallen into the river, or at least not entirely. I could go up.

Straining my back and pressing hard with my thighs against the table, I lifted myself into a position that would once have been upright. Placing both hands on its edge, I dragged my legs from underneath. I then twisted and grabbed the back of the seat with one hand and pulled both feet out from under the table. Setting my heels on its edge, I straightened and looked back. The younger man, still in his seat, sat stunned – and not just because of the full view I was giving him. The snot-faced boy, though, stared at the window glass – and the growing spider in its corner.

Drool ebbed out of Plump-Face's mouth and slid down the table towards the boy. The bile returned to my throat in sympathy.

With a crack, the window shattered, splintering out from the spider's legs. Dank water rushed in, flooding everything below my feet with debris churned up by the collision of the train engine and the riverbed. The snot-faced boy vanished, ripped from his seat by a spiteful tide.

The younger man reached out to catch the child. Instead, his wrist found glass, and a puff of vermillion bloomed in the floodwater. He fell back in disbelief, literally in shock. Horrified, I looked away and again across the aisle. While the old man hadn't moved, his jawbone now angled tenuously like a jigsaw piece out of place.

The exotic had vanished.

I tried to steel myself but couldn't resist one last glance at the younger man. His head hung back, his eyes stayed open, and his mouth sagged agape beneath a foot of stinking water.

The surge rose to caress my heels, then feet, then calves. Caress and firmly grip with cold. I looked up. Those that once were behind were now above and ahead. I tried to climb, but the others forced me back. There were too many. The dead and the stupefied blocked the aisle. Flailing corpses and the near departed filled the space between the headrests and the ceiling. I was going to die. I was going to drown.

A body fell past. As I looked through the new gap above, I saw the exotic nod and turn away.

It was the strangest thing.

The water reached my knees, shaking me out of my trance. Scrambling, I launched myself through the divide.

Others still writhed above me, all trying to escape. Trapped below and kicked in the chest, the arm, the face, the rising tide gained. By the time it grasped my hips, I'd lost sight of places above to find a grip. I fought for more height. If I didn't exactly hold others back, I still squirmed as a fish might among a captured shoal that sought to escape the closing net.

A few yards ahead, beyond the chaos of hands, of feet, of arms, of legs, of screaming mouths, and voluminous stomachs, hung the exit door. The water had reached my chest, but there was only a short distance to go now – only a few feet.

The train settled on the riverbed with a metallic yawn.

As the carriage shook, the window to my left shattered, and another torrent of water cascaded in. Like the fish I pretended to be, my lungs sucked in a draught of putrid liquid.

It tasted of peat.

I thrashed. I screamed. I think I drowned, or as near so as it made no difference.

I did not die.

Instead, a hand brushed mine.

At first, and to a blackening mind, its touch felt insubstantial. A passing through, perhaps. A blending. But then its borders firmed, and it strengthened, and it gripped.

The exotic drew me up to and beyond the internal door before closing it with her feet. It barely slowed the rising tide.

I looked around but saw no one else. I heard no sound except for the exotic's breath. When I peered down through the door glass, I saw nothing but black. Was anyone in there still alive? Was I willing to challenge the woman who had blocked their exit?

No.

I threw up.

'Better?' she asked. Her voice made me think of weathered brick.

I nodded.

The water oozed past the door seams, washing the discharge off my feet.

The exotic studied me. 'Do you have the amulet?'

Amulet?

'*Do you have the fucking amulet*?' she said again, but louder this time and with an added swear.

I stared back. Shivering and feeling sick again I… *Oh*. Reaching into my blouse, I scooped out Iresh's locket.

'Do you mean this?' I asked.

While the chain was gold, the locket itself was blue. Indeed, that was why I took it. Its colour almost matched my tuft. I took it and then forgot.

She nodded. 'Yeah, that. Pretty, don't you think? Now, let's go.'

The exotic pulled a thin, elongated V-shaped blade out from behind her back. She turned towards the outer door and cautiously pushed it open with her right palm while probing the growing space with her knife.

The door slammed closed, catching and shattering the blade.

'Cunt!' the exotic spat, dropping the knife. Balling her fingers into a fist, she lashed out at the window of the train door. To my surprise, the glass shattered, and I saw a woman's skirt and leg through the gap. The exotic stretched through the breach with a now bloody hand, grabbed a fistful of material and pulled.

It was only when I saw the woman's face as she fell that I realised it was the window mother. The poor creature seemed more confused than anything as she passed by the gap and down. She certainly didn't scream.

But neither did I.

I tried to tell myself it was the cold that had numbed my throat, but I knew better. It was fear of what the exotic might do next that had left me complicit.

The exotic looked down at her damaged hand and tutted before wrapping her palm with a strip of material. No blood leaked through. She smiled and tugged a long sliver of glass free from the window with her bandaged hand.

'A girl always needs a knife,' she said.

I stared back.

'We *really* need to go,' she added, before opening the door and slithering into the dark.

I looked down. The water was already above my ankles. Although terrified of the exotic, I had no choice but to follow.

Beyond the door was a stone pillar. Fixed to it was a ladder, and above it, yet another woman's foot – that quickly disappeared into the dark.

Again, I followed. Again, I climbed. This time, though, the water did not claim me and I managed on my own. I cleared the top in what felt like seconds.

There was no sign of the exotic.

I tried to stand and walk to safety but, from nowhere, a punch to my back sent me spiralling to the ground.

I landed on my front.

Almost instinctively, I reached around with my left hand and found something digging into my back. Grasping it, I pulled – and screamed. The pain made my vision double. But as quickly as it arrived, that same pain... just... went.

I stared in disbelief at the exotic's makeshift knife now in my hand. The upper half of the glass was speckled with dirt and flecks of blood from my fingers. The lower half was a darker red.

Understanding dawned.

Ahead, a woman shuffled, crouched against the storm. Her left arm held the pinkest of pink bundles against a shoulder. Would the aisle mother escape? I wondered. After all, the exotic no longer had her knife.

I realised soon it wouldn't matter that I cared.

My vision narrowed. My ears buzzed. To my almost acceptance, I sensed the blood pulsing from my back begin to slow.

I twisted with my remaining strength and rolled onto my back. To my surprise, the action didn't hurt. Indeed, I felt little of anything – except perhaps some anger at the black cloud now above me, obscuring the sky.

'Why?' I asked the cloud. I might have shouted the question, the accusation, but this time my lungs wouldn't comply. This time, my heart struggled to beat. This time, I failed even to vomit.

All I could manage were tears.

The cloud, my exotic, looked down. 'I'm sorry,' she said, before kneeling and retrieving the glass shard from my hand.

A gash ran from behind the exotic's left ear to her throat. Strangely, for so large and fresh a wound, it had already clotted. I looked into her eyes. Beyond the brown, and flecks of almost glowing orange, I saw only darkness.

The exotic tore open the thin cotton of my blouse.

Time slowed. I stared at my exposed skin and watched as the individual raindrops hit. They fractured and spread across the surface like ash.

The exotic ran a finger down the edge of the glass, gathered the diluted remains of blood onto its tip and dripped them onto my chest. Grasping Iresh's locket, she gently placed the glass beneath my breasts and traced the locket's shape in the blood. Removing the locket from my skin, the image that remained quickly watered.

'I have no choice,' she said.

The exotic drove the glass blade through the picture drawn, through the surface of my skin and through into my heart.

Lightning cracked one final time. It sounded like laughter.

And then it went quiet.

And then it went dark.

Chapter Two

Dust

I dreamt of a fire. I did! I dreamt of a large fireplace, its mantle dominating the room. Above it was a picture of a boy I did not know, gaudy ornaments and a clock. In this dream, I was a child. As a child, time passed slowly; the seconds seemed like minutes, the minutes like hours. I felt tortured in that room, sitting, waiting, watching that clock.

In this dream, as dusk settled on the day, I remember that an angel, who could never be my mother, unlocked the door and entered the room. I remember this mercy set light to the kindling and logs that lay dry in the hearth. She wiped away my tears and comforted me, as if recognising my punishment was excessive. Yet, once the fire was ablaze, this creature turned away. As the wilful sprite left the room, I remember hearing her mumble something before locking the door again behind her. It pains me to know the only words spoken were words I did not understand.

In this dream, I turned to stare into the fire. For hours, I watched as fireflies weaved and danced their magical patterns. I remember them blazing. I remember them shimmering. I *remember them glowing. In the end, however, as with all things, they gradually dimmed... and faded... and finally turned to dust.*

Then I found a key and knew it not to be a dream.

CHAPTER THREE

CHILDISH THINGS

The room was cold. Its floorboards were naked to the chill. Its fireplace was black as an open crypt. Walls that would be so white in the day luminesced blue in a night with no hint of cloud. The room was so very cold.

The rocking chair in which he sat creaked back and forth. As a measure, it was an impure timepiece but one that revealed his caution. When it stopped, and the man spoke, we both knew his words would never be unfelt.

I looked at the ice on the window glass. 'Is it still June?' I asked, confused. How long had I slept?

The man did not respond.

I exhaled, my breath flowing from my mouth like a harsh fog. 'Whatever happened to summer?' I asked more reasonably. The question felt familiar.

No response.

The shift I wore was flimsy, a silken thing, tinged cobalt by the flicker of the stars. Where were my clothes I wondered? The material was thin. It was so, so thin. Had all the warmth gone out of the world?

I pulled my knees into my chest. 'Why is it so cold?' I pleaded.

Nothing.

I looked at my feet. The blanket I sat on was an impostor. In the half-light, I concluded it was a cloak. I scrunched my toes – it felt ridged and seamed. Would it be warmer on top?

The rocking chair stopped. 'What do you remember?' he asked.

I was right. Like a shard of glass, some words can never be unfelt. I remembered… I remembered *everything*.

I reached around and touched my back. Nothing. I moved my hand to my chest. Nothing. There was no yawning wound that drained my very essence. There was no pain. Nothing. I felt nothing but a glacial, numbing cold. Its meaning took from me all hope. As lime cast into a grave, my grave if I had one, it devoured me. I was frightened. I knew, I knew, and I hated knowing.

The man exhaled heavily. The vaporous plume reminded me of the exhaust discharged from that wretched train. This room wasn't hell, not technically, but I still wondered whether his breath might smell of sulphur.

'What would you have done?' I asked.

'What?'

'If it had been you on the train rather than her?' I hated knowing, but I had to know.

He moved his chair closer. 'So, you do remember?'

Another plume. This time it touched my face – and smelt of nothing. In the light, I could see him better. Although he'd tied his hair back, it was clearly longer than mine. He might have been handsome if it wasn't for the awkward frown and random stubble.

The man hadn't disagreed. He knew my killer.

'Would I have died?'

He puffed again. 'Your death was not her intent.'

Nevertheless, it happened.

'What's her name?' It seemed only fair to know my killer's name.

'Lilith,' he said.

'Lilith? The bitch who stabbed me is called Lilith?'

'Yes.'

'*She stabbed me!*'

'She was trying to save you.'

'*She killed me!*'

'I know, and I am *truly* sorry.' His eyes met mine. 'Do you remember your name?'

I struggled to answer. 'Siduri… I think?'

He smiled. 'Names are capricious things. Some people change them as often as their mood. My name is Dumuz.' He hesitated. 'Siduri, you died yesterday. It is now 3am, and the night is at its darkest. I am afraid that, for you, summer is forever gone.'

Oh, you… '*Why am I here?*'

'Here?'

'My house.' Should I have said that? Should I have admitted that?

He nodded. 'When we first manifest, it is in a place we know, or near someone with whom we have a strong emotional bond. You manifested in this house, your house.' His eyes widened slightly. 'Can I ask why this room?'

No, you cannot. 'How did you know I was here?'

'I…'

Wait a minute! 'You said "we"?'

Irritation turned to annoyance. 'You asked me why it was so cold. Siduri, you are cold because you are, as you say, dead. It is the unfortunate truth.'

'I hate you!' This man was truly up his own personal arse.

'And you should, for many reasons. For now, though, that cloak might help. If you pull it on top, you can at least pretend you are warm.'

I stared at him, defiant – but shivering.

'And more completely clothed,' he added.

He had a point. I edged off the cloak, reached down, and pulled it to my shoulders. If I used my imagination, I could believe myself to be warmer – and less exposed.

But now, my backside felt frozen to the floor.

'How can I touch the cloak?'

He shrugged. 'I did say "we". While the dead can touch, feel and interact with the living world, it takes practice. The cloak is not of the living world…'

Beyond the window, I heard a woman curse.

'…and unfortunately, neither am I.'

I knew that voice.

I stared, transfixed, as the door crashed open. The exotic appeared out of breath, shivering. In the cold, the vapour generated rose like steam above her head. While the wound on her face was still visible, it had almost healed. What was once a scrape of rusted iron was now grey and fading and turning to jet.

In the starlight, the exotic looked younger than on the train. Perhaps eight years, ten at most, older than me. I examined her clothes. I hadn't thought to look properly before. Black ankle boots with almost no heel rose into similarly coloured leather trousers. Her red jacket looked well-pocketed and dense enough to provide warmth on this chilliest of nights. While her clothes were no attempt at fashion, she still had that exotic elegance. Why had she shivered then? She was out of breath. She must have been running. With the heat generated under all that clothing, how did she still feel cold?

And then I knew.

'Our mutual acquaintance is also corporeally challenged,' Dumuz confirmed.

Lilith? A ghost? Like me, a ghost?

I was a ghost!

Outside, I heard the beginnings of a bizarre medieval chant.

Lilith tracked my eyes. '*Quim scum!*' she snarled.

Terrified, I pulled the cloak up to my eyes in a childish attempt to hide. I hugged my knees further into my body to compensate for the shortening length. The exotic noticed and snorted.

Dumuz sighed. 'Lilith, this is Siduri.'

'We've met,' she said, eyeing me doubtfully. 'Have you asked her?'

Dumuz shook his head. 'I thought there would be more time.'

'There isn't. That's not exactly a mutual masturbation society out there.'

'The Fedhyow?' I asked.

Lilith licked her lips and grinned. 'Yup – and they're not here for a sherry and a séance.' Her teeth glinted pearl blue in the starlight. 'They're here for that sorry backside you're now flashing. Deep-fried, if possible. No need to add seasoning.'

'*Why?*' I squeaked.

'You mean, "Why do a shitful of religious arseholes want

to purge the world of a classic proverbial poltergeist?" Oh, I don't know, empathy?'

'But… But how did they know I'd be here?'

Like this?

Lilith glanced at Dumuz. She seemed uncertain.

Dumuz nodded and took over. 'Siduri, I am afraid that will take too long to explain. I doubt the Fedhyow will remain outside much longer. While I believe we can save you from them, there is something I must ask first – *do you have faith?*'

What?

Where did that come from? Yes, I used to have faith, but that was long ago and had nothing to do with Fedhyow. I hesitated, letting my eyes drift towards the fireplace. What should I say?

The clock remained on the mantle – unlike the sun-scorched picture of a boy that had once hung above. One day ago, I unlocked a door and entered a room. This room. A room I'd forgotten. How could I forget? How can anyone forget the attic of their own house?

I entered and noticed a chair that had once rocked, but no longer moved. There was a large chest that had been closed but was now open. I saw toys, lots of toys, all over the floor. It wasn't until then that I realised Iresh had lied. She'd lied without saying a word. This room was a shrine violated by a young girl – all those years ago.

I glanced at the ash still in the grate. This was a shrine never visited again after that day.

In the room, there was a desk with a locket sitting on top. The locket, though, wasn't the sort that held a picture. I wouldn't have put it on if it had held a picture. I remember the blueness of it matched my tuft.

I remember the locket burning against my heart and thinking it should be green. Jealousy can sneak up on you at the strangest times.

Hours later, I remember a pile of debris on the lawn. Bizarrely set atop a garden well, the resultant cone resembled a Christmas tree. Or perhaps not. While I'd laid the toys out like presents, I hadn't been in the mood to wrap them.

I remember a fire. I remember setting the heap ablaze.

I remember staring into the haze of super-heated air. At the heart of the blaze were fragments of a wooden desk, and above it, the boy's image was still intact in its frame.

Then the first lick of flame touched his chin.

Before entering this room, all those years ago, I believed, faithfully, that my mother loved me. Even after, when I only thought of her as Iresh, I...

'So?' Dumuz asked.

'I had hope,' I said. Of course, one day ago, even that turned to ash.

'*That's not an answer!*' Lilith trilled. 'What of those that promised a beyond? Salvation if you behaved in a particular way, bring others to that way? What did you say to them?'

I mannequined a smile. 'Nothing.'

Dumuz tsked. Lilith looked apoplectic.

I wrinkled my nose. 'Growing up, I learnt that it's pointless to question those who, by their very nature, refuse to give a proper account.'

Including Iresh.

'Good enough?' Dumuz asked Lilith.

'No,' she said, stepping into the room.

As she did, the hole in my chest, the one that wasn't there, spasmed.

'*Stay away from me!*'

'Nowhere near good enough.'

'*Please!*' I cried.

Lilith stopped. 'Still, given how you dress, you're not one of them. No Fedhyow would dare attempt that little "stand behind me while I pick up a penny" look of yours. If it was unique and bold, I might admire it. But it is not, and so I do not. It is a tribal disguise not dissimilar to others worn by those of your age. You tell yourself it is to mark you out, but you know in the place that was once your heart, it is simply a mask behind which you hide. Your clothing is a façade, just like that pathetic equivocation.'

'*Leave me alone!*'

'Resentment?' Lilith said. 'Good! Resentment is better than fear. Resentment lets you do the thing that needs doing. The only thing fear is good for is a colon cleanse.' She raised an eyebrow. 'Of course, given your preference for short skirts, that might be one of your kinks.' Her face tightened. 'You *will* say more, but it can wait. Now, you need to come with us.'

Seriously? After what she had done?

Lilith sensed my doubts. 'Can you remember what happened on the bridge? Did you see me stab you in the back?'

I said nothing.

Lilith knelt in front of me. 'No, of course not – but I also did not.'

I watched, terrified, as the soft smile on her lips slowly sagged. She continued. 'That joyless twat was waiting for me. I climbed onto the bridge, and the cum-faced clit hit me from behind. She poleaxed me. And then, as I lay there stunned, eating sleeper, rock shrapnel and moss, she took my *fucking* glass from my *fucking* hand and cut my *fucking* throat.'

My jaw fell open in shock as flecks of her sputum splattered my face. Lilith snorted crudely as some of it seeped into my mouth.

I hastily wiped my lips. 'Then it was her? The mother? She stabbed me in the back?'

Lilith nodded. 'As I lay there pumping effluent, I watched her sneak up behind you. Just as I sucked up a final breath, I watched her drive my very *fucking* glass into your very *fucking* back.'

Lilith scrunched her nose. 'Still upset about her sister, I guess,' she added.

Dumuz, who'd been quiet during the exchange, said, 'We have to go.'

I ignored him and considered the sequence of events. 'The mother cut your throat?'

Lilith nodded. 'Ghosts are as fragile as mortals when they fully form.'

'Fully form?'

'Become physical, solid and properly seen.'

'So, you died? Again?'

'Uh-huh. Painful as fuck as well.'

'But you didn't stay dead.'

'I misspoke. Ghosts can't really die again. Or at least not just because of a poxy bit of glass. Let us just say the twat somewhat inanimated me for a bit. Then I animated again.'

This was getting ridiculous. 'But why's there still a cut on your neck? I died too. What about my back? My chest? There's nothing.'

'Oh, my sweet girl. Your carcass is still full of holes. The shell you're now in is as fresh as a... well as a corpse, but at least one that bathes regularly. This shell, your ethereal form, can still be damaged, though. Small stuff, like this scratch on my neck, will heal faster than on living flesh. Big stuff, however? Well, with that, you're still quite seriously fucked.'

I'd had enough. '*Big stuff? You mean big stuff like cutting out my heart?*'

Lilith snickered. 'Actual anger? Even better. But honestly, dear girl, I didn't have a choice. You were dead… well… the happening dead. You would still have died if I had left you on that bridge, but it would have been a "final death". There would be nothing after. This way, you get to live. Well, sort of.'

Final death? I never thought that death could be so granular. 'Did you drink my blood afterwards?' I asked, letting the bitterness seep into my voice.

Lilith grimaced. 'No. That's a different ritual. Anyway, I didn't have a cup.'

'So, you're telling me you used the locket in a literal rite of passage?'

'*Amulet!*'

'*Locket!*'

'Amulet,' Lilith repeated. 'The fact that you're dead and it's still around your neck makes it yours. That you're dead and still talking makes it an amulet. Amulets allow our kind to continue – to die but also remain.'

'Our kind?'

Her eyes lit up. 'My dear, surely you must realise you're a witch?'

A witch? What, outside of folk tales, was a witch? But, if I exploded again, I might let slip that I'd only found the amulet. That it wasn't mine. If so, would Lilith take it from my neck in anger – or perhaps just spite?

Would I cease to exist?

Did I deserve to exist?

'No,' I said.

Lilith's pupils expanded. Already primed and coiled, she hunched like a panther ready to leap – but did not.

Instead, she stood and cackled. '*Time to go!*' she cried. Cackling is what witches do best, I guess.

Pulling the cloak off me, she threw it over to Dumuz. I shivered at the sudden exposure.

'Cold, are we?' Lilith asked, her voice softening. 'You poor baby. Just look at you, still half-naked with only that fake shroud for warmth. Dumuz, what were you thinking?'

'*Lilith.* Not now,' Dumuz said, standing and putting on the cloak.

She ignored him. 'Was it below? Were you lying on it?'

I nodded.

She continued, 'I thought as much. Dumuz had you draped on that pretentious rug like a whore in a tuppenny brothel.'

'Em… *Lilith*!' Dumuz warned.

She snorted in response. 'Try this, little girl,' she said.

She grabbed my frozen hands and put them on my chest before running them down to my stomach and hips. The caress slipped past my thighs, calves and ankles before concluding with my feet. At each touch, everything – my jacket, my skirt, my boots – everything I had dressed in the morning before returned. I still felt colder than I'd ever been in life, but now, adequately clothed, I could at least pretend I was warm.

I guess I looked confused. I certainly felt violated. Lilith just laughed. 'The living have preconceptions about what the dead can do and how they should look. These prejudices carry beyond the grave and take on tangible form. In this, your subconscious convinced you that you should wear that… somewhat tarty nightdress. Therefore, you did. Simply put, through touch, I helped you break the limitation.' She looked at my clothing and added, 'Of course, some limitations are more difficult to…'

The window shattered. I watched, bewildered, as a brick skated across the wooden floor.

'…break,' she completed.

Sniffing, Lilith grabbed my wrists and pulled me up. 'We really should go.'

'Why?'

'The Fedhyow know how to do "big stuff".'

She spun around and left the room, giving me no chance to reply.

Damn.

The exotic, my panther, was a killer. That was the black and not-so-white of it. Forgetting, for the moment, what she did to me, Lilith was a killer. While I've never liked the Fedhyow, I'd kept well short of slaughtering them. To be honest, I'd lacked the nerve to even shout at them. Lilith had dragged that woman to her death on the train. Why? Because she shared the Fedhyow beliefs? Or because she was in the way? Could Lilith have killed the mother on the bridge? Might she have killed the child?

I had no idea.

From below, I heard the creak and crack of buckling wood.

I had no idea, but did it matter *right now?* The mob, it appeared, wanted my blood – even if it was pretty much vapour.

'We have to leave,' Dumuz said.

'I know.'

'But?'

'Why do they *really* want me?' I asked, repeating the question from before.

The corner of one side of his mouth twitched. 'The Fedhyow detest our kind – and you, Siduri, are one of our kind.'

Not funny, not appropriate, and still not an answer. Shaking my head in disgust, I turned and left the room.

Dumuz followed right behind.

After drifting down two flights of stairs, I crossed the hallway and entered the kitchen. It had been a place I'd rarely visited in recent days. A place I imagine I might never visit again. Ghosts, I was certain, do not have stomachs.

The door to the garden was already open. Lilith stood on the grass, waiting. I tried to join her but failed. Nothing blocked my exit, but I could not pass. Something within me wouldn't allow it. I felt faint. Was this house to be my prison?

In the end, though, my legs did not buckle. Dumuz appeared beside me. Up close, he was taller than I had first thought. The cloak on his shoulders hung open. Beneath it, he wore a thick shirt that might have been useful against the cold when alive – and if the top three buttons weren't undone. Copious amounts of hair sprouted through the gap. I looked into his eyes. They were emerald green, just like his ridiculous cloak, and just as uncompromising as Lilith's. Dumuz placed a hand under my upper arm, accidentally brushing my right breast, seeking to prevent my fall.

It all felt very Gothic.

And then his *strength* poured into me, and, with it, the threads that held me to this place disappeared. Dumuz let go and stepped past and through the doorway.

I followed with ease.

Beneath the moonlight, the overgrown lawn shimmered as each blade of grass refracted and reflected its burden of dew. In the middle sat a circle of black that hadn't been there a day earlier. In the centre of the circle, there was once a garden well. Now all that remained was a hole.

I looked away.

To my right, a line of elm, beech and sycamore stood above all else. To my left, and far less imposing, ran a length of flowerbed and trellis. The flowerbed had been Iresh's treasure. Even in this year of drought, it had produced flowers that were truly sublime. The aquifer that fed the well had helped. Not mentioning it to the authorities did, at least the flora, no harm either.

The trellis stretched fifty yards before buttressing against and merging into a maze of bushes and shrubs. Although I couldn't see it, I knew all this domesticated greenery ended at an old garden gate. Beyond it lay a small thicket of trees. Beyond the trees?

I didn't know where we were going, but the screams behind us made one direction clear.

I ran.

Lilith and Dumuz followed behind as I raced across the grass, spraying fragments of moist glitter into the air. I clipped the edge of the dark circle, only to crack its surface and throw up a dust storm of still-glowing embers. If I were alive, the cinders would have singed my skin. Now that I was dead, it was my regret at their origin that stung the most.

I felt afraid. But it wasn't fear of those now in the house that worried me. Nor, after looking back, was it the flames I could see from a fire someone had started in Iresh's bedroom. No, what frightened me was what I saw to my left.

I shouldn't have run.

Just beyond the trellis stood a jury of the devout. Shoulder to shoulder, they lined its frame, their faces pressed hard against both wood and autumn rose. As they caught sight of our trail, they first kept quiet and still – before then screaming and moving as a mass to block our escape.

While some clambered and climbed, most just smashed through the fence. These differed from the Fedhyow of my past, who only offered casual slights and barefaced contempt. These Fedhyow wore rage as their uniform and my ruin as their goal.

We slowed to round a large holly bush that marked the start of the garden's lower half.

Out of view of the mob, Lilith took her chance. Grabbing my left hand, she dragged me to a halt. Dumuz, behind her, pulled up to my right. 'Now hush, little girl,' Lilith said. 'Be silent. This may feel a little strange.'

I opened my mouth to ask why, but before I could, she squeezed.

Whatever colour there had been in the night vanished, with its spectrum replaced by a scale of greys through to silver. It was like staring at a scene in brilliant sunlight and then shutting your eyes. Like that, the after-image remained. Unlike that, the more malevolent of those blurred artworks still moved.

I felt colder than I had before. It didn't seem possible. The ice forming in my veins wasn't a metaphor. Rooted and truly petrified, it became uncomfortably easy to remain quiet.

Those dressed once in black but now in marbled shades of silver shambled away, their focus lost. They couldn't see us. Most surrendered quickly and retreated towards the house. The remaining few wandered blindly among the maze of bushes, looking for something that was no longer there. Some slipped and fell in the shadows under the trees. In the lower garden, the Fedhyow were on uncertain ground. Moles, to Iresh, were not a burden. To her, they were living things beyond the need to harm. In return, they showed scant empathy for her vision of managed nature. This night, however, as belated compensation, their hidden runs challenged every Fedhyow ankle and each Fedhyow knee.

Suddenly, a man passed through me from behind. Initially, it felt like Lilith's hand on the train. Something insubstantial, a thing not quite there. But an entire body is not a hand, and his presence became far more intimate. Before I could react, however, the man stepped forward, and we parted. To him, I imagine, I was nothing but a breath of wind, just another space to be ignored.

For my part, my ectoplasmic skin crawled. How could such an unknowing act feel so deliberate? It was near enough a violation.

Perhaps Lilith agreed. The woman beside me strained against her solidifying form and drew out her glass blade, its handle now wrapped in a fresh rag and some tape. Fortunately for the man, Dumuz caught Lilith's eye and shook his head. I watched with mixed emotions as Lilith scowled and put the knife away.

And so we waited, and my joints got colder.

Eventually, those remaining under the trees withdrew. I didn't know whether the cold had defeated them, or the dark, or the minefield of a plucky mole, but I hoped it was the last.

To my right, Dumuz stretched his arms first forward and then up. To my left, Lilith did the same. Both yawned and smiled as my hands followed their lead above my head.

Reality returned.

I gazed back beyond the holly bush. What was once a

sequence of flickering white lights was now orange and red as the fire in the house took hold.

Both let go, and we walked silently past the remaining bushes and shrubs to the gate. While, strangely, Dumuz fumbled awkwardly with the latch, I took a last look at the house. The blaze had reached the roof, the plumes of smoke surpassing my pitiful efforts of the previous day.

I shook my head and turned back.

Another man stood before me, not four feet away. The man also wore a cloak, but his robe was white. He was thin, his frame almost skeletal. Just like us, the man didn't seem whole. Unlike us, he cast a shadow. Oddly, though, it fell towards and not away from the flames.

I might have called out a warning, but the man put a finger to his lips.

And… I said nothing.

The man nodded in acknowledgement, mouthed two words, shimmered briefly and was gone.

My eyes pulsed. The words were, "*Save me!*" Words that can lead to an entire quiz book of questions, with "*Why?*" being the most pertinent. Normally, "*What from?*" would fill that role, and it might have if I hadn't recognised him from the many wanted posters around the town.

Stephen Izdubar. My father.

Ahead, Dumuz and Lilith were through the gate and waiting. From their impatient expressions, it was clear they hadn't seen my father.

How could they not have seen?

I sighed and headed to join them. After all, I couldn't go back. To choose a blindingly obvious metaphor – behind me, there were only flames.

CHAPTER FOUR

WHERE MONSTERS LIE

A head, there was only ice.

A scowl can shout "shut up" as easily as words. Alive, Lilith's scowl would have withered. Dead, it merely chafed. Once beyond the gate, I tried to speak, but Lilith glared me into silence. After my misjudged sprint in the garden, I gave her the benefit of the doubt. As a recently dead, I had a lot to learn and knowing when not to run across wet grass was likely the least of it.

We set off through a length of scrub that lay beyond the garden. I passed one bush where, as a child, I'd found a path to its hidden centre. At age six, I had tea parties with my dolls, and by twelve, I discovered new delights that needed absolute privacy. At seventeen? At seventeen, as I passed it by, I could see the reflections of leftover detritus at its heart. Just as on the lawn, I guess the concept of "being invisible" is never as absolute as one might hope.

Breaking cover from the brush, we found ourselves in an open field. Row upon row of white stubble broke through the earth. In the day, it would be golden, but at night it rose from the ground like mottled lead. This year there had been no harvest. The heat and the drought had seen to that. The crops lay in the ground as planted, lifeless and unable to reach their potential.

Yeah.

On the far side of the field, we entered the remains of Marhasyow forest. The forest once stretched across large swathes of the countryside. Now cropped and burnt, mankind had confined the remaining trees to a strip of land hugging the coast.

However, a forest, ravaged though it might be, is still dark. Even in daylight, the lingering shade of Marhasyow forest felt like a monster's fingers waiting to take hold and to *crush*. At night, this night, the blackness should be complete, and I should be pap. It was not, and I was almost not. To my surprise, decanted moonlight lit my path through bramble, nettle and bracken. I took my first few steps, brushing against each and felt almost nothing. The nettles stroked but didn't sting. The brambles dragged but didn't cut. And the bracken? The bracken was as inconsequential as I. Neither of us had sufficient substance to interact with anything that mattered.

Now within the boundary of the sound-dampening trees, I asked, 'What happened in the garden? What did you do to me?'

Lilith turned and re-glared.

This time, it did not work. Giving someone the benefit of the doubt has its limits, especially if they've recently cut out your actual once-living heart.

'It's a simple enough question. Actually, I have lots of questions.'

Lilith pouted. 'Simple to ask, more difficult to…'

I interrupted. 'No, Dumuz tried that. Call me picky, but I've never actually killed anyone. I've also never felt the desire to associate with anyone who has. Why should I trust you?'

'You've trusted us so far.'

Well… not really. If I did, then I'd tell them I'd seen Izdubar in the garden. I'd tell them who he was to me and what he asked. I might have even asked their opinion on the "saving him" thing – once I understood what "saving" actually meant.

'Until now, I had no choice,' I said.

Behind me, the subliminal screams of wood and brick rose from a distant quiet to the loud before falling into silence. I turned to look. A ball of flame rose from where my house… had stood.

Lilith smirked. 'Dear girl, there's no such thing as choice.'

'We should keep moving,' Dumuz said. 'There is at least one Fedhyow who will work out where we're heading.'

The one who passed through me? 'Then why go?'

Lilith smiled. 'I have no choice.'

Before I could reply, Lilith turned and set off again. Within seconds, she had disappeared.

Dumuz took my wrist. 'I will explain on the way.'

I glared at his hand – which Dumuz removed. That, though, was as far as any resistance went, and I began to walk. Dumuz fell in alongside.

'You must first understand what we are,' he said. 'Much as I adore Lilith, she does like her mythology. The supernatural, the ghosts. While such things are true, they are also not true, or at least not the complete story.'

'You were the one who talked about ghosts.'

He laughed. 'That comes from taking the "*hypocritic*" oath. Still, I hope you agree it got the salient points across. That said, what it means to be genuinely incorporeal requires more explanation.'

I sensed a patronising lecture.

'As you know, there is height. There is width. There is depth. Also, you know you are born, that you live, and now, quite certainly, that you die. In other words, you understand time.'

As I thought, a patronising lecture.

He swept on. 'The universe is infinite. You, me, Lilith, and the few others like us are one turn of the screw from the norm.'

Wait a minute. What did he just say? 'Different dimensions? Is that where you're going? Seriously? Is that all you have?'

'Think of it this way. When death claims you, it seeks to cleave your essence from the mortal plane and cast it into the infinite other. Without an anchor, all that is you should dissipate. The cold you feel is the pull of the multiverse on your soul and when chaos finally claims you, there will be utterly nothing left.'

Gee, thanks. 'Yet I'm still here.'

'Yet you are still here – if there is truly a *here*. For that, you have Lilith to thank.'

'No problem,' Lilith sang from well out front.

'You said, "anchor"? Are you talking about the locket?'

'We are talking about the *amulet* you wear. Lilith used it to bind all that remained of you to this place.'

'You said, "all that remained"? What had I lost?'

He sighed. 'A witch is someone more sensitive to what might exist in the beyond. There is more *give* in our connection to this plane of existence than for others but it is not perfect.' Dumuz hesitated and looked ahead. 'Many, indeed most witches, cannot transition and those that do often fail to complete it… entirely.'

Which was a confirmation I did not want.

Dumuz continued. 'For those who succeed, this flexibility offers the dubious pleasure of a continued presence in this world, albeit slightly out of phase. However, this ongoing existence would still be short without a fixing place and a reason to remain. Unbound, a ghost quickly fragments. Your amulet is a mooring point. Each amulet is different and holds within it a symbol of some vital memory. Once formed, it allows its bearer to withstand even death – *if* they survive the change from skin and bone to ectoplasm.'

The message didn't get any better in its repeating. 'That sounds remarkably like the mythology that you claim to despise.'

'It is an analogy but nevertheless true.'

'How did you know the amulet was mine? It could have been my mother's.'

'Well…' he said. 'If it belonged to kin, it should still work.'

Why the hesitation? Was there a lie in there somewhere? But, if the amulet was mine, why did Iresh hide it? Why didn't she tell me what we were?

Why did she die and not come back?

I hated her more now than at any other time in my life – even yesterday.

Okay, not yesterday.

'Lilith!' I called.

'Yes, my precious?'

Bitch.

'On the bridge, when you stuck me like a pig, did you know the amulet would work?'

'It was a good way to find out.'

And a rather mean bitch at that. Still, I suspected what she said was also a fib. Or at least I hoped it was.

43

'Where was the amulet when your… mother died?' Dumuz asked.

Out front, Lilith tittered.

He shook his head and continued. 'Were you wearing it?'

'No,' I responded flatly, desperate to keep the fear out of my voice. If I told Dumuz how I found it, he might ask what I did next.

I didn't want to think about what I did next.

Dumuz nodded. 'It glows. When a witch first puts on an amulet, it glows. Yesterday, a shaft of brilliant light overtook the dawn. It drew us to you.'

Total nonsense.

I could tell it was nonsense because Lilith, yet again, cackled with laughter.

'You could see it then?' I asked. 'Yesterday morning? From where? From how far?'

'Oh… Oh, yes, a fair distance. I…' His voice trailed off.

I had him.

From in front, Lilith asked innocently, 'So, sweetness, when your… *mother* died, did you know where the amulet was but weren't wearing it? Or did you find it afterwards?'

Dumuz twitched. That was the only way to describe it. But then again, so did I. Did Lilith know the amulet wasn't mine? Somewhere in the dark, an owl hooted. Nearby, I heard a mouse slink under a leaf in response.

I would not be that mouse. There are other things you can do than hide.

I brought my hand to my throat. 'The amulet – why is it still here? *Lilith!* After what you did to me, how can it still be here?'

'Well,' she said. 'Because I shoved it into that hole in your chest, it…'

44

'…it stayed with you when you died,' Dumuz completed. 'The transition is smoother when placement and death co-occur. Unfortunately, that is not always the case.'

Smoother? 'Can your amulet be destroyed?'

He nodded. 'Yes, but if that happens, you will no longer have an anchor. Like any mortal, you would float away, adrift into the finality of nothing.'

Great.

I allowed myself a touch of anger. 'Okay. I get it. *Now, tell me what happened back there!* How did they see us in the garden, and then afterwards, how did they not? We're ghosts, after all!'

Dumuz sighed and looked at Lilith's back.

'Why won't you tell me?' I pleaded.

'She needs to know.' He spoke softly, kindly, and not to me.

Lilith kept on walking.

Dumuz sighed. 'In our normal form, we can see and hear as clearly as when alive. Touching, however, is more problematic.'

I thought of the nettles and his struggle with the latch on the gate.

He continued. 'How others perceive us depends on several factors. The physics of existing in a different phase determines both when and how mortals see us… but there are exceptions.'

'Exceptions?'

'The Fedhyow are an exception. At night, though, we are shadows and more difficult to see – even for them.' He paused for effect. 'Unless, of course, we do something to reveal our presence.'

'*Seriously?* How was I supposed to know? Nothing I've ever read suggested a ghost can kick up a fog when running across a bit of wet grass.' And dust and ash from a fire.

'You have studied the topic?'

Well, I've studied girly Gothic romances, but still.

'What did you mean by "*how mortals see us*"?' I asked instead, ignoring his question.

Dumuz let me. 'In the day,' he said, 'we look quite human, at least to a sideways glance.'

'And if it's not sideways?' Perhaps I should have read a better quality of book while growing up – less romance, still Gothic, more fact.

I'd have missed the romance though.

'Unfortunately,' he said, 'we appear rather odd. Remember, we only have a toehold in the mortal realm. In daylight, we shimmer. We best resemble a picture that has aged and blurred. When it is dark, we are far more difficult to see.'

I wasn't fond of his "picture" analogy. Did he know about the portrait in the attic? That had also faded with age. Yesterday, I could hardly make out that it was a boy.

Even less so after I burnt it.

And then I realised something. 'The Fedhyow saw us at night – and what about Lilith on the train?' I asked. 'She could touch. She looked real!'

'Real?' Lilith muttered. She seemed closer now. Had she slowed down?

'Real,' I repeated, adding a touch of petulance.

Dumuz answered. 'You are a witch and have an affinity with others like you. It matters little whether they are living or dead. Still, being ignorant, it is not surprising you found it difficult to tell the difference between a ghost and a mortal.'

Git.

'And non-witches?' I asked. 'The two that sat opposite Lilith on the train, just for example.'

'Because we only exist one step out of phase, we can retune and allow others to more properly see us for a time. It is tiring and difficult to do, but possible. On the train, Lilith would have appeared quite "real". Real enough to be thought human – and solid enough to be damaged by mundane weapons.'

'I told you she cut me,' Lilith complained. Did she sound nervous?

'What went wrong?'

Again, it was Dumuz who replied. 'Yesterday, Lilith made a mistake.'

'Thanks,' Lilith whispered. It was almost a whimper.

'What mistake?'

'You had a question about the garden first,' Dumuz said. 'It's a better place to start.'

I rather doubted that.

Dumuz continued. 'On the grass, we detuned and drifted further out of phase.'

'That simple?'

'Not that simple. As Lilith knows from the bridge, a transition in either direction is not instantaneous. With that said, detuning is relatively easy, and, in that state, even the Fedhyow cannot see you. However, drifting further out of phase weakens the bond you have with your anchor. If it breaks, there is no way back. Eventually, you become a "nothing", a none-thing without conscious thought that is everywhere and nowhere at the same time.'

'So, not a good thing. But you did it anyway?'

'We had no choice.'

'*We need to talk about the difference between choice and consent!*'

'But not now.'

'Not now? *Seriously?* Okay, let's try the question you said you *would* answer. *Why should I go with you?*'

He hesitated. 'You have another question. Its answer is what you really want to know.'

'Another question?'

'Yes,' he said, watching Lilith. 'The one you are too afraid to ask.'

He was right, of course.

Lost in the woods with only two spirits for company, one of which I knew to be malign, I asked, 'Why did Lilith kill that woman on the train?' I looked at Dumuz. His eyes demanded the rest. I raised my voice. 'And did she kill the mother? Did she kill the child?'

Ahead, Lilith growled.

Dumuz tensed. 'There are a few more things you need to know about the Fedhyow first. It is not something they would acknowledge, but our kind and the Fedhyow share an ancestral root. That is why they can see us better than others. A long time ago, however, the Fedhyow took a different path.'

'Path?' I asked.

'The Fedhyow desire a different sort of afterlife. One that demands supplication and abstinence to achieve a life beyond its normal stretch. One that unfortunately lacks the usefulness of being real.'

'Is that fact… or faith?' I asked.

'Not faith,' Dumuz said wryly. 'But the Fedhyow consider us deviants. They contend we only achieve survival beyond death through a dark and evil act.'

'They're not wrong,' I said.

Dumuz ignored me. 'It is a tenet of their *faith* that all

witches are an abomination, one that must be destroyed.'

'And not in a good way,' Lilith said from just in front.

We had reached a clearing, or at least enough of a gap in the brush.

Lilith had stopped.

I drew alongside, and she started walking again. Dumuz drifted back.

'I had no choice,' she said. 'The mother saw it in my eyes.'

'What?'

'On the train. The mother saw it in my eyes. If you're not concentrating, your eyes are the first to go. Your pupils dilate. They extend. If you're lax, the blackness can expand to fill the socket.'

Her voice wavered. 'It was the child. I looked at the child. That smelly, noisy, flatulent child.'

Another quiver, and then, 'I had a baby once. Did I tell you that?'

I stopped and stared at her.

She turned. 'No?' she whispered. 'My boy, Dara, he died, and I couldn't bring him back. He had such pretty red lips... why couldn't I bring him back?'

I reached out to her, but she shrugged me off. 'I made a mistake. That woman saw it in my eyes. They're the first thing to go, the eyes. Did I tell you that? Or perhaps it was my mouth? The lips can turn blue if you're not concentrating. Did you know my Dara's lips turned blue? What was he thinking?' She swayed but pressed on. 'The mother on the train grabbed the baby and ran. Any mother would. Any mother who saw something that threatened her child would. I would have if...'

Her knees buckled.

I reached out to catch her, but she fended me off.

Lilith steadied herself. 'No,' she said. 'I'm not that woman. Not anymore.'

I didn't believe her.

I think she could tell. 'Afterwards,' Lilith snarled. 'I found a better way.'

Lilith paused and rubbed the vanishing scar on her cheek. 'But, it seems, so did that fucking bitch. After all, she did fillet my throat and shiv your spine. I wouldn't have hurt the baby, but put yourself in her position. She'd likely seen what I'd done to her sister. She definitely saw you follow me onto the bridge. It's not unreasonable for the twat to believe we were out for her arse.'

'Unreasonable?'

She smirked. 'It was a good thing she wasn't an actual Fedhyow. Her reaction on the train was instinctive. She had no idea what I was. Even after her sister died, that likely stayed true. She was running and was afraid. She struck first.'

'What if she'd been Fedhyow?'

'A Fedhyow would have known what I was and attacked. Immediately. It wouldn't matter if there were a child in the way.'

'They hate us that much?'

'Yes.'

'But when I was growing up?'

'You thought they were just your regular bunch of arseholes?'

'Em… yes.'

Lilith shook her head. 'The Fedhyow are like that fungus you get in your down-below. You know, the one all mothers warn about? Sure, it tingles all gentle at the start, but eventually

– well, my point is, with our kind, the fuckers tend to skip the *gentle* part. It takes just one whiff of our lady parts to make them turn all stabby-burny.'

I stared in disbelief. 'But… the mother on the train. You're saying she panicked and then, *oddly enough*, panicked more when you killed her sister?'

Lilith wrinkled her nose. 'Well… yeah. Personally, I don't get all the fuss about sisters. I had one once, loved her once as well – don't now and don't now.'

'Why did you kill the sister?'

'*She broke my knife!*'

'I thought it broke on the train door?'

'It did… but the cunt was the one who kicked it shut. It was my special knife. I'd had it for ages. I…'

Dumuz interrupted. 'The Fedhyow would have questioned her.'

Lilith turned and glared at him. I did as well. We all knew her action had been far more spontaneous. Far more elemental.

I really could believe it was because of the knife.

'So,' I said, holding my pseudo-breath. 'You killed the mother as well?'

Lilith grinned. 'No, unfortunately. One of my more major fuck-ups. I just couldn't do it. Not when she still had the child. That stupid pissing child.'

'Oh.'

'Yes, "oh". Even after the fucker cut my throat, even after that twat reamed you on the bridge, I still let her go. So, you see, those tuneless wanks turning up at your house truly is my bad. Dumuz was right. Little Miss Slit-Mouth was always going to turn tattletale. While your street-corner-slapper look is pretty generic, I've got to admit that blue birdshit in your hair does mark you out.'

'Oh,' I repeated.

'Exactly. While the Fedhyow didn't find your corpse, they still knew where to come a-knocking.' She hesitated before almost whispering, 'Well, one Fedhyow did.'

One Fedhyow? Again? Wait a minute. '*My body!* What happened to my body?'

Lilith sniffed. 'I rolled it into the river. After that storm, I imagine your carcass is arse high in a foot of silt.'

I didn't even bother with an "oh".

I never thought I could want someone dead. But now? Now I felt almost consumed with hate. My scourge, my killer, the aisle mother, was still alive and, to my shock, I so wished she wasn't. Unlike Lilith, who, to my surprise, still had some humanity, I had just discovered how little of mine remained.

Morality, it would seem, is nothing but a concept of the moment. In my new reality, I saw one woman killed and found I didn't care. One more survived, and I regretted she had. And the child? The infant? Before yesterday, I might have agreed with Lilith's choice. But now? Now I wasn't sure what I felt or believed. In these past few moments, if my heart wasn't already a ruin, it might have turned quite black.

How quickly things change. Twenty-four hours ago, I hadn't even had reason to set a fire.

Not until I saw a picture of a boy.

Damn.

For sanity's sake, I changed the subject. 'Where are you taking me?'

'You will see!' Dumuz said. He sounded tetchy. Perhaps I shouldn't have upset Lilith.

I left it. I think I already knew. 'Okay, then. How about telling me why Lilith was on the train in the first place? You might also want to add why you were there when I woke up?'

Staring at me.

When I was almost naked.

He grimaced. 'You are one of us. We felt obliged to…'

That hole just kept getting deeper. 'Obliged? You just "*saw the light*" and came running?'

'What?' Dumuz seemed confused. 'Oh, yes. Of course. That is an interesting way to put it, but yes.' He paused. 'Where were you going on the train anyway?'

I let him divert me. The hole would still be there in the morning. 'I was visiting my aunt.'

'Another wayward witch, no doubt. What is her name?'

'Eanna.'

He smirked. '*Aunt Eanna?*'

Lilith tsked. 'Why visit?'

'My mother died. I thought Eanna should know.'

Her eyes glinted. 'A letter would have done.'

I resisted the urge to check my jacket pocket. I suspected one was still there. Instead, I tried to sound hurt. 'No, it really wouldn't.'

I couldn't tell them the real reason I'd been going to Sulis. It was less about Iresh's death and more about my father's life – and where he was right now.

I couldn't tell them because they would then ask his name.

Dumuz, now enjoying himself, asked, 'Since Eanna is kin, perhaps you could still visit? I imagine she will be quite accommodating, particularly if I help persuade her.'

What?

'*Oh yes!*' Lilith said. '*We can both come!*'

Damn. Sorry, Eanna.

'You think she'll be able to see me?' I asked. 'That she'll know what I am?'

'Certainly,' Lilith said, her voice still tinkling.

I wondered. Would Eanna know why my father needed "saving"?

And being Izdubar, did I care?

Of course, I couldn't visit Eanna. Not now. Not with someone as deranged as Lilith in tow. You just don't do that to someone you've never met.

I changed the topic. Maybe they'd forget about Sulis. 'The Fedhyow in the garden,' I said. 'The one that passed through me. You knew him, didn't you?'

'That pig-fucker Hugo?' Lilith asked. She wasn't laughing anymore.

'Hugo? That was Hugo di Conte?'

'Unfortunately, yes,' Dumuz said.

Earlier this year, Hugo arrived from Guitt, home to the Fedhyow. He brought his son with him. The boy's name was Nicolò – although, by the start of summer, I called him Nikka.

'I haven't seen Hugo for months.' I hadn't seen Nicolò either.

'There's a reason for that,' Lilith said.

'What?' I tried to keep the quiver out of my voice. 'What reason?' Nicolò had ripped apart my heart long before Lilith took it with her knife.

Lilith glanced over my shoulder. Behind us, but still in the distance, the soulful marching chant of the Fedhyow had struck up again.

Even I knew it would only get louder.

'Can it wait until the morning?' Dumuz asked.

Did he think the Fedhyow might hear us? I doubted it. Not now. Not until they were closer. Dumuz just didn't want to answer my question. Perhaps he thought I might run off?

But, of course, I couldn't. Not in this dark. Not when, literally, I could see only a single path ahead.

I, therefore, bit my tongue and kept silent. There was always tomorrow. Tomorrow, with the return of light, when I could see far and run further, I'd make sure to ask again.

Chapter five

Castles in the Sand

Upon a precipice of chalk, three blind souls waited for sufficient light to allow the climb down to the beach below.

Then came the end of night.

Beneath my feet, a band of light rose to kiss away the mist with lips of ruby. If this growing luminescence thought to scour me of the bleakness that lay within, it failed.

Death, apparently, hadn't cured me of an addiction to the occasional florid metaphor.

Beyond the beach, and hugged on the other side by the ocean, stretched a bar of pebbles that ran parallel to the coast, towards a distant outcrop of rock. Filling the gap between the shoal and the mainland lay an uninviting, and not-so-tropical lagoon.

Seepage gave the shallow water a brackish look. With little plant life, this part of the lagoon would cause excitement only to academics and the manically depressed. Further in, the lagoon grew less salty and might have been more varied if it had still been May. I could imagine a field of yellow flag iris reflecting the sun at its glorious height. But that was imagination. In autumn, all there can be is brown and grey.

In the distance, atop the rock, lay the ruins of Izdubar's castle.

Lilith's mood had softened with the light and I wondered whether the dawn chorus drowning out the distant singing of the Fedhyow had helped. We'd kept a steady pace ahead of them throughout the night – at least judging by the unchanging volume. Even while waiting for the light, it hadn't substantially increased. Perhaps even fanatics need to rest.

I doubted it would be for long.

Still, it seemed there was enough light to start our descent.

'*Lilith! Please!*' Dumuz shouted from out front.

'Lilith?' she asked in a honeyed voice – before tickling his ribs.

Better her fingers than a knife, I guess.

Dumuz, squirming, fingers slipping, let go of the red guardrail that marked the way. Toppling forward, he squealed an "*Ea…!*" before his voice cut off.

Guffawing loudly, Lilith grabbed his collar and hauled him back to safety.

I let Lilith go next.

We reached the beach without further mishap. While crossing the sand to the pebble shoal, I recalled a picnic I had with my mother. It was once a happy memory, but now that I remember it fully, it can only be the most bitter.

It was my eighth birthday, and the picnic was a surprise. In the past, birthdays were strictly indoor affairs with candles, homemade cake and the occasional transitory friend.

Iresh had put little thought into the picnic's preparation. I remember the taste of old cheese on dried, almost desiccated bread and that we ate scones dampened with the scrapings from an old pot of jam. I even remember this odd liquid called breakfast tea, which seemed a strange name given it was midday. Whatever the quality, I did my best to show appreciation. On my special day, it was the company that brought joy.

After lunch, I built a sandcastle. I knew, even as a little girl, it wouldn't hold back the tide. Yet still I built more buttresses and still I built more walls. Back then, I believed the concepts of losing and loss were different, and that the latter is much less painful if you strive against the first.

I was wrong.

My mother walked along the pebble bar while I played. I remember seeing her stop near the far end and stare. She stared for a long time. I never found out why. Finally, though, she turned and walked back.

My mother seemed fine when she returned. In fact, she joined me and helped as the tide advanced on my failing construction. When the water swamped my castle, leaving it flat and nothing, my mother suggested we simply retreat a little and start again.

We stayed on the beach until the tide was fully in.

When we returned home, my mother rushed upstairs to the attic. She stayed there for ages before heading to the bathroom. For the first time, and the last, my mother left the attic door open.

We never built castles together again.

Beyond the sand, I followed Lilith and Dumuz as they climbed the pebble bar before starting a slow trudge along its top. The exposed ridge was barren and discoloured, bleached white by salt-burn and sun. Alive, I wouldn't have been shocked that each step sank into the unbound stones. Dead, I was at least initially surprised. Unlike the Fedhyow, gravity, it seemed, considered the concept of my continued existence worthy of at least some weight.

I might no longer be human, but only on the inside.

With no sight, and now no sound of the Fedhyow, I thought it safe to talk.

'Pretty, isn't it?' I asked.

Lilith grunted. Dumuz didn't even manage that.

'*Pretty, isn't it?*' I repeated.

'Yes, Siduri,' Dumuz said. 'Very pretty.' It was grudging, condescending, but at least an answer.

I bludgeoned on. 'You know, my mother took me to that beach.'

It was Dumuz's turn to grunt.

'We're going to the castle?' I asked.

'Given that's the only place this fucking bar goes, it's kind of obvious,' Lilith snapped.

'You haunt a castle? Seriously? An empty castle?'

'Never said empty.'

'What?'

'I saw her, you know,' Lilith said.

'Who?'

'Lilith!' Dumuz warned.

She ignored him. 'Blonde? Pretty? That was her, right? Yup, it must have been her. We don't get many visitors. A bit of an odd one. The icy tart walked the full length of this pissing dune, stared for an age and then fucked off. I guess she had to get back to change your nappy.'

'*Lilith!*' Dumuz repeated.

Icy? Wait a minute... 'I didn't wear...' My head buzzed.

Dazed, I slipped on the treacherous scattershot before landing on my backside – just like an infant might.

Lilith reached down, grabbed my left arm at the elbow, and hauled me to my feet. 'Are you okay?' she asked. The smirk showed she had got the whole "baby still in nappies, unable to walk" schtick.

Bitch.

'You've lived in the castle all these years?' I asked. Privately, I struggled with the correct use of the word "lived".

'Yup. It was likely I saw Iresh the day we moved in. It... It got rather busy after that. I...'

Dumuz interrupted. '*Ladies*, can we do this later? We are exposed out here.'

'Exposed?'

'Particularly against this backdrop.'

I looked at the blue ocean merging seamlessly into the sky. Oh yes, I'd forgotten. In daylight, I was somewhat refractive of light.

'Why mention my mother?'

'You mean Iresh? You were getting cocky,' Lilith fired back. She turned to Dumuz and repeated, '*She was getting cocky*.' They stared at each other, something passing between them. Lilith broke first and smirked. 'Do you seriously think I'm a lady? Well, fuck me.'

Dumuz sighed.

Damn, Lilith was annoying. I increased my stride, ignoring the hazards underfoot. If I fell and broke my neck, it would be painful, *really, really painful*, but most likely only temporary.

I fumed. Was Lilith the reason Iresh stopped before reaching the castle? Did they speak? They must have! How else could Lilith have known her name?

Why hadn't Iresh mentioned it?

And then I remembered. After that day, Iresh was different.

It wasn't immediately apparent. At first, the distance kept seemed natural. I went somewhere I should not have. Any child could do that, be punished, and eventually forgiven. However, in the days and weeks that followed, I never felt forgiven. Iresh provided food, clothing and the occasional word of encouragement, but there was no longer any warmth there.

Lilith had a point. Iresh became quite the icy tart.

It seems strange that I forgot what happened in the attic that day. How could I forget? My only explanation is that I simply decided not to know. I guess, as a child, that time was a horror. Its root, a frightening unknown. Perhaps I couldn't understand what I'd done so wrong. What else could I do but forget?

Still, that doesn't explain why I forgot the attic itself. That it became just another wall. How is that possible?

A gust of wind broke me out of my reverie. The onshore breeze scoured my pupils with salt, making my eyes seep – or so I told myself.

Apparently, I'd gone ahead.

In front of me was the castle. My first thought was that it was big. Ugly and pointless, but big. Broken, torn and shattered, it took the sun from the sky. The pebble bar stopped abruptly, ending fifty yards short of the island. Eighteen years ago, the storm that struck hit this section the hardest. When given a choice between solid island rock and the thin, almost organic curtain wall, the tidal surge took the easier path.

Here, the storm swept the pebble bar away.

I was confused though. Now closer to the edge, I realised

the drop wasn't complete. I'd expected the marsh to extend in a gradual transition from fen to sand to sea, but it did not. A barrier of pebbles and rock stood between the ocean proper and the lagoon. This lower bar rose well above the tidal high and looked much less weathered than on the one I stood.

Beyond the barrier began the castle proper, or what remained of it after the storm. The openings in the outer screen wall, created by the storm, remained at the mercy of the tide. Further in, while the keep's walls still stood, they weren't exactly proud. The damage to their balustrades was so severe that any attempt at actual defence looked impossible. To the right of the keep, I saw a cottage. Past that, there were a few lean-to sheds and a mesh cage that might have once held chickens.

Dumuz arrived and stood to my seaward side, sheltering me somewhat from the breeze. Lilith appeared on my other and wrapped an arm around my waist. Standing on this precipice, and given her recent history, I wasn't happy.

I swept an arm out in front of me. 'I thought the storm destroyed this end of the shoal?'

Lilith hacked and spat on the lower bar as if checking the drop. 'I thought you were getting smarter?'

I shook my head, refusing to rise to the bait.

Dumuz took pity. 'Lilith, stop teasing the poor girl.' He looked at me. 'Very few people have seen it. We do not get many visitors, particularly after…'

Lilith giggled. 'Oh yeah, but I apologised afterwards.'

Dumuz harrumphed. 'I was thinking more about the Wards I set.'

'Wards?' I asked.

He nodded. 'The mortal world and ours are out of phase. A Ward is a device that projects a bit of our world into theirs. The result makes it uncomfortable for a living creature trying to pass.'

'So, back there when I fell. That was a Ward?'

'Yes. A Ward works both ways. In our case, it merely affects our balance. I put another one up near the castle's entrance.'

Lilith added, 'Wards keep the curious away from things they shouldn't know. Me? I prefer a broomstick, what with being a witch and all. And as Dumuz knows, I do so like giving wood.'

Dumuz's face pinked. '*Yes, well*, after that incident, I came up with a less intrusive solution.'

Lilith mock-sulked. 'Spoilsport.'

'That *man* was quite upset,' Dumuz said.

Lilith winked at him. 'That *man* hung around for hours afterwards.'

'That man could not walk!'

Lilith smirked – audibly.

She was teasing Dumuz again, and I didn't know why. But I had other concerns. I looked again at the cottage. 'You said the castle wasn't empty. Are there others?'

'Some living, some dead. We're not fussy.'

'You never mentioned there would be others – never mind living others.' I failed to hide the quiver in my voice.

Lilith sniped back, 'So what?'

So what? The "so what" was that I would meet the still-living for the first time as a newly-dead.

I think Dumuz sensed my concern. 'Siduri?'

'Yes?'

'Do you know what happened after Izdubar disappeared?'

Or perhaps not. 'You mean after he robbed the town blind?'

'*He took far more than that!*' Lilith snarled.

Not a fan, then.

Even if I wanted to, getting her help to "save" my father was obviously off the cards. The way she spoke made it sound personal. What had he done to her that was so bad?

I didn't get a chance to ask.

'That night,' Dumuz said. 'The tidal surge flattened the pebble bar, swept over the port and excreted the detritus it had gathered into the river Koner.'

I gagged at his choice of words, but it was something I already knew.

Dumuz continued. 'With the bar gone, the causeway was passable only at low tide. With the river's main channel blocked, no cargo ship could dock – even if they had rebuilt the harbour. In the beginning, the townsfolk of Marhasyow tried to fix it all. They began by rebuilding the barrier.'

That I didn't know.

'And the harbour?' I asked.

'They never even finished the bar. Can you see that hole between the bank and the rocks? That is a pipe. Without it, the pressure would collapse the bar along its entire length. At least at high tide.'

'*The harbour?*'

Dumuz shook his head. 'They never began work on the harbour for the same reason they never cleared the river or finished the bar. They ran out of money. Do you see the gravel piled up on the rocks above? They intended that for the next layer, but it never happened.'

'Lilith said you arrived ten years ago?' I asked. Which was, of course, when my life fell apart.

'Yes,' he said, clearly cautious.

'Was the castle empty? Or did you have to… *evict* anyone?'

Again relief. 'Emptied and abandoned before we got there. The place was a ruin.'

'So why did you come to Marhasyow? To the island?'

'We needed a new home and Marhasyow seemed suitable. Lilith has history here.'

'Ancient history,' Lilith added quickly.

Dumuz nodded, acknowledging the interruption. 'Back then, the castle was quiet and grubby. Unfortunately, it still is.'

I looked again at the heap of stones. 'Why is the gravel still there? It looks dangerous. Couldn't you move it?'

Dumuz shrugged. 'You never know when you need to block a pipe.'

'Dumuz!' a voice squeaked in the distance – saving Lilith from a tart response.

A young boy scrambled down the rock face from the castle onto the lower ridge. He looked about three or perhaps a small four. Blond hair, thin, almost gaunt, he ran across the bank, sure-footed on the wayward surface. He ran and ran until he stopped just beneath my feet. '*Dada!*' he shouted. '*Pull me up!*'

Dada?

Dumuz looked down and laughed. 'Sorry, Kitten, not this time. Introduce yourself to the nice lady.' He glanced at me. 'Siduri, this is Kitten.'

Kitten?

Lilith sniffed. 'Lady? That's twice. How come she gets to be called a "lady" twice?'

To be fair, calling you a "lady" the first time was likely a mistake.

I looked at the boy. 'Hello,' I tried.

The child backed off warily.

There was something odd about him. 'Is he… like us?'

Lilith whispered, 'Yes. He was here the day we arrived. Almost gone.'

'Gone?'

'Dissipated, the final death. It's what happens when we give up.'

I looked closer. There was something about the boy's eyes, his face.

Lilith continued. 'When we found him, his skin was almost translucent. His lips…' Her voice increased in pitch and grew louder. 'The name Kitten came from me.'

I couldn't stop staring. 'That's unusual.'

The child wrinkled his nose. 'Don't like it. It's a girl's name.' I could almost see the whiskers. 'Er,' he added. 'Why is your hair blue?'

Yesterday, a different boy asked that same question.

'My hair is blue, or at least part of it, because it's in my nature for it to be so.'

That boy was also dead.

Lilith scowled, perhaps noting that the rest of my hair was black. Rather than a barb, though, she surprised me. 'Kittens are naughty. This one is forever underfoot.'

The child giggled. There was definitely something familiar about him.

Dumuz clambered down to the lower shoal. Ruffling the boy's hair, he said, 'Now, off you go. Tell them we are on our way.'

Kitten lifted his chin, grinning in mock defiance.

Dumuz sighed, bent down, and kissed the boy on the

right cheek. Before the child could protest, Dumuz spun him around, spanked him lightly on the backside, and sent him on his way.

Kitten skipped across the stones back to the castle.

'Them?' I asked.

In response, Lilith gave me a shove from behind with her hand. 'Your turn,' she said.

I landed painfully on the incline before sliding down. The stones sprayed across the bank as I stopped at the bottom.

Lilith skated gracefully down the slope to land beside me.

'How did he die?' I asked.

'What?' Lilith said, almost tripping as she rose.

She shouldn't have pushed me. 'How did Kitten die?'

'I…' she began.

Dumuz interrupted. 'Damn!'

'Damn?'

'Look back at the cliff.'

I turned. When I'd been at its top, I hadn't noticed this lower stretch of the bar. The gap was too narrow, the angle too acute. However, looking in the opposite direction, I could easily spot the white chalk bluff and the rickety steps that meandered down to the beach below. It was almost as easy to see the man at their head. Against a white background, the man wore black.

I suspected he'd been watching us for quite some time.

'*Hugo!*' Lilith hissed.

Even at this distance, I knew she was right.

Dumuz nodded. 'Kitten died in the storm. If anyone is to blame, it would be that creature back there.' He glanced then at Lilith. 'And, of course, Governor Stephen Izdubar.'

Oh, f… fudge.

CHAPTER SIX

RUIN

Real castles have walls that are solid and stout. I should know – castles feature in all the best Gothic romances. Izdubar's castle was so full of holes that it failed even to halt the breeze. If anything can pass through without block or challenge, then it is better named a ruin than a structure that suggests the possibility of defence.

I strolled through.

Once past the rubble of the outer bailey, the sand of the breach gave way to patches of coarse grass. I tried to imagine Dumuz hard at work with a scythe, or Lilith, but couldn't. Then I saw the sheep droppings and stuttered to a halt. Soon, there would be the living, and they would meet me, Siduri, the ghost.

I felt unready.

'What's wrong?' Lilith asked.

'You mean apart from Hugo spotting us?'

'Yes.'

'Nothing,' I said. Could I delay it?

No.

Kitten appeared from a turn in the track. Red-faced, he opened his mouth and bawled. He sobbed repeatedly, his wailing interrupted only by those sweet moments of silence as he dragged air into lungs that were not there.

'Whatever's the matter?' Lilith asked, in that voice used only by mothers.

'Rosalind's leaving!' he blubbed.

'*Fuck!*' Lilith spat, forgetting the boy was there – or perhaps not. She turned and sprinted off across the mud. Dumuz didn't try to keep up. He couldn't, not with a wailing child acting as a literal drag.

Who was Rosalind? I wondered.

⤹

Apparently, I'd picked up more than I first thought from my favourite genre of book. For example, I know a castle entrance only *appears* to be a two-dimensional affair. There is an essential third dimension that remains unseen. The entranceway of a correctly-built castle is not just a gate. It's more of a tunnel sealed at either end by a barrier, one grand and glorious and the other squat but just as functional. I can imagine attackers breaking through the outer gate, only to find themselves trapped in a narrowing passageway engulfed by arrows. As we approached what would have been the inner of the two gates, something was obviously wrong. Well, to be picky, three things. Having a missing inner and, far down the tunnel, outer gate was also somewhat problematic – particularly if you wanted to keep out those you didn't want in.

A single cart stood ahead of us. Hanging precariously off its rear was a trunk packed full of... stuff. From what I knew of the roads around Marhasyow, it wouldn't matter. The cart was uncovered, with seating made of wooden planks. A set of reins lay on an otherwise empty front bench. On their own, they wouldn't have been a concern. However, ahead of the cart and attached to it by a harness stood a pair of draught horses.

A mildly attractive, blond, round-faced girl about my age sat on the rear bench. In her lap was an infant, or what I thought was an infant. It was hard to be sure. The swaddled child had so much material around it there was no sight of skin. The bundle made me think of the baby from the day before, the one in the old man's lap. That man had been too old to hold a child. The girl? Surely she was too young?

Was this Rosalind?

Beside her sat a boy, or possibly a man. Since he was facing away from me, I couldn't tell. The girl had her left hand resting on his thigh. Even from the rear, he looked vaguely familiar. I wondered…

'*For fuck's sake, Freddie!*'

Lilith blocked the path of the nearest horse, arguing with a man and woman who hovered near its rear. Horses are skittish creatures and can take flight at the slightest sign of a breeze. Faced with a very sweary ghost troubling the air in front of them, these two looked particularly twitchy.

Lilith's voice got even louder. 'If not the dead, why don't you listen to the living? Even Adapa told you that leaving by road is crazy. He might be old. He might drool and occasionally piss his pants, but even that old fucker's lucid enough to know the idea is stupid.'

Adapa?

I looked around for Kitten. He'd gone strangely quiet.

A small child shouldn't be able to push an adult out of the way, but he did. An ability, I imagine, he learned from Lilith. I wavered but did not, quite, fall.

'Sorry!' he chirruped as he ran past.

'Who's the girl in the wagon?' I asked Dumuz.

'Rosalind Arden.'

'He cares for her?'

'Kitten? Yes. She grew up with him. They played, but then she got older. Now, I think she barely tolerates him. Not that Kitten notices.'

From the look of it, the girl had found a new pet. 'Perhaps when that baby grows up, Kitten will play with it too.'

'No doubt,' Dumuz said coolly.

Perhaps a tad tactless. 'Sorry,' I said.

Dumuz loosened. 'While Kitten will never grow old, he will also never become more than what you see. It is our lot. Kitten is like the shadow of a fly stuck in amber. The delight comes from watching his aspect change with the movement of the sun.'

'Deep,' I said. And twaddle, I hoped. I didn't like the use of the word "our".

Dumuz missed the sarcasm. 'It is. Still, I think we'd better prevent Lilith from doing something someone else might regret.'

I glanced at Lilith. Her left hand appeared to be drifting around her back – and towards the glass knife hooked in her belt. Dumuz stepped beside her and wrapped his fingers around her wrist.

The man Lilith was arguing with was of average height, balding, and had the most comical of condescending looks on his face. His chubby cheeks, now almost red enough to match his equally bulbous nose, suggested an excess of weight too common in the middle-aged man. I glanced down at his boots. Significantly, mud dotted the toes.

The thin-faced woman beside him, indeed almost physically attached, I took to be his wife. She looked a few years younger than the man and *a lot* shorter. The woman didn't speak. She just held on to him tightly, staring into her husband's eyes.

The woman also looked improbably fat around her belly.

Lilith's blistering attack continued. 'Cordelia, will you stop that doe-eyed-cack! Honestly, I am going to puke. There's a time and a place for such bollocks, and this isn't it. Man up for once and tell Freddie that he's wrong!'

The woman simpered.

'Frederick, where are the others?' Dumuz asked. His question was polite enough, but the subvocalised breaths before and after were audibly not.

The atmosphere was horrible. You could cut the air… with Lilith's knife. Keeping a wary eye on the horses, I stepped forward and stuck my hand out towards the man. 'Hello, I'm Siduri…' My voice trailed off as he stared at my fingers. I had not mastered touch.

The man's nasal twang was immediately irritating. 'Seriously? A dead girl? That's who you went looking for?'

Lilith wrinkled her nose. 'She was alive, at least to begin with.'

'But now?' he replied. 'Now, not so much.'

Git.

'And why is her hair blue?'

Oh, for…

'Up at the keep,' a voice said.

I knew that voice. 'What?'

The boy on the far side of the cart turned his head – and my stomach. 'The others, Mother and Adapa. They're up at the keep.'

He looked thinner than I remembered. I wonder if the girl beside him had anything to do with that. I looked into his eyes. They were green, although a small segment of brown broke the symmetry in his left. I knew him and felt sick.

'Hello, Nicolò,' I said.

'Hello, Siduri.' He looked nervous.

I smiled, almost baring my teeth. 'Hopefully, you'll never forget your first kiss, but it looks like you've moved on.'

Nervous and guilty.

I continued. 'I have as well. Death does that to you.'

Nicolò at least had the decency to look upset. There might even have been a tear. It wasn't the wailing and grief I might have wished for, but still. Maybe he saw the dead thing as not a big deal.

Or perhaps it mattered more that the girl beside him was alive.

'You know each other?' Frederick asked.

'Yes.' We both replied.

'*How well?*'

Nicolò's face blushed beetroot. I made sure mine did not.

'So, Nicolò, I guess you didn't tell Rosalind about Siduri?' Lilith lilted.

Rosalind turned to stare at Nicolò. Forget red. Nicolò was turning blue.

'He does like them cuddly,' Lilith said.

That was unfair. While the girl wasn't exactly thin, she wasn't much bigger than me.

Oh! Bitch!

Of course, there was a more pressing matter. After all, it'd only been a few months since I last… saw him.

'Boy or girl?' I asked.

'What?' Nicolò replied.

I nodded towards the blanketed ball in Rosalind's arms. 'Boy or girl?'

'Oh, him! A boy!' Nicolò said hastily. 'Tristan! He's Frederick's son. Rosalind's brother.'

'Yes,' Rosalind said, near enough hissing. She didn't seem to appreciate his urge to clarify.

I looked more carefully at Cordelia's waist – and the papoose fitted to it. It explained the excess. So, the child was actually hers, and Nicolò wasn't quite the devil I'd thought.

He still deserved a place in the lower reaches of Hell, though.

Before I could say as much, Dumuz interrupted. 'Nicolò, we saw Hugo.'

Nicolò looked stunned. 'He's alive?'

'Yes, and…'

'*And what!*' Frederick asked.

Dumuz grimaced. 'He followed us. The Fedhyow have followed us.'

'That's it. We're leaving!' Frederick warbled.

Lilith growled. '*Freddie, stop squeaking like a soggy twat!* Nicolò, don't you get it? Of course, we have to leave, *but by road?* Now? Go by road, and Hugo will catch us, *which is a bad thing!*'

Nicolò's face spasmed in pain. 'No, you don't get it. There is no "us".' He hesitated and glanced at me. 'There can't be. I…' He stopped and covered his face with his hand. 'My mother wants this,' he said. 'Even Adapa…'

74

Lilith interrupted. 'Adapa?'

Nicolò nodded.

Beside me, Lilith seemed a little... *lost.*

Rosalind slipped her left hand onto Nicolò's right knee. To comfort him? To own him? I could believe the latter. She seemed the sort. Still, and even forgetting the dead thing, I was a tad disappointed when Nicolò let her shuffle closer. As she drew near, the baby squeaked its displeasure.

I knew how it felt.

Frederick regarded the couple approvingly. 'Nicolò's right. What you've created is a charade. I mean, ghosts and humans living together? It's bizarre. I know we engaged in the fantasy but remember our predicament. We are grateful, yes, but now? Now Rosalind has grown.'

'Well, her tits have,' Lilith said, before glancing at my chest.

My bosom felt disappointingly slight.

Frederick didn't seem to hear. He continued, 'Cordelia was so ill that I kept on putting the decision off. But then Tristan came along.' He looked at Nicolò. 'And now this boy. You know, you should have told me who his father was. If I'd known when he first arrived, I might have stopped the two of them...'

'Papa!' Rosalind squeaked.

'*Papa, nothing,*' Frederick growled. 'Nevertheless, what's done is done.' He looked at me meaningfully. 'We all have to move on.'

'So, no word of goodbye then?' Dumuz asked. 'No proper thank you? The moment we turn our backs, you skulk off?'

Frederick clambered up onto the wagon. '*Skulk!* You'd have tried to stop us. For crying out loud, *you are trying.* I will not have another child suffer like Rosalind. She had no one to...'

75

'*No one?*' Lilith asked sharply, her gaze wavering between Rosalind and Kitten.

Frederick winced. 'I'm sorry. I truly am. But, be honest, look at you! No rational person can live with ghosts and fucking sheep forever. Ultimately, you're nothing but vapour.'

Lilith bared her teeth. 'I guess the sheep came in when Cordelia was up the duff?'

Frederick's face grew even pinker. He opened his mouth to respond – before noticing that Cordelia hadn't followed. She'd attempted the climb, slipped and landed on her backside. I tried not to laugh. The track was so muddy it could've been me. Mind you, being a ghost meant my clothing wasn't exactly absorbent.

Frederick harrumphed, leapt down and hauled his wife to her feet. After almost throwing her onto the wagon, he scrambled back up and grabbed the reins. Cordelia muttered a "thank you", which seemed entirely undeserved. Picking up on Frederick's grumpiness, she reached around, tore the infant from Rosalind's grasp and dropped it in the papoose.

Frederick was calmer when he finally spoke. 'I wish you well. You know I do. But this really has to be goodbye.'

With a shrug of his shoulders, he snapped the reins. The horses whinnied and shot forward.

It is one thing to share the same space as a human, but it's quite another to share it with a terrified horse. It stank of fear and testosterone as it passed through me. Still, I could only reflect that I felt far better sharing the same space with that horse than I had when sharing it with Hugo in the garden.

Not that I'd dare tell Lilith that.

'That went well,' Lilith said.

'Idiot,' Dumuz muttered.

They looked at each other. Underneath the bravado, Dumuz and Lilith were worried.

'The others then?' Dumuz asked.

'I guess so,' Lilith said.

I grimaced. 'I thought I knew him.'

'Who? Nicolò?' Lilith asked.

'Yes.'

'You truly don't.'

I looked up, expecting more. Lilith said nothing.

Again. Bitch.

Dumuz broke the silence. 'We need to round up Tiama and Adapa. We either go before the Fedhyow arrive or wait until dusk. They must not see us leave.'

'Leave? But you just said… if we're not going by road, then which way are you thinking of?'

Lilith fluttered her arm in the general direction of the sea. 'Thataway.'

'I couldn't swim before, and I'm pretty certain I can't now.'

'Don't be silly. Try again,' Lilith said.

'A boat?'

'Yup! It's pea green with a big white sail. You'll love it.'

Oh, dear. The idea of being stuck on a small, bleached island of wood surrounded by water nauseated me. 'And if I don't get on the boat?'

'You can always wait for the Fedhyow,' Dumuz said. 'It will be a short journey. We're going to Aberfal, just up the coast. When we land, you can go wherever you wish. Trust me.'

Lilith raised an eyebrow – so much for trust.

Aberfal? At least it was beyond the bridge.

'I'll get the boy,' Dumuz said.

The last time I'd seen Kitten, he'd been pleading with

Rosalind. I turned my head, searching, straining vertebrae that had, ironically, given up the ghost hours ago. And I saw him. The child was disappearing over the horizon, flapping his arms. From the annoying hum the boy was making, it looked like he was chasing a bee.

Dumuz stormed off after Kitten.

Lilith took my hand, and near enough dragged me up the hill towards the cottage.

'He's like that,' she said.

'Who?'

'Kitten. In life, they'd call it autistic. The little dear gets so easily distracted. This time, though, it might be a good thing.'

'Has it got anything to do with his death and his time here alone?'

'Yes,' she said.

I waited, just in case.

Nothing.

'Okay then,' I said. 'Tell me about Frederick.' And Rosalind. 'How did that family end up here?'

'Before Cordelia came here, her mind was broken.' Lilith hesitated. 'Really broken, I mean. We never forced them to stay. There were upsides. So, don't buy the line that cock-faced cantaloupe was selling back there.'

'He thought Cordelia would get better… here?'

'That wasn't the only consideration but, yes.'

'This place is hardly a hospital.'

'I'm not sure I agree. You'll have to trust me but Cordelia's mind really has improved.'

The cynic in me spotted what she hadn't said. 'What did you get out of it?' I asked.

Lilith laughed. 'There was a small matter of ownership.

78

Although we had the money, we still needed a mortal as our front. While we never asked, only an idiot might believe a ghost can hold title. Can you imagine the dilemma if the cash-strapped of Marhasyow realised who the buyers were?'

'I guess.'

'So, we bought the place in Freddie's name. He thought he was onto a good thing. The ungrateful fuck.'

'*Seriously*?'

'Seriously,' she said. 'Anyway, it didn't work out as Freddie hoped. To be fair, the dilapidated nature of the dump came as a shock. Even the best plans can go wrong, I guess.' She looked at me as if what she'd said was significant.

I stared back, baffled.

Lilith shrugged. 'Of course, Freddie turned out to be a complete tit, with an ego directly in inverse proportion to the size of his…' She chuckled. 'You know, I caught sight of it once. Dumuz and I had gone for a romantic night-time walk along the shoal. And, well, I think Freddie and Cordelia had the same idea. Unfortunately, they'd sipped too much of the old sherry and…'

'Lilith,' I warned.

'Don't shush me. With a dick that size, I don't know how they managed it. Still, out popped Tristan nine months later, so I guess they did. How he fathered Rosalind in the first place, I've no idea. Although he must have. With that girl's snotty attitude to life, she's certainly Freddie's progeny.'

'As well as a boyfriend-stealing trollop,' I snapped.

'It wasn't all Rosalind's fault,' she said cryptically. 'So, anyhow,' she added, rushing to continue. 'Freddie is a bit of a tit, yes, but the man turned out to be well-intentioned. Without that saving grace, I would have cut off his cock a long time ago. He even put up some ginormous fuck-off signs at the other end of the causeway. Don't tell Dumuz, but I suspect it was the signs that stopped any visitors well before they got to the Ward.'

Lilith glanced up the hill. 'Ultimately, though, Freddie's right. You, me, Dumuz and Kitten? We are dead. Being dead makes us different. We can laugh and play with them, but we'll always be different. We never age, we can walk through walls, but we also find it difficult to hold, to touch.' She sniffed. 'And we are all damaged.'

'Damaged?'

The left side of her mouth twitched. 'I'm one of the better examples. We each have our flaws, our fixations. Often, something is missing, and you so wish it were not. Still, we make do. We have no choice.'

My heart, *which was not there*, skipped a beat. 'You're saying the living consider us a bunch of infirm, mentally-challenged country cousins?'

Nicolò was alive. So was Rosalind.

'If you add the word deviant somewhere in that, then yes. It doesn't surprise me they're leaving. To leave now, though, and in that direction, is beyond stupid. It's likely to be terminal.' Her voice lightened as she caught my eye. 'If that were the case, and, Nicolò survived the transition, would you still welcome him into our little fold?' Glancing at my groin, she added tunefully, 'Or, at least, yours.'

I said nothing.

I didn't dare.

Chapter seven

The Black Void

The lush grass gradually thinned as we neared the cottage. By the time we reached the entrance, any sign of organic life underfoot had vanished. From its sight and smell, the remaining substance was a composite of sandy, shitty mud, which, I guess, made it organic after all.

The cottage was built out of cobblestone and knapped flint. Despite its obvious age and exposed position, I was surprised the lime that glued it together had not eroded more than it had. However, the deep welts gouged between the stones still made me think of the teeth of a sugar-hungry child.

A feed trough sat just below a window – which probably explained the shit.

The door was open. Against my better judgement, I looked inside. Beyond a few initial patches of dirt, the floor was clean. Further in, there was the traditional set of soft and hard furnishings with chairs, a table, and even an old oil lamp. Straining my eyes through the gloomy half-light of the hallway, I looked into the kitchen.

It was empty save for a table with plates. Each plate was covered in dust.

Lilith bumped a knee against the back of my thighs. 'Don't be so nosy,' she said before pushing past. 'A girl's house is like her knickers. Only the privileged get a peek inside.'

Even ghosts need a home, I guess.

'I'll only be a minute,' she said from somewhere inside.

'Why rush? Won't the Wards stop the Fedhyow?'

'No, not en masse, and the Fedhyow are likely to send a mass. It might slow them a bit, and I'm hoping a few will puke up their guts, but that's about it.'

I looked out towards the pebble bar. Hugo and the Fedhyow were not there… yet.

They soon would be.

Lilith clipped the back of my head.

Bitch.

As I stepped aside, my eyes still popping, my killer, my saviour, walked out into the light.

She was carrying a teddy bear.

'What the…'

'It's Kitten's,' Lilith said.

I should hope so. However, '*We came all this way for a stuffed toy?*'

The yellow fur was thin and stained. Judging by the stitching on its chest, it was a thing repaired, a thing much-loved.

'*Kitten needs it*,' she snapped. 'It's important.'

Apparently.

'Why?' I asked.

Lilith glowered. 'He can't sleep without it.'

Possibly true, but not enough reason for a detour, not with the Fedhyow bearing down. There was something about that bear Lilith didn't want me to know. Something important.

Something she wasn't going to tell me.

So, instead, I asked the other obvious question. 'I can sleep?'

'Well… what else would you do in bed?' Lilith asked, flicking out her tongue. The sweetness in her voice made me think of treacle.

I shook my head in despair and turned away.

We set off along the track towards the keep. The mud remained just as shitty.

With the bear off-limits, I asked Lilith something else that bothered me. 'Why describe us as witches? I know there needs to be a term for what we are, but I didn't exactly see a cauldron or a wand inside your house.'

'Cauldron?' she trilled. 'No… but I've always considered Dumuz a wizard with his wa…'

'Or a spellbook,' I added hastily.

Lilith's lips tightened, her voice deepening again. 'Wards are not spells. They're more like contracts. A contract the victim is unaware they've signed. But, of course, *witch* is simply a colloquial term. The correct name for witches, or at least in these parts, is Wycche.'

'*What?*'

Lilith laughed. 'So, you *did* learn something at school? It wasn't all "touch your toes" biology?'

Bitch.

'The Wycche of Marhasyow are gone,' I said. 'It was an exam question and everything.'

'The Wycche were here long before Marhasyow. But yes, you're right. The Wycche as a people no longer exist, but their heirs survived. Some in Marhasyow, some not.'

'My mother was Wycche?'

'Most definitely.'

'How do you know?'

She smirked, her voice switching back to the musical. 'Iresh and I were close once. There'll always be a place for your mother in my... heart.'

'You're saying that you and Iresh were...'

Lilith stopped me. 'Nicolò? Frederick and family? They're all Wycche. That's why they could see you so clearly.'

'Iresh...'

Again, she interrupted. 'Frederick's not from Marhasyow. But you already know that. Do you want to know how he ended up here?'

'Not right now, I...'

Lilith bludgeoned on. 'Freddie was a psychiatrist. I'm sure he made his parents proud, and then not so when one of his patients dropped a sprog.'

I gave up. 'Cordelia?'

She nodded. 'Apparently, giving her mind, and other parts, a proper pounding crossed the whole doctor-patient line. Who'd have thought? Freddie served three years for it.'

'And Cordelia?'

'Her family kicked her out. She ended up in a single room with only Rosalind gnawing at her tit for company. Of course, her poor noggin got worse after that. Then, three years later, Freddie got his get-out-of-jail and found her again.'

'Very... romantic?'

'Quite. Anyway, eventually, they upped sticks and made for Marhasyow, looking for a fresh start. The poor man didn't realise he'd end up de-scroting sheep for a living.'

'What about you? Why are you here?'

'*Me?*' she squeaked like an operatic mouse. 'Let's just say

84

that I didn't end up in Marhasyow out of choice.'

Our eyes met. Again, Lilith obviously didn't want to say any more.

'It seems I need to know more about the Wycche,' I tried instead.

'You studied them at school. You sat the exam.'

'I failed the exam.'

Lilith eyed me suspiciously. I smiled back. Smiling wasn't easy, what with the dead thing… and the Nicolò thing.

'All right,' she said. 'But where to start?' She snorted. 'How about with my best, Dumuz?'

My grin dropped.

Lilith's rose. 'Any conflict has its gaps, its contradictions. Particularly if one side ends up so shafted, the only thing left is a void.'

Okay, not quite Dumuz.

She continued. 'The victors write the history. The losers write fuck all. It doesn't take a genius to figure out which side qualifies as "the good". Awkward things, such as the black of some of their acts, never make the page.'

'You could have just said "*the history books are wrong*".'

She growled. 'Do you want to hear this or what?'

'No, no. Please continue.'

'Before the castle. Before Marhasyow, there was the Wycche. They built their homes near the floodplain of the Koner where the soil was good and kept their flocks on the moorland where the soil was… well… not so good. The Wycche grew vegetables in the silt, ate fish from the sea, and were quite the aficionados of the occasional lamb shank.'

I ignored the double entendre.

She added, 'Particularly the young and the singletons.'

85

Nope, not playing. 'What were the Fedhyow doing? With those cloaks, they wouldn't be much good in a field… or a river.'

'The Fedhyow fucked off before anything covered in the history books.'

'But… they were here?'

'Long ago, yes. In those days, the Fedhyow were pretty much Wycche. The cloaks and the "Fedhyow" name only came about when they moved to Guitt.'

'Why leave?'

'Few souls survive death. Even among the Wycche, it's a matter of parentage and luck. The Fedhyow were some of the not-so-lucky.'

I wasn't exactly feeling fortunate myself. 'They left because they were jealous?'

'They disliked some of the Wycche's lifestyle choices.'

'Such as the masturbation you were indelicately hinting at?'

She laughed. 'Well… yes. Still, human nature should tell you that's something they're hypocritical about. However, I'm talking about some of the more arcane rituals the Wycche took a fancy to over the years.'

'Rituals like cutting out someone's heart?' Not that I was bitter.

Lilith smirked. 'Yes, that kind of thing.' She grew more serious. 'Although there are some even I find distasteful.'

'Which ones?'

Lilith said nothing.

'You're not going to tell me, are you?'

'Not right now. No.'

Of course not.

Lilith continued. 'So, the Fedhyow left to seek a better way… if you consider prayer and piously treating women like shit, "better". Still, to be honest, their vision of immortality would be an improvement over reality. Pity, it's all bollocks.'

'I thought you hated the Fedhyow? You sound almost sympathetic.'

'I hate what they've become. I hate that they twat anything that as much as sniffs like a Wycche. However, before they left, the Fedhyow were just another bunch of prudish dicks.'

'How do you know? Were you there? You said you came from somewhere else?'

The youngish woman beside me snorted. 'I am not quite that old. It's something I read in a book, just not one you'd ever see at school.'

'You still haven't told me where you're from.'

'No, I haven't,' she said.

Again, Bitch.

'Anyway,' Lilith said. 'After the Fedhyow left, the Wycche settled back into their old ways – mostly. They built a wool mill and dock at the river's mouth to bring in some more income, but that's about it. The Wycche carried on happy enough until about sixty years ago…'

'What happened then?' I asked innocently.

Lilith glanced at me. 'The books you *should* have read in school and the actual truth match up, at least at the beginning. A group of settlers arrived. They were unexpected and most certainly not invited. They came from the north and seemed suspiciously uninformed about the principles of prior ownership. These same settlers, though, were experts on what an army was. Indeed, they made sure the Wycche knew they were on first-name terms with the commander of one just thirty miles up the coast.'

'But, of course, the settlers weren't farmers.'

'Nope,' she said. 'The new lot didn't know a sheep's arse end from its front – which was unfortunate for a few of the lonelier ones at night.'

I winced.

Lilith smirked. 'Yup. It's unsurprising the fucks turned out to be a bunch of cave jockeys, both literal and not so. After intimidating the Wycche with the army talk, they buggered off inland to mine a shitload of tin. Tin the Wycche wouldn't have given a toss about, even if they had known of its existence.'

'The school preferred books that told tales of derring-do and doughty souls. Legends that tamed the wilderness, living on the edge, that kind of thing.'

'So, you *did* read some of them?'

'A few. Still, the miner's sexual preferences never made the syllabus. I'm sure I'd have noticed.'

'Don't think I'm prejudiced,' Lilith tweeted. 'Every cocksmith needs a hobby. There was this one time with Dumuz when he…'

I interrupted. 'I did like the stories with a handsome hero, though, the one that battles against the odds.'

'But when the odds turned in his favour?'

'Well, I imagine that's when we get to the black and white of it.'

Lilith nodded. 'With the Wycche, in this case, being the black.' She squinted at me. 'You know, you're not as dumb as you pretend – or look.' The squint turned to amusement. 'Speaking of looks. You might want to do something about that skirt of yours. Especially when you bend over.'

'Why?'

'You'll see.'

I wouldn't let her distract me. 'I did fail the exam,' I said.

'But not because you hadn't read up on it.'

'No,' I admitted. 'Much of my essay paper was spent questioning why the Wycche were depicted as so one-dimensional. They didn't seem to have a past of their own. Now? Now I'm still struggling to accept that this Wycche past also includes the Fedhyow.'

'Very few know the two share the same ancestry. The Fedhyow certainly don't talk about it – unsurprisingly.' She paused. 'Perhaps it's time for you to take the lead. Consider it punishment for playing stupid.'

The glint in her eyes gave me little choice. Steeling myself, I began. 'One winter's day, a delegation of miners arrived at the wool mill. They offered the miller a small fortune in gold for the mill and a nearby dock.'

'It wasn't gold.'

'What?'

'It was tin, and even then, it was more like a promissory note.'

'What?'

'Just saying.'

'Have you finished "just saying"?'

'I thought I'd take a turn at the gaps.'

'Can you just stick with the significant ones?'

'Define significant?'

I glared at her.

'Okay, but I choose what's significant.'

I grimaced. 'While the miners found the tin easy to extract, transporting it over land proved difficult.'

'Yeah… the road through the bog has always been kind of "*sinky*".'

I nodded. 'So, the miners decided they needed the miller's dock to ship their ore by sea. Unfortunately, the mill caught fire during negotiations, and its owner died.'

'At least that's what the books say,' she said bitterly. 'They never mention the miller's wife and child. They certainly never mention that said wife and child burnt to death in the pyre.'

'He had a wife? A child?'

'Yup. One of your gaps no one bothered to write about. It had an upside, though. The miners got their dock.'

'Was that why the Wycche behaved as they did?'

'Wycche?'

'Are you saying what happened next wasn't in revenge for the fire?'

'Oh no,' she said. 'It was most definitely related.'

'*Anyway*,' I said. 'The books turn quite graphic when they get to the next bit. I know. I threw up when I read one of them. Supposedly, that same night, the Wycche snuck into every hovel, crept into every home, and cut the throats of every man they found.'

'The idea of gaping wounds and pools of blood makes you queasy?'

'As I said, I threw up.'

'So yesterday?'

'Yesterday, if I hadn't bled out, I'd have choked on my own vomit.'

'Not a good way to go,' she agreed.

'To be fair, having my heart cut out wasn't much better,' I said pointedly.

Lilith sniffed.

I shook my head. '*Anyway*,' I continued. 'It was my commentary on the *bit after the next bit* that got me that fail in the exam. Those next few months were particularly abridged. While I understood the moral outrage, I explored the possibility that the punishment the army doled out was a tad more collective than necessary. I don't really know the details but certainly, by the end, there were no more Wycche.'

'It wasn't moral outrage, not from those that mattered anyway.'

'Mattered?'

'The ones who financed the venture. Those twats only ever cared about the tin, or at least the fuckload of cash they got for it.'

'So, what actually happened to the Wycche?'

'You've pretty much already nailed it, just like the army did when it arrived soon after. They crucified every man they could find.'

'What about the women? The children?'

'The wives and daughters worked in the fields, supervised by a soldier's cock. The sons were sent to the mines. Their fate was pretty much the same.'

'But,' I said, 'given that I'm here, some must have survived. Some escaped?'

'A few. Those who survived changed their names and did their best to forget what they once were. They certainly hid it from their children. There were some mementoes, of course, but the danger back then was so great that the Wycche gave up on anything that marked them out.'

'Like the witchy stuff? Like the... oh, I don't know... ghost stuff?'

'Precisely. Still, some truly pissed-off exceptions hung around for a while. Those exceptions sliced up the newly-landed at quite the rate. So much so that the citizens of the new port town of Marhasyow finally demanded and got a castle.'

'With a garrison,' I added.

She snorted. 'Who were fuck all use. When the incidents stopped, it had nothing to do with them.'

'Who then?'

Lilith ignored me. 'A few years later, the tin petered out. The army left, and any wealth that was gained drifted away.'

I gave up. 'Until Izdubar,' I said.

∽

Approaching the keep, we reached the remains of a dry-stone wall. Like the cottage, it looked older than the castle. That said, it still seemed capable of deterring wandering livestock – and anyone who couldn't find a stile.

'Did you say our kind can walk through walls?' I asked.

'Yes,' Lilith replied – and goosed me.

I tumbled through as if it wasn't there, landing on my elbows.

'Or at least you can when you learn how,' Lilith added. 'The barrier is only in your mind. The trick is to pretend it's not there.' She snickered. 'It also works if you're distracted.'

Is every unhinged killer quite this annoying?

Well… probably.

Ahead of me, a noise made me look up.

An old man and a middle-aged woman sat on a bench. The old man was laughing, although it might have been a consumptive cough. The woman stared blankly.

Lilith flicked her hand towards me. 'This is Siduri. As you can see, you can forget any hope she was worth the trip.'

'Gee, thanks.'

Lilith nodded towards the old man. 'Siduri, this is Adapa. I'd like to say that, as the grandfather of the group, he's respected by all, but…'

The old man broke wind, loudly, before coughing and spitting a wad of phlegm bloodily onto the grass. I wrinkled my nose in disgust. In response, his creamy, watery eyes sparkled with amusement. I looked down. His clothing was a traditional mix of brown and grey interspersed with the occasional vomit stain.

'See what I mean?' Lilith added.

He pulled out a pipe and coughed again. Perhaps lung cancer?

'You're alive?' I asked. It was a reasonable question, given his condition. I was also beginning to wonder about his mental capacity.

He guffawed, spat again, and spoke. His voice made me think of air bubbles popping in tar. 'Alive? Of course, girlie. I haven't earned my eye pennies yet. I'm Adapa Dubar. Good to meet you, lass.' He stood and wrapped his arms around me.

Then three further thoughts snapped into my head: If he's still living, how can he touch me? Are his clothes really smearing me with *expelate*? And is he actually fondling my arse?

A mass of stubble scratched my skin as he pecked me on the cheek.

'How did you do that? How can you touch me so easily?' I asked, bewildered.

'Dumuz reckons it's due to me being nearly dead and all.' He pinched Lilith's bottom, who yelped. Adapa's eyes twinkled. 'I like to think it's because I'm still alive.'

I smiled. I'd always be a fan of someone who could put Lilith in her place.

Lilith frowned at him. In response, Adapa blew her a kiss – followed by a raspberry.

Yes, I really might like him.

Lilith sighed and turned towards the woman. 'Siduri, this is Nicolò's mother, Tiama.'

I looked at the woman beyond Adapa. Her hair, backcombed, was the colour of strawberries. The face underneath was both blotchy and heavily lined. Her body looked thin and worn and tired. I stretched out a hand in greeting, confident that contact was possible. Her feet were bare and unspotted. The woman was just as dead as me.

'Hello, I'm Siduri. I don't think we ever met?'

The woman, Tiama, stared at it. What a cow! Contempt I'll take from a mortal, or perhaps Lilith, but not from a poxy scarecrow!

Adapa answered instead. 'Ah, lass, you'll have to forgive her. New people and situations only confuse. You see, Tiama's transition didn't go well. The poor woman is mute, and her mind is mostly haar.'

I gave up. These two were the last of my companions. I had hoped for someone who was at least heroic, and, if not that, then at least good-looking, and, if not that, at least my age. I guess "living" was also no longer mandatory. Actually, aside from Adapa, I was developing a low opinion of the living. The Fedhyow were alive. Nicolò and Rosalind were alive.

Of course, if Lilith was right about the road, then for the latter two, that might change. Did I want that? Might Nicolò then…

No, Siduri. Get real. Wishes are like kisses. Both end in regret.

Iresh taught me that. Nicolò taught me that.

Of course, getting real isn't much better. Getting real let me hear that noise I'd done my best to ignore.

And still wish I could ignore.

CHAPTER EIGHT

IF GOLD RUSTS

At first, I thought it was a gull. Even as the screeching grew more plaintive, that impression remained. Tiama was the first to realise the truth. The furrow of her wizened brow furrowed even more. Her eyes, blank and wide until that moment, crumpled into slits.

Dumuz, with Kitten in tow, appeared at the entrance to the keep. He looked upset. Distressed, even.

For the first time, I truly heard the screams.

'They've been caught?' Lilith asked.

Dumuz nodded. 'The wagon hardly got off the causeway. Frederick, Rosalind and Nicolò are there, tied up in front of it. Cordelia...' He couldn't bring himself to finish.

Behind me, Kitten hummed an old folk song.

Dumuz and Lilith held each other's gaze for quite some time and I waited. What was there to say?

Finally, though, Lilith turned towards me. Absurdly, she was clutching Kitten's teddy bear. 'It is part of the real world,' she said. 'This is your next lesson. Hold it.'

I reached out. It tingled, but I couldn't maintain a grip.

'*Concentrate!* Force yourself into their realm.'

I focused and firmed my hands. As I took the stuffed toy from Lilith, I almost felt alive.

'Now, put it in your jacket. The action itself will make it part of our world.' Lilith hesitated. 'He will need it,' she added.

Dumuz turned to Kitten, bent down, and kissed his forehead. Lilith allowed herself a single stroke of the boy's hair.

Lilith raised her chin. 'Okay. They're here now, so we can't leave. Not yet. Not until dark. Until then, we must stop them from getting in.' She stared at everything but Dumuz. 'The shingle bank?'

Dumuz nodded gruffly and set off.

Kitten tried to follow, but Adapa grasped his wispy hand. 'Not now, son,' he said. 'It's best you stay with me.' His voice lacked any humour.

Lilith pursed her lips. 'Can you take him to the wharf? It's out of sight from most things.'

Adapa hacked a "yes". The tears in his eyes betrayed his concern.

'Kitten,' Lilith said. 'Can you go with Adapa? Maybe you can help him prepare the boat. That'll be fun, won't it?'

Kitten looked apprehensive. 'Where's Rosalind?'

Lilith bit her bottom lip. 'Rosalind went ahead. You'll see her soon.'

I thought about the screams. Some promises are hard to keep.

Kitten squinted warily. 'Okay. But I'll want a story later!'

Lilith smiled. I suspected she didn't dare speak. Frowning, Kitten let Adapa lead him to the keep and into the blackness beyond.

Oh, sh…

Kitten shouldn't have turned. He really shouldn't have turned. If he hadn't, I wouldn't have seen that face, now barely visible in the shadows. Without the lack of light, I wouldn't have recognised…

I remember a fire. I remember a large fireplace, its mantle dominating the room. Above it was a faded picture of a boy.

A boy I didn't know.

I do now.

Who was the boy in the painting?

Kitten. My brother.

Damn.

The boy in the painting ruined my life. He took my mother's heart and kept it captive in his grubby little paws. He…

Lilith found her misplaced voice. 'Siduri, can you get that arse of yours up on the roof of the keep?'

'What?' I asked, still in shock.

'You can go with Adapa if you like, but you'd be more useful up there on lookout. If things turn to shit in a puddle, make for the boat. Leave. Take Kitten and Adapa and leave. Once safe, you can go wherever the fuck you want.'

'Sulis,' I said. I had more questions for my aunt.

'Your… aunt?' she asked, sounding oddly amused. 'Then, could you take Kitten with you? He'll be happy there.'

Happy? Eventually, perhaps, but by then I wouldn't be around to see it. Anyone with a heart would know the boy wasn't to blame for how Iresh treated me.

But I no longer had a heart.

I nodded. It was easier than saying no.

Lilith seemed satisfied. 'Okay,' she said. 'Inside the keep entrance, on the left, you'll find the lever that drops the portcullis. That'll slow them down if they get past me. Beyond the lever, there's a staircase. It'll take you to the roof.'

She turned towards Tiama. 'Tiama. Can you show Siduri how to get there?'

Tiama looked doubtful.

'After that, you can join Kitten on the wharf if you like,' Lilith said.

Tiama's face lit up. It seemed enough.

'Thank you,' Lilith said, before spinning around and running down the hill.

Tiama ambled towards the keep. All I could do was follow.

Of course, the inside of the keep had to be dark. When searching for a hidden lever, it's usually better to have it a tad murky.

I reached out with my fingers.

On the upside, I found the lever. On the down, my hand slid through it and beyond. As Lilith had taught me, I focused and tried again. Perspiring sham beads of sweat, I met resistance. I shut my eyes and pressed down more forcefully through my shoulder. The lever jarred and moved several inches. I stepped back, astonished. Then, moments later, I almost jumped out of my pseudo-skin as the poorly-geared portcullis slammed down onto, and, to a certain extent, into the ground.

That done, I stepped into a closet that I hoped was the entrance to the stairwell. I would have asked Tiama, but she had vanished.

Ghosts do that, I guess.

Forget murky. The room was pitch black, and I nearly fell flat on my face as I clipped the edge of the first step. I only managed to stop by grabbing an old rusty handrail. Perhaps I was getting better at the touch thing?

Thankfully, it turned out I was – even though the dark required a firmer grip on the loose rail than I might have liked.

At the top, much to my disgust, the exit was astonishingly narrow. Only someone young, or thin, or very determined could pass through.

Oh, and ghosts, of course.

Daylight.

The keep's roof was a makeshift affair, cobbled together from wooden offcuts of variable length. There was also a lot of canvas – a lot of canvas. At a guess, the keep had been Frederick's home, he'd been no carpenter, and he'd been much skinnier back then to have got through the doorway. I looked at the front parapet. What was left of it appeared near to collapse. If you were bold and lacked a rational fear of heights, you might imagine it offered some defence. I kept well back. Ghost, though I might be, the contemplation time available in so significant a drop didn't appeal.

I looked out… and wished I hadn't.

What was once a harbour was to my left. If there had been buildings that had survived the storm, they had long since collapsed. Touched by the salted blessings of the sea, nothing vertical of interest remained. Even the gulls stayed distant. In contrast, the mouth of the Koner itself glistened with life. A dam of silt and debris slowed the river's natural exit to the sea. It was a place where wading birds obviously felt at home.

To my right was the shingle bank. From this angle, it resembled a slash of golden ink scribed onto a sheet of turquoise parchment. An expanding dot in a darker shade shimmered as it grew closer.

The dot was not ink.

Closer, just beyond the castle walls at the junction between rock and pebble bar, Dumuz sat patiently, his legs dangling. His left arm rested on a pole that grew out of the mound of gravel just below him. If he lifted that pole and held it high, he would look like a fisherman.

He didn't lift it.

I couldn't avoid it any longer. I stared ahead at the crowd gathered on the pebble beach beyond the lagoon. An ankle-deep film of water covered the causeway between the beach and the castle. As its lines rippled and fractured under the sun, I could see that the causeway was passable despite it being high water.

For the moment, though, the crowd was too busy to show interest in the castle. Dressed in anything but black, these were natives of the town I thought I knew. They were workers, doctors, teachers and classmates. None, though, were friends. All had supped upon the chalice of the Fedhyow, but, until this moment, I had never known them capable…

…I saw a woman staked to a tall wooden post. Squinting tears into makeshift prisms, I recognised her face, just. It was difficult. The fire made it difficult. I watched, tapping my lips with my fingers as the crackle and snap of flames reached higher and higher. I listened, although my hands had now moved to my ears, to the whoosh of air as it screamed. I stared and couldn't cover my eyes as I saw its source vanish into a cloud of black.

Cordelia.

I refocused. The road beyond the causeway was once a major highway. Not now. The edges had weathered badly. Even from this distance, I saw crumbled road metal lying loose on the top of ditches already full of silt. The only thing left of the thoroughfare was a track capable of passing traffic in a single direction – a track that was blocked. Rather than the regular four wheels on the wagon, only the two at the rear remained. The front wheels were missing. Bizarrely, the image of a cat came to mind, with its belly on the floor, its hind legs set higher than its head, toying with its prey. Frederick, sat just in front, was wearing Tristan's papoose. Beside him were Rosalind and Nicolò.

They must have been terrified. Surely. Instead, bound by rope, they seemed oddly calm. After Cordelia's death, had they given up? Or perhaps even faced with all that was fact, they still doubted the imminence of their demise. I gazed across at the remains of Cordelia's pyre. Beside the glowing embers were three more posts. Fate doesn't do clemency. I'd learnt that the hard way. In fact, Fate was a bit of a shit, really.

The causeway raised into a ramp against the seawall. On the ramp's left, and away from the townsfolk, the joining point offered a place to hide if they were daring or foolhardy. Lilith, naturally, was both. To put words in her mouth, Lilith was about to tell Fate to "go f… flip itself".

No doubt she'd claim it was through lack of choice.

My panther flowed over the concrete ramp and towards the wagon. Lilith moved quickly, but without the jerkiness that might catch an eye. She grew more substantial in form as she glided across the shattered road. As Lilith approached the prisoners, she drew her knife.

A chance wind caught the last remnants of the rising smoke and pushed it back down. Those gathered nearest the pyre felt its stinging touch on their throats. They coughed, they spluttered, they turned – and saw Lilith.

It wasn't a coincidence. If it hadn't been the smoke, it

would've been a noise, a glance away, or a decision to begin the next act of this most passionate of plays.

Lilith's knife darted out. The blade flashed first towards Nicolò, then Rosalind, and finally Frederick. To my pleasure and, guiltily, my pain, it was the ropes that fell.

Still dazed, they didn't move.

Lilith reached down and tugged at Nicolò's arm.

Initially, I wasn't sure what would win, Nicolò's weight or Lilith's determination. I should have known Lilith would cheat. She let go, and Nicolò fell back onto Rosalind. The collision broke Nicolò out of his stupor. He leapt to his feet almost on the bounce and set off at pace towards the causeway. With Nicolò's fingers wrapped around Rosalind's wrist, the poor girl could only follow.

Burdened by the bulk of Tristan's papoose, Frederick rose awkwardly. The sudden flight of his daughter had sparked him into motion. "Following the herd", one might say. But that, of course, would make his daughter a "cow".

And I was happy with that.

Lilith hung back to give them some distance before trailing behind. This time, she wasn't a panther at all. This time, she was protecting the game.

Nicolò and Rosalind quickly reached the causeway and didn't stop as they splashed into the shallow waters across its top.

Frederick lagged, but Lilith wouldn't let him slow. She chivvied and chased, swearing so loudly that even I could hear. Even so, her focus wasn't just on Frederick. Lilith's head swept from side to side, from front to back. The movements weren't of panic, but of a worldly warrior looking to strike at anyone who might come close.

They were coming close.

In the end, it wasn't Lilith's fault. Lilith would blame herself, but it wasn't her fault.

Frederick slipped off the ramp and fell into deeper water.

He did not rise.

You do not rise if your skull makes so hard a contact with the edge of a concrete slipway.

I wasn't close enough to see the pooling blood and splinters of skull. Nor see the ruddy ooze slap back against his hair and turn to foam. But I was sure it would be so. Frederick floated on his back in the shallow waters by the ramp. He looked like an upturned turtle with his arms apart and legs asunder in classic man-spreading repose. Perhaps that was the wrong metaphor. A beetle might be a better choice as two smaller legs were kicking out from his waist.

Tristan.

Nicolò and Rosalind, now keep-side of the castle wall, couldn't have seen. The entrance to the castle was far too narrow. Instead, they waited patiently, calmly, Nicolò with his left arm draped loosely around Rosalind's waist.

Lilith must have known that Frederick was dead, gone, lost even to the sacrificial cut of her knife. She could have made it to safety but didn't try. Instead, Lilith knelt and reached out for Frederick's corpse. I think she intended to pull Frederick close and free Tristan.

She was far too late.

A wave of the vengeful swept down from the land, onto the ramp, and into the sea beside it. Grasping hands took hold of Frederick and Tristan, sucking them into their mass and out of view. Those on the slippery ramp were less successful. Unable to stop, they met the kneeling and very solid form of

Lilith with untargeted force. The collision sent them flying through the air and onto the causeway behind her.

I could almost see Lilith sigh as she stood, knife in hand, backing up beyond the fallen... but she didn't flee.

Why did she stay?

And then I saw why. When Lilith moved, she limped heavily, favouring her left leg. The collision with that first wave had taken its toll.

Lilith angled her knife towards the closing mob, the blade glinting in the sun.

I made myself look away. Why should I care? She took my heart.

Dumuz, the fisherman, sat to my right. His left hand remained on the metal pole embedded within the mound of small boulders and rock. I wondered if he could hear the shouts from the causeway and guessed how Lilith's story had played out.

Would he want to know?

Dumuz, the fisherman, didn't have time to consider anything beyond the immediate. He had a catch to make.

Beneath him and closing rapidly along the reconstructed dyke, ran the Fedhyow. Once fine and pure, the golden sand of the shingle bank was now marked and pocked with black scratches that ran along its length.

As the vanguard of the Fedhyow approached the rocks of the castle proper, Dumuz stood and leaned on the metal pole. He strained, he pushed and pulled, but it refused to move. Dumuz stopped and turned to look at me. I waved and pointed to the front. I tried to tell him. What? What could I say through gesture or even sound that might change what he was about to do? Dumuz sighed and shook his head. I think he understood. Dumuz arched his back and pulled even harder on the rod. To my surprise, he glowed. He began to flare and fire. If he could be more than real, Dumuz was more than real. That wasn't right. That wasn't human – or inhuman. Ghosts should be less substantial, not more.

If asked, most people would describe rock as a solid. It is a simple fact. If you tap a rock or hit it, it does not give or bend. Rock just looks back and dares you to do your best. However, a rock's inability to soften can make it the thing it is not. To Dumuz, rock can also be a liquid. The metal pole moved, and gravity did the rest. The gravel heap intended once for the pebble bar faltered and failed and slid into the sea.

The Fedhyow, not on the temporary dyke, shuddered to a halt.

Leading this second group was Hugo.

Nicolò's father always had a slight limp, but now it looked more pronounced. Shaking his head, Hugo seemed to mutter something to a Fedhyow on his right. The man nodded, drew out a glass orb, arced his arm, and *threw*. It fell short of its target, but the effort was impressive. The globe shattered where the gravel pile had been, spraying a fine mist. A translucent fog hung briefly between the Fedhyow and their prey before momentum moved it on.

It touched Dumuz. It blended, it merged, and when it cleared, Dumuz was simply not there.

Those on the dyke were also not there. For that matter, neither was the dyke. Thirty yards of it, all gone, washed away in that instant. The noise was deafening. The bang carried from the collapsing bank to my ears, to my teeth, and to my toes – which curled. Dumuz had been right, again, but apparently for the last time, when he said, "You never know

106

when you need to block a pipe". With no vent, the pressure of high tide quickly broke the dam.

I blinked away the compression wrought on my eyeballs by the sound wave. Turning, I watched as the wall of water, foam and rock swept across the lagoon towards the causeway and…

Lilith had not fallen.

There were many lying dead in front of her or the water to her side, but Lilith still stood.

At the sight of the wave, the remaining citizens of Marhasyow tried to flee. They barely managed to turn. The ocean swept over them, and Lilith, as if they were not there.

And, after its passing, they were not.

Beneath me, and still safe, Rosalind buried her face into Nicolò's chest. Perhaps she'd seen the rising tide through the entranceway. Rosalind would certainly have heard the noise. Either way, she must have understood that she'd never see her father or brother again.

I bit my lip and watched as Nicolò pulled her close.

⌐

Smoke billowed, almost vertically, on a hill beyond the landward side of the causeway. Now late into dusk, the sea breeze was just a memory. The air, however, was anything but still. As the sun set, a war of volume began as energetic gusts of breath pushed out from land to sea. The dominance of the ocean was under threat. For now, it was a stalemate. By nightfall, I knew that the land would have its triumph.

While Hugo and the remaining Fedhyow on the shingle bank had retired to lick their wounds, the townsfolk weren't as lucky. The wave had smeared many of them across the harbour ruins. Others were carried to the silt banks of the Koner's mouth and laid to rest – or they would have been if it wasn't for a growing flock of seriously unfussy birds. The few corpses that remained in the lagoon had settled among the iris. It was a fleeting sight. The bodies and what once were flowers would soon rot and sink into the now tidal mud.

Never to be seen again.

The hours had passed slowly and quietly apart from the tears. Nicolò and Rosalind had walked hand in hand across the castle grounds to join Adapa and Kitten on the wharf. With nothing left to see beyond the castle walls, I followed. Tiama had already gone ahead.

Sat at the small dock, they waited and cried a lot. Adapa wanted to leave immediately, but I insisted we stay until dark. The timing between our departure and the arrival at low tide of the Fedhyow would be close, but I reasoned it would be our only chance. When logic failed, I invoked Lilith, or at least her name. I told them it was her last wish. Adapa went quiet when he heard it was her idea.

I left them again at dusk.

Now, one last time on the ramparts of the keep, I looked out, wanting only darkness, but it refused to come.

A small fire had been lit on the hill opposite. The fire was about level with, or perhaps just a little higher than I. In all the chaos, I hadn't thought of looking beyond or above the causeway, beach or road. Of course, there is a hill, and, of course, it is higher. There is always something higher.

He stood to the fire's left, cloaked in white, a creature who cast a shadow that leant towards a flame and not away. A man who looked to all the world as if he had no need of saving.

His eyes were on me.

My father wasn't alone. To his front, and so near the flames, was Hugo. Once night fell and the tide retreated, I imagine they'd find it easy to take a night-time stroll across an emptied moat, along with the remaining Fedhyow.

Looking closer, I saw a child in Hugo's arms and felt confused. The fire didn't seem necessary to keep the infant warm, swaddled as it was. As I stared harder, though, I realised the swaddling looked loose. Perhaps it was still wet from its time in the water only a few hours before? Maybe the child needed the heat to dry it? I tried not to think about why else Hugo might want to hold Tristan above such an all-consuming flame.

I didn't cry out. There was no point. I lacked the heart to cry out, but I also wouldn't tell Rosalind. I wouldn't have her be braver than me.

As night fell, I turned away and walked towards the winding staircase. Even when there is no choice, there is still a choice.

I chose not to look.

Chapter nine

Queen of the Castle

Like a river, all faiths must have a source, a fount of wisdom that is pure and sweet. A true believer will consider any suggestion otherwise to be heresy. However, even the most pious accept that an *actual* river is better off bland, and, if not, then it makes sense to discover why before supping upon its waters again.

At the end of the summer, the river Koner turned bitter.

⤳

Early one morning, just as the sun was rising, I woke from a sleep that held me still. Unlike the old folk tune, I didn't feel like singing, and I was no longer a maiden, but "early" was sadly correct. "Woke" was also an exaggeration, almost as much as "sleep" and "still". The summer for me had been a forever dusk with humid nights filled with sweat and tears and an almost manic shuffling under a single sheet. The days weren't much better. In the light, I moped around, eyes half shut, incapable of anything practical.

But at least in daylight, I didn't cry. I didn't dare, not in front of Iresh.

That morning, four weeks ago, getting up proved particularly difficult. Indeed, I was so sleepy I put my knickers on inside out – twice. Even before Iresh opened her mouth, I knew it would be a bad day.

Awful.

'*Are you out of that bed yet?*'

Well, obviously, given the clumping around. Still, Iresh found it funny. That was the main thing.

The next tease came when I entered the kitchen.

'*Water?*'

I didn't do water. Iresh knew I didn't do water, not since the river had begun to smell. Of course, she might not have either, but her water, she repeated incessantly, came from the garden well.

'Lemonade?' I suggested instead, already knowing the answer.

Her glare didn't wither as much as it once had.

'Okay then. Milk, please.'

'What's wrong with water?'

I watched, horrified, as she dipped a calcified glass into a bucket of the stuff that sat beside her knee. What indeed? It always surprised me she never spilt a drop.

I ignored the question and spooned out some homemade muesli that I kept in an old biscuit tin. After popping it into a bowl, I waited.

And waited.

Iresh grudgingly shoved the milk bottle across the table. I poured some into the bowl and much of the rest into a large tumbler.

'Toast?' she asked, munching a black slice of the stuff that could only taste like charcoal. There was once a time when we made cakes together, and Iresh was a genius at the breakfast bun.

But that was long ago.

'What will you do now you've left school?' she asked.

Ah, yes, the ritual. One we now played out every morning. There were three parts to it – the bed bit, the breakfast bit and the question. Iresh had metaphorically been packing my case since the start of summer. Indeed, she had been packing it since that picnic all those years ago.

I didn't bother expressing *yet again* the pain I felt inside. To her, my failed romance was a mere paper cut in the grand scheme of things. No doubt she'd seen far worse. Not that she ever told me. To me, Iresh's history was a blank page. The only smudge I knew was that there must have been at least one man in her life. A couple of lessons at school taught me that. A midnight fumble with a boy told me that.

I'd taken a risk and got away with it. Iresh, it turned out, was less fortunate.

'Have you thought about college?'

Maybe the blank page bit was just down to her flaky memory. The college question was at least a weekly occurrence.

And so was my answer.

'The one in Marhasyow has stopped taking girls – thanks to the Fedhyow.'

'What about Sulis?'

That was new. Iresh usually suggested Aberfal at this point. A town just beyond the moor. If I'd been more awake, I'd have realised she was telling me something – and not just to pack a bigger case. Sulis was much further away. Maybe, if I'd let her continue, she might have explained. I might even have gone if I'd known her disreputable sister was there.

But I was a teenager.

'Sulis? Is that where *my father* lives now?'

Questions about that man were always likely to provoke.

'I'll need an address,' I added, twisting the knife. A girl from the regions wouldn't get into a college in Sulis anyway, particularly with my exam results.

Her nostrils flared, but she said nothing. I should've realised she was waiting for the next question.

'A name might also be useful,' I said sourly.

Her blue eyes clouded to aquamarine – the colour of ice.

'Izdubar.'

'*What?*' My hearing was terrible first thing in the morning. I thought she said...

'Your father's name is "Stephen Izdubar". I have my doubts he'd be in Sulis though. Sulis is full of people who'd gladly turn him in for the reward.'

There is that moment when incredulity has not yet turned to anger. Sheer disbelief dampens the embers. The sudden knot in your stomach calms the acid. The sharp intake of breath leaves you wondering whether you will ever exhale again.

It never lasts long.

'*Governor Izdubar?*'

'Ex-Governor.'

'But... how?'

She raised an eyebrow knowingly, and evasively, in response. Pushing her glass towards the middle of the table, she stood.

Our conversations were forever thus. Brief, staccato, and filled with hidden meaning.

'Think about Sulis,' she said.

Okay, sometimes not so hidden.

I sniffed in disgust… before glancing at her glass on the table. 'That water smells off.'

Iresh sighed. 'A girl can only drink what's set before her – even if she knows it will turn out foul.'

I refused to be baited. The woman just wanted me to fledge. 'Izdubar…' I began.

'*Later!*'

I thought I knew her.

'Later,' Iresh repeated more gently before turning and opening the door to the garden. After stepping through, the woman who was once my mother made sure to shut it behind her.

She didn't look back.

There was never a later.

⤸

I was the queen of the castle.

It was Iresh that gave me the idea. Why did the glass of water smell so bad and why did the river? As I stared at the closed kitchen door, I decided to find out. While I didn't care if I succeeded or failed, I needed the distraction.

I mean, seriously, Izdubar? How could she?

The journey was hard, with even its start in Marhasyow being unexpectedly torturous. My favourite short skirt, leather jacket and black-ash make-up always upset the Fedhyow – but that was the point. I dressed to rebel. By summer's end, though, what had once been joyfully ignorable catcalls had liquified into actual phlegm. If they'd bothered to ask, I'd have told them that spitting wasn't advisable, given the desiccating heat of the day.

They didn't ask.

Of course, with sweat running down my ribcage, I also had issues with dehydration. Possibly, I shouldn't have worn the jacket. Still, I suspect if I'd just worn a thin summer blouse, the consequences of the phlegm would have been far, far worse.

It wasn't until I left the town and the abuse behind that it became possible to dry.

I followed the river north of the town for perhaps two or three hours. I followed it further as it narrowed into a stream. I climbed until there was no tree or hedge. I climbed until all the grass was gone. I climbed until the coolness of altitude overwhelmed the heat, leaving me chilled. It was only then I found the river's source. Before me, liquid oozed like plasma from a rocky throat. I pooled my hands and took a draught. It was neither sweet nor sour.

I gazed back down the path and saw a series of large shadows on either side of the Koner. If I were a girl, I might believe them to be the footprints of a giant.

I was no longer a girl.

The indentations were simply a legacy of the past. Tin mines that were abandoned long ago. Mines with still-open shafts that offered, for example, no barrier to an errant flock of fluffy white sheep.

Now necrotic fluffy white sheep.

I should have paid more attention during the walk. I should have paid more attention at school. It was well past noon, and I'd walked much further than a basic understanding of watercourses, and their pollutants, might reasonably require. Annoyed, I looked up. The summit appeared to be just ahead. Determined to avoid the day being a total loss, I carried on.

It took an hour.

I was starving when I finally reached the top. Finding a natural shale dip to shelter in, I delayed taking in the view. Instead, I dug into my knapsack for the dried-out sandwich I'd put there before setting off.

I've no idea how Iresh managed it, but she'd replaced the sandwich with fresh homemade buttered rolls and lemonade. The gesture salved less than she might have hoped. Breaking bread is something you do together.

Still, I ate and drank the lot. It was only when I was full that I looked back down towards the town.

The glass of Marhasyow's windows glinted chaotically in the afternoon sun, making the sight of any detail impossible. But, I didn't care. I was the ice queen on a castle tall. I'd lost the heart to care.

Sighing, I turned around.

On the other side of the hill, the rail track morphed into a waggling line before vanishing into the haze. I saw the bridges of Marhasyow and the bog they crossed, but little else. It was into that unknown that Iresh would have me go.

And I would go.

There was nothing left in Marhasyow I wished to see.

⌣

It was well past dusk before I got home, but Iresh wasn't around to criticise. She'd gone to bed with a fever.

Typhoid, apparently.

Three weeks later, she was dead.

Three days after that, I found and opened the attic door.
And after that?
After that, I never ate nor drank again.

Chapter ten

By the Light

Well, this is pleasant.

You can forget owls, you can forget pussycats, and don't get me started about the missing light of the moon, silvery or not. Instead, I sat among an emotionally bollocked-up mix of ghosts and mortals who went to sea in a piss-poor excuse for a boat. The boat was neither pea green nor beautiful. It was fug ugly. In daylight, the colour had made me think more of bile than any variety of the legume family. Now, long past dusk, I could still taste its scent. The sail also didn't live up to Lilith's billing. In the faint luminescence cast by ethereal flesh, it wasn't so much white as different shades of grey. Black mould bled from the edges of the canvas and along the folds, leaving only a small patch of fabric at the centre that, at a pinch, could be called alabaster.

The absence of that pathetic piece of rock in the sky had one benefit. In the almost-dark, it made it easier to ignore the sight of the occasional pulse of seawater as it squirted through a gap in the hull. Adapa, our self-selected choice of captain, assured us it wouldn't be a problem if someone operated the hand pump… which Nicolò did at the thin end of the boat.

Rhythmically.

Someone is "morose" only in novels or medical reports. You never hear anyone saying, "I'm feeling morose today". I never knew it was an actual "thing". It was my second day dead, and I felt a tad morose. Seeing Lilith and Dumuz erased hadn't helped. Indeed, after the shock wore off, I found I was actually upset – much to my surprise.

The moroseness thing, though, also came from seeing Tristan held above a fire. Not a surprise, really, but not telling anyone had seriously spiced up the guilt. It had been a difficult decision, but I truly believed that a petulant Rosalind might insist on staying – and that a doe-eyed Nicolò would have held her hand.

The Fedhyow would have caught both and turned them into ash. While Rosalind and my ex had more than a pocket's worth of blame for Lilith's fate, they didn't deserve that.

Surely?

Kitten also didn't deserve such a fate – or its Dumuz equivalent. It wasn't the boy's fault that Iresh had no place left in her heart for me.

Again… Surely?

Of course, Kitten didn't know that Iresh was our mother. The only mother he knew was his foster one, Lilith. Indeed, it had been a struggle to get the boy on board the boat without her acerbic tongue. Even Adapa's sticky fingers couldn't hang on to a squirming ghost child who had no wish to leave. I might have offered a hand but didn't. To mortals, the ridiculous amount of snot the child produced might be ethereal ectoplasm. However, to me, it looked very moist and very real.

Much to my surprise, it was Tiama who took charge. When Kitten freed himself from Adapa, there was no escape from an experienced mother's arms. Tiama reached out, grabbed the boy, and didn't let go until we were well out to sea.

Four hours later, I found myself at the boat's fat end beside Adapa. On a normal day, not the best choice of seating arrangements. This night, though, I needed to be as far away as possible from Nicolò. Unfortunately, that left Tiama sitting in the middle and Rosalind and Kitten lying, pretty much catatonic, at my feet.

Both stared at me... blankly... which wasn't freaky at all.

It hadn't taken much to convince Adapa and Nicolò we should make for Sulis. I needed to talk to my aunt. I hoped she might know why my father would... I mean, how could he? He stood there while Hugo held Tristan above the fire. Couldn't he do anything to stop it? Was it cowardice? It looked to me like he just didn't care.

Adapa's enthusiasm to take charge of the boat had bordered on the suspicious, especially coming from a man with such foul, alcohol-soured breath. First impressions are usually accurate. It was only when we'd set sail that Adapa confessed to being "somewhat underskilled in real-life waterborne vessel management". Still, Adapa grasped the impossible, gobbed on it, and made it practical. He suggested we follow the coast to Aberfal.

'The journey should only take the night,' he said.

'We should be fine,' he said.

'Just as long as Nicolò's hand stays in motion.' Well, this last one I'm paraphrasing.

After that, we'd catch a train to Sulis.

The plan seemed reasonable while waiting for an attack

by the Fedhyow. Now, four hours into the journey, I felt the idea lacked a worrying amount of detail. I opened my mouth to question this travesty of planning – before quickly closing it. Adapa had farted again. I gagged. What could this old... fart... have eaten that could threaten the senses of those of either realm?

'Do you mind?' I asked.

'No, lass. Why would I?'

Oh great.

'Please!'

'It never bothered Lilith.'

Of all of us, Adapa was dealing best with the loss. The man had no respect for the dead – or the *seriously* dead.

'You mention her name so casually.'

'Not casually. Lilith was never a creature to be casual with. But if she were here, she wouldn't tolerate all this sulking and certainly not from you.'

'Why me?'

'Girl, you've crossed over. You, for one, should realise how weak mankind's grasp on existence is. I suggest you make the most of the time you have without fretting about the past. Things that are past are, by definition, past.'

Condescending git.

'So,' I said. 'How about you? Losing Lilith and Dumuz must surely hurt?'

'I'm too old and full of wind to fret about such things.'

'Full of wind certainly, but too old? I thought old people spent their daylight hours griping, and their nights worrying about making it to dawn?'

'True, true, but even that's just a phase. I got *really* old. When you're this old, you've already lost most of those dear to you. It's a statistical probability. If you survive the shock of a broken heart once, you can do it twice. This is my third time – and I'm finding it so much easier. Trust me. There's been many a pretty nurse who has pissed her pants when she met her first corpse. In the end, all they could do was change their underwear and keep going. So should you.'

'*Me?* I wasn't talking about me!'

He moved his face closer to mine. The foulness of his breath made me nauseous. 'Lass, we're on either side of the mirror, with you on the wrong side. You need to learn to cope better.' He licked my nose and guffawed as I shrank back in disgust.

'You…' I calmed myself. 'Who was the first person you lost?' I asked. How does he manage that touching-a-ghost trick? For crying out loud, my nose was wet!

His glaucomatic eyes fixed on me. 'Oh no, dearie, not now. I don't know you well enough for that. Well, not yet.' He put his hand on my knee.

And I eased it off. My touch skills were definitely improving.

'I'm not buying this demented pervert routine,' I said. 'It's a distraction. Lilith was odd, but I think perceptive. She liked you.' I glanced at Kitten. Not that perceptive though. Not after leaving me to look after my mother-heart-grasping brother.

Adapa looked embarrassed. 'Our relationship was way more complicated than "like", but…' He smiled. 'Damn it, girl, you almost got me there. I'm still not telling you squat.' As punctuation, Adapa stuck his right arm down his trousers and demonstrably scratched his balls. All this was bad enough, but now there was only one hand on the tiller.

'Okay, captain. How about answering the question I was about to ask before you…'

He cocked an eye and moved a buttock threateningly. 'Yes?'

'This idea of yours.' I refused to grace it with the word "plan". 'This idea, oh Captain. This idea to land in Aberfal, it's…'

'Yes?' If it had been possible to raise his other buttock, I think he would have.

'It's… it's deranged.'

He chose not to break wind.

'Why?' Adapa seemed genuinely curious.

'There might be Fedhyow there.'

He nodded. 'There was the last time I visited. At least around the port. Is that all?'

'All!'

'Yes, all.'

'Okay then. When we arrive, won't the Fedhyow be curious when they see three mortals limping in at dawn, sitting on something that's more driftwood than a boat?'

'Good point. The Fedhyow are nosy by nature. Still, I'm sure I'll think of something.'

Oh, dear. 'That's it? That's all you've got?'

'Well, yes. But it might not matter.'

'Why?'

'Look behind you. Carefully though, you might do yourself a mischief.'

I snapped my head around – and winced at the resulting spasm. I hate being dead. There truly is no upside. Any text on the subject would suggest that ghosts can completely rotate their heads or even take them off and carry them under their arms – total claptrap. One sudden turn, and I get a crick. I winced and pressured the spasming muscle under my fingers.

'Told you so,' he said.

I ignored him. The pain was already beginning to recede. Okay, I forgot. We do at least heal quickly. And anyway, the sore neck wasn't the worst thing – what I saw was the worst thing.

A light in the dark.

'Fedhyow?' I whispered.

'Who else?' While his voice wasn't loud, he wasn't following my "keep quiet, or the bad guys will hear" lead.

'They'll be listening!' I said, in my best mumble.

'Probably,' he replied. His voice was even louder than before.

Before I could shush him, he continued, 'Have you ever heard the phrase, "You can't teach Grandma to suck eggs"?'

'Er… Yes?'

Adapa guffawed. 'Well, you can, and it's the best thing ever!'

I rolled my eyes. 'I assume you're making a point?'

'Oh yes, where was I? Eggs? No, that wasn't it. Life lessons? Yes! Life lessons.'

'Get on with it!' The light behind us was getting brighter.

'Patience, girlie, all in good time. There's a background first, and you need to know the background. I really have been in a boat before, you know. It was after Izdubar but… well, you'll see. Anyway, it all came about because I was at a loose end… being somewhat inhibited in the liberty department and all.'

'Uh?'

'Jail, or almost jail. Well, the vermin-infested cells beneath the magistrates' court in Aberfal. Vermin of all sorts there was. One, two, three and four-legged. I…'

'Oh, for… Just get on with it!'

'Anyway, in my case, I was down for a minor infraction, not that the Aberfal constabulary saw it that way. I also still had a blinding headache three weeks after the event. While it might have been the sugar-based bathtub beverage that my finances had limited me to, the more likely cause was a different type of cane.'

'Cane?'

'Bloody Fedhyow. Only the truly pious stay up to the wee small hours on the lookout for drunks to piss on with their verbals. When I challenged one or two of his tenets, he answered with one of those big sticks the so-called pious like to carry.'

'And then?'

He snorted. 'Never bring a stick to a knife fight, I always say.'

Oh.

He continued. 'After that, I was in something of a bind – what with the likelihood of the long drop and all.' He winced at the concept. 'Then Dumuz rescued me,' he said.

'Dumuz rescued you?'

'That's what I said.'

'What about Lilith? I thought she specialised in damsels in distress?'

'Damsel? Hardly. No, not Lilith. She was elsewhere. Anyway, so there I was, crouched in the corner of my cell, hovering over some straw. Dawn, it was, and a man has got to do…'

'*Moving on!*' I said.

'Well, movement indeed, that's what I was trying to say. So, anyhow, here I was focusing on old man stuff, and being this old, you need to focus, so I didn't see how he got into the cell.'

'Dumuz?'

'Yes. At the sight of him, up I jumped, pulling my skanks up faster than I ever had in the past thirty years. Well, twenty anyway. There was this woman, you see. Gorgeous she was. How was I to know she had a husband? Well, aside from the wedding ring. So, when he came home early I…'

'Dumuz!'

'Yes, dearie, Dumuz. So, there he was doing the vapour into solid thing, which is strange since I'd pretty much been heading in the opposite direction before I pulled my pants up.'

'Please. Just get on with it!'

'Well, that had been my thought, but… Oh, okay. So, this apparition appeared, offering to get me out of there. Bizarre, I thought, but since I had an appointment with Mr "Oh, I've got a great black cap for my pretty peruke", I said to myself, "What the hell!"'

'You didn't know him?'

'No.'

'You'd never met Dumuz?'

'No? Why would I?'

'Had you ever met a… em, a ghost before?' It seemed ridiculous saying it out loud.

Adapa hesitated. 'Well… I've dated quite a few "nearly theres".'

Yuck.

He continued. 'To be honest, dearie, I didn't particularly care about the ins and outs of it all apart from the fact that I was "ins" the cell and wanted to get "outs".'

Why was he dithering? It was a simple question. 'How did you get out of the cell?'

'It's obvious, really. Ghosts, apparently, make excellent pickpockets. Dumuz opened the cell door with the head warder's keys, and I strolled out.'

'As easy as that?'

'Well, that's what should have happened. The actual that happened was that the cell door creaked. I mean, "big-time creak". Cheapskates! They hadn't even bothered to oil the hinges. So, when Dumuz opened it, it squawked all haunted-house-like. Quite appropriate, really. Then, the head warder turned up alongside a couple of blokes with billhooks.'

'I guess they were unhappy?'

'Even unhappier after they failed to kick the living crap out of Dumuz. Tough bloke that Dumuz when he wants to be. Kind of glows and goes all hard, like.'

I thought back to the pebble bar by the castle. 'I've seen it,' I said.

Adapa's eyes flicked towards me before replying. 'Yeah. Mostly he just let them hit him, which didn't do squat. Once they'd tired themselves out, I snuck up behind and gave them a little goodnight tap when they weren't looking.'

'So, what were you doing when they were attacking Dumuz?'

'Mostly staying out of the way. More of a lover, me.'

'You killed them?'

'No. I didn't need to, or so I thought. All they got was a sore head and a bit more sleep. Mind you, if they had ended up dead, the pleasantries later might never have happened.'

'What pleasantries?'

'Getting to that, girlie, getting to that.'

'Well, hurry then!'

'*Okay. Okay,*' he said, his voice still far too loud. I was beginning to wonder whether he was deliberately trying to attract attention. 'So, bottom line, I escaped. We had no problems on the staircase from the dungeons to the courtrooms. Climbing that last step into the dock sent a shiver down my spine though. Of course, being that early, there was no one there. I hopped, well, climbed, well, crawled out of the dock and over to the judge's bench. Nicked his gavel – you never know when you might need a good gavel. We then scooted through the judge's office and out of the back of the court. Not a guard in sight, would you know! It was only then that Dumuz told me the rest of his plan.'

'Which was?'

'This boat. This bloody boat. Tied up in the harbour, it was. I tried to tell Dumuz I wasn't a sailor, but he pointed out the jailors would be coming around and raising the alarm. Once the word was out, I'd soon be caught – what with me being so distinguishable and all.'

'You mean fat?'

'You hurt my feelings. I consider myself big-boned. Well, so do the ladies. There was this one time I…'

I interrupted. 'So pretty much the same scenario as Marhasyow?'

He sniffed, disappointed. 'Unfortunately, yes. Except obviously in reverse. Fifteen years ago, we took this boat from Aberfal to Marhasyow. Leaks more than I remember though.'

'Is there any point to your story?'

He nodded. 'Oh yes, dearie. You see, back then, we also didn't get clean away.'

'They followed you?'

'Yup. I imagine the Feds thought my backstory deserved a proper full stop. One with my feet all twitchy, like – you know, at the end of a rope.'

He glanced back. 'They also had a bigger boat, just like that one. Their boat was also faster, just like that one. They caught up with us around about where we are now.'

'And?'

'And their boat had a deeper draught – just like that one.'

It loomed. The ship that was once so far, loomed, its lantern high above my head.

The next voice I heard came from beside the light.

'There!'

They'd found us. Adapa, Nicolò and Rosalind would die, most likely horribly. If the ship had those strange orbs on it, Kitten, Tiama, and I would also be ended – possibly even more horribly. Looking back, I knew it did. The ever-growing light let me put a face and name to the voice.

Hugo.

Nicolò saw him as well. 'Father,' he said. It was the first word he had spoken in hours. It came without emotion. Tiama, though, snarled. Or she would have if she'd been able to speak.

I looked again at Adapa. His eyes danced merrily. The old git looked like a peacock getting ready to strut. And, right then, I wished he would – if it were backwards, downwards, and out of sight.

Then... then I heard the other voices; panicking, fearful voices, and all from the ship.

When the noise came, all I could think of was the train. Obviously, there had been the bolt of lightning, but it was the screech of steam escaping from the engine that stayed with me the most. It had been an unearthly howl without peer in volume – until now.

Adapa had steered us to this point, knowing there would be rocks. Rocks, hidden just below the surface. This man, this, not-as-stupid-as-he-might-pretend-to-be man, knew what might pass and what might not.

We did nothing but watch as the ship went down, an island of quiet among the chaos. Still afraid, we ignored the cries of terror, the clamour for rescue. It was only when the voices faded and merged into the slapping of waves on the hull of our boat that I realised how little I'd seen of our enemy. There had been no mass of something either brighter or darker than night. I saw no masts, no sails, no false idols mounted on a bow. I saw nothing. Nothing but a light that fell from so very high, to level, and then below. As a child, I never realised that entropy could be so sudden, so commonplace and, at the same time, so astonishingly messy.

I was learning, but only a smidge. Again, I missed the obvious.

At first, I thought the noise from the front of the boat was Nicolò struggling with the pump. Then I thought it was a corpse banging against the bow in the bobbing waves. Then Nicolò hauled it aboard, and it groaned, and I saw it was alive.

'Father,' Nicolò repeated.

Chapter eleven

A Touch of Darkness

So, third day dead, third dawn dead. Yes, if you want to be pedantic, it was only my second one as Ghost Girl Walking, but that was hardly a comfort or, I might argue, accurate. I died the moment I found a key to the attic door.

I could tell it was dawn. Like an ageing head of hair, the relentless blackness of the sky ebbed into nothing, consumed without fuss by a blanket of grey. I contemplated the result. Unlike dawn, the need for a blue rinse was a problem I would now never have.

Unlike yesterday, this wouldn't be a sunny morning. When someone said the past is a different country, I wouldn't have thought that included three days, or two, or even one. Three days ago, I boarded a train and allowed myself a few moments of hope. Brief and quite limited, but hope all the same. Now even that felt dashed as a ship might, or a Lilith, against the rocks.

As the sky fleshed out into the colour and consistency of curdled milk, I was glad my first journey at sea approached its end. That it met expectations said more about my state of mind than any judgement about what might be reasonable. Reason and hope had joined the past and fled abroad. Given what happened, I couldn't blame them.

Hugo was a problem. The minute Nicolò hauled him on board, dead to the world but not quite a corpse. It was clear he was a problem. If I'd been capable, I might have drowned the murderous shit myself – I'd never forget Hugo, Tristan and the fire. But I wasn't capable. Anyway, I would then have to explain why.

I wasn't yet that cruel.

I was also sensible. Rosalind, like Kitten, had remained pretty much in a coma. Neither noticed Hugo's arrival. While I could wake Rosalind with memories of the hilltop, I did not. When sitting in a vessel as small as this one, the phrase "don't rock the boat" should be etched in big letters on its side.

Tiama, of course, was doing her best to sink us. An alphabet writ large in blood on the sails wouldn't have stopped her. The woman was freaking out. She was *really, really* freaking out and had been ever since Nicolò had landed his catch. Fortunately, her opinion carried no weight.

Literally.

It was apparent the marriage of Hugo and Tiama hadn't ended well. Actually, given Tiama's current physical state, possibly far, far less than well. All this made Nicolò's actions last night somewhat odd. It had taken a while, but my curiosity finally piqued. '*Why did you do it?*' I shouted across the length of the boat. '*Why save him?*'

Nicolò ignored me and continued syphoning water from onboard to off. He would have to look at me, and his remonstrating mother, to answer.

'Let him be!' Adapa said.

'Why?' I asked, letting the bitterness simmer on my tongue.

'It would be a long story, and the boy is still busy on the pump.'

'So?'

'The weather's closing in. We need to get past that bluff up ahead before it gets bumpy. You might laugh at my skills, but even I know boats are better off above the water than below. They're easier to steer as well.' He paused. 'Obviously, I'd offer to take over on the pump myself, but…'

'But you've got arthritis?'

'Well, I am quite old.'

'Your hands were in fine fettle a few hours ago.'

He smiled. 'Some pains just come and go, dearie.'

I'll bet. I still wasn't planning on tying a shoelace in front of this man – not ever.

'What about Rosalind then?' I asked, staring directly into the girl's bloodshot eyes. A mix of salt in the air and a lack of blinking will do that.

'Leave the poor lass alone as well. She's had a shock.'

Shock? Really? I would have laughed in his face if he hadn't been looking ahead. Shock? He honestly didn't see the irony. I had her well beaten on the shock front.

'Then, you tell me!' I spat back.

He feigned confusion. 'Tell you what?'

Oh, for crying out loud. 'Why did Nicolò save him? What happened to Tiama?' I glanced again at the coiffured scarecrow. 'At a guess, something not good.'

'It's not my place to say, dearie. Ask the boy again when we get to land. Better still, ask Hugo when he wakes – if he wakes. I'd like to hear that conversation.'

I gave up. Was it possible to drown in the cesspit that is the silence of others? Sat in the middle of the ocean, on yet another backside-numbing bench, would I succumb? It certainly felt like everyone had my suffocation as their prime and common goal. Slumping back, I allowed my spine to engage with the boat's rim, noting, almost subliminally, that it was another item for my ghostly diary of painful "do nots". Maybe I should have offered to take a turn on the pump myself? Okay, perhaps not. I'd be as successful as a halibut and look just as stupid as one if I tried.

So, instead, like Adapa, I looked ahead.

Beyond the dead and almost dead at my feet, beyond the angry matchstick, beyond the son and prodigal father, I looked ahead. When I was younger, time passed slowly – like a flame ebbing, like embers. For an old man like Adapa, I imagine time passed by like the beating heart of a butterfly – quick and ephemeral. For someone in the not-so either, time can pass unnoticed, without weight or value. For me, time just passed. Only afterwards did I realise these were the last few moments I was the self I once was but could never be again. On the railway bridge, I changed from something solid to pretty much mist. But I was still me – opinionated, petulant, spiteful *me* – a creature with darkness in thought but not in act. I wish I had paid more attention to this final quiet. In my last moments of innocence, I think I would have appreciated its vividity.

Instead, the next thirty minutes were a blur. They were a pastel palette of memories that tended towards the abstract. If it had been a fine day, I might have first delighted in the opals of the sea as they contrasted against the green and brown of a pastoral headland. After rounding it, I might have then marvelled at the more cubist reds and shades of white that made up Aberfal. Much of that detail should have remained, even on a day like this. Instead, all I can remember is the bleeding of colour, the slow motion of brown into grey into black. In this memory, the only things with any definition were the flecks of sleet that speckled the view – and my eyeballs.

Finally, though, we saw the harbour and the dock, and I came alive again. A reception committee waited at the nearest vacant wharf. Five minutes out, they were still black insects, but that would change.

Nicolò's mother faded, and I did the same. Why risk detection? After placing my left hand on Kitten's ankle, I found, to my surprise, that it took little effort to shed all substance. Perhaps I was getting better at this ghost thing. Under my fingers, I felt Kitten grow cold. Above them, two small hands slipped on top of mine. Instinctively, the child followed my lead, and we soon disappeared from mortal sight.

Dumuz the wise, or perhaps, more accurately, Dumuz the once and therefore not so wise, said we exist out of phase. He claimed that this "fading" was a further distancing from humanity's realm. It was a rotation, perhaps, into a colder place. Dumuz also said that we might completely dissipate if we went too far. Now safe from view, I made to stop.

Kitten wouldn't stop.

From his fingers, now entwined with mine, I felt this corruption prick into me, its tendrils scouring me clean of all hope. Kitten had little reason to stay and, in this weakest of moments, neither did I. Deep within, I knew this colder place was my ultimate destination. One that I should have reached three days before, and one that I could reach now if I let my brother lead me.

But I refused.

Maybe it was stubbornness, but I wouldn't be the subject of the boy's whim or timing. I refused to travel there. Not yet. Not if my brother wished it.

I could have let him go, but that also did not happen. A release from agony wasn't for the child to decide, not after the misery his first death had caused me.

So I held on, just. If there's nothing left in the present, if the future is a void, then reach back into the past. My right hand navigated the frayed and broken seams inside my jacket and found the bear – the scuffed, torn and surely flea-ridden teddy bear. I moved it from my chest to his… and Kitten released my hand. He took hold of the teddy bear and pulled it close. He let us stop. Instinctively, I knew it wouldn't last. The memories fixed around this one item wouldn't keep him in this world for long – but perhaps long enough.

I drew us back to the real world, or at least its nearest silver alternate. Far enough to avoid being seen. Near enough to still move and function.

Letting Kitten go, I leant back and turned towards Adapa. Snot drifted down from his nostrils like mercury. Would he still hear me in this new state? Lilith mentioned some nonsense about an "affinity" between our kind. Did it stretch this far?

'They're waiting for us,' I said.

'Yes,' Adapa replied, also answering my other question.

'I assume you have a plan?' I asked unhopefully.

'Yes,' he repeated, still gazing ahead.

'A good one?'

'Yes.'

'And?'

'And what?'

'And it is?'

'I'm not telling you.'

'Why not?'

'You won't like it.'

I suppressed an unusually long stream of Lilith-inspired four-letter words.

'So, you're not telling me your plan, in case I object? You're setting it in motion without review, without comment? You, the brain-pickled captain of this ship, will have us rely on your *unique wisdom?*'

'Pretty much.'

'It'd better be a cunning plan.'

'It is. I didn't get where I am today without a degree of cunning.'

'Oh – f... fabulous! What happens if, and when, it all goes wrong? A little foreknowledge would be helpful. Let's face it, most of us won't be much use in a fight.'

'While somewhat true, I'm afraid it doesn't work that way. You or someone else on this... fishing vessel might want to change it, and it's too late to change now.'

I guess the use of the word "fishing" was a hint. However, Adapa was baiting me, and I refused to bite. 'Did you say you had a degree *in* cunning?' I asked.

'*Of* cunning, not *in*, I'm afraid. I'm somewhat self-schooled in such things. Still, have faith, girlie, have faith.'

Faith? If he'd said that to Lilith, she would have gutted him. Ahead, the number of Fedhyow was growing. I wondered what the collective name for a group of praying mantises was – for this lot, probably the same as a bunch of crows. A few minutes left then. There was time for a few last words with Adapa. Although I hoped "last" wasn't too literal.

'So, when did you meet her?' I asked. To be honest, I didn't expect a helpful reply. His track record wasn't brilliant, and the man was distracted. Adapa was trying – and very much failing – to look as if he knew what he was doing.

'Who?' he replied.

'Lilith.'

'Lilith? As in dead and rational? On this boat. She was on this boat when I escaped from prison. Sat right where you are now. Do you remember that rumpus I mentioned when I jumped on board? That was Lilith, that was. Scared the living daylights out of me, she did. I squawked like a girl. Back then, she was quite good at that sort of thing. Terror was her forte, you might say. In recent times, not so much. I reckon it's...' Adapa paused, apparently changing his mind. 'It's the boy's fault. Kitten made her a touch gooey.'

My brother twitched as Adapa spoke, his eyelids flickering briefly. I felt like doing the same, and not just because my veins had filled with slushy ice. The idea that a Lilith of the past was even more terrifying than the one I'd known was difficult to contemplate.

Then I realised I'd missed something. 'Dead? You said dead?'

And rational?

'Oh, yes. I knew Lilith when she was alive – knew her very well, in fact. Even though I was already well into my first bit of age-related paunch.' He chuckled, turning his head towards me. 'You'd better watch out, girlie. It happens quicker than you might think! Still, I guess that's not a problem you're going to have – or at least not get any bigger.' The smile on his face became a grimace as the boat veered right as an unsighted wave caught the bow. Adapa turned back and looked ahead.

Cheeky sod – but the look proved he could still see me.

'You knew Lilith from before? When she was alive?'

Much to my surprise, the side of his face blanked. Adapa again risked a glance into my eyes – a decision made. 'How well do you truly know anyone when you think about it? You might meet someone and make a snap judgement, only to find out later that you were wrong. Or you might have lived with them for years before discovering that you never really knew them at all.'

Was he talking about me?

'I never knew Lilith, not really,' he said. 'I had no idea what she might become – not even when she was my wife.'

What the…

'Exactly,' he said, replying to words I didn't air, before turning back to the waiting crowd.

'*Ahoy there!*' he cried, waving his right hand.

Oh, please, no!

Rather than returning to the tiller, Adapa's hand dropped onto my left knee. Touch, it appeared, was also a thing still possible. Copying Kitten, I placed my left hand on top… and let it chill. Adapa's fingers moved smartly away.

I looked at Rosalind. She was waking up a little, no doubt because of the growing racket from those in black. The girl seemed troubled, and I couldn't blame her. The last time we'd heard a din like that was yesterday – when Cordelia burned.

An old Fedhyow threw a rope to Nicolò at the front of the boat. Nicolò, to my amazement, caught it nimbly and tied it off. Sadly, that's all he did. Having completed the task, Man-boy Nicolò turned to his father and moped. I almost felt sorry for the elderly Fedhyow as he pulled us close.

The boat banged hard against the brick wall of the jetty. Wood ruptured, and yet another puddle formed just beneath my feet.

The Fedhyow, though, weren't going to let anyone drown. Not unless they were the ones doing the drowning. Nicolò pretty much flew off the deck as they dragged him up the steps running alongside the seawall. They were gentler with Rosalind, although some hands lingered on her body longer than was strictly necessary. At a guess, it was men beneath those cloaks. Quite desperate ones if they felt the need to fondle Little Miss Plump. Adapa was next. Him, they chose not to grope.

Finally, there was Hugo, a man who drew recognition. Even though he was unconscious, his face bruised and battered, and his black clothes torn, they still knew him. Or at least it seemed that way as they carried him carefully on to land.

As the crowd gathered on the quay, Tiama, now carrying Kitten, and I, climbed the steps. We had barely reached halfway when the Good Ship *Risible* rolled over and died. I suspect I was the only one who noticed the involuntary and immodest flash of its barnacles. Unlike it, I couldn't fathom whether its death was because of a mortal wound, sudden loneliness, or simply embarrassment.

When I got to the top, my living companions surprised me by being neither shackled nor gagged. As I looked across a shimmering palette of black and silver, the scene on display wasn't one of conflict but of almost tea-house discourse.

'…I told you we found him in the water. Look at him – he's still bloated!' Adapa said calmly.

It was true. Hugo undoubtedly looked bloated. The Fedhyow had propped the unconscious sod up against a bollard, his excessive gut flopping over his groin. One Fedhyow must have removed his cloak and used it as a pillow for Hugo's head. Three more must have served up their clothing as cushions, one for his back and one for each arse cheek.

The Fedhyow didn't grant Adapa, Nicolò, and a now awake Rosalind such comforts. Facing Hugo and the rest of the Fedhyow, they sat on a cold, wet concrete path with their backs to a literal wall on the opposite side of the jetty. They'd be staring at the sea if the crowd hadn't been there. But the Fedhyow were, and the scene looked like an execution waiting to happen.

Approaching from the side, I circled behind Hugo to get a better view of the proceedings. Out of respect, or perhaps merely the mildest ability to smell, the Fedhyow had given Hugo plenty of room. Room which I now filled.

I peered over Hugo's shoulder. Sitting on their hands, my companions made me think of a trio of naughty schoolchildren. Adapa, though, as was his wont, quickly broke the illusion. '*Okay!*' he said. 'I can see you have your doubts, but think for a moment. Why else would we have him on the boat?' Adapa's acting abilities were better than I imagined. In fact, he delivered the line with only the slightest sign of a quiver on his upper lip – and that was likely because of nasal mucus. 'I told you before. I was showing these kids how to sail at night. You know, navigate using the stars. They didn't learn that much in the end, unfortunately. It was just too cloudy, you see. It would've been a complete waste of time except that we found him – just floating.'

A Fedhyow to the front and right of me screeched, exasperated. 'But where did he come from?' It was the old Fedhyow.

'I told you! The water!' Adapa repeated dumbly.

Too dumb, judging by the Fedhyow's response. '*You know what I mean!*' the old Fedhyow shouted, almost stammering, apoplectic with rage.

Adapa wrinkled his nose. 'Well, assuming he didn't walk on it, I'm guessing he must have fallen off his boat.'

'You saw his ship?' The Fedhyow asked, trying to rein in his anger.

'Ship? Boat? I wouldn't know. Mostly, all we saw was a light. That likely means he was out fishing. Lamping, it's called. You hold a lamp over the side, the fish get curious, and, if you're lucky, you might catch yourself a big fish. Not that I'd know, of course. I don't have a permit for that sort of thing. Finding him in the water was an accident.'

The Fedhyow grimaced. 'So, you're saying that he fell into the water and you pulled him out? Wasn't there anyone else on his ship to save him?'

Adapa looked baffled. 'I didn't see a ship or anyone else. I also didn't hear a sound, so I'm sort of guessing his vessel must have been empty. It's all a bit of a puzzle, really.'

Okay, Adapa was now aiming for a doctorate in stupidity rather than cunning. Personally, I'd always kept the lies I told Iresh simple. Growing up, I realised that half-truths were often better than lies. While I liked what he did with the light, the comment about bigger fish was cocky. If the Fedhyow understood the reference, they would be toast. If they also knew that empty vessels are famed for making a hell of a lot of sound, my mortal companions would be seriously burnt toast.

Of course, all this was moot. This was the Fedhyow. They'd never accept a word he said unless it was an out-and-out confession. Adapa was getting nowhere fast. One might even say he was sinking – just like the boat.

Hugo suddenly lifted his head and groaned, muttering something worryingly close to English.

Almost without thought, I reached into Hugo's back. My left hand passed through his skin as if it were not there. Transiting the layers of fat didn't slow it, nor did the muscle or the spine. Nothing hindered its progress – not until my index finger touched and entered the left ventricle of Hugo di Conte's heart.

I let the tip solidify slightly, just enough to detect the pulse of blood. I then made my finger harden further, and it pressed against the aortic valve. The sensation felt more like an intimate caress than anything else.

Or so I told myself.

Hugo's whole body spasmed. His belly and chest thrust up from his seated position, bowing his body into something that best resembled a fat banana. As he did so, I pulled my fingertip back and away. I let it soften. I returned it to the ether from which it came.

'*Father!*' Nicolò shouted.

Adapa added quickly, 'He means "Father above, save him".'

No one was listening.

Once again, Hugo was unconscious, frothing out bloody drool from the corner of his mouth. The Fedhyow immediately surrounded him and started to shout and argue – so much so they forgot everything else.

Which was my intent.

From within the huddle, the high-pitched voice of the older Fedhyow shouted, '*Give him air,*' and then, '*Give me room,*' and then, '*Let me breathe.*' The others ignored him as they all fought to give Hugo aid. I wasn't surprised when the old man's screeching turned into a sharp wail of pain as some younger, clumsier Fedhyow trampled him underfoot.

My conscience caught up with what I had done and it took an effort to reassure it. Hugo would survive, I insisted. The man had suffered only a *little death* – just not the sort you find in Gothic novels.

Despite appearances.

Amongst the prisoners, Adapa was the first to react. The old soz wouldn't have survived for so long if he couldn't seize an opportunity when he saw one. He was also sprightlier than I'd imagined. He leapt to his feet, pulling a surprised Nicolò up with him and, in chain, the overstuffed rag doll that was Rosalind. Nicolò was smart enough not to cry out. Rosalind wasn't sufficiently lucid for it to be a possibility. Stealthily, at least as much as a man that large could manage, Adapa led the other two away. Nicolò moved… well, perhaps what he thought was carefully. Rosalind, though, glided. Her toes, which I imagined to be the size of plums, had more strength in them than I gave credit for.

Watching, I waited until they reached the end of the jetty. The smooth concrete surface looked difficult to cross in the damp, but the trio managed it well. Beyond the jetty was the magistrates' court that Adapa had mentioned earlier. If it had once been imposing, then it wasn't now. The building sat squat against a background of poorly-constructed tenements. Since the slum likely provided much of the court's business, its location was at least convenient, although the locals might not see it that way.

I looked ahead. Adapa was now encouraging Nicolò and Rosalind into the bowels of a black coach that had bars instead of walls.

I stepped out from behind the ongoing huddle of Fedhyow and made to catch up with the escape. I…

Tiama was staring at me. In horror? Had she seen what I had done and not approved? How could she not approve?

I met her gaze and hardened my eyes. We both knew I had taken another step into a new beyond.

And that there was no way back.

I hurried to catch up with the coach before it left. Behind, without hearing her step or breathe, I knew Tiama would follow with Kitten. She had nowhere else to go.

Neither did Kitten.

CHAPTER TWELVE

THROUGH A GLASS, DARKLY

Unlike Marhasyow's pathetic attempt at a terminus, Aberfal train station was vast. Its size became apparent as a pair of matching cart horses dragged the wagon around almost the entire circumference of the site. The horses, black like the coach, were, thankfully, blinkered. With three powder-puff ghosts as cargo on the upper deck, the word "spooked" might otherwise have proved literal.

When setting out, I noticed the station had an entrance next to the dockyard. At a guess, Adapa was trying to avoid any possibility of pursuit. It was that or Adapa had an abysmal sense of direction. As we travelled, I sat beside Mr Morning-Breath, with Tiama and Kitten behind. The locked-up lovers were in the cage below, no doubt contending with the residue left by previous residents – which was pleasing. With Tiama's eyes forever on the back of my neck, I wasn't in the mood to talk, or frankly, had any wish to explain what I had done. Thankfully, Adapa didn't care. For the next twenty minutes, he seemed happy enough to regale me with the history of every rusting hulk we passed that might once have carried goods. I almost expected him to whip out a little black book filled with block rows of steam engine serial numbers. While he didn't do that, he did bore me to tears, which made a pleasant change from the recent trauma.

The railway station's scale reflected the bloat the town had achieved. With a natural harbour much larger than Marhasyow's, Aberfal was once a major port. If Marhasyow were alive, it might have cried in jealousy at the benefits nature offered its rival just up the coast. It wasn't. It was dead. So, it didn't. However, Adapa's impromptu tour also revealed that its success was relative, and if Aberfal had glory days, they were in the past. The warehouses were mostly empty, their broken windows covered in grime. The stock pens were also fallow. It looked as if some bright spark actually believed crop rotation also applied to sheep.

Adapa halted the wagon a few hundred yards from the actual station. Given his nearly disastrous encounter earlier, it appeared Adapa had learned some humility.

'*Get yer arses up and off. We could all use a walk,*' he shouted.

Or perhaps not. I looked him up and down and raised an eyebrow.

In response, Adapa gasped in shock and pointed behind me. As I turned to look, he pinched my bum as it lifted from the seat. 'Yeah, well, even you've got an overhang that could do with some work,' he said, sniggering.

I spun back and slapped him across the face with my left hand. The crack was satisfyingly loud. Even more satisfying was that I'd accomplished it with little thought.

'*Will you not do that!*' I said, giving him my best stare.

Adapa rubbed a cheek that had already turned purple,

his expression wavering somewhere between surprise and respect…

…before settling into a smirk. 'Of course, I guess exercise doesn't make much difference to the dead.'

If Lilith couldn't control him, what chance did I have?

He moved his hand from the higher cheek to one that was lower and much larger than mine. He scratched. 'Where was I?' he said. 'Oh yes. A walk. As well as a desire to avoid our mono-coloured friends, we need to do a bit of scouting. Methinks a more irregular route on to the train is required.'

'Why?'

'Well, lass, with all the shenanigans when we left, I forgot to bring any money. Those of us who aren't as wanting in the weight department are expected to pay for their tickets.'

'Ah,' I said and risked a glance at the locked-up lovers.

'Oh, don't look at them,' Adapa said. 'They don't have a coin between them.'

That brought a protesting 'Hey' from Nicolò and an echoing whimper from Rosalind.

'Still true, though,' Adapa said.

Moving my eyes to Rosalind, I smiled and asked Nicolò, 'I take it she's back with us?'

Rosalind's cutting response came out as a mewl.

'No change in her diction skills, I see,' I said, before turning to Adapa. 'Okay, the sleet has now turned to rain so I suspect some of us will now get properly wet.' I beamed at Nicolò and Rosalind. 'Why not go for a stroll and take in the air? It'll do my sense of humour no end of good.'

Adapa shook his head, disappointed at my vindictiveness. He didn't linger, though, and climbed down from the wagon, walked behind, and unlocked the padlock that kept Mr Bill and Little Miss Coo in their cage. Stepping out from the rear, Adapa set off at what he no doubt believed was the pace and gait of a soldier.

Unfortunately, and not for the first time, he better resembled a sailor. Or at least one early in the morning.

Tiama floated to the ground, letting Kitten slip from her arms as she touched down. While still visibly traumatised, Kitten stayed on his feet. Tiama retook his hand and led him away in pursuit of Adapa. It wasn't exactly a surprise when the right horse bucked as they passed.

In the distance, a sign hung across the width of the road. For the not-completely blind, it spelt the words "TO THE PLATFORMS" in a font that was as large as it was functional. On either side of the sign and supporting it stood two brick buildings. It was obvious the building on the left had been vacant for a while. While I suspected the one on the right housed the ticket and other sundry offices, the one on the left better resembled a rescue centre for damp pigeons.

Adapa was veering left.

I jumped down. 'We need to talk,' I said to Nicolò – before looking at Rosalind directly.

'Alone,' I added.

Rosalind's eyes flickered with emotion. I sighed and placed my right hand on hers, drawing her aside. If he'd seen, Adapa would have laughed as the girl pirouetted very much like a ballerina. I'm certain Lilith would have. We ended up with my left hand on her left shoulder and my right bumping against her stomach – which, disappointingly, wasn't as lardy as I had hoped.

I opened my mouth to talk, but before I could, she interrupted. 'You can't…'

My icicle-like fingers tightened on Rosalind's hand, cutting off her words in an expulsion of air. I can't have Nicolò? Seriously? Was she that insecure?

I almost bit her ear. 'Don't be silly,' I said. 'Think about it! I wouldn't have thought the phrase "you are dead to me" could be so literal, but it is. I am dead to him, and even before my not-so-celebrated departure, he was dead to me. He still is.'

I only wish the last were true.

'Oh,' she managed, or perhaps it was 'Ow' as I crushed her fingers.

'Times change, interests diverge. We all need to move on,' I said. I may have been speaking about myself and Nicolò, but it could have been about Rosalind and her family.

'Yes,' she replied, more assertive than I thought she'd manage. From the side, however, the pasty-faced grimace she attempted could never pass as a smile. Pain, perhaps, but not a smile. Still, she agreed, even if only to get me to release her hand.

As I let go, Rosalind spun back to face Nicolò with me in between. From behind, Nicolò asked, 'Are you sure?'

Rosalind, her eyes on mine, lips locked tight, nodded rapidly. By the end, her face was turning blue. I almost felt guilty. Almost.

Without further words, Rosalind turned away and ran to catch up with the others.

Nicolò and I followed at a more leisurely pace. The left-hand carthorse snapped out a bite as I passed. I was both pleased and relieved to react quickly enough so that it found only air. I really was getting better at this.

We both waited until Rosalind was out of earshot.

'Why?' I asked.

'Sorry?'

'Don't play dumb. You know what I'm asking. Why did you leave after we…?'

'Oh, that.' His upper lip flickered into a brief and *very* inappropriate smile. Then he blinked as his mouth caught up with his brain and whatever grain of decency remained within it. He jutted out his lower teeth, grasped the lip and drew it back towards his mouth.

'Were you rebelling?' I snarled. 'Or was it ego? Did you find it kinky having sex with the strange girl?'

'No.' He looked stunned. 'How could you think that? No, no. It was never that.'

'*Then what?*'

He stepped in front of me to block my path. I knew I could have passed through him but didn't. Instead, I watched as Nicolò reached out. Instead, I let my body firm and allowed him to touch my shoulders. I shook, just like in the heat and sweat of that midsummer night. This time, however, it was in disgust at my weakness.

'It was Mother!' Nicolò said. 'That was the night he killed my mother!' His eyes welled with tears.

'He?' It was all I could ask.

'*My father!*'

Oh.

At that moment, if he'd wanted it, if he'd needed it, I might have let him pull me close. But Nicolò's elbows remained locked. The distance between us kept safe. I glanced over his shoulder at Rosalind. The girl had caught up with Tiama, and although her neck was likely twitching, I knew she wouldn't look back. With his hands on my shoulders, not looking back was probably best.

For everyone.

The moment passed. I strengthened and stared at Nicolò's intruding hands until he let go. We gazed into each other's eyes for a few moments more, but not at all like lovers. Finally, he turned away, and we resumed walking.

The rain was growing heavier. Nicolò, it seemed, had regained his composure. When he spoke again, it was without emotion or emphasis. It was like an aria recited by an automaton.

'He never really knew her. From the beginning to the end, he never knew her. Father has always been a large man. More so when younger. His one sin was gluttony, but that was a sin the Fedhyow could forgive. One thing they wouldn't forgive, however, was bachelorhood. The Fedhyow are unusually rational when it comes to children. Bringing others into faith is fine, but breeding your own is better. They tend to be more reliable.'

'Not always,' I said.

Nicolò snorted. 'Okay, not always,' he agreed. 'Still, while a strong lineage is important, the Fedhyow also realise that too much inbreeding can lead to deformity... both physical and mental.'

Nicolò paused, waiting for the obligatory comment.

I saw no need to give it.

He kept going. 'For much of their existence, the Fedhyow were just another small sect. Fanatical, but localised. Even before they turned to missionary work, the Fedhyow sent their menfolk into the world when they reached adulthood. It was just, back then, more to do with acquiring good breeding stock. It wasn't unusual that, at twenty, they sent Father out into the wilderness to find a wife.'

Nicolò laughed bitterly. 'It probably comes as no surprise that for many years he failed.'

His voice switched back to monotone. 'Eventually, Father found himself in Marhasyow – working for the Governor, oddly enough. And it was in Marhasyow that Father's luck changed. I can't imagine it was all his work, but he found a woman who'd marry him. Mother never told me why she agreed, but the subtext was that she had no choice.

'She was a bit wild, but he could always beat some discipline into her. At least, so he thought. Either way, it didn't really matter. She was a means to an end, and that end was me.

'Mother became quite adept at playing the devout wife, if only to avoid the beatings. She wasn't a believer. Of course, neither was I – not that Father knew that until the end. He put my lapses down to being a bit of a mummy's boy.'

I snorted but didn't comment. Instead, and staring ahead at Tiama, I stated the blindingly obvious. 'Your mother was Wycche.'

'Yes,' he said. 'She didn't tell me until I reached my teens. With a Fedhyow in the house, even telling me then was a risk. She waited until I understood the consequences of Father finding out. She waited until my life choices became unavoidable, and then she waited a little bit more. Mother only told me when we came to Marhasyow. It was like finding out about the facts of life all over again – except scarier.'

I thought of Iresh and her secrets. She should have told me.

'She shouldn't have told me,' Nicolò said.

He continued, 'That night after we… I didn't head directly home. Instead, I went down to the river. There's a bench just south of town. It was my favourite place, especially at night.' He laughed without humour. 'I loved staring at the reflections

153

of the streetlights in the water. I remember them dancing and skipping, refusing to be moved by the flow. After a while, every time, I'd turn my head and follow the water into the dark. Before that day, I always drew my eyes back towards the light.'

He tilted his head and glanced at me. 'That night, I did not.'

It was becoming an effort to ignore him.

Nicolò shrugged. 'It was after midnight before I got home. Mother was still up, waiting in the kitchen. I didn't need to ask about Father. He was always in bed by ten. Mother and Father didn't just lead different lives, they pretty much lived in different time zones.

'We argued when I told her I wanted to leave.'

'I guess she lost,' I said, trying and failing to keep the bitterness out of my voice.

Nicolò looked confused. 'Don't you remember talking about leaving, saying we should run away together? Don't you remember me agreeing?'

Damn! I did, didn't I? I had forgotten after he disappeared.

He continued, 'I hesitated when Mother said she didn't want to be left with him. One minute, I'd agree that leaving was ridiculous. But the next one? Well, I was at the point of suggesting that she should come with us.'

He stopped and turned to me. 'You would have agreed to that? Surely?'

'I…'

'It doesn't matter. It didn't matter. In the heat of it, I asked what would happen if Father found out I was Wycche… Well, you can imagine the rest.'

Perhaps, but after seeing Hugo hold Tristan above a fire, I needed Nicolò to say it. 'Tell me anyway,' I said.

Nicolò gulped, but I wasn't about to back down.

'Father was listening. It's not surprising, really. I suspect he'd been in the hallway for much of the shouting match. It surprised me, though, that he left the kitchen door closed for so long. Father was never a man to hold back. Of course, when he heard we were Wycche, any restraint vanished.'

He grimaced. 'Almost as quickly as the kitchen door.'

I tensed but said nothing.

Nicolò took a deep breath. 'The butcher's knife in the kitchen was never that sharp. However, the edge was keen enough to cut Mother's throat when she threw herself between us. I still remember Mother gasping out air and blood and... other stuff from a hole just below her chin. At night, when I close my eyes, I can still see her falling to the floor, her hands tight around her neck. I...

'Father just stood there, staring at his dying wife. I remember his eyes almost glowing with such divine wonder.

'I threw myself at him.'

He snorted. 'Of course, Father cast me down... *literally*. Lying on the floor, I waited helplessly for Father's next cut... but it didn't come.

'Instead, I heard a squeal and then a thump as Father landed on the floor beside me. I remember looking up.'

Nicolò stopped walking. 'Above me, there was a woman,' he said.

I turned to face him. 'Lilith?'

'Yes. Although, of course, that night, she was just someone I didn't know. I... I remember forcing myself to my feet. I remember looking down at Father. He was rolling around in agony. I remember he had both hands on the back of his left thigh... The butcher's knife was lying beside him.'

'You…' I began.

Nicolò interrupted. 'I remember this woman, Lilith, had a strange sliver of metal in her left hand. I remember she looked at him and said, "That's both now".'

'Both?' I asked.

Nicolò wrinkled his nose. 'She never did explain.'

Nicolò took another breath. 'Lilith kicked the butcher's knife away when I tried to pick it up. She wouldn't let me… Her first words to me were "Not in anger".'

'*Seriously?*'

He sighed. 'Lilith wasn't one for taking her own advice, was she?

'Anyway,' he continued. 'Lilith grabbed my arm, opened the back door, and pushed me into the garden. She… she then stepped back into the kitchen and shut the door.'

'Lilith took Tiama's heart,' I said.

'Yes. Although I only found out afterwards.'

'Your mother had an amulet?'

'Yes'

'And then?'

'Lilith burnt down the house.'

'*What? Really?*'

'She set it on fire. When she came out, I saw Father on the floor. I… I didn't see Mother.'

I was speechless.

Nicolò looked at me quizzically… before deciding to continue. 'Lilith made me leave. It felt like a dream. I couldn't believe it was happening.'

My house also burnt down. I had thought it was the Fedhyow… but could it have been Lilith?

'And then your mother… manifested?' I asked.

156

Nicolò paused for a moment before answering. 'Yes,' he said. 'At the castle the next day. It was a shock to see her that way. It was a shock…'

Again, I thought of Tristan. 'Why did you do it? Why did you pull Hugo out of the water?'

'I needed to know why he killed Mother.'

'You know why.'

'Do I? Even for a Fedhyow, it can't be all absolutes. There must be some room for doubt. I lived with the man for almost eighteen years. I know he had a temper, but I thought he had limits.'

'Really?' My voice was harsher than I intended.

'Oh, don't get all worthy. There were good times sprinkled with the bad. No one is that two-dimensional. He taught me to sing, he…'

'He cut Tiama's throat.'

Nicolò didn't bother to challenge.

'Why was she there?' I asked.

'Who?'

'Lilith. Why was she at your house in the first place?'

'She…'

I never let him finish. 'Did she know about us?'

'What?'

'Afterwards. Did you tell Lilith about us?'

He seemed relieved by the change of tack. 'I… Only in the briefest of terms. I didn't want you involved. At the start, I was… just running. I didn't know where I would end up. I… I was protecting you.'

Oh, for crying out loud. '*Protecting me?*'

'Yes,' he said, already knowing what was coming next.

'But then you met Rosalind?' Oh, sod it. I let him see the

full depth of my bitterness. 'It was only three months ago.'

He didn't answer.

'Three months,' I repeated.

'I was upset… and Rosalind was there.'

'I could have been. I would have been,' I said, almost whimpering.

Tears welled up in his eyes. 'If I had known what you were, what you are, then possibly, but back then? Really?' He paused and looked away. 'And it turned out to be more complicated than I first thought.'

I waited for more, but he kept quiet.

Eventually, I asked. 'Are you happy… with her?' I was trying to sound calm.

Nicolò turned back, staring cautiously. 'We've become pretty close.'

I was glad he didn't smile. The double entendre *might not* have been deliberate. He also, I noted, hadn't… quite… agreed with "Happy".

'When I turned up at the castle… obviously a Wycche… you still left.'

'Yes,' he said, with just a hint of shame.

Of course, the obvious bit was me being dead so I guess "Yes" was the only reasonable answer. At least Nicolò sounded sad about it, which was good. Perhaps it might have been different if I were alive… but I wasn't. At childhood's end, we put away our childish things and look to see the path ahead.

I was his childish thing.

And it was my turn to look ahead.

Rosalind was loitering alone at the entrance to the building on the left. I guess the others had gone inside. Rosalind wasn't alone though. Beside her was a man wearing a white cloak with a hood that hid everything but his eyes. In the overcast sky, the lights from the building opposite blazed brightly. It no longer seemed strange that his shadow fell towards the light and not away.

Could she see my father? I wondered. Had they talked? If so, what had he said?

'Go to her,' I said to Nicolò.

He looked undecided. Finally, and far too late, he looked undecided. 'Go!' I repeated.

At least this time, I saw him run away.

'*Are you sure Lilith said, "Not in anger"?*' I shouted.

His laughter, nervous though it was, sounded as tuneful as the chiming of bells.

Chapter thirteen

Into the Black

The street was empty. Nicolò and Rosalind had vanished into a maze of concrete that appeared almost subterranean. Ironically, the façade of the dilapidated building actually rose high from the ground as if trying to be the monolith it so obviously wasn't. Even given my recent experience, I would take a failed castle over this superficial monstrosity. A castle's walls are at least thick. This partition merely separated the out from the in.

Stephen Izdubar, ex-governor of Marhasyow and, unfortunately, my father stood at the building's entrance.

In daylight, I could see his face better than I had that first night, and, although I wish I didn't remember it, the second. It helped that Izdubar had pulled back his hood. It was a stern face. A face scoured raw by experience. His lips looked chapped, his mouth severe, and his eyes... his eyes were black pools that drew a watcher in and drowned them in their depths. It was a face that demanded trust. Trust I could not give. He'd been with Hugo. He'd watched while that creature held Tristan over a fire.

'It's too bad he won't live,' he said.

'What?'

'The infant. It's too bad he won't live.'

'Tristan? Do you mean Tristan? He's alive?'

He laughed. 'Damn it. You didn't see? Yes, *Tristan* is safe for now, but it won't last.'

Last? No, I'm not playing this game. 'Is it a penis thing?' I asked.

It was his turn to be surprised. 'Pardon?'

I smiled and channelled my best Lilith. 'Why do that? Why do you bad guys always have to do that? We've just met, and your first words are a tease and a barb. Have you considered trying a bit of sweet-talk first? I've heard it works sometimes. Or is it all testosterone with you?'

I wasn't very good at Lilith.

He grimaced. 'Testosterone? I've had no need for it in recent years. I'm unable to... Well, let's just say it's an old injury but a debilitating one. Still, it serves as a reminder to never expose your back to... anyone.'

Was he talking about himself or me? I stared at him for a while, both of us knowing who would break first.

'How might I *save you*... Father?'

He smiled. 'A girl who gets straight to the point, good. Evasion and deceit were Iresh's least desirable traits. I'm glad she didn't pass them on to you.'

'I am only what you see,' I said.

Izdubar's eyes drifted across my ethereal form – lingering in places where a father's eyes *really* should not.

Finally, he looked up. 'You have very nice... hair.'

Now wasn't the time to throw up.

'Are you dead?' I asked, still feeling sick. The question would have been strange a few days ago.

He sighed, disappointed. 'No,' he said. 'Of course not.'

I pushed on. 'Yet, here you are, a man talking to a ghost. A man whose face looks the same as on that wanted poster – the one from long ago. How is that possible?'

He chuckled. 'Dear girl, what you see is a projection, although admittedly a vain one. I'm actually on Guitt. These days I rarely leave my room.'

'Guitt?'

'Yes.'

'The isle of Guitt?'

'And the home of the Fedhyow. Yes.'

I persisted. 'Are you Fedhyow? You were with them in the garden… and on that hill.'

'I was never *with* them. In each case, I was present, but the Fedhyow never knew it.'

'They couldn't see you?' I asked.

'Like this, I am only seen when I want to be seen and heard when I want to be heard.' He paused. 'However… Also like this, I can *whisper*. I can *suggest*. When a Fedhyow hears, they think it's…'

'Divine intervention?'

He nodded. 'Sometimes they listen. Sometimes not. The Fedhyow aren't the greatest listeners. It must be something they might anyway have done.'

I realised where he was heading. 'You convinced Hugo not to kill Tristan?'

He nodded.

'While most people consider infanticide a bad thing, Hugo's sense of what is right and wrong is quite obviously warped. Why would he even hesitate?'

Izdubar's cheek twitched. 'I'll explain in a second,' he said.

'Will you accept the infant is alive?'

'I'll accept it's possible.'

'Good. You see, Siduri, I need your help.'

'I know,' I said. 'You want me to *save you*. To be honest, this whole "saving" thing sounds a tad "Fedhyowy" to me.'

And then I realised.

I wasn't at my best. Death does that to you. Sleep deprivation also doesn't help. 'I hope you don't mean "rescue" because there is no way I'm going to Guitt.'

He raised an eyebrow.

'Seriously?'

'If you come, I guarantee the infant will be freed.'

'Blackmail? Is that why you convinced Hugo to keep Tristan alive? Oh, you are a real piece of work. For a second, I was almost sympathetic.'

Izdubar rolled his eyes. 'Blackmail is such an ugly word. Still, let's try again, shall we? I can ensure that *both Tristan and Nicolò* will be free.'

My heart, which was still not there, missed a beat. 'Nicolò?'

'I said I'd tell you. You see, while Hugo is impulsive, he's still open to *suggestion*. Hugo knew there was always a chance you might escape.'

'You *whispered* and convinced Hugo to take Tristan as insurance?'

Izdubar nodded. 'Hugo's son is smart enough to know where the Fedhyow will take the child.'

Guitt.

But. 'What makes you think Nicolò will try to rescue Tristan?'

'The boy's family were quite talkative when first captured. My sources tell me they considered Nicolò to be near enough the child's uncle.'

That shouldn't have hurt as much as it did. Still, there was a problem with Izdubar's plan.

'Nicolò doesn't know that Tristan's alive. I didn't know.'

He smiled again, this time exposing his teeth. 'But you do now.'

Okay then, a second problem.

'Why should I tell Nicolò? You've already admitted that Tristan is bait. The moment Nicolò steps on to Guitt, the Fedhyow will grab him, and this time Hugo will personally fire up the barbecue.'

My father's eyes narrowed. 'I told you before. That won't happen.'

I wasn't convinced.

He could tell. 'What did… Iresh tell you about me?' he asked.

'Not much. Just a name. Still, it shouldn't come as a surprise that I find it difficult to trust a thief who abandoned his family.'

He rolled his eyes. 'Speaking of family,' he said. 'Was that your dead brother I saw on the dock?'

Well, that was a mistake. 'You were on the dock?' I asked.

Izdubar hesitated. 'I'm surprised you didn't see me.'

A mistake that had just been compounded. 'I'm surprised you saw us when even the Fedhyow couldn't. I'm surprised you knew about the shipwreck.'

He winced.

'Do you know how your brother died?' Izdubar asked. No doubt he was trying to distract me.

I let him, at least for the moment.

'No, not really,' I said. 'All I know is that it happened during the storm.'

'There's little I can add,' he said. 'Your mother and her sister and I had a fight that night. They told me the boy had snuck into the castle and didn't come home. Unfortunately, I didn't believe them.'

'A child's death is not simply *unfortunate*!'

'No, sorry, you're missing the point. I'm not talking about the boy. I didn't even know he was dead until months later. No, the unfortunate thing was that Eanna thought I was lying… and stuck a knife in my back.'

Right now, I was struggling to blame her. 'You were still fit enough to leave with the gold though.'

'Just about,' he grumped. Surely, he didn't expect sympathy?

'From what you've said, I guess you and Iresh had already split up by then?' Was I the result of a goodbye fling?

He snorted. 'You silly girl. Iresh and I were never a couple, or at least not in the conventional sense. Iresh… well, where do you think the money came from to pay for your house, your food, your education?'

'*Are you saying Iresh was a whore?*'

He snorted again. 'Let's just say Iresh was more of a courtesan who welcomed gifts.'

I… I took a mock breath and tried to stay calm. 'And when Iresh had a son?' I asked.

His face grew serious. 'That was problematic.'

I looked at him, but he wouldn't expand.

'Okay,' I said. 'Let's try something different. You say you were injured?'

'Stabbed.'

'Fine, stabbed. If that was the case, why did you leave that night? Anyone with sense would call a doctor.'

He peered at the dead girl in front of him. 'You didn't. Sometimes it's just not possible.'

Git.

He continued, 'The economy was falling apart. People were suddenly a lot poorer. The farmers reached for their pitchforks... and the doctors for their scalpels. Back then, a doctor would've made my problems worse, not better.'

'I thought the recession happened after the storm? You know, after you stole the gold.'

'No. But the writing was already on the wall. Before I arrived, Marhasyow was just another crappy backwater. Under my guidance, it was briefly rich. By taking the gold, all I really did was let Marhasyow return to what it was.'

Izdubar's body started to shimmer. 'So, will you come?' he asked.

I tilted my head and squinted. 'How did you find us, anyway?'

'You mean, how did I find you at the train station in Aberfal? You know, the one next door to the harbour and the only realistic way out? Oh, I don't know. Just lucky, I guess.'

He had a point.

'Tristan will be safe if you do what I ask,' he added.

'You said that before.'

'So will Nicolò.'

'And also that. I'm sorry, Father, but no. We both know which of us ends up in a vat of ghost-girl-dissolving liquid.'

'That's not true. I promise.'

'Promise? After what they did to Cordelia? For crying out loud, the only thing left of her was smoke.'

'Cordelia? Do you mean that unfortunate woman on the beach? There was nothing I could have done to stop that.'

'But you can on the island? You're saying you can *convince* the Fedhyow not to turn me into "ecto-mush"? No. I'm not buying it.'

His image was fading badly now – so was his voice. 'Don't you care?' he gasped. 'Are you really that heartless?'

I laughed in his face. Loudly. If there had been proper spittle, and he'd been a proper man, it'd be running down his face. But he wasn't, and it wasn't.

And his mistake of a pun wasn't that funny anyway.

I let the laughter die. 'I told you, Father, I am only what you see. We both know I'd be inhuman not to care.'

He stared in disbelief as I literally walked through him and into the labyrinth of concrete beyond.

Unfortunately, as I passed through, he *whispered* one last time. The words felt as much a prediction as a *suggestion*. A serpent's hiss that I couldn't ignore.

'In the end, Siduri, you will have no choice.'

I knew he might well be right.

⌐

The journey through the darkness inside the building wasn't quick. As I stumbled and slipped, I kept asking myself the question I should have thought of before. Why were there no Fedhyow? Even if I thought Izdubar wasn't Fedhyow himself, why were they not there? Surely, they could also work out where we had gone.

As I stepped into the light, I got an answer.

They had.

The enclosures of wood and metal to my front stood empty, the gates towards the tracks open. Judging by the clumps of wool caught on barbed-wire spikes, the pens once contained sheep. The narrowing path towards a row of cattle wagons was also devoid of life – or should have been.

Tiama and Kitten were aboard a wagon of what appeared to be a soon-to-depart train. Its door was open, inviting anyone who might want to enter to do so.

Next to the door and struggling with two of the Fedhyow were Nicolò and Adapa. It looked like something of a mismatch. Still, Nicolò and Adapa weren't ready to give up anytime soon. Nicolò, with boyish enthusiasm, danced around his opponent, offering the occasional jab. One grab of his leading arm by the large Fedhyow he faced, though, and Nicolò would soon be splat.

On the other hand, Adapa had the mass and, apparently, the experience to deal with an opponent who was almost as big and unquestionably younger than him. How he'd managed it I've no idea, but Adapa was sitting on the Fedhyow's head, forcing the man's face into the mud. On dry ground, there would be no contest. The Fedhyow would roll and squirm until he threw Adapa off. However, he struggled to find a grip on the rain-soaked, shit-laced earth.

A third Fedhyow strode towards me. His face said it all. It was obvious I'd been seen.

I could have done with a knife right then.

The Fedhyow carried a staff capped with a weighted head and topped off with a small glass sphere. Knowing what an orb had done to Dumuz, it didn't take much of a guess to realise the sphere's contents were equally lethal. The Fedhyow's right hand was similarly full, filled as it was with some poor girl's hair.

Rosalind twisted and turned as he dragged her behind.

I solidified and tried not to overthink what I would do next – which pretty much consisted of clenching my hands into girlie fists.

Still, the pathetic and harmless look seemed to work.

The Fedhyow growled, yanked on Rosalind's hair, and threw her into a nearby water trough.

Git.

He then advanced, swung his staff and… missed.

I'd faded and stepped into his swing. So much so that the lethal sphere passed behind my back. I might not have a heart, and, to me, courage was a different country, but sometimes I can do better than stupid. As the Fedhyow's weapon continued its arc, he lost his balance, slipped on the almost fluid surface, fell, slid, and quickly became entangled in the rungs of a perfectly situated barbed-wire fence. He struggled, obviously, and bled, obviously, and found himself trapped even more than before.

I looked for Rosalind. The poor girl was still in the trough. Almost without thought, I firmed again, reached down, and dragged her out. Putting an arm around her waist, we staggered forward, eyes on the ground, the shit-covered surface demanding more than just a touch of respect.

I wouldn't have known what to do about the other two Fedhyow. Flooring the first was more instinct than skill. There was no way it would work again. I risked a look up at the fight.

There was no fight.

Nicolò was moving towards us, no doubt coming to his girlfriend's aid. Beyond him were two bodies. The first lay crumpled, with his head at an impossible angle. The second was still twitching, a dark red pool growing out of his lower back. I recognised that stain and knew its cause – and that the twitching would soon stop.

Beyond them stood Adapa. Physically, he looked just as decrepit as he had before. His eyes, though. His eyes lit with a flame, a fire, a furnace of certainty that spoke of a younger man – a younger man hidden until now. Adapa lifted an eyebrow and smiled. This was a side of him Adapa hadn't intended to show.

He winked.

It was only then I noticed he carried a knife, a knife almost identical to the one Lilith broke on the train. His blade dripped with the same dark blood I saw on the sliver of glass she held on the bridge. The one that Lilith placed so carefully on my chest.

I wasn't sure that I wanted a knife after all.

A thunderous blast of a horn brought me back to my senses as the train announced its intention to depart. It lurched forward with a shudder as Adapa landed his arse cheeks on the floorboards of the wagon. The two events were unrelated... probably.

For a while, I didn't think we'd make it. Rosalind, her clothes soaked and heavy, remained dazed from her unexpected bath. Despite Nicolò supporting her other side, I still struggled to carry my share of Rosalind's increased weight.

Behind us, the trapped Fedhyow began to shout.

As we edged towards the train, the calls in answer grew. By the time we reached the wagon, the replies had transformed into threats.

Adapa backed off to allow Nicolò on board. Nicolò let go of Rosalind and grabbed my right hand to pull me up. Rosalind would be last. It would take our joint strength to haul the, admittedly temporarily, overweight girl safely up.

At that moment, I could have let go. No one would have

blamed me. It was awkward hanging on as I climbed. As a ghost, one slight fade and Rosalind would have slipped from my fingers. By the time Nicolò realised my error, she would be gone. Even if he threw himself off the train, he'd be unable to save her. Left at the station, her life would be forfeit, and, if Nicolò also stayed, so would his. I didn't think he would do that. It wouldn't be cowardice that held him back. It wouldn't be for a better chance of revenge. No, it would just be me. It would be my hands, my firm, and suddenly so very solid hands.

But I didn't let go. Just like Kitten, I didn't let go.

Which was a surprise.

Chapter fourteen

When All the Colour Has Bled

My left hand hung in the gap between the wooden bars of the cattle wagon. Fully firm, it swayed in the breeze, allowing nature's breath to buffet what once was skin. As it flapped in the air, my fingers toyed with a single stalk of straw, teasing it playfully, pretending to let go.

I sensed a fall.

Cast aside and bewildered, the straw hung in the air longer than expected. Eventually, however, understanding came. Realising the truth, the stalk surrendered. Only a dark soul acts differently when they discover they've been betrayed.

It seems I am like chaff – my soul is not that dark.

Twice now, with Kitten and Rosalind, I held on when a desire for vengeance demanded I should not. Even Hugo, whose heart I should have crushed, I let live. To my disgust, I realise now that I am like the many. A creature that is good and bad but mostly in between. If I stared into a mirror, I would find that my tuft would be gone, my uniqueness gone. If there had once been any colour to me, that colour had long since bled.

I no longer felt morose. I was beyond morose.

Withdrawing my hand from the gap, I dragged what once was flesh across the rough surface of the wood before letting it flop onto my chest. Sighing with resolve, I pushed my fingers into the breast pocket of my jacket. The envelope was still there. My desire to deliver it to Eanna had not changed. The discovery that Izdubar was an utter shit had merely removed any codicil. There was nothing left to ask about my father. In those few minutes in Aberfal, I'd learnt more about him than any daughter would wish to know.

⌒

No one else joined the train during the journey. Not surprising, really, but still, overall, Adapa had chosen well. That the straw on which we sat stank wasn't his fault. Well, mostly not his fault.

The bleating from the sheep at the far end of the wagon was incessant. In comparison, my companions and I kept to ourselves. I had the scenery to dwell on. Kitten and Adapa spent the journey snoring. Tiama watched the pair with ambiguous interest. Nicolò? Nicolò cuddled Rosalind and offered words of comfort. To be honest, there was far too much bodily warmth going on for my liking. Still, I found it interesting that while she soggily accepted the warmth, Nicolò's words fell on deaf ears.

After a long journey across high moorland, we'd dropped into a winding river valley where we met the first few rustic outcrops of civilisation. As we drew closer to Sulis, corrugated-iron-roof barns, whose purpose I understood, gradually mutated into a quainter thatched variety. They flowed past, each unique and each the same and each with chimneys that puffed out smoke in the absolute faith that straw does not catch fire. Fifty minutes ago, the train had slowed to a near crawl before entering a long and mostly dark tunnel. The artificial lights that lit our way seemed an afterthought. They were things without true purpose, offering nothing but varying shades of grey.

Just like me.

⤳

While the sun had not yet set when we entered the tunnel, it was undoubtedly dusk by our exit. A cheerless evening fog worsened the sense that little had changed – except that my ears popped. Which, again, was something that seemed very not possible.

I stuck my head out of the gap between the boards of the wagon wall – decapitation being the least of my worries. I watched as the sheen of sickly white fog first brightened and then yellowed as the nearing city streetlights grew dominant. The houses that now backed onto the railway tracks looked nowhere near as pricey as those cottages of the recent past. In their way, they also were identikit in nature, each with tacked-on extensions that matched their neighbours'. I briefly wondered how quickly this ripple of desire for indoor plumbing took to cascade down the street – but then decided not to pursue the thought. Inappropriate metaphors can lead a mind into some sticky cul-de-sacs.

Speaking of inappropriate.

'It's near time to go, dearie,' a now-awake Adapa said – before licking my ear.

I turned, pulling my head back to avoid further saliva.

'Go?'

Adapa nodded. 'The train has to slow down before it reaches the platform. We can hop off then.'

'But it's heading for the stockyards. Why does it need to slow down?'

His eyes wrinkled. 'Health and safety regulations require that a train mustn't enter the station at excess speed. The locals are quite touchy about it. There was an unfortunate incident a while back.'

'And you know this how?'

He sighed. 'Lilith.'

'Is that how she died? Hit by a train? Here? In Sulis?'

'No. Well, not quite. The authorities thought so, though.' His eyes suggested I shouldn't push for more.

'Won't someone see you?' I asked instead. While apparitions can take care of themselves, and Nicolò and Rosalind might slip down unnoticed, I wasn't so sure about someone as large as Adapa.

He smiled. 'If the station staff have any sense, they'll be inside with a nice cup of cocoa. I also wouldn't worry about anyone waiting for a passenger train. The platform's long, and that fog's looking pretty dense. Even if they see us, they'll take us for a bunch of free-riders. They might sniff a bit... well, they will sniff a bit, but they have better things to do than fuss. Anyway, we'll be off this thing before we reach the platform.'

'*Before we reach it?*'

'Oh, yes!' he said, putting his right hand into a gap in the wagon door. Adapa pulled. The door drew back a couple of feet.

I glanced at his belly. 'A little more, perhaps?'

Adapa looked insulted but complied. The door slid back three more feet.

'Better?' he asked.

I raised an eyebrow. Behind me, the sheep bleated at the sudden draught. I knew how they felt. Closer still, I sensed a different kind of sheep forming a queue.

Adapa sat down on the wooden board and swung his feet out. He started to mumble but was gone before the sound could reach my ears. Nicolò and Rosalind, hand in hand, leapt and tumbled after. Tiama, arms around Kitten, stepped out, floated briefly, and sank into the mist. I...

Oh, f... fiddlesticks!

I looked down. The embankment was still made of earth, even this far into town. As the station lights grew brighter, I knew that would change.

Oh, what the hell. I was dead anyway. Like Tiama, I sprang into the air. Unlike her, my still solid right boot clipped the wagon door. I corkscrewed, my skirt flying out in all directions. In the half-light, I hoped no one could see.

Fortunately, I landed with a squelch rather than a thump.

Sitting up, I reached down and took off my right boot. My throbbing big toe was even whiter than the rest. I put the boot back on. Obviously, I still had a few lessons to learn about this ghost thing. For example, when should a girl fade, and when should she not? Leaping from trains, I guess, was one of the "shoulds". I honestly wasn't that clumsy when alive. Death and dissipation were getting the better of me.

As I stood, and briefly hopped, my unusual companions gathered around.

Adapa was suppressing a snigger, Nicolò wouldn't dare. Tiama looked serene, and none looked the worse for wear. There is always someone to see.

And Rosalind? Rosalind stood in the background with Kitten.

'So?' I asked.

'We're here,' Adapa replied. 'This is where you wanted us to go.'

'This is where I needed to go. You're free to do as you please.'

'But... you invited us?'

'I suggested we travel to Sulis. I didn't say what would happen after we arrived.'

Nicolò looked shocked. Surely, he must have expected this? Sulis was merely a waypoint for them. They still had lives to lead.

Well, except for Tiama and Kitten.

Oh, and I suspect Adapa didn't see the value of a five-year diary, either.

The truth was that the idea of turning up at Eanna's door with an old git and a couple of lovey-dovey spit-in-mouths filled me with dread. Oh yes, and when I think about it, there was also the minor fact that I was a tad deceased. I hoped my aunt could look past that small detail and welcome me anyway. Of course, I also had my wisp of a brother in tow. Eanna would undoubtedly remember him and adore him because everyone, apart from his sister, did.

And, annoyingly, I was having some doubts about her.

With Kitten there, I knew I would find it uncomfortable. Eanna would ask the next question and then the next. Almost subconsciously, I fingered Iresh's amulet still hanging from my neck. Eanna might recognise it and learn more about her niece than I might want her to know.

Adapa interrupted my thoughts. 'You have an address?' he asked.

'Yes,' I said.

'And do you know how to get there?'

'Well…'

'Well?' he mirrored. Adapa, the almost sailor, knew how to bait a hook.

'No… I don't.'

He winked. 'I know Sulis from way back. I can help you find your way if you like?'

'I…'

The old git was enjoying himself. 'We've come all this way, dearie. A touch further shouldn't hurt. Maybe you can convince your aunt to put us up for the night?'

Damn.

'One night,' I said.

'Of course,' he replied, his eyes glinting in amusement like the yolks of two soft-boiled eggs.

How had his victims let him live so long?

＞

Sulis, or at least its centre, was a culture shock. As we walked out onto the still-bustling streets, the young adult population was notable for its absence. It was as if, against all nature, the local youth preferred to stay home after sunset. It was much more likely that this part of Sulis had few residents of my age, or, more correctly, what had been my age. In front of me stood and walked and waddled the middle-to-aged. As a group, they were all a decade past their prime and all wearing the most current of fashions – if the fashion was beige.

The sight of them confirmed my long-held belief that Sulis was a tumour, albeit in an insipid disguise. It was an inflated retirement village where those beyond the first bloom of youth made up for their lack of dress sense with better money management. The suburban housing I saw on our arrival strengthened, rather than weakened, this view. There were no slums, but there were no factories either. Sulis was an onion where the affluent lived at its centre, and the wealthier still lived on landed estates beyond the outskirts of the town. Sandwiched in the middle was a servant class that wouldn't think of themselves as such – but they were. They provided the shopkeepers, the plumbers, the cleaners, the street sweepers and the suppliers of whatever the rich might need.

There were no Fedhyow though. Not one.

This was the real reason for the shock, culture or not. The Fedhyow had adorned Marhasyow's streets. Their presence sucked the air out of the sky. As they ranted and raved and tutted and tsked, it wasn't surprising that some of the more oxygen-starved were malleable. Here, though, there were none. Here I could breathe – at least metaphorically.

Behind me, a sudden noise made me jump. Should I fade further? Although it was night, could those dressed in beige still see me?

Adapa drew up next to me and repeated his raspberry.

Git – and I reconsidered whether the first noise came from his mouth.

'Your point being?' I asked. It was difficult to keep the disgust from my face.

Adapa strode past me, smirking. 'Nothing, dearie. Nothing. Well… It's just that you seem to find it hard to both gawp and walk.'

'I don't…' Oh, what was the use. 'I haven't told you the address yet,' I said.

179

Adapa halted. Was he embarrassed? It looked more like guilt.

Rosalind snarled, 'Oh, for crying out loud, hurry and tell him then! Eventually, someone will notice that the man's talking to literally thin air. You...' Her mouth snapped shut. Her eyes now desperately staring anywhere but at me.

I looked at her, surprised. Rosalind stood beside Adapa, her right hand bound tightly to Kitten's. Nicolò and his mother hung further back. Still, she had a point. Mortal eyes would only see the girl, Adapa and Nicolò. That was likely why she shut up so quickly. The poor dear realised she was compounding the issue. I glanced down at her right hand, clamped onto something that was nothing, and imagined how abnormally twisted it might look to the mundane. I didn't have the heart to comment – I didn't have a heart.

Still, I wasn't in the mood to put up with her nonsense. Ignoring her, I spoke again to Adapa. 'Where was I? Oh yes. My aunt's address is number one, the Royal Crescent, which sounds nice.'

Rosalind wouldn't let it go. 'I assume you're talking about a house, not a museum?'

Cheeky git. 'Why don't you...' I began.

Adapa interrupted. 'Pricey neighbourhood, the Crescent. I wonder how she affords it?'

It's odd how deflection can deflate a conflict where a straight "leave it" would escalate. If you let someone deflect, that is. I stared back for longer than a moment, but then let him. He was right. Who seriously wanted to see a catfight between a ghost girl and a live girl in the middle of the street? Well, quite a few pervs would, but only if they could see the ghost girl, which most couldn't.

I twitched out a smile.

Adapa beamed back. 'Anyway,' he said. 'Rosy-Paws is right. Some of these stares are looking somewhat severe. Perhaps we should move.'

He set off again up the street.

Rosy-Paws? Thank you, Adapa.

Rosalind, obviously embarrassed, followed, dragging poor Kitten behind. As she passed by, she breathed into my ear.

'I know,' she said.

What did she know? What could she know? It was only when she caught up with Adapa that I realised. Rosalind had been on her own at the station in Aberfal, waiting for Nicolò.

Waiting beside my father.

I've never liked the word "interesting". Whenever I hear it, I always add the word "times" and consider it a curse. However, it was the only word I could use. Rosalind's comment was "interesting". Had she seen my father? Did he tell her that Tristan was still alive?

Yes.

The times might soon get interesting. I wasn't in Izdubar's league.

Nicolò drew beside me and slowed. Tiama scuttled past, almost at a run, chasing after the others... Well, Kitten anyway.

'So here we are again,' Nicolò muttered. It was a weak opening.

'Lover's tiff?' I asked... almost kindly.

'Not exactly. I think Rosalind's still in shock after the spat back in Aberfal.'

Spat? Okay, not the most appropriate word, but it suggested that she hadn't told him about Tristan.

'What will you do after tonight?' I asked, trying to sound as if I didn't care.

'I don't know. I honestly don't know.'

A week ago, I would have found the sadness in his voice pathetic. A day ago, I might have been angry. Now? Now I knew how he felt. I glanced at his face. He looked disappointed. Why would he look disappointed?

He forced a sad smile. 'What about you?' he asked. 'How do you think your aunt will react when we all troop up?' He took a breath. 'Particularly those of us who are deficient in the skin and bone department?'

'Yeah. I was wondering about that. I know so little about her. It would be hard enough if it were just me and I wasn't dead. Now? Well, Iresh always described Eanna as the wild one of the family. I'm sort of hoping this feral side of her is a sign that she also likes cats – as well as brooms and bespoke pointy headgear.'

'You think she'll still welcome you?'

'"Welcome" might be pushing it. It will be an imposition, and she'll deduct some points for the lack of a hat, but hopefully, my aunt will let me stay.'

I looked ahead at Kitten. Tiama had caught up with Rosalind and taken his other hand. I continued, 'She'll take pity on the boy. However, the rest of you?' I smiled. 'Well, I imagine she'll let you stay the night – as long as Adapa keeps his hands to himself.'

Nicolò sniggered. 'Trust me. Watching him when he does isn't pleasant either.'

I got the giggles. I got the giggles for the first time in a long time – far more than his quip deserved. Nicolò laughed alongside me, not really understanding the excess. He had no idea it was the forced laugh of the condemned, the laugh you make before an ending, a parting of ways. You laugh because you don't want to be seen to cry.

Adapa led our little flock beyond the grand into the mildly dilapidated. The shops here were smaller and less flashy. The ones with clothes had several knick-knacks that might pass indeed for fashion. All seemed reasonably priced, or, unlike the town centre, priced. These were shops for the workers and servants then. The hodge-podge periphery of commerce didn't last long. We soon meandered into something that resembled parkland – except that the roads and pavements remained. And then we turned a corner, and then we were there, and then I knew I was wrong. I was wrong about my onion metaphor for Sulis. The onion had a baby onion, a pocket of wealth set out well beyond the centre. But even a baby onion has variation, variegation and rot.

At first sight, number one, the Royal Crescent, did its best to disappoint. Unlike the other houses that looked expensively pristine, Eanna's appeared a tad run-down. Walls once whitewashed were weathered, and the guttering more resembled second-hand planters for weeds. The front garden also had a somewhat bohemian look with its brambles, nettles and an astonishing variety of fungi. Iresh would have been apoplectic. I liked it. I wondered, though, how dark it might be inside with all that ivy covering the windows. If I had to guess which house on the Crescent belonged to a witch, this would be it.

Adapa stopped at the front gate to let me pass. I felt oddly nervous and fumbled for an age at the latch. Adapa noticed and helped me work the mechanism. Once the gate was open, Adapa removed his hand from mine and didn't even try to cop a feel.

At my mission's end, I felt surprisingly ambivalent about that.

I walked alone to the porch and knocked on the door. Would Eanna resemble her sister? Iresh, even at her worst, had always been well-kempt. I noticed the paint peeling on the wood in front of me. Would Eanna have even brushed her hair?

The door swung open with the most clichéd of creaks.

'It's about time you fucking got here,' Lilith said. And then added maternally, 'Whatever's the matter? You've gone quite pale.'

Oh!

The world swayed and turned silver as I fell into the most Gothic of romantic swoons.

'And why is there a puddle of piss at your feet?'

Bitch.

Chapter fifteen

A Surfeit of Light

When I awoke, my first thought was, *Ouch!* The brightness was so intense that my first thought became my second and third. My eyelids offered scant protection against the intensity of brain-mangling light. My fourth thought was something other than *Ouch*. Given the stimulus, I did what any sane person would do and scrunched my eyes. The pain lessened somewhat – only to be replaced by a sudden spasm. In my forehead! Seriously, in my forehead, of all places! That had never happened when I was alive.

I was still not alive.

Eventually, I reached an equilibrium. I could relax my eyelids to a point where the cramp receded and my false retina didn't complain – or not so much.

It took longer before I could open my eyes.

To my front and left, I saw faded, but I think once-golden curtains. Tied back, a creature of malign intent had neutered their volume and purpose – or that is what my throbbing brain again screamed. For sanity's sake, I looked right and towards the sight of black and the sound of a mouse rustling.

I couldn't see it at first. I couldn't see much of anything. The transition from light to dark took away any possibility of that. I heard the mouse curse under her breath though. Which was odd. To the centre of this non-sight, a sudden flare sufficiently singed my optic nerves to make me question my choice. But the flames didn't get much brighter, and those gossamer threads that now made up my only transit of light – calmed. It was a fire then, in a fireplace. Although I couldn't see clearly yet, I heard it cough. I heard it bark.

I rested my hands on the fabric I was lying on. Silk, I thought, although it did smell oddly acrid. But still a bed then. A bed furnished with mortal linen that I couldn't lie beneath. That would explain why I felt cold. Being dead, of course, didn't help. The shaft of autumn light through the window also didn't help and wouldn't help. Perhaps once the fire was fully aflame, I might feel warm. At least I appreciated the attempt.

As time passed, and my eyes adjusted, that thing I knew to be a mouse grew and grew until it wasn't a mouse but a woman – as it could only be. My memory, the thing no longer a dream, reminded me I'd once thought of her as an angel. More recently, I had regarded her first as an exotic and then as a panther, but again, I was wrong. The creature was merely a woman.

Forgetting the dead thing, of course.

'What was it you said?' I asked.

Lilith turned so I could now see her face. 'What?'

'When I was a little girl in the attic. That was you, wasn't it? You lit the fire.'

'Yes,' she said, before slipping back from her haunches onto her buttocks and crossing her legs. Her leather trousers creaked as they bent. From experience, I knew the action shouldn't be possible. Leather is just not that flexible. The trousers were a fake then, a glamour, just like their host.

Her shift in position had blocked my view of the flames. Now, on her right, I could see some shelves. They were empty save for a single book. The book looked old. I could just about make out the word "Wycche" among the scuff marks on its spine.

'So, when I was a little girl, what did you say when you left the attic? *You know, just before you left and locked the door?*' I kept my eyes on the book. 'It's bothered me ever since.'

'You don't remember?'

'I didn't hear.'

'I said I had no choice… and I didn't.'

Sitting up, I let my eyes drift back to hers. 'That's kind of vague, isn't it?'

She flared her nostrils but said nothing.

Damn, that headboard felt painful against my spine. I adjusted the pillow before continuing. 'It seems you survived then… and Dumuz?'

'Dumuz is downstairs.' Yet again, there was that odd, musical trill.

'That's nice,' I said. This wasn't the moment to tell her how happy I was they'd both survived. 'So,' I continued. 'How did you manage it? I only ask because I might need to know. In fact, how did you get here ahead of us? That's one trick I would've liked to have learnt earlier.'

Lilith smirked. 'My, we are the talkative one. I blame Adapa. That old goat brings out the strop in the best of us.'

'Which you are not.'

'Which I am not,' she agreed… before pursing her lips.

Okay, later then. We both knew there were other questions I wanted to ask.

Although, hopefully, she didn't expect the first. 'Did you have faith… in me?'

Lilith smiled wistfully. 'When you were a little girl? Back then, I had hope.'

'You were a hopeless guardian angel.'

Lilith raised an eyebrow. 'True, but I had my reasons.'

'And I'll want to know them,' I said. 'But how about starting with why you locked the door again after you left? Was the thing I'd done *really* that bad?'

'Are you sure you want to go down this path?' she asked.

I gave my best impression of granite.

Her eyes twinkled. 'Okay. The two are related anyhow.'

They would be.

'*What do you remember*?' she asked.

It was the way she said it. I felt like a child caught in the glare of a lie. 'I remember watching the flames,' I said. 'I remember the waiting. I remember the only thing left was dust.'

'You learnt about entropy. You learnt that even the infinite must eventually pass. You found out that a fire makes an excellent distraction for a little girl who can't go out to play.'

Bitch… but I suppose it was true, except, 'You could have left the door unlocked.'

'No… I couldn't. It wasn't my place to interfere with your day-to-day. You were not the reason I entered that room. Or at least not the main one.'

What?

She continued. 'I went there to deliver a… let's call it a covenant. Although Iresh had little choice in the matter.'

Oh shit.

'Covenant? Do you mean...' I dragged out the piece of parchment from the inside of my jacket. The letter wrapped within popped out and flew towards her. 'You wrote this?'

Lilith picked up the envelope at her feet and played with its seam. She took a deep breath. 'You were right,' she said. 'I was a piss-poor guardian angel, but I was still better at that than as a mother.'

Was she about to fall apart again? Was she about to tell me again about her baby – the one who died?

No.

Her skin melted but didn't fade. The blackness of it glowed, it luminesced, it lightened. As a wisp of errant smoke from the fire washed the resultant sheen from her face, the skin that was left wasn't dark. What was almost bald was now shoulder-length, raven and tightly-curled. The woman, the girl before me, was barely older than me. She had shrunk, was slight – and she wore a skirt.

Her voice also was nothing like before – but the words were. 'Oh, stop gawping. I've seen whores on their knees with less drool than that dribbling from their gobs. Honestly, if you weren't already dead, you'd be dehydrated by now.'

Okay, still Lilith then. Even if she looked like butter wouldn't melt in her mouth – although perhaps not the most appropriate metaphor.

I scrunched my nose. 'Eanna?' I asked. The concept seemed ridiculous.

Her voice softened. 'Yes. Although *Mother* might be more appropriate.'

What?

'*Mother,*' she repeated. '*Your mother.*'

My mother? Was she trying to wind me up? How dare she!

'*My mother is dead!*'

'I am.'

'Your child died!'

'You did, and I cut out your heart. Does that make me a bad parent?'

Well, objectively…

'You had a baby boy. It died,' I said.

'Lilith had a baby, a boy, and it died. Eanna had a little girl who grew up and lived until she was seventeen. You lived until you were seventeen.'

'*But you are Lilith!*' I said.

She rose and crossed the floor to stand by the bed. 'And Eanna,' she said. 'You see, we are Legion, for we are many. Well, we are two, and it's still frigging crowded in here. It's not something you want to try out on a whim. Seriously, even the pronouns can blister your, er, well, your brainstem thingy.'

'Hypothalamus?' I said, bewildered.

'Yup. That's the almond. Anyway, that's why, for the day-to-day, we are typically Lilith.' She sniggered. 'But when we're alone with Dumuz, then we are Eanna… and most definitely not thinking with our head.'

'What?' I was beginning to detect the saliva Lilith had mentioned.

The lilt in her response was almost musical. 'Although Lilith likes to watch – the perv.' She paused and reflected, 'Given our situation, it's strange we never considered whether it might be possible for a bit of *girl-in-girl*.'

'*On,*' I corrected.

Eanna smiled sweetly. 'No. *In.*'

I wiped my face with the back of my hand. 'Um… But what about my mother?'

'You mean Iresh? Well, it has been eighteen years, and her sexual tastes are now irrelevant – what with her being proper dead and all.'

I glared.

'*Ah*, you don't mean that,' she said. 'Okay, I'll try again, using words of one syllable this time. *I... resh* is not your *mo... ther*. I am. *I... resh* is your aunt – or was.'

'Oh,' I said.

She snorted. 'Just don't expect any cake-making. That was Iresh's thing. Me? I'd burn water.'

'Oh,' I said again.

Or at least I thought I did. My skin, if there had been any, felt clammy. Once again, my world turned to silver. I started to fade and sink into the mattress. I...

Eanna sat on the bed, stretched down with a hand, and hauled me back up. As I rose, I gasped for air – which I did not need. Even now, not all of me would accept my death. The woman, *who claimed to be my mother*, smiled. And I stabilised. And I was whole again.

I reached out.

This time, it was Lilith who spoke. 'Girl, I hope you're not going to let go again,' she growled. 'The piss pot for that kind of effluent doesn't exist. There was never a need before you came along.'

All I wanted to do was hug her. A mother should welcome that. Mothers always spoil things. Well, any mother of mine does. My murderer, my angel, claimed to be my mother... and I had to accept that it was true.

Which deserved another "Oh".

She, Lilith, had been in the house. All those years ago, she'd been in the attic. She'd seen the picture of Kitten.

Oh… and… fuzz.

She'd known days ago. Lilith knew the picture was no longer there, that the furniture that had filled the room had vanished. She was beside me when I ran through the ash on the lawn.

This woman might be my mother, but my angel was also my watcher.

And she knew everything.

'*Ah*,' I said.

Eanna's eyes glinted silver at my realisation and then amber as her form shimmered back into Lilith. 'Ah… *yes*,' she said.

Standing again, she returned to the fire.

I was glad of the distance.

'It's time to ante up, oh daughter of mine. Well, mostly mine, well, Eanna's.' She smoothed the leather of her trousers. As she did so, I could imagine the glass knife currently secured on her belt dripping again with… well, not exactly blood.

'I'll tell you mine if you tell me yours,' I said. It sounded weak, even to me.

Lilith smiled as a panther might. 'I already know yours. I want you to say it.'

'Not all of it.' I wasn't sure I wanted to talk about my encounter with Izdubar.

'Perhaps not all,' she agreed. The amber in her eyes seemed to glow.

I confirmed what she already knew. 'Kitten is my brother.'

Lilith hesitated, as if about to probe for what I was hiding… before letting it go. 'Half-brother,' she said.

'And my cousin,' I said.

'Complicated, isn't it? That's your father for you. Too busy getting his end away to worry about a legible family tree.'

She looked at me coldly, knowing what I would say next, but demanding it all the same.

'I was jealous,' I said. It came out as a stutter. Tears rose from a well no longer there. I almost said I'd wanted Kitten gone, which in Lilith's eyes would be unforgivable.

And, as it turned out, never true.

I tried once more. 'The day I left Marhasyow, I found a key to the attic door. It's strange that as I grew up, I never again wondered what was behind it. Not until…' I stopped, confused, and then not. 'Oh, damn. It was you!'

She nodded. 'It's called a Geas. A Geas is a bit more focused than a Ward. Don't feel too bad. Iresh couldn't go into the attic either. We needed her to forget Kitten. We needed her to forget anything that reminded her of him.'

'Why?'

'You should start with "how". How I made her forget. That night, you know, back when you were being such a whiny brat, I put two things on her desk. The first one was the parchment you carried. Iresh read it and invoked the Geas. I love it when a plan comes together.' She looked wistful. 'Which it almost…'

I interrupted. 'Too complicated. And anyway, there were only a couple of sentences.' I glanced at the book on the shelf. 'While I haven't read a copy of "Incantations for Girls", surely you'd need more than that.'

Lilith followed my eyes. 'Invisible ink. An ink that turns invisible once it's read or, actually, once it's "*red*".' She pulled out her knife and pricked a finger.

I blinked as I watched it fade.

She continued. 'If Iresh had bothered to read the full thing, the Geas would have worked rather than mostly worked, but she skipped a bit.'

'The bit that was left on the page?'

'Yes… which had consequences.'

I felt cold, but not ghost *cold*. 'From that day on, we were never close.'

About to vomit *cold*.

Lilith met my eyes. 'While you proved to be an adequate substitute for the day-to-day, you could never replace her child. After the whole "let's rebuild the castle" thing ran out of steam, Iresh felt drawn back to the ruins.'

That hurt – a lot. But before I was even close to saying so, Lilith gave me her best "don't even try it" look. Which was unfair, but at least it stopped me from *unnecessarily* asking about the use of words like "adequate" and "substitute".

Lilith continued. 'So, imagine the scene. The townsfolk are gone, the castle's quiet, and there's not a soul to be seen – except one.'

'Kitten,' I said.

'Kitten… But not the Kitten that you know now. This Kitten couldn't speak. This Kitten couldn't see her, never mind recognise her. This Kitten spent his days and nights searching. He searched the walls, the cottage, the keep, the entire island for something that was never there.'

She sniffed. 'I imagine Iresh wanted to hold him, love him, take him home, but that was impossible.'

She met my eyes. 'So, she made do.'

I winced.

Lilith's face tightened. 'Iresh wasn't a hypocrite. In those early years, her affection for you wasn't false. It may not make sense, but no human is binary. It's only when they're forced to choose that they discover they have no choice.'

Was she talking about Iresh? Or herself?

Lilith gave me no opportunity to ask. 'It wouldn't have lasted,' she said. 'It wasn't lasting.'

She took a deep breath. 'So, we fixed it. While he couldn't see her, he could see us. While he couldn't remember her, he could learn to love Dumuz and me as parents. With us, he could firm again, see again, view the mortals of this world again. What we *couldn't* let him do was meet his true mother. It would have broken him.' She looked away. 'It would bring back memories that…'

I tried to speak, but Lilith held up a hand. She continued, 'The only way to make sure was to use the Geas and the Wards. Once in place, while Iresh still knew that Kitten had died, she forgot that a part of him remained. That's what I designed the Geas to do. But, as I said, it didn't work. Not completely. To Iresh, that missing thing was like a scab she couldn't scratch. It changed her and not for the better.'

Lilith again met my gaze. 'I couldn't lose my child again. I just couldn't. We gave him a purpose, a new family. We had to…'

'*You had to do what?* Mess Iresh up? Mess me up?'

Eanna's voice took over. 'We didn't mean to.'

'You destroyed my life!'

'Yes,' she whispered.

'A life you didn't try to fix!'

'And risked Kitten's?'

Yes!

Or no. Could I blame her? Really? At some level, I understood. I so needed to blame her. If not for that, then…

Oh.

'The Geas collapsed when Iresh died,' I said.

'Yes.'

Once the Geas was gone, I could enter the attic.

I screamed incoherently.

Eanna waited until I fell silent. 'You have a letter for me,' she said.

'What?'

Her eyes flamed. '*You have a letter for me,*' she repeated, before ripping open the envelope I'd thrown at her. Taking out a slip of paper, she read it. Even from a distance, I recognised Iresh's handwriting. Sighing, the creature, the woman, my mother, tossed it onto the fire.

'*What are you doing?*'

'That… you should not read,' she said.

Eanna then drew out a smaller letter from within the envelope. A letter addressed to me. 'And this you should. When I left, I asked Iresh to give it to you when you grew up. Apparently, she didn't. Actually, it looks like she was planning to send it to me – but again, she didn't.'

The flame in her eyes grew cold. 'There is a kind of hope in that, don't you think?'

I stared in disbelief.

'You should take it.'

She spun the letter into my lap.

I didn't move. 'It'll say why you ran away?'

'Yes.'

'Why won't you tell me to my face?'

She looked at me sadly. 'Some things are better read.'

'Does it say how you died?'

'I told you. I wrote it before I left.' She smiled. 'Unfortunately, Lilith wasn't around then to improve my vocabulary.'

'You mentioned two things,' I said.

'What?'

'You left two things on the desk. What was the second?'

It was Lilith who answered. 'Your amulet, of course. What else?'

'I'd always thought it was Iresh's… or Kitten's?' I was secretly afraid it was Kitten's.

'*What?* No, no. The amulet around your neck is yours. Kitten has his own.'

'He does? Where?' I'd never seen it.

She laughed – there was a brightness to her voice that I'd never heard before. 'It's inside his teddy bear, silly. I knew I'd find it in the attic. I should never have given it to Iresh.'

'You took Kitten's teddy bear?'

'Yes.'

'And left the parchment and my amulet behind?'

'Yes,' she said carefully.

'Where did it come from?'

Lilith hesitated. 'Your amulet?'

'Yes.'

'Yeah… well… I have a confession. A few days ago when you put your amulet on, we didn't actually see a light.'

'No? Dumuz lied?' Oh, call me surprised. 'But… how did you know I'd put it on?'

She bit her bottom lip. 'The maker of the amulet always knows where it is… and if the new owner is wearing it.'

Oh.

'Did Eanna make it?' I asked.

She shook her head quietly, again embarrassed.

'*Then, who?*'

Lilith bared her teeth a little. 'I have certain skills. I know how to collect tears of a vital memory – and how to distil them into an amulet.'

She then sniffed in distaste. 'Although, after all that blubbing you did that night, I'd have been better off with a quart jug than a hanky.'

Oh my.

Oh dear.

Lilith stood up and walked into the hallway. 'Now, will you just read the *fucking* letter!' she snarled, although not unkindly.

As she closed the door behind her, she muttered something. This time, though, I heard. 'Back then, I had no choice,' she said, 'but I wish I'd done better.'

As I unfolded the paper, I found the pages, stiffened by age, difficult to turn.

And, after reading them, wished I hadn't.

Chapter sixteen

The Place of Many Tribes

Having read, no, change that, having consumed the letter, I found myself in an empty room with the fire damped down, which pretty much represented how I felt. I was no longer in a state of woe, precisely, or anger. "Hollow", yes, that was the word. I felt "hollow". It should have been "harrowed", really. If Eanna had kept me, if we had bonded, it would have been. She didn't, so the word was "hollow".

I rolled my legs off the bed and walked over to the fireplace. Consciously, I forced the fingers of my left hand to fade and watched while the pages fell onto the embers. The fire reborn flamed briefly before darkening again to ash. If that wasn't a metaphor for life as a ghost, I've no idea what would be.

I didn't need those yellowed scraps of paper to remind me of what she had said – the words were etched into my synapses. However, I felt no immediate need to accuse or offer sympathy. Both were waiting for an out, and they would have it, but only when I was ready, and only when Eanna was not.

The staircase beyond the bedroom was Grand (the capital G was necessary). It swept down from both sides like an hourglass. Its mandatory red carpet cascaded like a waterfall before pooling at the bottom like… well, like blood. Lilith was a bad influence on my similes. Still, I felt like a debutante at her first ball. On a whim, I visualised myself as a princess out of one of my favourite Gothic novels – and suddenly I was so dressed. I was definitely getting the hang of the more useful aspects of this ghost thing. I took my first step – and tripped on my underskirts. I only avoided a painful descent by grabbing a handrail.

Bloody gown! I changed back into my regular clothes.

Upon reaching the bottom of the stairs, I heard laughter from behind a closed door to my left. I walked through the door without opening it. The last time I used this phasing skill, I had briefly stopped Hugo's heart. It was nice to know I could also use it for something more mundane. I found myself in a dining room – the size of a small ballroom. I crossed the floor, passed through the open French doors at the far end… and encountered one of the more peculiar variants of people hitting balls with sticks.

The lawn was flat and clear of leaves and twigs. If it hadn't been, then the game of croquet being played would have been far more difficult. There was one thing I couldn't understand, though. The grass itself never seemed to end. Instead, it merged into the field beyond without a barrier to separate them – a beyond absolutely brimming with cows.

Why hadn't the cows trampled the lawn?

To my front, Adapa looked on from a patio, guffawing while sipping something that smelt ridiculously alcoholic. He wasn't laughing at the lack of skill. Team Living, Nicolò and Rosalind seemed quite proficient. And the Team Spirit? Well, if you give Lilith something that looked like a brain-mashing club, then it was an odds-on bet that she'd know how to use it. Adapa wasn't laughing at Dumuz, who looked like he knew every divot on the lawn. No, Adapa was laughing at Kitten. My semi-brother-from-once-my-mother had got it into his head that every time a ball went through a hoop, it would be a hoot to kick it back out again. Still, it evened up the game. Kitten only kicked Dumuz's ball back.

Team Spirit's defeat seemed inevitable until Tiama walked onto the pitch, scragged Kitten by the collar, and hauled him away. She then dumped the boy into the waiting arms of Adapa. Adapa's arms were only waiting, of course, because he'd been reaching out to refill his glass.

Team Spirit won.

As the teams returned from the croquet pitch, Dumuz caught my eye. He looked good for a guy whose ectoplasmic flesh had recently been vaporised. Dumuz glanced at an arch cut into a tall beech hedge that led… somewhere else. I took the hint and moved towards it. Dumuz followed. Lilith, though, held back. Was she avoiding me?

Well… probably. Now that I'd read the letter.

Beyond the hedge was another lawn. Surrounding the grass was a herbaceous border containing the last remnants of green stuff that looked expensive and not in the least bit hardy. At the end of the lawn stood a structure with an ornate, impractical and ridiculously large wooden bucket suspended on a rope above it. Simply put, someone had taken something useful and made a folly out of it.

Behind me stood the man who I suspected had arranged its construction.

I turned. Close up, he looked pretty dreamy. Another death had been good for him. Dumuz had more hair on his head and fewer lines on his face. He still wore that stupid cloak though. He still had far too many buttons undone, and, apparently, he was snogging my mother – and had been for years. So, on balance, I made up my mind to stop fancying my almost stepfather.

Not that I ever did.

There was something else different about him. Dumuz now wore an amulet. It hadn't been there when we first met. That chest hair had most certainly been unadorned with decoration. When I saw Lilith in the bedroom, she hadn't been wearing hers – not even when she was Eanna. While I wasn't as fixated on her chest as Dumuz's, I'm sure I would have noticed. Even if it were only to plot a bit of revenge "trace 'n' cut".

'I assume this is your family's house?' I said, beginning with the simple.

'Yes,' Dumuz replied. He looked uncomfortable.

Not so simple then. 'Should I have used a capital F?'

He rolled his eyes. 'It is just that the word "family" is not exactly appropriate. I never had a mother – nor much of a father.'

'You're saying you were the classic poor little rich boy?' I wasn't at my most sympathetic.

Dumuz smiled. 'My father got bored with me early on and packed me off to boarding school pretty much as soon as I was toilet-trained. I rarely saw him outside of holidays.'

Okay, slight sympathy.

His smile faded. 'University continued the pattern. It was only after I graduated things changed. We had a spectacular argument, and I left home again. This time for good. I thought I could become your classical romantic degenerate, albeit one with a dislike for poetry – and syphilis.'

That explained the cloak and unbuttoned shirt. 'You mean a wastrel then?'

He raised an eyebrow. 'Yes, but one with a large stipend. My father went to great lengths to ensure the strings were not entirely cut. Me? I still feel ashamed that I let them remain.'

'You never saw him again?'

He sighed. 'No.'

I looked around. 'When did you inherit this... pile?'

Dumuz tongued a cheek. 'Fifteen years ago,' he said. 'You see, my father had a thing for tropical plants and he kept many of them in a conservatory – actually, where the patio sits now. Unfortunately, tropical plants need heat in winter to stay alive. This proved somewhat problematic when that same heat set the entire conservatory on fire.'

'He burnt to death?'

Dumuz lifted his chin slightly. 'Not exactly. Did you know that glass falls ridiculously hard and fast and sharply when there are insufficient roof struts to hold it in place?' He sniffed. 'After that, there was a lot more of the red stuff and far less of my father... at least in any specific spot.'

'Er... Sorry?'

Dumuz's eyes flickered. 'Anyway,' he said. 'Much to my surprise, I found his death traumatic. It made me consider my mortality, my place in the universe, my... it got so bad I wrote a poem.'

'You had a full-blown "mid-life"?'

'In a way... but I was also trying to understand what it meant to be Wycche.'

I looked at the dead man before me. 'When did you find out?'

'After I graduated. My father had waited until then to tell me my mother was Wycche. He thought I would find it funny.'

'So that's where you get your sense of humour.'

He ignored me. 'My father found the Wycche fascinating. He even owned a book on the topic. One he never let me read.'

'The book in the bedroom where I woke?'

Dumuz nodded. 'My falling out with my father had nothing to do with my lifestyle choice. The trouble with people with the morals of a skunk is their lack of nuance. If he had just told me she was Wycche, I wouldn't have reacted as I did. Unfortunately, he thought I would be mature.'

I waited.

'My mother was a servant, indentured, and probably not that willing. She died giving birth.'

'Em. Can I take back my earlier *sorry*?'

Dumuz glared. 'What he did to her was inconsequential compared to some of his other acts.' He hesitated. 'After he died, I read his book myself.'

'You wanted to know about the whole "life after death scary ghost" thing, didn't you?'

His feet shuffled. 'Well, yes,' he said.

Sweet.

Dumuz lifted his head. 'I tried to find other Wycche. Ones that understood what they were. I succeeded only with the first, and that was only once. I guess I turned in on myself. I rarely ventured out. I rarely spoke to anyone. I…'

'What changed? Ah… Lilith.'

'Actually, Eanna. Although to begin with, we found a better use for our tongues than speech.'

'*Eeew…*'

He smiled in amusement. 'Anyway. While ultimately my death was unexpected, I still had time to plan for it.'

'Unexpected?'

'Very much so. Eanna feels guilty about it, even now. Although it was never her fault.'

'She...' I began.

Dumuz interrupted. 'It was also her death. I think you should ask her.'

'You died together...'

Dumuz's eyes hardened.

Okay. Yet another question for Eanna.

Dumuz continued. 'I made sure my affairs were in order. When I died and hopefully returned, my household would function much as it had before. I established a trust fund to pay my staff, provided they met a few conditions. For example, to discourage visitors, I asked them to let the front of the house fall into disrepair. Of course, the plan changed when Eanna and I moved to Marhasyow.'

'It didn't faze them that their employer was... no longer present?'

'They hardly saw me even when I was alive. Dead, ideally not at all. I was paying them to, essentially, dust, and cut the grass.'

'But you left them in the house on their own. What if they had taken liberties?'

'Not completely on their own. I rented the house out. There were a few void weeks each spring and autumn without tenants – thankfully, this is one now. During them, Eanna and I returned to see how things were going. As you can see by the lack of staff today, they take their holidays at the first hint of a visit... particularly after that first year.'

'Lilith?' I asked. I could almost guess what was coming next.

He snorted. 'Yes, Lilith. She discovered that one unfortunate was selling off the contents of my wine cellar.'

'And?'

Dumuz looked over my shoulder.

Lilith whispered in my ear from behind. 'Polyembolokoilamania.'

I jumped and spun around. 'What?'

Lilith's eyes lit up. 'The doctors thought he had Polyembolokoilamania – the self-insertion of a foreign object into one's body for pleasure. Here, the object was a wine bottle. It wasn't self-inserted, and, from his reaction, it wasn't pleasurable.'

'Hello, *Mother*,' I said caustically. I wasn't ready.

Lilith glowered at me. 'I haven't changed, you know.'

'Meaning?'

'Don't expect any bonding. I don't bond. Mass slaughter would be more my speed – if it weren't for Eanna.'

'But then you are Eanna,' I said.

Lilith re-glowered. 'Okay then, I *am* Eanna, and just like her, I don't make cakes. At least not as a team activity.'

'I did, or I used to when I was young. Of course, that was when I thought Iresh was my mother and when she treated me as a daughter. You know, just before you destroyed everything.' I smiled politely – just to show I could.

Lilith looked at me oddly. It appeared that "bitter and twisted" was acceptable if I avoided the whiny tone.

Her lips tightened. 'We have a problem.'

'What problem?' I asked.

Lilith's eyes pulsed. 'Kitten's asking questions. About what happened, about why we had to leave. He is asking about you.'

'So?' I asked.

'It was always likely,' Dumuz said.

The tension in Lilith's voice was palpable. 'He's been through so much.'

'*I know,*' I said sarcastically. 'You told me that. *Remember*?'

Lilith scowled, which, apparently, was higher on the glower scale than glower.

I scowled right back. 'Kitten survived the journey to Sulis, believing you were gone. Surely that suggests he's stable. Not particularly interesting, but stable.'

'Kitten's grasp on this plane of existence is tenuous,' Dumuz said. 'As well as an amulet, a ghost also needs a reason to remain.'

Oh, for pity's sake. 'You're not saying Kitten had unfinished business? That old cliché?'

Dumuz nodded. 'Kitten was looking for something.'

'What?'

Did I have *unfinished business*?

Lilith's eyes glistened. 'Every child needs their teddy bear.'

I shook my head. Of course.

Dumuz continued. 'After Lilith found and returned it, we gave Kitten a new purpose. We gave him a family. Together, that was enough for him to remain and, perhaps, even grow a little.'

'I take it you're not talking about his height?'

Dumuz didn't respond. Instead, he turned to Lilith and stroked the short bristles of her hair – no doubt imagining them longer. 'On reflection,' he said to her. 'Siduri is right. To survive that journey, Kitten must have been stronger than either of us thought. We need to tell him who she is.'

'We have no choice,' he added.

Lilith froze – apart from the trembling.

When she finally spoke, it was with Eanna's dulcet warble.

'Wait here,' she said. 'We'll talk to Kitten. I'll call you over when we've told him who you are.'

She then put her hand on Dumuz's lower back and guided him through the arch. As they arrived on the main lawn, the hand slipped further down and into his back trouser pocket. I couldn't believe it. The woman was fondling my sort-of-stepfather's arse.

It was while watching the vomit-inducing pair walk across the grass that I remembered a word from one of my favourite romantic Gothic novels. The word was "ha-ha". A "ha-ha" is *"a recessed landscape design element that creates a vertical barrier while preserving an uninterrupted view of the landscape beyond"*. Dumuz's lawn had a ha-ha. It was there to keep the cows out. This non-fence also proved an excellent place for the Fedhyow to hide while preparing to attack.

Somehow, they'd found us.

There were over thirty of them, almost forty. Let's call it forty as they sought to steal away whatever family I had left. They swept across the lawn like a black tide of oil.

Lilith and Dumuz had their backs to the onrushing mass. Although I screamed something that, on reflection, was more like a gargle, it was too late. A glass orb exploded behind Dumuz's heels, spewing liquid onto the back of his legs. Dumuz's lower limbs dissolved. Or I wish they had because what remained wasn't exactly functional. He fell to the ground, dragging a semi-attached Lilith with him. Lilith regained her feet quickly. She snarled and turned, pulling out her glass knife. I glanced at the leather trouser leg below her right knee – which was just not there. Neither was there any skin on her calf. The damage didn't initially appear to bother her, but then one of her muscles snapped and tore, and Lilith fell again.

The Fedhyow swept past the couple and towards the house, ignoring the already-fallen. That Lilith hamstrung one Fedhyow with her knife made no difference in the broader scheme of things.

Not quite the coward I thought I was, I raced to help.

When I got there, Dumuz was already unconscious – which, given the ongoing disintegration of his lower half, was a good thing.

Lilith was still trying and failing to stand. Seeing me, she held out her glass knife.

'Take it!' she said. 'You're their only hope.'

'What? Seriously?' I couldn't. I…

'You have no choice,' she added in a voice that made me think of honeydew.

And then she passed out.

Bitch.

But she was right. I picked up the glass shard and turned towards the fight.

Adapa was still on the patio, covered in a heap of Fedhyow. Judging by the broken furniture lying on the ground, they'd never given him a chance to stand. I looked on, appalled, as a Fedhyow hit Adapa's head with a broken chair leg. Adapa sank into the mass and didn't rise again.

I suspected he never would.

On the lawn, two Fedhyow had forced Nicolò to the ground. One Fedhyow stood behind him, twisting his right arm, driving his shoulder into the grass. The second Fedhyow was on Nicolò's left, grasping his hair, pulling Nicolò's head back with his right hand. His other held a knife.

This second Fedhyow, I knew. He was a man difficult to forget, particularly since I'd touched his heart and let him live.

Hugo.

Almost anyone would have struggled at that moment, fighting for their life. But not Nicolò. Nicolò, face splattered with mud and grass, hardly moved as he stared back at the house.

Horrified at Hugo's obvious intention, I ran again to help. As I sprinted, I glanced at the house and whatever had caught Nicolò's eye.

Rosalind watched from just inside the dining room. That it doubled as a ballroom felt even more true. Rosalind held Kitten in a dancer's embrace – or she would have if she'd allowed Kitten's feet to touch the floor. Beside Rosalind were two men. Both wore white cloaks rather than black. One was as substantial as any Fedhyow.

The other was my father.

I could hate Rosalind now. I could hate her without worrying about whether it was jealousy. While I knew Izdubar had told her Tristan was alive, it still never crossed my mind that Rosalind would sell us out. How had the Fedhyow known we'd be here?

Rosalind must have told my father.

Who had then *whispered* it to Hugo.

No doubt Izdubar had offered her Tristan, but only if she gave up Kitten in exchange. I couldn't believe Rosalind would betray Nicolò for anything less. When Izdubar tried to blackmail me to go to Guitt, I'd refused. Did taking Kitten there mean Izdubar no longer needed his daughter?

Would either of his children do?

Suddenly, Rosalind bit her bottom lip and turned away.

Ahead, I saw Hugo's left arm tense for the killing stroke and knew I was too late. I ran on anyway, panting, eyes wide open, screaming incoherently as the knife drew across Nicolò's throat.

Tiama, though, was not too late.

Before Hugo's blade could cut skin, she appeared behind him and stretched out her arm – just like I had at the dock. Her arm blended into Hugo's back. Unlike mine, though, it didn't fade. Instead, Tiama's arm grew more substantial as it passed through and out of the front of his chest.

Hugo screamed in pain – briefly. Indeed, he was quite silent by the time he slipped off Tiama's arm and onto the ground. As I closed the distance, it surprised me to still see a hole. I had expected blood, a lot of spurting blood, but there was remarkably little. It took a while to realise there was no longer a source to power the action.

Above him, Tiama didn't move. She was a woman neither ashamed nor proud, a ghost neither solid nor shadow. Her hand was still solid, though, as was Hugo's heart. Well, the heart was until Tiama's fingers crushed it. My stomach heaved as I watched the resultant fatty pulp slop onto the perfectly manicured lawn.

The Fedhyow who still held Nicolò had experience, at least in dealing with resistance. He didn't freeze in shock at the sudden loss of his master. Instead, and in almost one motion, he pushed Nicolò onto the grass, turned, drew a pair of glass spheres from his robe and *threw*.

As they hit, Tiama literally dissolved. Her feet, her legs, her torso, everything but her amulet turned to mist. The last thing to go was her face. She seemed younger in those last moments. A woman who was finally at peace.

I looked again at Hugo's corpse. Back in Marhasyow, Tiama had failed to protect her son. This time, she'd succeeded. Her unfinished business was done.

The remaining Fedhyow picked up Tiama's amulet. It

looked more like a sugar cage than the thing it was before. With unnecessary drama, he snapped his fingers to his palm before relaxing again and letting the resultant dust fall away. This was a man, though, who had made a mistake. This was a man who had messed up his priorities.

Nicolò slammed into the Fedhyow's back, catching an elbow in the face for his troubles. Both hit the grass *hard*.

When I arrived, the Fedhyow was still face down, panting for a breath he hadn't expected to lose. I knelt and placed the tip of the glass knife on his neck. The daughter of Lilith would drive it into his brainstem. The daughter of Lilith could kill when necessity demanded it and sometimes when not.

I was Eanna's daughter, not Lilith's, but, even so, the Fedhyow took the choice away from me.

He rose! The idiot turned his head and rose! Did he sense weakness? Or did he want to be a martyr? Did he think my arm would bend, or did he desire the most classic short-cut to a holy place? Unfortunately for him, the first option didn't exist. I couldn't relax my arm that fast. The Fedhyow, therefore, got the second – with added hole and deeper cut.

The result was almost risible before the Fedhyow got a hand on it. It didn't stop the man from slumping to the ground though. It didn't stop the blood that continued to pulse through his fingers with a regularity that surpassed the best comic timing.

I stood and tried to pull Nicolò back up, but couldn't. On the ground, Nicolò looked dazed, his eyes meandering worryingly. Was it just the concussion that kept him from moving? Within minutes, Nicolò had lost his mother and been so basely betrayed. That his father was at the root of much of this shouldn't have made it worse. But even now, I think it did.

I looked again towards the dining room. Those inside had gone. The Fedhyow on the patio, though, were not gone. Indeed, they had turned like the tide and were now rushing back across the lawn.

Towards me.

Which was a bad thing.

I tugged once more at Nicolò's arm, but again he wouldn't move.

Lilith hobbled into view, white as a proverbial... ghost. Her right leg beneath the knee looked almost entirely withered.

In her left hand was Dumuz's amulet.

I glanced back to where Dumuz lay – had lain. Nothing of him remained.

Lilith put the amulet over Nicolò's head.

The effect was immediate, if not a little worrying. Nicolò shuddered as if having a fit. The shaking passed quickly, though, and Nicolò stood, his face a mask of concentration. It almost looked as if he wasn't entirely in charge of his own body.

He wasn't.

When Nicolò's lips moved, the word choice and tone were all Dumuz. 'We have little time,' he said. 'I can only stay in control because of Nicolò's emotional state. If we can get into the side garden without being seen, we might still survive this.'

Oh.

Okay, that's another one for my list. Apparently, we can do *possession*.

We hauled Lilith towards the gap in the hedge. By necessity, we moved slowly. I didn't dare look back though. On that day at the beach, the tide destroyed my castle of sand. It wasn't the castle's fault or the tides. It was an irresistible force meeting...

well, not so much an unmovable object as a dissolvable one. I felt a bit like that castle right then – but I was a castle with no desire to meet the tide.

We were not dissolved. The Fedhyow never got close to dissolving us.

The difference between that little girl's castle and this one was that it was moving. After passing through the gap in the hedge, Lilith demanded we stop. Releasing Dumuz/Nicolò, she leant against me, before pulling a small canister out of her pocket. Lilith then poured its contents on everything green and behind us. Once empty, she tossed it aside before reaching back into her jacket. Pale, clammy and about to go into shock, she pulled out a box of matches.

Of course, Lilith was a pyromaniac.

Lilith removed a match from the box, struck it alight, and threw it at the hedge – the entrance went up in flames.

'*So, you did burn down my house!*'

'It was never your house,' she said.

Dropping the matchbox into my left hand, she continued. 'Keep them. You never know when you might need a distraction.'

Then she passed out.

Again.

Bitch.

Dumuz/Nicolò caught Lilith before she fell.

'While the flames are impressive,' Dumuz said, 'we have to move before they fade. We don't want the Fedhyow to see where we are going.'

I looked at the side lawn, the brick wall and the absolute f… folly of a well.

'And that would be?' I asked.

Chapter seventeen

The Thing That Is Real

Siduri,

My name is Eanna, and I'm your mother. Your real mother.

There, I said it. It's best to get the truth out there. I tried to come up with fancy ways of being all subtle, but that's not me.

When I told Iresh I had to leave Marhasyow, we agreed it'd be better if she brought you up as her own. Better for you, better for me, and I think better for Iresh, although she won't admit it. I'll get to the details later, but some bad things happened a year ago. There are a few that even Iresh doesn't know, and I don't want her to know. However, the result is that I'm leaving, and you are staying behind. As I said, it's for the best.

To help you understand, I need to go back to six years ago when I was ten, and Iresh was nineteen.

Back then, Iresh was more of a mother to me than a sister. She didn't have a choice. Mum died the year before. Dad? He disappeared the very next day.

We lived in an attic above an inn. It wasn't much of a room, but it had one benefit. It was the landlord's bedroom below us and not the bar. The drunks never kept me awake, but the racket he made banging my Iresh certainly did.

Are you shocked? You shouldn't be. There's not much work around for a girl with a kid sister in tow. Although she was hired as a "barmaid", Iresh always knew that a bit of humping was also required.

The landlord got himself a bargain. Iresh was pretty and blonde and carried jugs of ale without spilling a drop. She wore a dress that showed the right things and often the wrong. It was good for business, and Iresh ignored any wandering hands with a professional smile.

Then one night, everything changed.

That night, instead of just groping her, some prick tore off her entire top. Still, I've always thought sticking him with a knife in response was a bit much. Not my sister's response, of course. The poor girl was too busy covering her tits. No, it was another customer. Some helpful doorman gave him a knife, and he used it.

Weird, eh?

I don't know what Stephen Izdubar was doing there. The inn was as rough as you get. But what I do know is that just after cutting out some poor bloke's guts, Izdubar then put his cloak around Iresh. I guess it looked all gentlemanly to the regulars. Or at least the ones not looking at the blood. Mind you, it wasn't so much the blood but the swelling in Izdubar's trousers that got Iresh all scared.

Stephen Izdubar bought the house where you were born. He wasn't being generous. The randy sod needed somewhere to bang my sister and have no one find out. Izdubar may have been horny, but he was also the governor of Marhasyow. The man had to be seen as moral and law-abiding. Izdubar was good at covering things up. So good that I also heard no more about the perv he stabbed in the bar.

The secret relationship thingy started well, and Iresh warmed to the upsides. Izdubar still frightened her, of course, but we had our own place, and he gave her some money. In fact, Iresh even enjoyed the bed-bouncing in the end.

Well, sometimes.

Then she got knocked up.

Looking back, I'm amazed Izdubar let her live, never mind keep the house and a bit of cash. We just had to stay quiet, avoid the castle, and never ever mention her new kid's dad.

Iresh had a boy, Suranu, but I've always called him "Kitten". My brother mewled as a baby and then never stopped. While I tried to avoid the boy, Iresh went big on motherhood. It didn't surprise me. Her near-enough adoption of her sister had shown she liked that sort of thing.

I was twelve by then and more independent. Izdubar's money paid for my schooling. Outside of it, I found other ways to avoid my whiny brother. I spent a lot of time exploring. While I found the fields and forests just fine, walking along the pebble bar to the castle was always the best. I knew I wasn't supposed to go near the place after what Izdubar said, but I was always careful. I never tried to get in.

Other things distracted me as I got older. Boy things. I'd kept to myself in the beginning. There were just too many questions my classmates might ask. By fourteen, this became a major problem. Or at least that's what my down-below told me. Desperate for, I don't know what. I felt a sudden need to fit in.

Iresh was sympathetic. She taught me about make-up, hair, and how to lie to boys. It worked. I was pretty, not as pretty as Iresh, but pretty all the same. Being chased by boys told me that. Being caught told me that. For the next two years, I spent my time wandering the lads-scape rather than the landscape and never went back to the castle.

That all changed a year ago.

I woke up that morning to the delightful sound of Kitten whining. I gave him his usual feed and looked for Iresh. She was still in bed. Strangely, she'd spent the day before digging a flowerbed for fun.

She'd then spent much of the following night suffering for it. Iresh should've known. Her back wasn't as flexible as it used to be. After Izdubar, she'd never had time for a man.

Anyway, while the pain in her back was a bit less, Iresh wasn't getting out of bed anytime soon. To get some peace, Iresh suggested I take Kitten to the beach. She didn't remind me to stay away from the castle though. Which was a mistake.

The walk would've been nice if I hadn't had a whimpering brother by my side. We'd barely entered the woods before Kitten turned all "cryity".

When I asked what was wrong, Kitten held up the teddy bear he'd brought and said he needed both hands to put down a paper trail "just in case we get lost". I told him it was a single path to the sea, but he kept mewling.

I carried the bear.

He was right about the path. After two years, it had overgrown. He was wrong about the paper though. We didn't have any. So, he made little piles of branches to mark our way.

The walk took an age.

I'd hoped Kitten would settle down when we got to the beach, but no. As I handed back the bear, Kitten started complaining again. This time, he wanted to see the castle up close. I know I should've refused, but I had been there before, and, well, I just couldn't cope with any more tears.

After a long, but thankfully quiet, trek along the pebbly ridge, we reached the castle wall and the point where we had to turn around.

Kitten didn't turn around. Instead, the little shit sprang up onto the rocks and was gone. I chased after him. I knew if we were caught, that meant the end of the deal made with Izdubar. We would be poor again.

Or worse.

I followed Kitten around the castle to the bit that faced the sea. Just before I got my hands on my idiot brother, Kitten climbed through a gap he'd found in the wall.

I followed.

It wasn't just a gap. Someone must've merged the castle wall with an existing building and filled in the windows to make it look secure. It could never last and it didn't. Facing the ocean on the unseen backside of the castle was a hollow that was also a room.

I'd heard the story. Everyone had. There was a mill on the river Koner. A few years ago, a fire broke out, the mill burnt down, and its owner died. There was also something about a fight, but I don't remember the details. Still, it turns out that the story had at least one fib. The mill that burnt down wasn't on the Koner.

There was soot on the walls, a skeleton on the floor and a large round stone trapping its legs. Still, I only really knew the place was the actual mill when I touched the locket around the skeleton's neck.

Something made me put the locket on.

I saw a second locket on the floor. Kitten saw it as well. He grabbed it and tried to copy me but the chain was too small.

So, he put it on his teddy bear.

The locket on my chest hated him for it. Hated him for treating the small locket so cheaply.

I saw an odd V-shaped knife on the floor near the skeleton's left hand and picked it up. I remember shouting that Kitten had to die for what he'd done.

My brother scampered away.

Although they'd been bent by the fire, the metal shelves on the far wall were still deep. Kitten, squealing, dived under the one closest to the floor.

I was shocked by what the locket had made me do and begged it to let me throw away the knife. It refused. Reluctantly, though, it allowed me to put it into the belt behind my back.

As I released the handle, the thing in the locket moved into my heart. Love. I felt a mother's love for her child and her pain at its loss.

I made myself calm.

I walked over to the shelves and asked Kitten to come out. He ignored me. I knelt and reached for him, but my brother just wriggled away. I thought he'd cry or beg, or at least something, but Kitten stayed quiet. Perhaps he hoped I'd leave.

Or perhaps he heard the bang at the door.

The bang turned into a crash as the melted lock that'd kept it closed all these years shattered, and the door flew open.

A guard stepped in.

I wasn't calm when the ugliest, tallest, scariest man I had ever seen grabbed and dragged me out of the room. I didn't tell him about Kitten though. Me being caught was one thing, but I didn't know what Izdubar would do if he knew his son was in the castle.

I told myself Kitten would make his own way home, that Kitten had his "paper trail" and he would find the way.

Izdubar was in a meeting when the guard brought me to him. If you call a shouting match, a meeting. Most of the shouting was one-way, and it amazed me that Izdubar could keep quiet with so many posh people yelling at him.

Still, I'd never seen his face quite that pink, not even after a full-on rump with Iresh.

Izdubar ordered the guard to take me to his apartment. It didn't look good. Could he take away our house? Just like that? I thought about the man he'd stabbed at the inn. Of course he could. Izdubar could do whatever he wanted.

When Izdubar walked through the door to his apartment, I realised that "whatever he wanted" was different from what I'd thought.

Izdubar hadn't changed, but I had. The first thing Izdubar said was that I looked like my sister. He called me a "knock-off Iresh in a frizzy black wig but with smaller tits and a skinnier arse".

Before I could answer, Izdubar headbutted my mouth with his face and pushed me onto his bed. It was horrible, but I didn't resist. We both knew what he was doing and why he could. To him, I was Iresh again, but with tinier boobs and a tighter fanny. Izdubar wanted to wind down with an old friend after a tough meeting. But since Iresh wasn't available, her sister would have to do.

A sister who didn't want to be poor again.

It hurt. If I'd known how painful it'd be, I would've fought. I didn't fight though. When Izdubar pushed my legs apart, I let him. When he pulled down my knickers, I lifted my arse to allow it.

And when Izdubar pushed in, I cried and cried.

Not once, though, did I think about sticking him with the knife. Neither did the thing still in my heart. We were both too frightened.

There was blood and cum all over my thighs when it was over. After that, I never felt whole again.

Once he got his breath back, Izdubar wiped himself against my skirt, pulled up his trousers, opened the door and left. The bastard never said a word.

I pulled up my knickers and followed him out. Izdubar was already gone, but the guard from earlier was there. He didn't smirk or look disgusted. He just took my arm, led me to the castle gate, and let me go. It was only when the guard went back through the gate that I remembered I'd seen him before. The guard had been that doorman at the inn. The one who handed Izdubar the knife. This was a man who had seen it all before.

Kitten wasn't there when I got home.

I told Iresh most of what happened, but not everything. The locket wouldn't let me tell her why Kitten had run away from me or where he'd hidden. As Iresh listened, I'd expected her to scream or something. But she didn't. Instead, she just stared at me, taking deep, deep breaths. Her eyes frightened me though. They were still blue, but now that blue made me think of ice. The cold had reached her voice when she finally spoke. The guards must've found Kitten, she said. She wouldn't let me suggest anything else.

Iresh told me to have a bath, iron straight my hair, and put on my prettiest clothes. After I'd done that, she told me I had to go back to the castle. I cried and refused, but Iresh insisted. Iresh said she'd also put on some of her best clothes and come with me. She told me it was the only way Izdubar would give Kitten back. Iresh gave me no choice.

The sun hadn't set when we reached the castle, but the sky was already black. It was also warmer and properly windy. A girl of Marhasyow knows when a storm is coming.

There was a wagon just past the gate with the tall, scary guard sitting in the driver's seat. As Iresh got closer, another man stepped out from behind the wagon. I recognised him as well. He'd been standing behind Izdubar in the meeting earlier. Wearing that stupid black cloak, he was hard to forget. Iresh asked this new man to take us to the governor. The man in black looked her up and down, slapped her face, and called her a whore. Even the tall, scary guard in the wagon looked a bit surprised at that. He was the one, though, who pointed out to the man in black that Iresh had once been Izdubar's whore.

I remember the man in black just stared at the guard for ages before he finally turned and went into the castle.

We followed.

When we arrived at Izdubar's apartment, the man in black opened the door, let us through and shut it behind us. Maybe he didn't want to explain the marks on Iresh's face.

Izdubar looked annoyed when he saw us. There were two half-filled chests and discarded clothing all over the floor. Izdubar was obviously preparing to leave. His annoyance turned into confusion when Iresh demanded that he give back her son. Izdubar said he didn't have him. Iresh offered payment. Given how she had us dress, that's always how she thought it'd go.

It might have worked if Izdubar hadn't had other priorities. Given the sudden size of his cock, it should've worked. Instead, he spat in her face and told her to take our "overused twats" elsewhere.

Iresh chucked herself at him. Izdubar blocked a knee aimed at his balls and threw her onto the bed. Iresh didn't have time to scream before Izdubar put his hands around her throat.

It was the thing in my heart that made me bring the knife. It made me pull it out from behind my back and stick it into Izdubar's side.

Izdubar cried like a baby, rolled off and bled.

I felt pleased, and then not pleased when I realised he'd been telling the truth. Izdubar hadn't seen Kitten.

No one had.

I'd heard the storm outside and knew what it might mean.

I took a last look at Izdubar. Iresh was using the bottom of her skirt to stop the bleeding. She stared at me, oddly disappointed. But Iresh didn't know what I knew.

I ran to the room where I had left Kitten. The corridor outside was an inch deep in seawater when I arrived. As I forced the door open, more water rushed out. I crawled, fighting against the current, across the floor to the shelves.

I reached underneath.

Kitten was still there. He'd hooked himself on a splinter of broken metal. I imagine my brother was still alive when the storm surge raced through the window.

But he wasn't now.

I unhooked him, dragged him out, and rolled him onto his back. Kitten still held his teddy bear. The stuffed toy sat on his chest, still wearing the necklace.

The thing in my heart made me do what was necessary. We drove the knife through teddy-bear fur and little-boy skin. We cut out a little boy's heart.

I threw up.

It was then the man in the black cloak arrived and hauled me back into the corridor. Unfortunately, he didn't realise I had a knife.

I was the one who spiked his left knee.

It wasn't surprising that he dropped like a stone to the floor and squealed. It was a noise I could get used to, or so the thing in my heart told me.

I looked back into the room. The tide swept in again, this time dragging my Kitten, our child, with it. All I had left of him was the teddy bear I still held and a memory. The bear had a bloody slash on its chest. The memory, or memories, weren't as clear. The first was that of a Kitten torn, whose face and lips were ocean grey. The second was of an infant I'd never known, an infant whose lips were blue.

Somewhere within, the thing in my heart moved into my head, and the memories merged into one.

I went back to Izdubar's apartment. Iresh's skirt was a bloody mess, but she'd stopped the bleeding. That was before I told her that Kitten was dead. To be honest, I couldn't blame her when she screamed and punched Izdubar's wound, undoing all her work. It took a few more thumps before I convinced Iresh to leave. She didn't even ask how Kitten died. Perhaps she couldn't face the details, but, and more likely, it was the way I spoke that told her not to ask.

I whispered, but the whispering didn't come from me. It came from the other "me". The one inside my head. The thing that knew both hate and guilt and what it meant to lose a child.

The causeway was still there when we crossed it. It was probably still there an hour later. Beyond that? The pebble bank broke during the night. Nothing in the path of the wave that followed stood a chance.

That night, no one came for us. The next day, no one came either.

Iresh went back the day after that. She saw what was left of the castle and the port. She asked anyone she could find whether they'd seen Kitten's body.

They hadn't.

I lost my sister that day. She could barely tolerate me and I couldn't talk to her. How can you tell a mother you cut out her dead child's heart? How can you explain why when you can't explain it to yourself? If possession is a thing, then I was possessed. I certainly had no control.

One year on, I still have no control.

I still hear whispers, you see. They won't let me take off my amulet or throw away the knife. The whispers beg me to find a child that cannot be there. A child once dead and dust, but also a child now washed away.

The whispers now say I must go to Sulis, and I will go, but I must also leave you behind.

I knew I was pregnant before the throwing up started, and the bleeding did not. The whispers told me. I knew, and I hated knowing. You, Siduri, are my punishment and my pain.

However, after saying that, you might find it strange that I can still wish you well. In fact, you might find it odd that I let you live.

That I didn't find some back-street doctor to cut you out of my womb
and throw you away.

And in the dark, so do I.

But today, the day is bright, and I do wish you well. When I look
at you in the light, I know that while you might be his child, you're
also yourself. It's not your fault how you came about, and it's not your
fault I'm leaving.

It's just that I have no choice.
Eanna

Chapter eighteen

The Well of Truth

Who'd have thought you could fit a ladder in a well? Dumuz had, but I couldn't imagine anyone else would. At least not this well. The large bucket's position ensured nobody would see the climb down. Zombie-boy Nicolò went first, pretty much to prove the ladder was there, and fainty-hop-a-long Lilith went next, mainly because I was better than stupid.

It didn't shock me that there was a chamber just above the waterline. If you go to that much trouble, there will always be a chamber. The armchairs were a surprise though.

Reaching Dumuz's subterranean man cave, we slumped down to rest and, somewhat ironically, to play dead. Of course, Nicolò and Lilith then took the concept more literally and passed out.

Again.

I sat there for hours, studying the lines on Lilith's face. Watching them flex, harden, and then relax. Lilith looked disturbed. I knew her well enough now to see the pain beneath the veneer of skin and sleep. When she woke, I could hurt her with a few simple words if I so chose.

And I would.

It was almost dusk when her eyes fluttered open.

'What happens next?' I asked.

Lilith lay slumped in the armchair, her legs spread. 'Uh?' she replied, yawning.

She had good reason to keep her legs apart. It was grotesquely clear they wouldn't be functional by the morning. Whatever had been in those orbs was stopping her muscles from knitting, her veins from forming, and her skin to grow. She wasn't healing, and I wondered why – in between finding it all quite seriously icky.

I looked at the impressive lump on Nicolò's forehead. 'Who'll be in charge when they wake up?'

'Oh. Nicolò. Unless something's broken in his head. Still, I wouldn't worry. I've seen worse.' Behind the casualness, her voice was strained.

'But were they dead at the time?'

Lilith snorted. 'Unfortunately, Nicolò will be a bit grumpy when he wakes up. Having so large a parasite inside you just isn't pleasant.'

'Been there, done that?'

Lilith raised an eyebrow before smiling.

'So, how long then?' I asked.

'Dumuz, you mean? It'll take another day or two inside his boy-oven before he can refill his tank with ecto-juice. After that, he'll separate from Nicolò, manifest and be as solid as before. And, trust me, Eanna will want him solid.'

I wasn't ready for Eanna. Not yet. 'Will they still be up there?'

'The Fedhyow? Probably not. The whole thing was quite a disturbance – at least for Sulis.'

'Should I take a look?'

Lilith glanced back up at the entrance. Sunlight still lit the bricks at the bottom of the well. 'No. The local watch will still be there. Best wait until dark.'

Lilith looked down at her gammy leg. 'I'll also have a shopping list for you.'

I thought she might. The wound was getting worse. 'How do those orbs work anyway?'

Lilith sighed. 'Dumuz would use words like "ionise" and "catalyst" to explain how that gunk can slime our form across an entire clock face of "phases". Unfortunately, you're stuck with me. So, and keep in mind I'm not a cook, I suggest you prefix the word "water" with the word "holy". Then try stirring in some secret sauce, and you'll find the resultant salty crap reduces nicely into a consommé of "painful as fuck".'

But… 'Back at the castle. The people you were fighting didn't have orbs?'

'That's why I used words like "reduce" and "consommé". A large body of water, such as Dumuz's sudden tide, can have a similar effect, particularly if it's powerful enough to smash you against the rocks. In that case, it doesn't matter whether you are a mortal or a ghost. Both are going to suffer a sudden loss of self. Mostly, all the Fedhyow did was concentrate the bad stuff in seawater. Bad from our perspective anyway.'

Which was "ouch"! As well as something I wish I'd known before getting on that boat. However, knowing it now wasn't going to help. I didn't need a fortune-teller to tell me I had another "journey across open water" in my future.

'The Fedhyow took Kitten,' I said. Knowing it would hurt.

She blinked. 'I know. I saw. That cunt Rosalind and some weird white-cloaked fuck had him. I couldn't do anything. My leg…'

'But you'll try to get him back.' I almost felt guilty.

'Of course. As soon as I can walk, I… will you help?'

The desperation in her voice was palpable.

I ignored it. 'How did you end up here? You've just told me you were pretty much bisque.'

Lilith looked at me, knowing I was toying with her, but not understanding why. 'When you die, you manifest in a place you know well or near someone with whom you have a strong emotional bond.'

'Yes. Dumuz said.'

'However, if our ethereal form is destroyed, we manifest beside our amulet, wherever that might be. Dumuz kept his amulet in his study. Mine?' She smiled again. 'Well… it's somewhere about.'

'Why keep them here?'

'Here is as safe a place as any.'

I looked at her throat. 'Dumuz wore his amulet earlier in the garden. Actually, Nicolò's wearing it now. You, though? Your neck is quite bare. Don't you do jewellery?'

'Only when necessary. Back in Marhasyow, all I got was an arse full of ocean. Dumuz was whacked by an actual *fucking orb*. The cum in those baubles is so concentrated it frays the connection we have to our amulets. Manifesting afterwards isn't enough to fix it.'

'And if the bond to his amulet, his anchor, breaks, there's nothing left to keep him in the mortal realm?'

She squinted. 'You sound just like Dumuz. But yeah. Those twats in black call it exorcism for good reason.' Her eyes drifted to her calf. 'However, the bond will repair if your amulet stays close. It also speeds up fixing anything physical.'

Ah, of course. 'Your shopping list.'

Lilith wrinkled her nose. 'Yeah. One item only. Could you fetch my amulet? I guess I need it after all.'

I would, but I wasn't ready to be that accommodating. Not yet. Instead, I asked, 'Tiama was wearing her amulet. Was it still repairing the damage done in her transition?'

Lilith looked at me coldly. 'No... Sometimes it only preserves what is left.'

We were no longer talking about Tiama – and I was nearly ready.

'Kitten is on Guitt,' I said.

She sniffed. 'It's the likeliest place they'll take him, so yeah.'

'Definitely,' I said, meeting her eyes.

'Definitely?'

'I bumped into my father when we were in Aberfal.'

'What do you mean, *bumped?*'

'Well, not really "bumped". Technically, he wasn't there. Words like "projection" were used.'

Lilith nodded as if she understood.

It was only then that I realised she did. 'You like to pretend that Dumuz is the expert on all things mystical,' I said. 'I suspect you know at least as much.'

'Perhaps... But Dumuz is the one who studied it more recently.'

Possibly, but the guilt writ large on her face told me it wasn't the whole truth.

Or maybe the pain in her leg was getting to her. Lilith grimaced. 'Now. You were telling me about Izdubar?'

'Physically, my father is on Guitt. He tried to blackmail me into going there.' I paused and met her eyes. 'I refused,' I said.

Lilith stared back, saying nothing.

I continued, 'The next time I saw him was a few hours ago.

He was in the house above, standing next to the Fedhyow in the white cloak. I take it you missed him?'

'It's an upside of projecting. You get to pick who's allowed to see. Why did he want you on Guitt anyway?'

I mimicked a breath. 'My father claimed I could *save him* – whatever that means.'

Lilith slammed a fist down on the arm of the chair. The resulting vibration made her right leg bounce.

'Fuck,' she said.

Painfully, it seemed.

'Do you know what this *saving* thing actually means?' I asked.

It was her turn to fake a breath. 'I hope not. I…' She paused and considered. 'But it's something I hope you never need to know.'

'You're not really a "truth will set you free" type of girl, are you?' I spat back.

Lilith gave me her best glare. 'Izdubar let you see him for a reason.'

I gave up. 'He wanted me to know, or at least guess, where they were taking my brother. It's taken me a few hours to work it out. It's another attempt to get me to Guitt. For some reason, my father wants both of us and he's hoping I'll try to rescue Kitten.'

Her eyes pulsed. 'Will it work?'

Again, I ignored her.

Lilith shook her head, confused. 'Okay then,' she said. 'Do you at least know why Rosalind betrayed us? Particularly Kitten?' she said. 'Something must have happened on the way here. I can't imagine what would make her…'

I tilted my head.

Her eyes widened. '*Wet my biscuit!* Tristan's alive?'

I nodded. 'That's what Izdubar told me. I imagine he offered Rosalind an exchange.'

'You didn't think to mention this before?'

'I had other things on my mind.' I could do callous as well.

'So will…'

I interrupted. 'You have to cross the sea to get to Guitt.'

She shook her head, annoyed now. 'It's a short hop across a very narrow strait, but yes.'

'Filled with water.'

'Of course.'

'Water of the bad kind?'

'Yes, but a bit of sea air or bilge water won't harm you.'

'And if I fell in?' I asked.

Lilith thought she understood. 'Well. Harm.'

'The Fedhyow come from Guitt. There will be orbs. Lots of orbs.'

'Yes.'

'It's a terrible idea,' I said sourly. 'We have practically no chance.'

'I know,' Lilith said. 'But will you come?'

'Eanna,' I said with a smile… or perhaps a panther's grin.

She stared at me.

'Eanna,' I repeated. 'I want to talk to Eanna first.' One pathetic letter would never be enough. I needed answers.

Lilith's eyes hardened in realisation.

'If you want my help…' I began. I almost hoped my saviour, my killer, would know it was a lie.

She didn't.

The woman before me melted but didn't dissolve as Tiama

had. The thing on the chair was a young woman and not an empty space.

I stared at her jet-black curly hair, and yes, if you were unkind, you could describe it as frizzy. It was also true her bosom and bottom were smaller than Iresh's – and mine. She was pretty, though, at least on the surface.

And perhaps only on the surface.

I looked down. If there was any glamour left, that sight vanquished it. Just like Lilith, her legs were inelegantly apart. Just like me, she wore a skirt. Unlike me, Eanna wore nothing underneath.

She smirked. Closing her legs carefully, she asked, 'Been there, done that?'

I lifted my gaze. 'Mother,' I said.

'I might have guessed you'd try to catch me with my pants down.'

'Only in metaphor,' I said, trying to keep calm. 'Speaking of metaphors. Today is not a day that is bright.'

'The day was bright when I wrote the letter. It started that way this morning. Now, not so much,' she agreed. 'You realise I'm not that little mouse anymore? I'm older now and know bigger words. I think I'm wiser.'

'But also dead,' I noted.

'There is that. Yes.'

I thought for a moment. 'Was it Lilith that taught you *big words*? Is that the way it works? Did she teach you to talk dirty, or was it the other way around? You both specialise in innuendo.'

Eanna giggled. 'Do you *really* think I'm a *cunning linguist*? Well, thank you!' Her face straightened. 'I'd argue that what comes out of her mouth now is more carnivorous than carnal. Still, we influence each other.'

I still didn't get it. 'Where did your obsession with sex stuff come from, then? It couldn't have been Iresh. She taught me basic biology and the occasional swear word. While I heard more in the playground, she never let me bring any of it home. Back then, I never got a sniff of the libertine about her.'

Eanna raised an eyebrow.

Oh, dear.

Eanna snorted. 'You forget, I *saw* a lot of the libertine. It was only after Izdubar that my sister turned all proper. Still, my passion for all things throbbing and pink doesn't come from Iresh. At least not directly. Back in the day, I did a lot of watching… and listening. The *sex stuff* always fascinated me, even when I didn't know much. Of course, now that I do, I love it even more.'

'But there was a gap.'

'You mean my… oh, you don't mean that. You're talking about the "rape and baby" thing?'

I bit my lip. 'You agree it was rape? In the letter, you didn't seem so sure.'

'I told you, I'm older and wiser. The blackmail was implied, and permission never got a mention. Mr Cum-Needle just locked the door and jumped my bones. So, yes, it was rape and yes, I lost my appetite for it for a while.'

'But you got it back.'

She nodded like a woodpecker. 'Uh-huh. Thanks to Dumuz, that tingle in my twat is entirely renewed. Did you know that he's got a seriously impressive lode hammer? No? He really does. Promise. It goes so well with my welcoming, but very monogamous, fissure.'

Time, I guess, to change the subject. 'I assume it was Lilith's amulet that you found?'

Her eyes bulged. 'Yes, but I didn't figure out what it was until too late – as in dead kind of late.'

I wasn't listening. Lilith had said her baby's lips were blue. 'There was no air. It was Lilith and her baby that died in the fire.'

'Yes.'

'And that would make Adapa the miller of the tale.' I didn't want to believe it.

Eanna's eyes glittered.

I continued. 'If you want me to accept that you're older and wiser, then I'll need more.'

'I don't even remember large parts of it, and it doesn't matter to me what you're willing to accept.'

I still had to know. 'Okay. If I agree that you're both ancient and smart, will you tell me how you can be here, dead, staring at someone you once considered *throwing away*?'

Eanna opted for fake Dumuz. '*That is* a complex question. Are you asking why I am dead or why am I here?' Before I could answer, she continued. 'That was rhetorical – a trait I picked up from my man. Thankfully, it's the only thing I've picked up. It seems he's been monogamous as well. The two are linked, obviously. Being dead and here, I mean. Not…'

'*Mother, focus!*' I spat.

She laughed again. '*Okay. Okay.* But now you've read the letter and know it was Lilith's amulet I found. How much of the rest can you put together?'

I blinked. 'When Kitten put the necklace on the bear, and you picked up the knife… that was Lilith? She wanted to kill the boy for defiling her baby's amulet. Seriously?'

She nodded. 'I guess it sounds odd, but yes. The creature that did that wasn't the Lilith you know now. That Lilith was an elemental, incapable of conscious thought. Back then, there was little left of her but hate and a desire for vengeance.'

'Why?'

Her eyes turned to steel.

Sometimes it's easier to give up. 'Okay then. Afterwards, which of you was in control?'

'When you get angry, have you ever told yourself, "That wasn't me"? All I've got as a reference are the things I'd done before that day. I can compare, but that visit to the castle was so life-defining that it was always going to change how I thought. So, to answer your question, I genuinely don't know.' She switched to her best girlie-gossip voice. 'Except for the stabby stuff, that's always Lilith.'

'I'm confused. After you pulled Kitten from under the shelves, the thing that was Lilith cut out his heart and made him like us. Why? It was only hours before that she hated Kitten.'

'Seepage – and I'm not talking about the funny thing that happens when I look at Dumuz.'

'What do you mean?'

'When I said there were two of us in here, I might have left the impression that we are wholly separate. That's not quite true, and it's becoming less so as time passes. Each day, each month, each year and certainly each traumatic event, Lilith becomes more like Eanna and Eanna more like Lilith. Who knows, but there might come a time when there is only room for a single mind. What physical form we take then is also unknown. Although if it's Lilith, Dumuz will have to make a few adjustments.'

'Are you suggesting that when Lilith first, and I still snigger each time I say the word, but when Lilith "possessed" you, she also absorbed your *love* for Kitten?'

'Love? I wouldn't call it "love" exactly, but there was something. The creature that became Lilith found it easy to amplify and merge whatever it was with the memory of her baby. To her, or it, Kitten *became* her boy. So, I guess the answer is yes.'

'I thought that possession required a willing participant?'

'It does. But the participant doesn't have to be aware. After that day, Lilith became my crutch and, for good and bad, my protector. While we might be merging, we are still currently and literally of two minds. Lilith has her loves…' Eanna winced. 'Or perhaps love, singular, and I have mine.' She smirked. 'Mine has a bigger cock though.'

I shook my head. It would never be the right time, but I couldn't wait any longer. 'Why did you abandon me?'

She looked confused. 'I explained that in the letter.'

'No, you didn't. I want the real reason.' Although I already had my suspicions.

Eanna sighed. 'Siduri. You need to understand that I wasn't at my most rational. I could never love the result of what Izdubar did without reservation. Lilith's obsession merely pushed me further down that path. I didn't hate you. I couldn't hate you. But that thing Lilith once was *screamed* you were a changeling. You were not Kitten. You were not her child. Given what happened later, I'm certain that Lilith's knife would eventually have found more work.'

I wasn't feeling rational either. '*You would have killed me! Your daughter!*'

'Yes,' she said.

'So, why did you come back…? Oh, of course. Kitten.'

'Siduri, I am no longer a young woman with some serious post-natal depression issues. I no longer have a banshee of unknown origin screaming kill, kill, kill in my ear.'

'Yeah, you know her name now.'

'We are in balance. That Lilith wasn't self-aware. She is now. Still, some things can never change. I'm sorry, but I cannot love you as a mother should.'

'Well, sod you too.' Did I sound needy?

Eanna smiled. 'Not possible without a strap-on, my dear. To repeat, *I do not hate you*, and neither does Lilith. Actually, I think she likes you. My not-so-twin tried to save you, after all. That's got to be far more than a simple duty of care.'

Eanna grimaced. 'That was a kick from Lilith. She says she doesn't do affection.' She glanced over my shoulder. 'More of a master and apprentice type of thing then?' she asked.

'What!'

'Or maybe not,' she acknowledged, wincing again.

I let it go. 'Does Nicolò know what's in the letter? Does he know who you are?'

'He knows I exist, but not my back story. Rosalind knows even less. Part of our deal with Freddie was to keep things as simple as possible for his daughter.'

'Simple!'

'Relatively.'

I was getting nowhere. 'Okay then. How did you die? How did Dumuz die?'

Eanna sniffed. 'All the pieces are there.'

I said nothing.

'But you'll still have me say it?'

It was my turn to raise an eyebrow.

'Very well. To pick up where the letter left off. I went to Sulis. It was far enough to let me forget but still near enough to Marhasyow in case I didn't.'

I felt something like hope. 'You mean…'

'No,' she said caustically – and then added more salt. 'Of course, the decision was never mine.'

'Lilith,' I said.

'The creature she was then, yes. But again, I didn't know that then. Anyway, compared to Marhasyow, work in Sulis turned out to be amazingly easy to come by – I didn't even have to shag the boss! For two years, Dumuz's father employed me as a dogsbody and occasional shit-tank cleaner. Not that I ever saw him – what with the smell and all. While the hours were long, I was happy with the distraction. It meant I didn't have time to think about you or Kitten.

'Unfortunately, the other side of that lack-of-thought coin is that I don't remember much of those early years – not even the whispers. I didn't know anything was still wrong – not even when Dumuz's father died.'

Oh… 'Are you saying Lilith killed him?'

She nodded. 'But I didn't find out until after I died.'

'Why?'

'Lilith might have lit the match, but the spark came from many years before.'

Oh, damn. Dumuz had almost told me. His mother wasn't the only reason he'd left home. She wasn't even the main reason.

'It was Dumuz's father who financed the miners in Marhasyow,' I said in disbelief.

Eanna nodded. 'Not on his own, but the expedition was his idea. When the miners were killed, he was the one who persuaded the state to send in the troops.'

She pouted. 'Given what happened to Lilith at the mill, you can understand why she went all "burny" on him.

'Anyway, my ability to remember returned after that and the whispers did not. At the time, I assumed that this improving awareness of all things "else" was due to the return of the not-so-prodigal *Dumuz*. To me, that man was, is, and always will be Mr Dark, Mr Brooding and Mr Fuck-Me Sexy. A Gothic wet dream, you might say.'

I pretty much once thought the same – and now regretted it.

Eanna pulled a face. 'Not that there was much luck over that first year – Dumuz was hardly in the mood. The poor dear was going through a whole "Oh woe is me, tears before bedtime, mid-life". And all because Lilith had turned his father into crispy bits, who'd have thought?

'Still, I spent as much time as I could upstairs rather than down. I volunteered for stuff I didn't need to do, hoping Dumuz would notice me. Really notice me. It took a year of me flicking my bean, usually in my off-hours and mostly unnoticed, before he did. By then, the bean was more like a pea…'

'*Mother!*'

'Oh, be quiet. With your parentage, I'll bet you've also had the occasional twitch or three yourself. I mean, you built a den in that bush – don't think I didn't notice. I'll bet it wasn't just dolls you played with in there?'

Can ghostly cheeks turn pink? They can, I think.

'So, how did you and Dumuz get together then?' I asked in desperation.

It was her turn to look embarrassed. 'My twenty-first birthday didn't turn out to be my finest hour, or twenty-four, or whatever. On reflection, the first twenty were fine. It was only in the last four, when I got drunk and celebrated, that the problems started. In fact, the only really bad bit was the last hour, which makes it the one that wasn't my finest. So, forget about the previous twenty-three.'

'And?'

She squirmed. 'That's when I got bollock naked. That's when I went upstairs to shag the boss.'

'Oh,' I said.

'Not "Oh", unfortunately, or even "Uh", but at least he wasn't cross. It turned out that Dumuz was a gentleman – frustratingly. And didn't think it was something a boss should do – even more frustratingly. He carried me to his bed, put me in it, and slept on the sofa.'

I looked at her. 'That was decent of him.'

'Yup. What was even more decent, though, was the following day he changed his mind, and every day after that, he shagged me *every-which-way-left-but-Tuesday*.'

'I don't think I wanted to know that.'

'Perhaps not. But it does lead to how we died.'

'What?'

'After two years of *fun-time-bouncy-bouncy*, Dumuz suggested we get married. He wanted a kid. I could have said, "Sorry, I don't want my labia stretched that far again – or at least from the inside out". But I didn't. I couldn't. He knew nothing about my past.'

She pursed her lips. 'It was the talk of children, you see. The whispers returned. They demanded I return to Marhasyow and find our child.' Eanna looked at me. 'Kitten,' she clarified.

I stared back – what else could I do?

She continued. 'I imagine it was about then I started speaking in tongues – and not the sort Dumuz liked because he took me to a doctor. The kind of doctor who throws you in a padded cell if you fail the questionnaire. It was after finishing the interview, and failing the questionnaire, that I made a run for it.'

She paused. 'Shame, really. It turns out the doctor had lost his licence. The man wouldn't have been able to lock me up even if he'd been willing.'

I made the leap. 'You're talking about Frederick! Rosalind's father.'

'Yup,' she said. 'Dumuz tracked him down. Freddie and Cordelia were the only Wycche that Dumuz ever found. The newspapers had backgrounded Freddie three years earlier, looking for more dirt. They discovered that Freddie's parents originally came from Marhasyow. When Dumuz visited Freddie, he outright asked him if he was Wycche. Freddie denied it at first. It was only when Dumuz showed him his massive… manual on all things Wycche that Freddie fessed up. Afterwards, when we were dead, Dumuz visited Freddie again and offered him the castle in Marhasyow…'

'You ran away,' I said, bringing her back to what I really wanted to know.

Eanna quietened. 'I got as far as the railway station before Dumuz caught up with me.'

She swallowed. 'I don't know how it got there. I thought I'd left it in Marhasyow, in the attic. When I pulled the knife from the back of my skirt, I remember it glinting in the station lights though. I do remember that. It was dusk, you see. I…'

'You stabbed…' I began.

She put up a hand. 'I… I remember Dumuz wouldn't let me go. He didn't understand. When I started crying, I remember he put his arms around me.

'It was difficult to get the damned thing into his chest. His amulet blocked it the first time. Mostly, though, all I remember is Dumuz falling onto the tracks. It was only then I woke up.

243

It was only then I finally understood. About the knife, about Lilith, about what she'd just made me do.'

'Oh shit,' I muttered.

Eanna didn't seem to hear. 'I had no choice… I couldn't leave him. I remember pushing the blade into my chest… and falling onto Dumuz. I remember rolling onto the tracks. I remember the train.'

'Oh shit, oh shit, oh shit,' I said, louder now.

'Exactly.' Her voice was both cold and warm.

'And you forgave Lilith?' I asked. 'Dumuz forgave you?'

Her shredded calf twitched. 'You're missing the point. If you want to understand anything about what happened, you need to understand the point. Can you think of any moment in my story where I made a decision that was wrong? I can't. Not really. *Each time I had no choice.*'

I looked away.

'Oh, grow up!' she snapped. 'There was nothing to forgive!'

'How can I grow up? *Lilith killed me!* That had to be a choice.'

Sweat was forming on her brow. Her ghostly pale skin was growing even most ghostly – and pale. She sighed. 'Lilith kept you… *you.* That's not a proper choice.'

Still, she could have asked me.

I tried to meet Eanna's eyes but couldn't. She'd fixed her gaze at a point over my left shoulder. I wasn't buying the whole forgiveness thing – at least when it came to Dumuz. There might be no need, but there was certainly a desire for it.

I desperately wanted to strangle her then – or comfort her. Instead, I said, 'Hugo had a limp.'

'What?'

'When Hugo first arrived in Marhasyow, he already had a limp. Left leg. Stiff knee.'

'Er… Yes.'

'The man, the Fedhyow, in your letter. The one you spiked. That was Hugo?'

Her eyes drifted back to mine. 'Yeah.'

'It was Hugo that took Izdubar to Guitt,' I said, beginning to understand.

Eanna nodded. 'If your father's on Guitt, then that's probably how he got there. I never knew where he went. I guess his falling out with the townsfolk of Marhasyow was worse than I thought. That said, the price for sanctuary on Guitt still feels steep.'

'The wagon of gold?'

Eanna swallowed. 'There were enough coins in it to reboot an entire polygamy of religions.'

'You mean plurality.'

'I know what I said… Still, I'll bet your father didn't expect to travel to Guitt arse-high on a wagon.'

I hesitated and thought for a moment. 'Do you think it was the *tall scary guard* that rescued him from the castle?'

Eanna smiled… or winced. 'You've already worked that one out as well, haven't you?'

'If you mean, am I asking, "Was it the *tall scary guard in the big white sheet* I saw with Rosalind", then, yes.'

'Again, I think so, although he wasn't wearing that bedsheet back then. With Izdubar and Hugo the worse for wear, it's likely he hopped off his big wagon of gold, saved them both, and hopped back on again. To be honest, just seeing that ghoul again made me shiver.'

I could tell. 'Did Nicolò know where the money came from?'

She squirmed, now clearly in pain. 'I don't think so. We never told him, and Nicolò had other things to think about when he arrived. The Fedhyow had good reason to keep the whole thing secret. There's no way they'd confess to help from a thief as infamous as Izdubar.'

'Tiama then. Did she know?'

'I don't think so. Tiama was on Guitt the night of the storm. Like all Fedhyow women, she had to return to the island to give birth.'

'Surely Hugo would have told her afterwards?'

'I doubt it. They were never close. It seems unlikely Hugo would tell her about the questionable source of his sudden popularity within the Fedhyow.'

Speaking of sudden.

Eanna squeaked, puffed out her cheeks, slumped back in the chair, and forced her legs apart, vainly trying to find some relief from the pain. Forget abyss, this was like looking at the origins of the universe.

Or at least my universe.

'Do you remember Lilith mentioned her amulet?' she said. 'I think I need you to go fetch it.'

And then she told me where… or possibly where.

And then she fainted.

I'd like to say her collapse was as messy as the one her daughter had the day before. But no, not a chance. Eanna's legs drew elegantly together as her head rolled slowly to the side.

Of course, with all that sticky gunk still oozing from her damaged calf, Eanna might wake up to the most unfortunate of mermaid scenarios.

Which was a shame.

Chapter nineteen

That Which We Call a Rose

I found climbing the ladder in the dark even more difficult than going down it during the day. The metal rungs felt so slick with condensation that they may as well have been made of soap.

Once up, I passed through the gap in the hedge, which was a mess, and onto the croquet lawn, which was worse. Even with the corpses removed, enough debris remained to make the pitch unplayable. Not that I was in the mood to play or had anyone to play with. It was also difficult to see, which also didn't help. Although the moon was still mostly full, it hung so low in the sky that its light was subject to the whims and wiles of the surrounding trees. While the shadows cast were atmospheric, they would be a pig to contend with when lining up a shot. So, no, I wasn't in the mood for games. Instead, I strolled across the grass, wispy enough not to be noticed, solid enough to allow me to move.

I left my feet bare. It was the closest thing to penance I could get for my accidental, but ultimately successful, "first life took". With the company I kept, and a travel plan agreed, I knew there might well be others.

The grass ended abruptly at the edge of the lawn – not one blade dared to cross into the realm of man. Had it not been for the day's events, the patio would have been a kaleidoscope of the geometric. I could imagine the chairs set in a line and the tables neatly stacked. I could picture the flagstones, glistening in the night's humidity like a checkerboard of soft yellows and greys.

All that might have been possible before today, but not now.

As I looked through the moonlit dark, I saw chair and table legs strewn across the ground like broken spaghetti. Although the flagstones remained untouched, they lacked the regularity they had before. In one corner of the patio, a place lit brightly by light from the house, a large splattering of copperish red ruined the simple certainty of the dichromatic.

I couldn't see Adapa's corpse, though, nor any remnants of the Fedhyow. Indeed, I imagine Hugo, Rosalind and Kitten were probably already on their way to Guitt.

And I would follow.

Still, I wasn't alone. Beneath one of the few upright chairs sat the smallest and blackest of cats I'd ever seen. As I stared, the cat scrunched its toes… and then relaxed. On impulse, I mirrored the action. The dew gathered from the grass streamed back into the ground. It seemed the hydrophobic nature of ghosts ensured nothing could stick.

Not even regret.

I stepped off the grass and onto the patio. The cat stayed calm as I approached. While it kept an eye, and an ear, on me, its reaction appeared more to do with form than necessity. Still, it was only when I stretched out my right hand in greeting that the cat rose and purred.

Lilith's amulet was on a chain around its neck.

Taking the purr as permission, my right hand continued into a stroke – before following through and uncoupling the amulet from its chain. The cat looked affronted, betrayed even, and I guess it had a point. The cat did look stupid with a chain and a hook with nothing attached.

Perhaps...

I undid my amulet from its chain and fastened it to the one on the cat. That should be better, at least from the cat's perspective. The cat, as cats do, I guess, squirmed unappreciatively in protest. I gave it a final scratch behind the ears and let it go. Almost immediately, the cat jumped away, arched its back and exhaled something I could only interpret as a harrumph.

The cat had no tail.

'Don't ask,' it said, the words resonating in my head long after I'd heard them spoken.

What I saw was the cat's mouth open into a massive yawn before snapping shut with a click. I hadn't realised cats flattened their ears when they did that. While the yawn and the voice didn't appear connected, I was sure they had the same source.

'Don't ask what?' I said.

'You don't seem surprised,' the cat answered sniffily. This time, there was no movement at all.

'I'm surprised you can snap your jaw closed that violently without breaking it.'

'Uh? Oh yeah. Practice, I guess. The first time I did it, I almost broke a canine. My jaw ached for literally seconds afterwards. No, you don't seem surprised that I'm here, that I can see you *and that I can talk*.' She added a loud meow to emphasise the difference.

'Shush,' I whispered, concerned a human might hear.

'Oh. Don't worry. The black crows are long gone. Bloody vermin, messed up my hunting ground good and proper. Most of the local watch have clocked off as well – not that they were any more careful. The only one left is a single, new-hire, quota-achieved, night-watch grump of a girl at the front door.'

'Grump?' Okay. This was getting unexpected.

'Hormonal.' The cat twitched her left cheek to expose a fang. I think, and hoped, it was an attempt at a smile. 'At least from the smell of her. She's also constantly crying. From what I know about humans, the junior help always gets the crappy jobs. If they stink, are female, and are whiningly annoying, that likelihood approaches certainty.'

'And you know this how?' Definitely weird.

'Have you ever met a pre-menopausal feline at 3am? You know – when the season is right?'

'Er. Maybe?'

'She'd either be living it up with the boys or have missed her chance like this one and be forever whining about it.'

'I'm guessing you're not in the "pre" camp yourself?' I asked.

She sat on her haunches and looked at me. 'Not as such. Back in the day, though, I was never much of a crier anyway. To be honest, I wasn't much of a lover either. I was too busy strategising how to give the boys a serious clawing to engage in any proper romance. Dumuz's right hand, of course, was another matter. When I was on for it, and he wasn't looking or didn't move fast enough. Well, let's just say I was rather good at reversing back in the day.'

'*Yuck.*'

The front paws went down. The cat now resembled a roosting hen. 'Don't judge if you haven't tried it.'

Maybe I should change the subject. 'Why are you here and not curled up somewhere inside?' I asked. 'That's where Eanna thought you'd be. I nearly missed you under that chair.'

'You don't know cats, do you? There's no way I'm heading indoors until I'm certain the house is back to its steady, nothing-scary-might-happen state. Shame, really. There's a bed upstairs with a pillow that I've curved my groove into – if you get my drift.'

I suddenly remembered the aroma I'd smelt when I awoke. 'Unfortunately, I think I do.'

'So, anyway,' she said. 'Now that's settled, how about this lack of surprise?'

'That a cat can talk? No way. Now, being a ghost, that came as a surprise.'

'Yeah, I spotted that. Recent?'

'How did you know?'

'I'm not your proverbial wise owl, but I like to keep an eye and an ear open. I can observe. I even do it in my sleep. Have you seen a cat's ears and whiskers twitch when it's napping? It's not fantasising about little edible birds. It's *thinking*. It's planning. Us cats know our limitations – if we survive beyond the age of two, that is. By the way, it's a myth that owls are smart. They're as thick as those cling-ons that are impossible to gnaw off. They're only good mousers because they have wings.'

The cat sniffed. 'Wish I had wings.'

I tried not to let my jaw drop. 'You're saying that you're nosy?'

'*Observant.*'

'Quite.'

'Anyway, don't ask.'

'Don't ask what? Don't ask why you haven't got a tail? I wouldn't be so rude.'

'Thank you.'

'So, why don't you have a tail?'

She ignored me – haughtily. 'My name is Pollyanna.'

'What?'

'*My name is Pollyanna.* I didn't like the one Eanna gave me. So, I changed it.'

'Oh… okay,' I said, feigning comprehension. 'My name is Siduri.'

Her front paws pushed up, raising her chest off the ground. '*Siduri?*' she said with an edge. 'Did Eanna give you that as well? She's not very good with names.'

'Maybe,' I said, realising it was a possibility – and that I'd just annoyed her. 'I can't be sure though. I've only recently learnt that Eanna is my mother.'

'I know,' she said. 'I was outside the bedroom when she told you.'

'*Observing?*'

Pollyanna twitched her back end – probably subconsciously. 'Em… Waiting to get my bed back?'

I glanced again at her missing tail.

'Did Eanna really call you *Stumpy*?' I asked in sudden comprehension… only to realise my mistake.

Pollyanna's ears flattened slightly.

'Perhaps we should start again,' I said quickly. 'It's nice to meet you, *Pollyanna*. Your name suits you perfectly. I might even be jealous.'

Pollyanna straightened her back paws, lifting herself back

to full height. I watched quietly as her ears stayed down. I imagine she was wondering whether I was being sarcastic.

I wasn't.

Pollyanna's ears popped up. It seemed she agreed. 'Never had anyone jealous of me before,' she said. 'Obviously, I'd offer it to you…' she blinked, '…but it's taken.'

I forced a smile. 'Funny,' I said. No doubt Pollyanna got her sense of humour from Dumuz.

Pollyanna yawned. 'Speaking of Eanna,' she said casually. 'I assume she was the one that put you up to this?'

Not so casual. 'What do you mean?'

'Eanna. She's chickened out and got you to collect her amulet.'

'No,' I said.

'No?'

'Eanna can't walk and couldn't do it herself. She needs the amulet to fix her leg.' Which was true – at least at a factual level.

'I thought it might be something like that,' she lied. This cat wasn't stupid.

She continued. 'Not sure if you know this, but when I wore Eanna's amulet, it… it kind of made me her familiar. Not that familiar, of course. You shouldn't listen to rumours. You know what a familiar is, don't you? What they let you do.' There was some nervousness in her voice.

I hesitated. 'No, I'm afraid I don't. What does a familiar allow you to do?'

'Well, for one thing, it allows you to talk to a cat,' she said stroppily. 'While you don't seem to find interspecies dialogue remarkable, I'll bet you're in the minority. Anyway, from my perspective, I reckon it's why my coat is still shiny. I don't seem to get as sleepy or thirsty as other cats my age, not that there are many – well, any.'

'You're that old?'

'A lady doesn't like to admit her age, but since I'm not, then yeah.'

'So, you need an amulet to stay alive?'

'Oh. I see what you mean. I never quite thought of it that way, but yes, probably. It's not why I'm asking, of course. It's just quite nice to have someone to talk to occasionally.'

'What about Eanna?' I think I already knew where this was heading.

Pollyanna sighed. 'I wasn't exactly a kitten when Eanna and Dumuz picked me up from the cat home. Felt like one, though, when she put that amulet around me a couple of years later. But then she died and moved away.' Pollyanna tried to sound chirpier. 'Although she did still visit occasionally. We've had some nice chats.'

'And between visits?'

She sniffed. 'To be honest, it gets a bit quiet. Even the staff are snotty when they feed me, but I guess Dumuz must have insisted.' Her head tilted upwards. 'So, can I be your familiar?' she asked. 'I'm already wearing your amulet, and we've got the verbal stuff down pat.'

Oh shit. 'Well, okay. But I've also got to go away for a while.' Was I just like Eanna when it came right down to it?

Pollyanna squeaked. 'Yes? Brilliant. Don't worry. I'll be here when you get back. Unless you want me to come with you?'

'Probably not a good idea – but I will be back. I promise.'

I wasn't Eanna.

'Cross your heart and hope to die?' She sprung up into the

air like a lamb – and landed on my toes. The slight merger of claw and ethereal skin didn't hurt. Well, not *that* much.

I smiled. 'Oh. Very clever. And yes.' I was committed.

Pollyanna spun around and stepped away. 'Good,' she said. 'Well, now that's sorted, you don't mind if I go for a stroll? I hear a rustling in the bushes and... well... you know.'

'Oh, okay then,' I said. 'Er... good luck?'

For the first time since the bridge, the hole that was now my heart felt warm. As the cat, my cat, strolled off into the undergrowth, I was certain she felt the same.

It was only after Pollyanna had entirely disappeared from view that I looked down. Although I still stood on concrete slabs, both my feet were wet. At first, I attributed the dampness to the creeping onslaught of a hydrophilic night, but then I noticed the acrid smell... and that the liquid was notably tepid.

Pollyanna's sense of humour had nothing to do with Dumuz.

CHAPTER TWENTY

A LAND OF SEPARATE STONES

We left at dawn, rising from our underground retreat into an early morning fog. If Dumuz could still speak, he'd *wittily* suggest that this "mist-icle" scene appeared somewhat "spirit-ual". But he couldn't – thankfully. Anyway, I'd already made sure no one was there to see.

Except for Pollyanna, of course, who I caught watching from a distance.

Nicolò woke a few hours before and was as crabby as predicted. Not that I could blame him. Rosalind had sold us out and Nicolò's father had come close to killing him. He'd seen his mother dissolve and still carried a passenger whose departure date and method Lilith had left worryingly vague. I was surprised that Nicolò agreed to come with us at all. I'd like to believe he was doing it because he thought he owed Lilith a favour rather than a desire for revenge. But I suspect revenge played a part. After all, why wouldn't it?

We travelled to Guitt, departing from the same station where my mother killed her lover, herself, and introduced the word "splat" into the vocabulary of the traumatised driver whose engine had rolled right over them.

Our train, minus any optional "splat", travelled due south.

Lilith sat opposite. Her leg had healed, her trousers were spotless, and her right cheek stuck to the window like glue. She looked tired, and not only because of recent events. We were both finding the "let's pretend I'm not dead" thing quite gruelling. I could understand why she'd messed up last time. Hopefully, this time she'd do better. We'd do better. That said, I still wasn't taking off my boots.

The seat next to Lilith was empty and was likely to stay that way. Lilith didn't need a floral handbag as a prop to finesse some extra space. The foul expression on her face worked just fine. Nicolò sat beside me, sullen and silent, quite unwilling to use his recovered voice. So, yet again, I spent much of the trip staring out of the window. The only difference was that I also had to deal with Lilith's outstretched feet.

The view at the start was almost identical to the one when I arrived. This time, however, there was no tunnel, and the fog only intensified as the train began a slow climb. The mist didn't release its grip until we cleared the top. As we levelled out, it seemed reasonable to expect a repetition of the high marsh and bog-land of the last journey. Nature doesn't do reasonable. It took little wit to describe the sight of flat green ground stretching into infinity as... well... "plain". In a steady breeze, clouds raced across the open sky, the light alternating sharply between dim and blinding scalpel. Beneath, the stunted grass glittered and paled through an entire rainbow of green. Variety is always there if you look hard enough for it.

And variety will arrive even when you don't.

Gradually, and sadly, the joyous fusion of the uniform and

anarchic broke down. Variegated shades of sage and mint took on streaks of white as the surface cracked into growing fissures of chalk. By the time the train turned sharply left and began a slow descent, what remained of the grass had vanished, leaving only a distant memory of what once had been.

On flat ground, the train twisted right and resumed its journey south. If the natural world of the plain had made a case for glorious monoculture, what faced me now was humanity's superficial response. The grass returned, but this time without the grandeur of the unchecked. Although the rule of humanity in this lower place was absolute, it was also subtle. There were no farms or fences. There were no houses, gardens or grand estates, but mankind's influence was still obvious. If left to nature's will, I could imagine that this place might become a forest. I could imagine trees as high as the equinox sun at its zenith. Not here. Not now. They might still call it forest, but gorse on its own isn't forest. Clumps of bracken without shade are not forest. Cart tracks and footpaths are most certainly not forest.

The clues to the lack of anything tall were the herds of deer and flocks of pheasants. Each was startled into its own form of flight by the mischievous toot of an otherwise pointless steam whistle. No. This was a pleasure palace for the rich or the wannabe. A curated, box-ticked, lookalike wilderness that guaranteed a high kill rate. I suspected the once-governor of Marhasyow would love it.

The charade of supposed wilderness ended in fits and starts. A thatched cottage here, a more pragmatic build there. However, I could only tell we were in true suburbia when I spied one of the more sensible houses sporting a vegetable patch surrounded by a tall net-topped fence. In amongst the woodchip weed suppressant, compost bins, and the occasional slug-eaten strawberry sat a bored cat. We exchanged the briefest of glances. Only a civilised man would trap the instinctively feral "for their own good". It made me wonder which of us was the more trapped. I thought back to my encounter with Pollyanna. She didn't seem to care about life beyond the metaphorical fences of her existence. While I…

Bang!

Given my history with trains, "Bang" wasn't a sound I wanted to hear. I looked around. That was when the screeching began – as well as the smell of urine. I was kind of hoping the latter came from the brakes.

The train slowed.

When Nicolò spoke, it was almost a growl. 'Haefen?'

Lilith didn't bother to respond. Nor did I. Instead, I squinted and gazed into the middle distance. There were buildings, to be sure, more than a few, but not as much as many. Beyond the buildings, there ran a strip of blue. Beyond the blue? Just a blur of grey.

There be dragons. Lots of them, and all dressed in black.

Haefen was a place famous only by association. Guitt was only a short ferry trip away.

Disembarking from the train was a novel experience for me. For once, I didn't have to jump off while it was still moving or fight my way through the soon-to-be-dead. Nicolò and I simply stepped onto the platform. We best resembled your standard "nice" young couple. The kind who frequent out-of-the-way hotels looking for the most biological of weekends. The problem with this image was that we were in Haefen, which is as next door as you get to the prudish Fedhyow, and, of course, I was also dead.

Lilith walked behind us like a servant, but most definitely didn't carry our baggage – baggage that comprised just one case. The case resembled Iresh's original one and was just as heavy – which is why Nicolò carried it. He didn't have it because he was particularly strong. It was more that he was particularly alive. Ghosts are not weightlifters. Lilith suggested we bring it as a prop. Despite not carrying it, I still felt tired though. Holding focus and form is tiring. I needed that hotel – and soon.

It was Nicolò's plan and a risky one at that, but we were down to Eanna's no-choice thing again.

The Fedhyow are a pious lot, and even I knew they preferred to spend the early hours in pseudo-masturbatory worship – or for the singletons, likely not so pseudo. Dawn, therefore, was when the black plague that was the Fedhyow would be at its whitest and the only time Nicolò's plan might work. The early ferry would be least likely to be filled with Fedhyow.

Of course, that didn't mean there weren't any Fedhyow in Haefen right now. We still needed to find cover until dawn. Well, cover in Nicolò's case. My ex was tired as well. Tomorrow, he would need to be at his best to play the role of acolyte. Something, I imagine, his father once wanted him to be.

'Can you manage this?' Lilith muttered into my right ear.

'Of course.'

'Are you sure? I could do it. We could change into Eanna. She'd like to be there if Nicolò pops early.'

'Hey!' Nicolò snapped back. 'What do you mean by "pop"?'

I rested my left hand on his right elbow and let it sink slightly into his skin. My thumb brushed against a nerve.

'Shush,' I said.

Nicolò pulled his arm away, rubbing it furiously.

I continued, 'We all know I'm the one who needs hiding. I can't keep this up much longer.'

'So, I end up in the stables?' Lilith grumbled.

'At least it's not the streets. While you're obviously into leather, I can't imagine you want to be seen as a prosti…'

Lilith glared. 'I don't like horses,' she muttered.

'I'll bet Eanna does,' I chimed.

'Well…' she lilted musically.

'Thought so.'

Lilith shut up but continued to look grumpy.

The name, The Ferryboat Inn, was misleading, and once inside, the deception became quickly apparent. There was no bar – or sawdust on the floor. But there were enough Fedhyow to spit at if you felt inclined.

I didn't spit.

Nicolò took my left hand with his right before fumbling something onto my fourth finger. I looked down. It was silver and embossed with the symbol of the Fedhyow.

What the…

'Lilith took it from Mother when she died,' he whispered. 'She thought I'd want it.'

'Seriously?'

'Let me do the talking,' he said.

Nicolò made his way to the counter. A counter spanning the entire width of the other side of the room. I meekly followed. Decades of alcohol served on its wooden surface had left it dented and scuffed.

Now, there wasn't a drink to be seen.

The receptionist was female, young and soberly dressed.

'Yes?' she said.

'My *wife* and I would like a room.' Nicolò's voice sounded a few years deeper than reality.

The woman glanced at my tuft and then at my knees – still naked below my skirt. Why hadn't I changed to blend in? She looked back into my eyes nervously before looking behind us and finally to either side. No one was watching. Nicolò wrapped his fingers around the palm of my left hand before casually placing it on the counter.

He spoke again. 'Sorry, I don't want to sound particular, but could we have the quietest room available? It's been a long journey, and we must be up early to catch the first ferry to Guitt.' He laughed. 'The double B's will take much of the day.'

'Double B's?'

'Baptism and Blessing. My wife's a convert. First, there'll be a formal baptism. Then there'll be the traditional blessing of our marriage. Not that the last matters – Lord Hugo performed the actual service himself, after all!'

She signed us in and handed Nicolò a key. Written on the fob was the word "Attic".

Of course.

It took even longer than I thought, but we made it to the room. After entering, Nicolò slammed the door behind him before dumping the heavy case into the gap between an old wooden wardrobe and the door. A storm of disturbed dust fountained into the air, coating his sweating face. The change in complexion made me think of a corpse many days old.

Just like me then.

'You did well,' I said, slipping from solid into the semi-substantial.

'I didn't think she'd buy it,' he replied, almost stumbling over the words.

'She wasn't Fedhyow. Receptionist for her is just a job. Oh, and you also name-checked your father. Nice.'

'I…'

'Sorry,' I said. 'It's Lilith's influence. Almost everyone I've met in recent days seems to have issues. Particularly the dead.'

He looked offended. 'You would have liked Mother when she was alive.'

'Sorry. I…'

Nicolò ignored me. 'The way she died would give anyone *issues*. You'd have also liked Adapa.'

'I did – when he kept his hands to himself.'

Nicolò took a deep breath. 'Adapa was my grandfather. My mother's father.'

I stared. '*Seriously?*'

'Perhaps I should have told you before,' Nicolò said, looking sheepish.

'*You really should have.*' I was stunned. So was Lilith his… 'What happened to your grandmother?'

Nicolò sniffed. 'Adapa said she died giving birth.'

Not Lilith, then.

Hang about. 'So… did Adapa bring Tiama up on his own?'

Nicolò smiled weakly. 'No. By then, Grandfather was well on the way to becoming the fine upstanding man you… knew. He told me it was a one-night stand.'

I shook my head in disbelief. 'Are you saying that Adapa ditched her? *Just like his grandson did to me.*'

Nicolò winced – and I wanted to kick myself. I thought I was past all that.

'Your mother ended up in an orphanage?' I asked.

'Yes. In Aberfal. All Adapa left Tiama was her amulet and a note telling her she was Wycche. The orphanage gave them to Mother when she came of age.'

I didn't get this thing the Wycche had about letters. 'What about Lilith?'

He shook his head, confused. 'Lilith?'

'Oh… nothing,' I said. It seemed Nicolò really didn't know about Lilith and Adapa. I continued. 'You first met Adapa the night we…'

'Yes.' He snorted inappropriately. 'It was a night of firsts for me.'

I kept my expression stern and said nothing.

Nicolò duly calmed. 'After what happened, I wasn't exactly in the mood for any more family, particularly a grandfather who'd dumped Mother at the earliest…'

I interrupted. 'Does that explain why Lilith was outside your house that night?'

Nicolò hesitated. 'When we first arrived in Marhasyow, Grandfather asked Lilith to keep an eye on us. It was nowhere near enough to compensate for abandoning Mother when she was a baby – and it turned out not to be enough for Mother at her end.'

'But… you forgave him?'

'Grandfather had a good heart,' he said.

That was evasive.

Nicolò continued. 'Lilith trusted him. She didn't even mind the odd southerly paw – which is weird, don't you think?'

I kept my face a mask. Hopefully, Nicolò couldn't read me as well as I could him. So, Lilith had been spying on Nicolò since he arrived? In fact, if Eanna had anything to do with it, she might well have been watching when we – oh shit.

My face went beetroot. The ethereal skin of it flooded with heat and blood that I surely did not have.

'What?' Nicolò asked.

'Lilith. She was watching us that night.'

Nicolò frowned, confused for a moment, before smiling slyly. 'Possibly,' he said.

I hadn't seen that smile for months. Not that one. The one he flashed the first time we met. It had been raining. A day to get home quickly after the last lesson's end – but there is always another lesson. This one came when a Fedhyow wannabe brat started taunting me about my holiday-whim-installed ultramarine flick of hair. I should have expected it, but the ferocity surprised me. Hugo had only been there for a week. I tried to run away but tripped. It was Nicolò's hand that helped me to my feet and his parentage that sent the bully on his way. It was Nicolò's smile that took my heart – long before Lilith's knife.

We made sure never to meet in public again.

I thought I'd resolved the hurt. In Sulis, we'd made peace. A peace that could turn into a proper friendship once…

'I had no choice,' Nicolò whispered. There was that phrase again.

'About what?' I said, tilting my head.

Nicolò inched closer. I didn't step back.

'That night. I had to disappear. Lilith made me disappear – and I couldn't tell you.'

'*Lilith?*' I spat back. 'Did she tell you to leave me behind?'

'Well, yes… It was just after Lilith returned from Mother. I wanted to go to you, but she wouldn't let me. Lilith made it clear there was no place for you on the island.'

He noticed the steel in my eyes.

Nicolò swallowed. 'Her concern was for you…'

I'll bet Eanna had a say. I let the steel take over my voice. 'You forgot me quickly enough – and you ran away when I arrived at the castle.'

'*They didn't tell me!* I didn't know you were coming – or what had happened to you. I… I didn't even know where Lilith had gone the morning you…'

'Died?' I completed.

He sniffed. Men should not sniff. 'I'm not entirely unobservant,' he said. 'When Lilith returned that afternoon, she was upset – and I was pretty certain it had nothing to do with the gash on her throat. She and Dumuz left soon after.'

He paused and then added, 'Why did Lilith come for you? Twice?'

Why indeed? It had nothing to do with Eanna. Not Eanna. But why then? Was it some latent guilt about the Geas she cast?

Was it more than that?

Oh my.

I didn't feel like heading down that path right now – and Nicolò's lips suddenly seemed so ridiculously close.

So, I ignored his question. 'You still left,' I said. 'You saw me and still left.'

Forgetting for the moment that I was also dead at that point.

Nicolò winced. 'They saved me. Lilith saved me. Dumuz, Grandfather… I owed Adapa. I helped… There is truth in what I said at the castle. Mother… even Grandfather in the end thought I should leave. They knew I could only have a normal life if I were away from… them.'

He shook his head. 'When I first arrived, Rosalind consoled me. She helped me get over Mother's death. We had a lot in common. I liked her!'

He was still hiding something. I told myself I didn't care.

'It's amazing,' I said. 'That you can hear someone speak, but sometimes you only remember a single word.'

Nicolò looked baffled.

I continued, 'For example. From what you've just said, I only remember the word "consoled".'

There was "like" as well, which wasn't "love". Why hadn't he used the word "love"?

Nicolò shuddered. 'When you arrived at the castle, we were already leaving. I didn't think Grandfather…' Again, he seemed to change his mind. 'I couldn't abandon Rosalind. Not then.'

'Twice,' I said, echoing the word from moments before. 'You abandoned me twice.'

'Twice,' he acknowledged, embarrassed. 'Don't you think Frederick was right, though? The worlds of the living and the dead should be separate?'

I shook my head. 'Sorry, I'm not buying this whole "separate worlds" nonsense. Yes, you and I obviously have quite different perspectives. But with that said, we still have more in common with each other than with the Fedhyow… or some others I could mention.'

He looked doubtful.

I ignored it. Well, I didn't. 'Rosalind *abandoned you.* How's that for irony? She sold you out. Do you really think you have more in common with her than with me?'

'But…'

'But nothing. When I first awoke, dead, I felt diminished, limited, an echo of what I once was. I wondered if I was even, conceptually, still human. But that's the wrong way to think about it. I may have transitioned from caterpillar to moth, but I haven't evolved or devolved. I am not separate from you. Inside, if I have one, I am the same. My values are the same.'

My mind, though, was contemplating a whole new set of deviances.

'You're harder than before. More confident,' Nicolò said.

'No,' I said. 'I've maimed. I've now even killed, albeit by accident. But I realise now that I was always capable of that. It was just that before I died, there was never a need.'

It suddenly came to me. 'I'm not Lilith though.' Or Eanna. 'She thinks herself a slave to fate. To me, that's an abdication of responsibility. It's a cop-out to protect yourself when things go bad. It's dogma to match that of any other creed – including the Fedhyow. But you can still like someone even if you disagree with them – even if they have done you wrong. Even if you believe they'll do so again.'

I could tell Nicolò thought I was talking about him. But I wasn't. Or not just him.

I didn't let up. 'It's the act of doing wrong that creates separation. Our state of being is not relevant. It's careless words or actions that create distance.' I smiled. 'But…! But! It is kindnesses done. It is the baring of souls. It is holding someone tight when they are at their weakest that brings us close.'

Nicolò pressed his lips to mine. I firmed and let him.

As we parted, I said, 'Kisses can work as well, I guess.'

'It was like kissing ice,' he said – before adding quickly, 'Strawberry ice, I mean. Soft and refreshing strawberry ice.'

Perhaps it was just as well that Lilith wasn't here. She wouldn't have let him get away with a line like that. The flutter in my belly, though, told me I would forgive it. Forgive more than that, in fact. Rosalind was gone. Now my Nikka had come up with an excuse that it was better not to over-analyse – at least while I was in his arms.

'What now?' I asked nervously.

'You know,' he replied. 'That day at school when we first met.'

'When you rescued me.'

'Where I stood there and helped you up. I never got around to telling you that… well… looking at you there, lying on the ground…'

'Skirt hitched up,' I teased.

Nicolò harrumphed but continued. 'That wasn't the first time I'd seen you.'

'No?'

'No. It was earlier in the day. You were climbing the stairs. I remember I was on the floor below, and for some reason, I looked up at…'

'My backside?'

He laughed. 'Yes, your backside, and your legs and your waist. Then you stopped at the midpoint, turned, and started again, up towards the next level. From below, I glimpsed your face – as well as that bizarre but rather alluring lick of blue hair.'

'Ultramarine,' I mumbled, not knowing what else to say.

'What?'

'Ultramarine,' I repeated. 'It's made from lapis lazuli. I…'

Nicolò interrupted. 'It was right then.'

'What? You saw my double chin? Because from that angle, that would always be the case. Why…'

'Well, to put it crudely, it was right then my…' He bit his bottom lip. 'Actually, to put it less crudely and far more accurately, *I knew.* I know it sounds pathetic, but even without speaking to you, I just knew.'

I blinked. 'Are you claiming it was *love at…?*'

'Yes,' he said.

Oh.

From the delight in his eyes, I knew my cheeks were flushing. There was no turning back from this. Some words cannot be unsaid – even when they're not.

If there were records, they would show that I'm not an expert in situations like this. To be honest, the only thing close was that one time with the… quite obviously man who stood before me. Still, as a girl raised on Gothic romances, I understood what should happen next. It would be dark, not light as it was now. We would have retired to our room after a drink (but only one) too many. We would kiss, and I would lightly touch my dress on the shoulder. The dress would slip to the floor, and then…

Well, the novels tended to skip the bit about the removal of socks, shoes and underclothes. They certainly didn't mention the tent pole that made it even more difficult for the man to get his pants off in a hurry. The reality, I imagine, is always a comedy of errors, hopping and pratfalls. Still, having done the "big death", I thought I might manage a Gothic "little death" with slightly more elegance than your typical "almost virgin".

I stepped back – and shimmered. My jacket, blouse, underwear and boots glowed briefly before vanishing into a fine mist. I then drew a smile on my lips and hardened as close to mortality as I could what lay beneath. After letting the mist tease and move for what seemed, hopefully to Nicolò, like an eternity, I finally let it dissipate.

Naked now and nipples hard, I felt pleased that his pupils

had almost consumed the brown and green of his irises – and that the tent pole remained.

Nicolò fell slowly to his knees, brushing my breasts with his mouth and tongue before reaching out and gliding his hands down past my waist and hips. Looking up again into my eyes, he kissed my stomach, which tickled and made me jump. We both giggled. Two fools standing (and kneeling) against a past we were convinced should not define us.

Unfortunately, this somewhat whimsical notion turned out to be a tad premature.

The door crashed open, smashing against the wardrobe before ricocheting back – and into the nose of the first white-cloaked man trying to enter. The crack was nearly as loud as the shattering of the door lock or the rebound from the wardrobe. The white-cloaked man fell like a plank, albeit a plank smeared with snot, blood and cartilage.

The second white-cloaked man tripped over the first and landed in a lump stopped only by the still-kneeling Nicolò. A short, third one fared better, stepping over the fallen and to my right.

The fourth I recognised.

He was too tall and too human to be my father – but he'd stood next to him just one day before. Close up, he looked old enough, and definitely scary enough, to be the guard Eanna had described in her letter.

The fifth wasn't Fedhyow at all.

Most definitely not.

Still in the doorway, Rosalind's face was bloated, her skin reddened by tears. At one level, it was understandable. After all, I was stark naked with her boyfriend's face near enough touching my groin. At the "let's get real" level, however,

Rosalind had betrayed us to my father and the white-cloaked men she was now with. Surely, she must have realised she'd never feel Nicolò's warm breath again.

I almost looked down – particularly *there*.

As if reading my thoughts, the tall, white-cloaked man grabbed Nicolò by the hair and pulled him aside. I watched, petrified, as Rosalind's eyes drifted to where Nicolò's head had been only moments before and... Well, it took time to force clothes upon my nakedness. Lilith wouldn't have bothered. Lilith would have attacked and not worried about what they saw. I was still modest enough to care and lost my chance. The short, white-cloaked man to my right pulled a pair of handcuffs out of a pocket and wrapped them around my still-firm wrists. The handcuffs were glass and looked easy to break, but I had enough sense not to try. Inside the hollow glass was a liquid that I almost felt. If I broke the glass or faded, I knew it would consume me.

By then, the tall, white-cloaked man had pulled Nicolò to his chest. While his left hand still gripped Nicolò's hair, his right now held a knife.

'Hammu! No!' Rosalind barked as she entered the room.

The tall, white-cloaked man — *Hammu* apparently — ignored her. His knife moved closer to Nicolò's throat.

'No,' she repeated. Her voice was quieter this time, but just as steady. 'That is not what *he* agreed.'

The knife didn't move.

Rosalind took a breath before continuing. 'You are not Hugo. You will do what was agreed.'

Hammu, almost twitching, moved the blade away.

Perhaps my father still thought he could use Nicolò to blackmail me. This time, he'd be right.

Hammu's right arm swung the knife high before bringing it abruptly down again.

Rosalind gasped in a breath that was all her own. I might have also if I thought myself capable. Thankfully, the knife only connected with Nicolò's neck with its hilt.

Nicolò's eyes were shut well before he hit the floor.

Hammu raised his head and caught her eye. 'I am to bring whoever we find to Guitt. *He* said nothing about their condition.'

As the short, white-cloaked man led me away, it got worse. Two things. The first was minor. The receptionist was standing at the head of the stairs. I could almost see the thirty pieces of silver lining her pockets. The second was pretty major. While the receptionist was at the top of the stairs, my panther was at their foot.

Lilith's hands were bound in glass like mine. Sensibly, at least from the perspective of the white-cloaked men, they'd also fitted her with a gag.

Chapter twenty-one

A Perfume Too Sweet

The thing about a dungeon is that it stinks. While Gothic romances go big on the damp and cold, they never mention the smell. Descriptions involving the stench of excrement, rotting limbs, and various forms of offal aren't exactly conducive to a swoon-worthy bedtime read.

Of course, when I arrived, my first thoughts weren't about the smell. Instead, terrified as I was, the senses of sight and hearing took over. Touch played its part, of course. Things that go squelch are never nice. But that uncomfortable feeling of ickiness was temporary, especially when there was soon another horror to be seen or heard or both. Touch, of course, also includes pain, and pain is always remembered. But the pain comes later. Pain was something I never wished to know.

I failed.

It took time before I truly could consider the stench. Once I was away from the working part of the dungeon, and in my cell behind the thick, sound-muffling stone, it became something I could *really* think about. Bound and fixed to a wall by rope, or chain, or, in my case, hollow, water-filled glass, there is little else to do, or consider, or want to consider.

Once I got past the gag reflex, I drew in the scent. At that moment, I pretended I was a perfumer, and the vile fragrance was the subject of a structured, but admittedly unscientific, analysis. My sense of smell at first refused to accept the metaphor, but I persisted. In my mind, I labelled the various ketones and acetones, assigning them a category and designating each a source. Separating the biological from the mere chemical was tricky. Humanity can produce the purest of fluids when given the right incentive. But even then, though, I succeeded. It just took longer.

Perverse though it was, it was still a better thing to do than consider what the future might hold. I wasn't worried about myself. Well, apart from the pain thing. But there were a couple of children, one alive, one dead, that deserved better than their likely lot.

And there was Nicolò.

After I completed my new, and likely forever undocumented, classification system, I moved on to another thing about dungeons that came as a surprise.

In a windowless room, I felt a draught.

To my disappointment, understanding came far too quickly. The wall at the rear of the cell was cold. I knew first-hand – I was glass-strapped-arse-hard against it. That the front, the wall with the door, was warmer was more deduction. The direction of the breeze suggested it, as well as the memory of the flames beyond.

I drew another waft of the sickly bouquet through my nose. Literally rising from nowhere, ectoplasmic bile filled my mouth. Joylessly unembarrassed, I opened my lips and let it dribble down my chin. I felt it string. I felt it string longer than might seem possible until time... just... stopped. And then time again began. When, finally, the transient teardrop splattered onto the floor, it disgusted me. In motion, it was a thing of wonder. When still? When still, it was just another stain.

I tongued my cheek. The taste left in my mouth was foul.

I had forgotten about taste.

$\backsim$

I'd like to say my long-fated journey across open water was eventful. Eventful, though, would suggest a change in circumstance, an education, a fresh experience, a sight, a sound, a touch, a smell... a taste. There was none. Oh, of course, my imagination could taste salt, could smell the seaweed, could sense a gentle rocking, could hear the lapping of waves... But my eyes? In the dark below deck, I could not see.

Lilith might have had some choice words on the subject, but she was still gagged and could not speak. Neither could I touch her. In that dark, I would have welcomed a hand of comfort, but both of us were still bound. Kept well apart, I couldn't even scent her. I would have liked to taste her lack of fear. As we travelled across the water to this place of dragons, I could have done with a companion I knew, with certainty, had no fear.

As always, I was to be disappointed.

They took me first. I didn't see Lilith then and haven't seen her since. It was the first time dead I had ever felt truly alone. The overwhelming senses thing began when the short, white-cloaked man from Haefen threw open the hatch and hauled me out like a choice piece of mackerel. There was no Nicolò, or Rosalind, to welcome me back into the light. There were no black Fedhyow either.

After that, the sights and sounds became jumbled. There was a cart, a track and a climb that rose high above the clifftops.

There was a castle.

Another castle.

This castle sat on a flat plateau atop a hill that was most definitely nowhere near the sea. It was also much larger than the one in Marhasyow. Much. Many times. Of course, having walls that hadn't fallen and guards who hadn't deserted their posts helped the overall *wow* factor. It was notable also that all the guards wore white instead of black.

Once inside the castle gates (that, unlike the previous castle, were present), the short, white-cloaked man handed me over to his fellows and left. While I wasn't expecting any real chivalry from them, a bit of civility wouldn't have gone amiss. They turned out to be just as shitty as your standard Fedhyow. They dragged me down and in and through. The pole they attached to the backs of my arms was also made of hollow glass, as were the hoops that held it in place. The water within it sloshed around every time I moved. Well, it sloshed around until they attached the pole to the wall. After that, I couldn't move much at all. Except for my feet, that is. They did a fantastic job of dangling. The pain thing was excruciating at first and only got worse. As it did, I thought about giving in. I thought about fading and letting the water within the glass consume me. But I decided not. There was no way I was dying my final death attached to a flipping coat hanger.

I know it wasn't minutes. It might have been hours, but I was reasonably confident it wasn't days. Let's just say the cell door opened after a time, and everyone's favourite rodent crept in. Behind her, the white-cloaked man looked a little sniffy about the situation, which was fair enough. He slammed the door closed as soon as Rosalind passed the entranceway.

'Hello, little mouse,' I said.

'What?' Rosalind replied, taken aback.

'Well, I could have called you a rat, which is undeniably true, but that'll hardly get me any sympathy – and I could do with some sympathy right now. An accomplice wouldn't go amiss either. I don't suppose you fancy helping me escape?'

Rosalind nervously turned her head towards the door. It stayed closed.

'Not going to happen?' I asked. Talking was better than screaming, but the pain made me a bit of a motormouth. 'Didn't think so. Perhaps I shouldn't have led with the "little mouse" thing either – although you did manage to gnaw Nicolò's nuts off. He grew them back, but I guess you didn't notice. After all, he had his back to you when his head was up against my…'

'Stop it!'

'Stop it? Really? After what you have done. Okay, how about another one – when?'

'What?' She seemed shaken by the verbal assault. 'When what?'

'Pick one. When did you decide you could do without Nicolò? I've heard of a lover's tiff but come on! Or, how about when did you decide to betray us? To be honest, I already know, but I do so wish it were earlier and that you're an utter villain. I do so hope it was back on the island. You know, before I was on the scene.'

'No.'

'No, it wasn't the castle? You didn't sacrifice your mother and father to Fedhyow? You know, the same religious f… fantasists you did the dirty with. Are you saying it was *after* they burnt your mother to charcoal? It was *after* they chased and killed your father. It was *after*…'

'It was *after* I found out my brother was still alive.'

'So, it was Aberfal then? At the train station?'

'What did you expect me to do? I had to get him back. He's all I have left… I…'

'What about Nicolò?' I asked, letting a chill drift into my voice.

'He said they'll let us go. The three of us, Me, Nicolò and Tristan. The agreement is to let us go.' She seemed unsure. 'Governor Izdubar promised.'

Former Governor, but now wasn't the time to get picky. 'In Sulis…' I began.

She interrupted. 'It was Hugo's fault. The Governor only wanted his son. Did you know Kitten was his son? I didn't, not until Aberfal. The Governor is dying…'

'*Dying?*' I shouted – and not just because of the pain.

The corner of her mouth twitched. 'Don't tell me there's something you don't know?'

The only thing worse than a ruminating cow is a smug, ruminating cow.

The twitch disappeared. 'I brought Kitten to him. I…'

She bit her lip. 'I wasn't happy Hammu put those glass handcuffs on Kitten, but the Governor said he had no choice.'

The bile rose again. 'No choice?'

Rosalind nodded. 'Kitten was upset, but the Governor said he thought he might run away. He promised Kitten would settle down once I was gone... He was right. I'd hardly left the room before Kitten stopped crying.'

The bile reached my throat. 'Why do Hammu and the rest wear white?' I asked. 'Are they Fedhyow?'

She hesitated. 'I'm not sure. But the others take orders from Hammu, and Hammu listens only to the Governor. I don't know much for certain. Besides the Governor, no one else will talk to me.'

I was struggling to blame them. 'Did Izdubar mention me?' I asked.

Her eyes flared. 'It's not *always* about you! I was there when Hammu told the Governor that Nicolò had been seen in Haefen. The Governor *most definitely* never asked about anybody else. I couldn't believe it when I saw...'

I smirked. '...saw Nicolò about to sup from the Holy Grail? Oh... you silly girl. Izdubar might not have asked who Nicolò was with, but he certainly knew.'

Rosalind's eyes pulsed.

I forced the bile into my mouth and spat it out. 'Hugo butchered Tiama the moment he found out she was Wycche. Back in Sulis, he tried to do the same to his son. If Izdubar dies, what's stopping the Fedhyow, be they black or white, putting you on the barbecue?'

'The agreement...'

'*Is worthless.* You are Wycche. Even if you are wrong and Izdubar lives, even if he could then save you, why would he bother? He has what he wants. Izdubar is not exactly famed for being honourable.'

Rosalind stared, bewildered.

'You do know Hugo was Nicolò's father?' I asked.

She turned pale. 'Hugo killed Tiama?'

'Yes,' I said.

'Nicolò never talked a lot about his past. All I knew was that he needed… comforting. Especially after Adapa…' Her voice trailed off.

Yes, little mouse. Mentioning Nicolò's grand-pappy was a mistake – particularly after that *comforting* remark.

I spat out another wad of ecto-phlegm. 'Let's talk about Adapa, shall we? Let's talk about Dumuz and Lilith. Oh, and what about Eanna? Were they all just collateral damage? I guess, unlike Nicolò, you just didn't give a…'

Rosalind interrupted. 'The Governor had also promised to let Adapa go. The rest of you? I knew you'd escape – what with being dead and all. I didn't want anyone hurt.' She paused before adding, 'Even you.'

Gee, thanks.

Another breeze forced the oil lamp on the wall to flicker and dim. Rosalind squinted. 'You mentioned Eanna? Do you mean the woman that Lilith changed into at night?'

She didn't know? 'Yes, that Eanna.'

'Kitten was calling for her.'

'What?'

Rosalind's eyes widened. 'When I took Kitten to the Governor. The boy was crying and shouting for Lilith and Dumuz… and Eanna. The Governor looked upset at first when he heard Eanna's name… and then happy. Scarily happy.'

Shit.

'They're not letting us go. Are they?' she said.

'No. You're a witch. The Fedhyow burn witches. If it were

just you, then I wouldn't be fussed. But it's not. Nicolò's also likely to have his chestnuts roasted.'

And Tristan.

Rosalind whimpered, exhaling sharply. On the subsequent inhale, she gagged as the putrid air lit the ember of that thing deep inside she knew to be the truth.

'Where's Nicolò?' I asked.

She tried to gather herself. 'He's in a cell one level up. They won't let me see him.' Rosalind glanced at the cuffs of glass that held me to the wall. 'They have beds up there,' she added.

Cute.

So, even dungeons have a hierarchy. Nicolò had a bed, and I couldn't even touch the floor with my feet. Not a great surprise, really. Still, we were going to be equally gone soon. Nicolò by fire and me by holy I-still-can't-believe-it water. I suspect it'll feel something akin to the sort of dissolve-u-like acid I guarantee I never saw in classroom chemistry. I do, though, wish I were in that bed with Nicolò and never mind the biological logistics.

I looked again at my little mouse. Her bottom lip was still trembling. Yup, dawn was properly rising above that empty glade she thought of as a brain. Rosy-paws was just as trapped as me, and now she knew it. She was going to die, and she now knew that as well. I was glad, though, I hadn't called her "little rat". Yes, she sold us out, but would I have done anything differently in her place? Sniffles here was just another victim. A rodent like me, really. Neither of us would get out of the maze, no matter how fast we ran. Neither of us would get the cheese or the happy ending.

'Why?' she asked.

'What?'

'Why does Izdubar want you… alive?'

Again, cute.

She continued. 'In Sulis, I knew you'd escape. In Haefen? Hammu could have destroyed you, but he didn't. Why?'

Why indeed?

'Kitten's my brother,' I said. 'Well, half-brother, if we're getting picky.'

'Uh?'

'Yeah. That's what I thought when I found out.' I glanced left and right at my glass manacles. 'I don't know why our father wants us here, but I suspect the future welfare of his children isn't high on his agenda.'

Rosalind was doing some serious re-evaluating. Of course, she'd never admit that she'd been wrong. Not to me, not when she still thought she still had a chance with Nicolò – which she didn't. And not just because we all would be dead, dead, dead – well before any fantasy make-up sex.

Oh, sod it. Let's get this over and done. They were just toying with us.

I looked beyond Rosalind and shouted, '*You out there. That's right, isn't it? There'll not be much left of Izdubar's slip-ups once this is over.*'

Not that there was much left anyway.

The door opened.

The man wasn't your typical Fedhyow but wasn't your standard boutique-styled *white cloak*, either. For one thing, he was far too old. Not Adapa old, but old all the same. Even in the half-light, I could tell the man was past caring about his appearance. Food stains ran right down the length of his tunic. His long hair approached the manic. Although untied, there seemed little chance of it blocking his vision. Not with the front half receding towards the back.

Hammu.

He… stared at me. While his left hand dangled loose, his right hand rested on a sword. In those watery blue eyes, I saw a bleakness beyond even that of a fanatic. I looked again at his sword. In the gutter channel was a tube of glass. I knew without asking that the tube didn't need to break to do its work.

Rosalind turned to the side and stepped back. It might have been carelessness. It might have been fright, but she fell arse first onto the ground and slid. The poor girl only came to rest when the curve of her back clattered into the side wall. I wondered whether I'd provided the lubricant that had facilitated her travel. She yelped but seemed otherwise unharmed. 'Is it true?' she asked. 'Is what she said true?'

The man glanced at her in contempt – which was answer enough. Lilith would have come up fighting. Rosalind just sat there and bawled. I tried to work up some sympathy. To my disgust, I succeeded. 'Let her go,' I said. 'At least let her and the baby go. You don't need them.'

His eyes again fixed on mine. Did I see a flicker of… *something*?

No.

It was just the light reflecting from the lamp on the wall above Rosalind's head. A lamp that appeared in danger of matting her hair with scalding oil – which would be a shame.

He crossed the gap from the door to the rear wall, reached up to my right wrist, and unbuckled it, freeing my hand from its glass restraint. I twisted in the air. While the trope of the slaughterhouse sprung to mind, I was as far from a lump of meat hanging on a chain as possible. The man reached into a pouch at the side of his robe and pulled out a pair of glass handcuffs and a matching collar. Attached to the collar was a lead – I might as well have barked. Both the collar and cuffs were hollow and filled with liquid.

He attached one cuff to my right wrist and the collar to my neck. Finally, he wrapped the other cuff around my left wrist and released me from the wall before stepping back. I fell to the floor. Hard. Only instinct made me use my knees, and only my knees, to take the hit from the ground. If I used my hands and tried to roll, the resulting pain I would feel from the shards of glass would merely be an inconsequential herald of the endless agony of the next.

It still hurt though.

From the side, I heard Rosalind mewl. It may have been due to hot oil dripping, but I preferred to think it was empathy for my pain. Still, she didn't help. To be honest, only a few days ago, I wouldn't have either.

The leash tugged. The hardened upper edge of my literal choker lifted my jaw from the horizontal to what seemed vertical. I rose painfully. Ironically, through his actions, my head remained unbowed. I walked without further comment through the door and into the place of scents and senselessness.

I heard the door close and knew without looking that the number of the cell's occupants remained at one.

∽

We climbed. With all its heat, I thought the smells emitted from the lower dungeon might rise to overwhelm the sensibilities of those above. I was wrong. On each floor, there was a door and a guard. Apparently, each door was a seal, or a sphincter, that separated one level from the next.

As a tour guide, Hammu was useless. He growled whenever I asked a question and tugged the leash around my neck. It took a while to realise I was getting off lightly. If he'd wanted to, Hammu could easily have manufactured a crack in my glass collar. I wondered what he'd do when the fluid released dissolved my pretty little neck into a pretty little puddle?

Probably suggest I carry my head under an arm.

The dungeon had four levels. I hadn't counted on the way down, but it seemed like more. The last level didn't even count as a dungeon. Not really. It better resembled a hospital – if you consider a morgue a sort of failed hospital.

On the ground floor, I literally saw the light. It was dusk again, so there wasn't much of it, but it was still something I'd never thought I'd see again. Looking through the windows as we climbed, I noticed an eclectic mix of stables and courtyards. Across one courtyard, where grown men played with sticks, I spotted a chapel and heard Evensong. In another, I saw bigger sticks, well, burnt posts, really. All vertical and surrounded by ash. A fresh set of posts lay nearby.

Sorry, Rosalind.

Sorry, Nicolò.

Above, for the next three levels, were dormitories. Mostly empty, it appeared the white-cloaked men took the concept of 'open-plan' to the extreme. Judging by the smell of misplaced urine, the male of the species inhabited the lower two floors. There is always misplaced urine when there are toilets and men. The female level wasn't any better though. The not-so-subtle scent of synchronised cycles made me think of rotting iron – and the place I had just left. Actually, at that point, I deliberately overdid the sniffing and gagging. Perhaps I could make this most male of males, colour.

I... suddenly, she was in front of me. How could she be there? When was the last time I'd seen her? The bridge? Was the aisle mother really the last mortal I'd encountered when alive?

She wasn't smiling. That deathly grin of hate could never be mistaken for a smile. While she wasn't wearing the black of a Fedhyow, neither was she wearing white. Magnolia might be the best description. I had to admit the full-length habit flattered her figure, pulling in at the right points, wider at the wrong. There was no cleavage on display, obviously, but still. In the artificial light of the dormitory, she seemed pretty enough – blue-eyed, with blonde hair poking out from under her habit. With a bit of make-up, she might have looked like Iresh in her earlier years.

Of course, after what I now knew about Iresh's previous profession, I suspect the woman before me wouldn't consider that a compliment.

The aisle mother spat in my face and pulled out a glass-channelled knife.

'No!' Hammu commanded. It was the first thing I'd heard him say since Haefen.

The aisle mother stared at me in disbelief, trembling. It took more than seconds, but eventually, she turned away.

As Hammu and I moved towards the door to the next level, I heard the beginnings of an infant's cry – and a cooing response. Perhaps there was something more to the aisle mother than hate?

Or perhaps not. A second infant echoed the first. That one she ignored.

Tristan?

Unlike the dormitories, the next level was as opulent as it was tacky. The vast hall had mirrored walls that reflected into infinity the light of any object in view. Its floor was a mosaic of varnished oak squares lit in a chessboard two-tone by a brilliant and blazing chandelier. The floor reminded me of Dumuz's patio in Sulis... but larger.

Much larger.

It wasn't a chessboard, and the hall was certainly not a patio. There was one more thing in the room.

The solid granite throne at the far end stood empty.

We crossed the floor to the throne and then behind. As we walked, Hammu's feet clattered and clumped and hopefully scuffed the surface. Only in my imagination did the man leave behind a trail of excrement and charnel fluid.

The door behind the throne was simple but solid – just like the short, white-cloaked man sitting by it on a chair. He, I remembered from Haefen. He was the one that brought me here. Alongside him, a Fedhyow staff and a halberd leant against the wall. The halberd seemed more for show than use. I couldn't imagine the man facing a cavalry troop in full charge, not across this floor. As we approached, the man casually leant back and opened the door. I walked through. Hammu, still holding my leash, followed. What I didn't expect, or see, was Hammu clipping something with a heel as he passed. I heard it though. I heard the guard falling off his chair. Was it possible that Hammu had a sense of humour? Probably not. No doubt Hammu had kicked away the chair leg because of a complete lack of one.

There were more steps, circular this time. They formed a staircase resembling another from my recent past, but better kept and better lit. And longer. And higher. After the first fifty steps, I was out of breath – not that I breathed, of course. My only satisfaction was that Hammu also panted. After a while, I gave up counting.

But even eternity has an end.

There was an entrance with an open door. Beyond the door, there was a bed, and in that bed, there lay an old, old man. The man had yellow-white hair, which had fluffed out. The hair, oddly, made me think of feathers. His nose also seemed even larger than when I last saw it. The ridge of cartilage was so crooked and hooked that it resembled the beak of a bird. In my mind, I could picture serpent scales beneath the sheets.

The cockatrice fixed me with a withering gaze. And when he spoke, I turned to stone.

Chapter twenty-two

There is Always a King

The room had six walls surrounding a bed that was nowhere near an edge. As I looked through the doorway, five large windows offered a failing panorama as dusk strengthened its grip. The bed had four posts that rose to waist height. Behind the bed were three torches on Gothic stands. Next to it, I saw two chairs. The chair on my left was empty save for an odd collection of instruments atop its seat. The chair on the right was… not empty.

In the bed was one total, complete and utterly literal… *motherfucker*.

I've never liked the Fedhyow's use of iconography. These days, I realise no one will buy into a religion that worships a statue of a bull, or the sun, or a fat woman with a big vulva, but still. The fact is that all the Fedhyow had done was codify something that was at least honest. The Fedhyow have their rituals and rites. They base their existence on a book of one-dimensional parables that seem as trite as they are malign. Talk about false idols. Their book is as false an idol as a slaughtered goat. Why else would they brimstone any who dare to challenge its words?

Of course, the Wycche also had a book. One I've never read and one I will never read, even though I knew it sat on a table nearby.

Beyond the geometric and numerical, the room was a maze of the eclectic. It was a muddle of rebranded symbols stolen in part or wholesale from earlier faiths that lacked the means to defend their flock, or copyright, from pillage. Take, for example, the quilt on the bed. Although the tapestry of squares had gone big with the abstraction, it clearly represented the liturgical year. It was obvious the slew of symbols for birth, death, ice, heat, drought, flood and the occasional wheat sheaf were hardly the product of an epiphany. Even a guy with a stone chisel and a flattish surface might have crafted them.

The creature in the bed spoke again, and the force that held me still... waned.

I almost fell forward and let the collar bite my neck. I almost became the thing I should have been on the bridge – but I did not. I had reason not. The serpent's voice was a rasping gasp among a background gurgle of fluid-filled lungs as the creature hissed what must be.

It wasn't his *whispers* that made me obey. It was my brother on the other seat that took away my will.

With my hands still cuffed, I walked to the left-hand chair, lifted the instruments off the seat, and took their place. I did not speak. Hammu stood behind me and tied my leash to the rightmost spoke of the chair's back. Tightly. The effect was to pull my head further away from the face on the pillow.

Positioned as I was, with my left hip lifted from the base and my right hip firmly pushed down, I couldn't reach out and kill – even if I had the choice. Hammu leaned over me and pulled the glass cuffs across my body before securing them to the chair's left arm.

He then took the instruments out of my fingers.

I felt a sharpness in my right arm, and my senses dulled. In turn, Stephen Izdubar, once Governor of Marhasyow but sadly still my father… groaned.

I waited until Hammu left the room before speaking. 'You look terrible,' I said.

'For now,' Izdubar replied. His voice already seemed stronger.

I glared at the tubing that connected us.

'Is this going to be our little secret?' I asked. 'Do the Fedhyow know you have a daughter?' I refused to look across the bed. 'Do they know you have a son?'

'Not a son.'

'A daughter?'

Izdubar coughed. 'Again, no. To be fair, I only found out recently myself.'

'It shouldn't have come as much of a surprise,' I said. 'It's the sort of thing that happens when you rape someone.'

Izdubar's eyes flared. '*I didn't rape her. I…*'

He calmed. 'As I remember it, Eanna was quite accommodating.'

'*She was just a girl!*'

'But old enough to do business.'

'*What the…*' The fake air I exhaled smelt of overripe fruit. 'What on earth are you talking about?'

'Iresh had agreed the sisters and the boy should stay away from the castle. Eanna broke that agreement, so some recompense was required. While my reward wasn't financial, I think the transaction still qualifies as *business.*'

My eyeballs pulsed with anger.

Izdubar lifted his head and puffed. His breath smelt of… nothing. 'It seems, at least from what you said, Eanna regretted it afterwards. I guess that's another thing I need to talk to her about. Unfortunately, the little tart's downstairs, refusing to come out of her shell.'

'Shell?'

'The black one. Hammu's done his best, but he's yet to crack it open.'

The trouble with pulsing your eyeballs is that eventually, they start to itch.

Thankfully, Izdubar changed the subject. 'Did you know the Fedhyow were once famed for their accountants? Arithmetic is one of the few things taught on Guitt without restriction.'

'Including girls?' I asked, finally blinking.

'Well… no,' he said. 'Still, the Fedhyow sent clever boys like Hugo out into the world to…'

'Find a wife?'

'Bring in a revenue stream. I made Hugo my treasurer, confident the people of Marhasyow would never believe a Fedhyow would steal from them.'

'No. That was your job.'

'Not at first. In fact, I spent my early years as governor fixing an economy that had been in the doldrums for years. I only brought Hugo in at the end. You see, while the town thrived, the state's coffers remained empty. I needed a specialist to help to reverse that… and Hugo was a very creative accountant.'

'But… why?'

'We needed Marhasyow's money. All of it.'

'We? Oh… shit… *You are Fedhyow!*'

He nodded. 'Lapsed... As is Hammu. Still, Hugo never understood how far we'd fallen.'

He paused for effect. 'What do you know about the Fedhyow and the Wycche?'

I was too weak for long speeches. 'The Fedhyow were once Wycche,' I said. 'But, unlike their cousins, a Fedhyow stays dead while a Wycche sometimes doesn't. It seems the Fedhyow are murderously jealous of that last bit.'

He shook his head. 'Not all Fedhyow. While the people from the north erased the Wycche decades ago, their encounter with the Fedhyow wasn't quite as life-defining. For the Fedhyow, though, it ended up almost as caustic. The temptations...'

Of course. 'You said lapsed.'

'Pardon?'

'How many Fedhyow sent out into the wilderness never returned?'

He lifted his chin – it looked ridiculously taut. 'Most of them. By the time I left, Guitt was already at a tipping point.'

I shook my head – and whimpered as the wattle around my throat moved with it. 'But you did return... eventually... *with a wagon of gold that wasn't yours.* Why would Hugo compromise his beliefs to help you?'

'A story about witches will always intrigue.'

'What?'

'Not every Fedhyow becomes an accountant. Hammu joined the army. Me? I went back to school.'

'University?'

He nodded. 'I didn't become Governor of Marhasyow by accident. I worked hard for it. My postgraduate thesis on urban renewal was visionary. I wanted Marhasyow.'

'But why?'

'Genocide has its drawbacks,' he said. 'Everyone believed the Wycche had left nothing behind. I was certain that wasn't true.'

'Certain?'

He ignored me. 'A governor has access to records no historian will see. Bureaucrats do like their paperwork – land seizures, crucifixion counts, that sort of thing. I found reams of them. But I'd bet much of my adult life that the pen-pushers would feel obligated to keep some other things as well. Things seized from the Wycche. Confiscated documents. Stories, legends... practices.'

'What did you find?'

Izdubar sighed. 'Absolutely nothing. That was the night I ventured into Marhasyow and got drunk. Very drunk. I only perked up when I spotted a barmaid with the most amazing décolletage. I...'

'Murdered the perv who mussed it up?'

Izdubar growled. 'I lost my temper. I...'

'You seem to do that a lot,' I said.

Izdubar paused and nodded. 'I do, don't I?' He calmed. 'Anyway, it wasn't Iresh's cleavage that caught my attention, magnificent though it was. It was the decoration on top.'

Of course. 'She was wearing an amulet.'

He nodded. 'Unfortunately, Iresh didn't know what it was. To her, it was a keepsake. She didn't even know she was Wycche... Of course, it took a lot of sweat and grunting to prove that beyond doubt.'

Izdubar briefly glanced at my groin. I *think* it was unintentional.

He continued. 'Iresh was as close as I got, but she gave me hope. There had to be more Wycche out there.'

'You hired Hugo after you… paid Iresh off?'

'I needed a Fedhyow.'

But… oh. What a complete and utter… 'You stole Iresh's amulet, didn't you? You used it to convince Hugo that some Wycche still lived.'

Izdubar tipped his head back in memory. 'I never told Hugo her name. Instead, I weaved a tale of a Wycche diaspora, knowing that the Fedhyow would be compelled to hunt them down.'

I still didn't get it. 'If it was just the Wycche you were after, why did you need the gold?'

'Guitt, even at its peak, was never rich. Without additional resources, their efforts, by necessity, would have been ad hoc and doomed to failure. I persuaded Hugo the Fedhyow would need Marhasyow's wealth to finance the search.'

'Conveniently obligating the Fedhyow to you.'

He smiled. 'The condition was that I would lead the project.' He looked around the bedroom. 'From this castle and with a few personal staff.'

'Really?'

'I convinced them I was still a Fedhyow at heart.'

'*Really?*'

Izdubar huffed. 'I offered a brighter future, a new-found purpose… and enough spare cash to evangelise properly.'

I glanced at the tubing. 'You never told the Fedhyow the real reason you were interested in the Wycche?'

He stared, surprised. Even with his eyebrows raised, his brow appeared unwrinkled. 'Other than to exterminate them? No, don't be foolish. That would've made me part of the problem.'

I grimaced. 'What happened next?' I asked. The cracks on my face felt like canals.

'Your mother stabbed me in the back, and I woke up on Guitt in different circumstances. Initially, I thought she hadn't hit anything vital. It took weeks to realise that an infection was destroying my kidneys. It nearly succeeded. I developed all the classic symptoms: fatigue, nausea, painful urination… impotence.'

'You poor dear – but, apart from pissing with difficulty, what else have you been doing all these years?'

Izdubar grimaced. 'As I said, *leading*.'

'*Whispering?*'

The scowl vanished. 'That too. Hugo became the face of the project abroad, and I supervised the… processing here. Hugo supplied a lot of candidates. It wasn't his fault they never met my needs. Of course, if Hugo had spent more time at home in the intervening years…'

'He'd have realised his wife was a witch?'

He smirked. 'Possibly, but Tiama did a good job hiding it.'

'So, those Hugo sent to Guitt…'

'Were like Iresh. While the Fedhyow found a lot of Wycche, none knew anything useful.'

'How can you be so certain?'

'You saw the cell and Hammu's tools.'

'Are you talking about the red-hot pokers, racks and other clichéd *bad guy* stuff?'

Izdubar laughed. 'Yes. The Fedhyow also provided some more customised equipment they knew would be useful against the mortally challenged.'

'You mean glass spheres, handcuffs, and the like?'

'And the like, yes. In fact, Hammu gave your mother's shell a rather unusual sponge bath a few hours ago.'

Nope… still not playing. 'What happened to the Wycche Hugo sent once you finished with them?'

Izdubar seemed disappointed by my resistance. 'Personally, I would have let them go, but that's not the Fedhyow way.'

My scalp itched. 'You bastard. You murdered a bunch of innocents for absolutely no gain?'

'I believe, daughter, that technically you're the bastard.'

He had a point. 'What finally made you change tack?'

'What do you mean?' he said smugly.

I hate smug. 'The Fedhyow have been in Marhasyow for years, but Hugo only arrived in spring. What changed?'

'Perhaps Hugo felt nostalgic.'

I shook my head in frustration, tears welling up. A clump of hair broke free from my scalp and slipped slowly down my cheek. '*What changed!*'

The few grey hairs on Izdubar's head were long gone. What replaced them was short but also full and black.

He waited for the sobbing to stop. 'Death comes to most. For some, it comes early. For others, it takes longer… but for a few, it need not come at all.'

I stared at the monster before me.

'For the past year,' he continued, 'I've been unable to get out of bed. I… I frequently shit and piss myself.'

'Too much information, but thank you.'

His cheeks pinked. 'I was clearly dying, but one thing kept me going.'

I looked down at my arm. 'This?'

'Still nothing that specific, but effectively, yes. I asked Hugo to return to Marhasyow to resume the search.'

'Didn't anyone recognise him?'

'If they did, they kept sensibly quiet. You must have noticed the Fedhyow's influence increased markedly after his arrival?'

'Er… Yes.'

'Subsuming local governance was always part of the Fedhyow's plan. I persuaded Hugo to hasten it. Marhasyow would be first and Aberfal next.'

'That's a lot more than evangelising.'

'It was the dream I sold them. Holding the levers of power lets you get away with many things not quite legal. With the Fedhyow in charge, I was confident Hugo would feel less constrained when hunting Wycche.'

'As Cordelia found out.'

Izdubar hesitated. 'That was a mob, not Hugo. Hugo would have sent her here. Still, it set about the chain of events that led to now.'

I shook my head in disgust – more hair fell. 'You asked Hugo to go to Marhasyow? I assume you mean you *whispered*? How long have you been doing that?'

'*Whispering?* Since I hired him twenty years ago. Why?'

'And the projection thing? I've seen you do it four times – my garden, your old castle, Aberfal station and Sulis. Each time…'

He raised an eyebrow. 'Each time with Hugo nearby? You're smarter than you look.'

'People keep saying that. To be honest, I'm beginning to have some doubts.'

He laughed. 'For projection to work, you need a host. Hugo was as oblivious to that as he was to the *whispering*. I managed four excursions. You can't travel far, particularly…'

'After the host dies.'

'Again, yes. I've known the theory for a while, but only recently tried it. Once cast, you might not return.'

'That's not sounding like a negative right now.'

Izdubar tutted. 'I think it's time for a story.'

'Why not,' I said. 'I'm sitting comfortably.'

Of course, I *really* wasn't. My right buttock had turned numb ages ago. If I was alive, I'd be worried about gangrene.

Cosy in his bed, Izdubar continued, 'Growing up on Guitt, I'd become disillusioned. As well as questioning the faith, I'd developed some doubts about what the Fedhyow considered a vice.'

'Yeah. Puberty's a bitch,' I said.

He smiled. 'And, on Guitt, very frustrating. There was this one time, during yet another lesson on the sins of the flesh, I got so frustrated I snuck out early and went for a walk.'

'Surely, that's not how you pronounce that last word,' I said. The numbness had reached my chest and head and, apparently, my sense of propriety.

Izdubar rolled his eyes.

'Okay. I assume you found something?' I croaked. My lungs felt more than a tad phlegmy.

'I came across a heap of rocks. Heaps of rock are not unusual on Guitt but human bones lying amongst them are. With them was a metal tin containing a sheaf of papers.'

'The book of the Wycche.' Forget phlegmy. I was almost drowning.

'Half of it was missing. Much of what remained was water-damaged.'

'But, from what was still legible, you learnt how to *whisper*?'

'And project. Beyond that, I could only make out hints of what was possible. There was enough there, though, to set me on a new path.'

'To be honest, the world would have been a better place if you'd just stuck to the... *walk*.'

The stare returned. '*Anyway*, as you can see, I've finally succeeded. Although it came down to a lucky coincidence in the end.'

'Coincidence?'

'Hugo's return to Marhasyow in the spring ended in disappointment – at least for him. Discovering that his offspring was an abomination really chafed.' He smiled. 'Not as much as the wound that black Wycche gave him though.' The smile broadened. 'And certainly not as much as when he realised what type of creature she was.'

I kept my face blank. It wasn't as difficult as I had hoped. The muscles in my face were solidifying. 'Did you tell him about me?' I asked.

Izdubar sighed. 'Not when Hugo first came back, no,' he said. 'I didn't know about you until...' He paused, embarrassed. 'I was in a bad way when I returned to Guitt on the back of that wagon. It wouldn't have taken much for the Fedhyow to look at gold, look at me and decide to cut their losses... and probably my throat. It took a year before I felt safe enough to ask Hammu to take a trip to Marhasyow and do something for me.'

'Something?'

'Perhaps I should have said "someone".'

A lump formed in my throat. 'Eanna,' I said.

He nodded. 'Unfortunately, the little tart was gone by the time he got there. Hammu's greatest strength, and weakness, is that he only ever does what he is told. It never crossed my mind to ask whether Iresh had anyone in the house. So Hammu, being Hammu, didn't mention you.'

'Pity that,' I said. At least the lump blocked some of the phlegm.

Izdubar could see I was struggling. He pushed on. 'Anyway,' he said. 'Back to Hugo. We agreed he should return to Marhasyow once he was able. He had a son to catch, and I, finally, had a lead on a practising Wycche.'

'You're talking about Lilith.'

'If you mean the bitch who attacked Hugo in his own kitchen, the one now downstairs in my best dungeon – then yes. Hugo spent his summer recovering and scouring the reports from Marhasyow, hoping for a hint that might lead to his son. You know, births, marriages, death certificates.'

'Death certificates?'

'Hugo thought I might find one interesting. It named a daughter as the next of kin. A daughter he'd discovered, far too late, had been dating his son.'

'But... I didn't know where Nicolò had gone.'

'You're missing the point. Hugo was at the castle during the storm. He met the sisters. That was the night he found out about my... rather sinful history with Iresh. He...'

'*He what?*' I asked. The man was enjoying himself far too much.

Izdubar smirked. 'He pointed out that your date of birth was on her death certificate and both Hugo and I could count.'

'You told him Eanna was my mother?'

'Don't be stupid... But I did admit to a lapse with Iresh. Of course, even then, I couldn't tell him I'd always known your family was Wycche.'

'Why not?'

'*You are Wycche!* Hugo only worked it out when he heard how you had died on the bridge. Instead of being suspicious, the poor man actually felt relieved I'd also been bewitched.'

Not even funny.

'How did you explain your wound?' I asked.

'I told him that Eanna was jealous. So much so that the bitch stabbed me in the back. Given that something similar had just happened to him, he at least was sympathetic – unlike you.'

'You sold him a hell of a story.'

'It's a strength of mine.'

'You *whispered* to him.'

Izdubar's upper lip twitched. 'Of course,' he said, before wincing again.

I watched in morbid fascination as his legs thrashed beneath the bedsheets. When he finally stopped, I knew without seeing that they had thickened. Depressed, I looked down. As expected, my calves looked quite spindly.

'I suspect I'm running out of time,' I said. 'Can we talk about the other thing now... if that's okay?'

He chuckled. 'Of course. We need to go back to the papers I found on the beach. As I mentioned, while most were illegible, some were quite clear.'

'*Whispering.* Projection... Ghosts.'

'Exactly, but there were also hints of something else. Something a Fedhyow could also do. Something so against the faith that when they moved to Guitt, the Fedhyow suppressed all knowledge of it.'

I looked down at what was, essentially, an umbilical cord transferring my essence from my arm into my father. From my position across the bed, I then looked at what remained of my brother – a brother still seeping ethereal substance from his wrists. I would have thought him gone, save for a single tear in his left eye. There was no breath. But then, why would there be?

'The thing about Gothic fiction is that it is fiction,' I snarled, rubbing my jaw against my shoulder. Something not quite saliva dribbled down my chin. 'I think I'm losing my taste for it.'

He smirked. 'What on earth are you drooling on about?'

'Ghosts are real,' I said, pushing on. 'Possession is real… Vampires are real.'

Izdubar glanced at the book sitting on the table. I recognised the scuffs and watermarks. 'After you disappeared from that house in Sulis,' he said, 'Hammu found this delightful tome in a bedroom. The only thing I knew for certain before I read it was that the Wycche could live a long time… and, in theory, the Fedhyow.'

My nostrils flared. 'And now you know how.'

Snot and ethereal blood now sat on my top lip. I ignored it. 'After all the suffering you've endured and caused, was it worth it?'

Izdubar snorted… elegantly. 'Why not?'

'Even the Fedhyow thought it unethical.'

'My dear, if our positions were reversed, you would…'

'No,' I said.

He shook his head. 'Seriously? Look at you! You are protoplasm. A wisp of almost nothing. In death, I wouldn't have even been that.'

'But now?' I prompted, needing to hear the rest.

He smirked again. 'Now, thanks to you, I will live longer. What now flows in my veins is better than blood.'

'Better?' I snapped.

I shouldn't have snapped. Reaching around my mouth with my tongue, I found, collected, and spat out a loose tooth. Exiting my body, it vanished as if it never was.

He guffawed. 'Theoretically, yes. Even the Wycche never managed it.'

'They didn't?'

'I suspect they lacked the tools. There are many things described they never tried.'

I didn't appreciate the hungry stare that went with his last few words.

Still, I stared right back. 'Maybe even the Wycche had standards.'

He said nothing.

My stare wasn't just because I was angry… or scared. My eyes needed more light. The world was getting darker.

'I don't understand,' I said. 'At my house, you asked for my help but hadn't yet read the book. You didn't know you needed my blood. Even at the station in Aberfal, you still demanded I come to Guitt – and that was after the deal you made with Rosalind to bring my brother. What were you after?'

'Do you want me to say I was dying? That I wanted my family with me when I passed?'

'It's the sort of thing normal families do.'

'I'm sure you agree that our family is not normal. I…'

'It was never me,' I said, finally realising the truth.

I could barely see him nodding. 'Not then. No. While Hugo thought you could lead him to his son, I was more interested in the creature that took Nicolò. I was especially interested when I heard that the same dead Wycche cut out your heart on the bridge.'

'You guessed I'd awaken at my house, and Lilith would be there?'

'I had people on the bridge too, but the house seemed more likely. It was disappointing when she escaped. It was more than disappointing when I thought I saw her destroyed.'

'But?' My guts ached.

'You kept on running. You had a place to go. There was still hope this Lilith told you something.'

'Nothing of use to you.' My guts *really* ached.

'Oh, I don't know,' he said. 'The result is that I will live, we will live, for longer than before.'

'We?'

'Hammu and some others. The white my staff wear is not a symbol of purity, no matter what I told the Fedhyow. It identifies those destined, if not for greatness, at least for longevity.'

'Hugo never wore white.'

And neither did the aisle mother.

'Once more, don't be stupid. I'd have been dead the day the Fedhyow found out. Now, though, I think I'm ready to tell them.'

'The Fedhyow?' I could no longer feel my legs. I could no longer feel my body outside my head, chest and screaming stomach.

'The people of Guitt are not as insular as they were, and the traditionalists are fewer than they might think. Once the Fedhyow realise how long they might live…'

'At a cost,' I croaked.

'All progress comes at a cost. In the beginning, the Fedhyow will search for more Wycche.'

'You've already made sure there aren't many left. What happens when they run out?'

I felt rather than saw the tap to my vein shut off.

'They'll turn on their own,' he said. The resonance in his voice was hypnotic. Bewitching, even. 'My people, of course, will always have enough to sustain themselves. For me? For me, I have better. I have you.'

I was glad I only heard rather than saw the quilt that covered him push down, his legs rotate, and the beast that was my father stand.

'You should be pleased,' he said. 'You have a family again.'

I could feel the heat emanating from the man before me, naked and in his prime.

My bowels spasmed… nothing.

Once more, my father snorted. I heard the floorboards creak as he stepped behind me and winced as he placed his hands on my shoulders. His left thumb rolled forward into the groove between my upper arm and breast. I sensed he wanted to move it further down, but he did not. Instead, he bent over me and *whispered* in my right ear, 'You did the right thing. Your brother still exists. Without what you gave me, that wouldn't be the case.' He kissed my cheek. 'I look forward to doing this again. I enjoyed our little chat.'

Izdubar didn't wait for a response. Instead, he turned, and I heard the rustle of clothing as my father pulled on a dressing gown I'd seen on the floor. Finally, I heard him walk towards the door and the stairs.

Soon he was gone.

I could no longer move. I could no longer see, but I could still stare without sight at that thing that used to be my brother and wait until the true darkness took me.

Finally, and after far too long, it did.

CHAPTER TWENTY-THREE

WHAT SHALL IRON DO?

A child's cry will pierce you if you let it. It'll draw blood from a vein if your fingernails are sharp enough and your arm is that tense. My arm was that tense, my nails that sharp, but strapped down as I was and without blood, it wasn't the most viable self-harm option available.

What I saw over my left shoulder took that prize.

My stomach didn't ache, which was a pleasant change. My intestines no longer had unrestricted access to the world, which was another. I took a breath that still wasn't there, and it came easily enough. I probed my mouth with my tongue. All my teeth seemed as present and correct as they'd ever been. When I moved my head, I felt my hair bounce in response, hair that included a tuft. I was still dead, of course, but I felt better than before.

Still, what was happening on the bed behind me would make any daughter's stomach flip a little.

'You escaped then?' I asked. My larynx seemed fine.

Nothing.

My ears worked as well, unfortunately. The wailing from the boy was incessant.

Given my improved condition, I must have slept a fair while and, given Kitten's, a fair bit more. I looked again over my shoulder and realised we'd both received help – which was the sight's only upside.

Eanna squeaked. Dumuz just groaned.

I wondered if untied I could run away. My legs still felt rather weak. 'Now that you've finished,' I said.

'You need to sort out your priorities,' Eanna replied, moving her right hand from where I'd rather it wasn't.

'*Priorities? Seriously?* I'm tied to a chair in a castle brimming with bad guys. The king of this cesspit, *who happens to be my father*, has drained me so dry that I'm likely stuck with a permanent pout. How can you talk about priorities when you're just lying there, *masturbating each other on his pissy bed?* Who knows when Izdubar's coming back?'

'There's no need to get biological,' Eanna tutted, panting.

And not quite finished.

The panting grew faster. 'Also, not sure about the just lying bit… Oh!'

'Dumuz?' I pleaded.

Dumuz looked over his shoulder. Unfortunately, his right hand remained in place.

'Pissy?' he asked.

I glared right back at him – mainly to stop my eyes from wandering.

He then gave me little choice as he rolled away from Eanna. Turning beetroot, I tried to look everywhere but *there*.

'Sorry about that,' he said, looking tired.

The cuff that secured my hands to the chair fell open.

'Would you mind doing the rest?' he added, before pushing what turned out to be a knife handle into my left hand.

I reached over and cut the strapping of my leash. My left buttock assumed its proper role on the chair. My right felt immediately relieved – and not particularly gangrenous.

'Why the mutual masturbation?' I asked, looking back at the bed, hoping they'd both manifested clothing.

They had.

Dumuz sighed. 'I am afraid you have discovered something about our kind that it would have been better for you not to know…'

I opened my mouth.

'…and it has nothing to do with what we have just been doing,' he added.

Beyond Dumuz, Eanna unplugged herself from my brother and sat up. She swayed drunkenly, her head almost falling back. I let my hackles fall – my mother wasn't at her best. Eanna forced herself up and fumbled at Kitten's tether.

'Are you talking about Izdubar turning me into a prune? That's one lesson I could have given a miss.'

Dumuz eyed the book on the bedside table. 'I imagine he read about it in that tome. As far as we know, this is the only copy left. Maybe we should have destroyed it years ago, but we always found a reason not to. While some of it is morally questionable, there are other bits I think you would find fascinating. For example, there is one chapter that details how mortals and ghosts can…'

Eanna sniggered. 'Dumuz, you're a *bad* boy.'

'Why?' I asked, confused.

'Dumuz was also in Haefen,' she said. 'At the hotel… *inside Nicolò*. He saw everything your boyfriend saw.'

I scowled at Dumuz, more angry than embarrassed. 'If you

were watching, you already know that our "make it up as you go" approach was working quite well. *Don't you dare say we still need an instruction manual!*

He wisely kept quiet.

Still sniffing in indignation, I looked at Eanna. She had Kitten on her lap, gently stroking his hair. My mother would never have done that to me.

The boy calmed down.

I bit back a snotty comment. Now wasn't the time to be churlish, and I would have been churlish.

'So, about the "masturbation thing"?' I asked them both.

Well, perhaps a bit churlish.

Dumuz kept his face straight. 'The intimacy you saw was necessary. The transfer of fluid takes its toll. Given the quantity needed, there was a danger that one of us might pass out…'

Eanna mimicked his expression. 'So, I suggested we try a touch of…Well, let's call it sensory stimulation.'

Straight became anything but as both of them broke down laughing.

Okay, I wasn't getting an apology, but there was still one thing. 'Why are you on this side of the bed and Eanna on the other?'

Dumuz swallowed, his giggles quickly suppressed. 'Eanna is Kitten's nearest relative. The closer the relationship, the greater the effect of the transference.'

My mother looked at me… not coldly, but the challenge was there.

Dumuz continued, 'In my case, I have only recently manifested. For a short period, my essence is universal. I knew it would work for you.'

I could have challenged the logic. Even after the most

cursory of considerations, it was obviously twaddle. But I like to think I have a certain grace – unlike the pair of wa… warren rabbits in front of me.

So, I let Dumuz talk.

I really shouldn't have.

'Yes, we escaped,' he said. 'And I am sure you want to know how,' he added, very much rhetorically. 'You see, while I know the book of the Wycche almost by rote, Izdubar only had it a few days. Despite your father's knowledge of transference, it appears he never made it to the chapter on possession. They took no special precautions when confining Nicolò. I…'

'What about Lilith?' I asked suddenly.

'What about her?'

'She was glass-tied? Tortured?'

'Yes.'

'What did Hammu do to her?' I wasn't sure I wanted to know.

Dumuz's eyes flared with anger. 'The large white-cloaked Fedhyow?'

I nodded.

'Let us just say that this *Hammu* enjoyed the hands-on aspects of his job.'

I winced.

Eanna wrinkled her nose. 'Lilith protected me.'

Because that is what my panther does, I thought. Or at least she tries to, in her peculiar, and only occasionally psychopathic, way.

'Lilith?' I asked quietly. 'Can you come out?'

Nothing.

'Please?'

Eanna's face hardened. 'She can't.'

'Why not?'

'Lilith told you it could happen. Maybe the final straw was the abuse she suffered down below,' Eanna said ambiguously. 'Or the nipple-twisting,' which was less so. 'I don't think the recent injuries have helped much, and her various "little deaths" in the lead-up weren't good for her either.'

I stared in shock – and not just because I'd witnessed Eanna at her insensitive best.

'She's gone?'

Dumuz clarified, 'No. Lilith can still talk, and, at least to some extent, act through Eanna. Physically, though, it seems likely they will remain in this form.'

Oh.

Eanna added, 'Still, I've always thought I had a better shape. Don't you? More womanly, you know? Of course, I guess some might prefer the Amazon type, especially when total mayhem is required. Unfortunately, I lack the physique for a serious session of slice and dice. My hands are built for smaller things.' She looked down at Dumuz's groin. 'Mostly.'

Again, not much empathy there, she… *Oh shit! Eanna was scared!* She knew that without Lilith, our chances of escape had turned from slight to almost mythical. The little girl still inside was afraid of what Izdubar would do if she were caught. Eanna was trying to be brave and to hide it in the only way she could. She was only pretending not to care. I imagine Eanna would have preferred it if Lilith was in front of me now rather than her.

And… so would I.

Still, grief, or whatever it might be called, was for later – if there was a later.

'I suspect,' I said calmly, 'Izdubar already knows you've escaped, so we don't have much time.'

Dumuz twitched, surprised at the change in topic. 'You…'

I glared at him. 'For once in your life, perhaps you could summarise? You did your newborn thing. Correct?'

He grunted.

Okay, good summary. I looked at Eanna. 'He freed you and…'

'Not quite,' Eanna interrupted. 'We were out cold when Dumuz found us. Glass-chained, strung up. Dumuz…'

'Been there. Done that,' I sniped back.

Eanna sniffed. 'Dumuz,' she repeated, 'woke us and suggested we should use my form. The clever darling reasoned that my dainty little paws would slip out of my cuffs and then… and then we couldn't change back.'

She hesitated. I knew what came next would be a lie.

'No matter,' she said.

Exactly.

'And then?' I asked.

'We came to collect Kitten… and you. We also picked up a few stragglers along the way.'

'Stragglers?'

Eanna smirked. 'We left Nicolò and Rosalind in the room below. Fortunate, really. If Nicolò had seen the state you were in, he might reconsider his love choices – again.'

I thought not… Still. 'After what happened to Tiama, they can't have made up?'

She snorted. 'Of course they have. Rosalind explained she was doing it for Tristan…'

Dumuz interrupted. '…And Nicolò understands what it means to be obligated to family.'

They both looked at me, wondering if I understood what Dumuz had just said... And I did, although I wish I didn't. We all knew that family, this time, didn't mean Hugo or Tiama.

I bit my tongue and said nothing. I had an accusation to make – just not one intended for Eanna or Dumuz.

Dumuz nodded, understanding my pain, acknowledging my silence for what it was.

Eanna didn't bother. 'So, anyway,' she said. 'Rosalind is most definitely with us – especially since we picked up her brother on the way up.' She smiled. 'Oh yeah. We also have a prisoner!'

'Prisoner?'

'Yes, and her baby. The mother's dressed differently than I remember from the bridge. The baby though? Well, the little dear's still wearing that unfortunate shade of pink.'

The aisle mother.

My stomach churned, but I had to ask. 'I imagine Izdubar's guards just nodded and let you pass... and that woman just let you tie her up?'

'Not so much,' Eanna said.

Dumuz spoke without inflection. 'I did what I had to do. There was a guard at the door on each level. I killed a guard on each level. It was the only way.'

Eanna rose from the bed. Her legs wobbled, but she kept her footing. Kitten slid onto the floor. To my surprise, the boy also remained vertical. He still grasped her hand, though, and she welcomed it.

Which again hurt more than it should.

Dumuz followed her lead and stood. 'We should say hello to your father, don't you think?'

315

'There's no other choice?' I asked, glancing at a random window.

'Choice? There is no…'

I interrupted. 'Just don't.'

Dumuz smiled. 'Even if we abandoned our still-living friends downstairs, the only other way out is a window. It is a *very* long drop though. Your shell would not survive the impact. Worse still, the transference has severely weakened the thing that binds us to this realm. Any mortal wound, even a fade, might break you free.'

'You're talking about the whole full-fat final death thing again, aren't you?'

The smile broadened. 'Yes.'

'Does wearing an amulet repair the damage?' I asked, studying the gold chain around his neck.

My neck was bare.

Dumuz's eyes tracked towards Eanna's chest – and lingered there. Her amulet set off her décolletage splendidly.

His eyes returned to mine, the grin still there. 'Eventually,' he said. 'But not in the short term.'

I sucked in a lungful of imaginary air. 'Okay,' I said. 'And just so I understand your plan. We first need to get past Izdubar and his men downstairs. After that, we have to escape an island swarming with Fedhyow, cross a body of water that is essentially acid and… then just hope they don't follow?'

'Yes,' he said.

I could see why Eanna was so afraid.

Dumuz took Kitten's hand from Eanna and walked through the doorway. The boy, trailing behind, had apparently recovered well enough to sing.

Tunelessly.

Eanna at first attempted to keep up, but then stopped. I watched, bewildered, as a recently-emptied hand tried to touch my damaged wrist – only to fail at the last moment to complete the move. My mother would never complete that move. Eanna smiled wanly. 'Are you coming? Nicolò is still downstairs. Do you want to leave him to Izdubar? Come to think of it, do you seriously want to leave him that long with his ex?'

CHAPTER TWENTY-FOUR

THE ROAD NOT TAKEN

I would like to say I bounded down the stairs from the bedroom, but I didn't. While I didn't, actually, slide down the steps one arse cheek at a time, it was a close-run thing. I was weak, tired, and more than a tad pissed off. To my surprise, though, I wasn't afraid. I had got past the whole frightened thing – and the need to describe every existential threat in oblique and florid metaphor.

Well, mostly.

We spilt out from the bottom of the stairs like a puddle of vomit. Dumuz and Kitten moved to the right of the throne, and Eanna and I to its left. The door guard was still there. He looked taller than before, but not by much. Perhaps it was because he was no longer sitting down. He wasn't exactly standing up, either. Not really. It was more like dangling. Forget petard. It was the spike of his own halberd that held him high. The entry wound in his throat was squeamishly ragged. Although the exit wound was smaller, there seemed little point in searching for his right eyeball. The tip of the weapon had embedded itself in the wood at the back

318

of the throne. Its shaft also seemed well fixed, driven as it was through the raised wooden floor into whatever existed beneath. The door guard dangled loosely, like the rotting corpse he was.

'Dumuz's work?' I asked my mother.

'No,' she said dryly. 'Although he helped Eanna with the flagpole aspects.'

'*Lilith?*'

Eanna's skin dimmed a little. 'I'm still here, you know. Shorter certainly, and with far too much hair, but I'm still here.' Her voice had a pleasing lack of melody. 'I'm also still the stabbiest fuck you'll ever see.'

The spring in my step returned, or at least some of it. I had an accusation to level, and Lilith knew it.

Eanna's skin lightened again.

Later then.

As we rounded the throne and entered the main hall, I encountered a few other things that toyed with my heart – some good, some not. Rosalind looked just like I remembered, or as I imagined, right down to her oil-matted hair. Nicolò was also worse for wear with a cut here and a bruise there. Still, he was vertical and looked pretty hot, wielding as he did a ginormous axe in his right hand. While his chopper made him look impressive, what made me tingle, and want to call him Nikka, was the distance he kept from Rosalind. Behind them, two infants lay on the throne seat, threatening to roll off. Amusingly, someone had used glass handcuffs to attach the aisle mother to a foot strut of the throne.

'Nikka,' I said.

'Siduri,' he replied. There was no need for words. Win, and we would come up with some way to make the relationship work. Lose? Well, then it wouldn't matter much, would it? Still, just looking into his eyes made me feel all…

A lump of phlegm hit my left calf.

I couldn't believe it. The aisle mother had spat on me. Again! And I was solid enough to feel it hit. Dumuz had said I mustn't fade. My sort-of-father-in-law could never understand the problems a girl has to face. I thought about returning the spittle-mouthed shrew's drool with interest. After my dicky tummy in the cell, I knew I could produce some serious ectoplasmic splatter, but what was the point? I could be magnanimous, but that also wouldn't happen. So, I went for smug. No doubt it would make her hate me more, but with our different loyalties, and the dead thing, we would never get along.

Dumuz and Kitten rounded their corner. Dumuz looked right and released Kitten immediately. For once, my brother showed some sense and moved towards the throne. Climbing it, he firmed further and secured the infants in their place. I glanced at the aisle mother. She looked grateful, but it wouldn't stop her from vaporising Kitten, given half a chance.

Dumuz snatched up a Fedhyow staff from the ground. At a guess, it once belonged to the Fedhyow now dangling behind the throne. I looked at the glass-topped head. The staff wasn't the safest weapon for our kind to wield. Still, Dumuz didn't appear particularly bothered. He winked at Eanna and turned to face our audience.

Who approached at quite a pace.

Gothic romances often stray into different genres to advance their plot. I can therefore say with a degree of armchair expertise that a chokepoint's purpose is to choke. The few and the brave use it to defend against the many. A many, who, admittedly, are equally brave but, with their numbers, just don't have the same drawbacks as the eponymous few. However, a chokepoint is only worthy of its name if the defenders use it to funnel an attack and avoid the outflank. Successfully employed, the many themselves become the few – as well as the more dead. If the defenders cannot wring the literal breath out of those attempting its passage, a chokepoint is just a gap, just like any other gap. Or it would be if you could still see it, which we couldn't. There were far too many in the way.

I imagine the door behind the approaching mass wouldn't have been there anyway – off its hinges, blown to smithereens, something serious. While Lilith liked to fly by the seat of her pants and Eanna without them, I was confident that Dumuz would have secured it somehow. Nicolò would know. I'd ask him, but we were about to be busy.

There were eleven of them in all. Well, twelve if you counted Izdubar, who kept well to the back. Or perhaps thirteen if you counted the aisle mother, which hopefully you couldn't. Hammu led them, and boy, did he look angry. So, five of us then, with a toddler as a backstop, facing twelve of the most bad. It didn't feel like it would end well. It certainly didn't start that way.

I'd forgotten the orbs. How could I forget about the glass orbs? They launched them in a volley just as I found my mark. It became more of a skid as I tried to duck out of the way. For all their training, it showed a lack of experience by 10 of them. I could tell because the larger of the remaining two seemed audibly disappointed. Judging by his Lilith-level language skills, Hammu was most definitely no longer Fedhyow. They'd thrown the orbs too early, giving me time to react. Not enough time, but you can't have everything. What I found appalling, though, was that they were all aimed at me. Not Eanna, not Dumuz. *Me!* I know she's prettier, and he's got a tad more gravitas, but come on! My face hit the parquet floor with more of a slap than I'd have liked. I wasn't going to make it. Dumuz said I mustn't fade. I...

While they were premature, Hammu had trained the throwers well. The orbs converged on a single spot and would have struck and dissolved everything they found – starting with my ever-so-slightly raised arse. Well, they would have, except for the one thing I hadn't thought possible.

Rosalind stepped in the way.

Really.

They all hit and broke short of their intended target. Rosalind didn't dissolve, but she did collapse in a spray of holy water, blood and glass. When she didn't move, I hoped, to my surprise, that Rosalind wasn't dead. For what must have been only moments, that hope was dashed – and then it was not. Suddenly, her chest heaved, and a pinkish air bubble grew out of her mouth. My traitor, my rival, my new best friend, exhaled. Yes, glass had lacerated her body, and yes, she was in shock, but she wasn't dead. My saviour wasn't dead, and I would forgive all her ill deeds.

But I still wanted a "sorry" first.

As I forced myself back to my feet, I winced. While Rosalind took most of the attack, the halo of spray that passed her by certainly hurt. I'd skipped the biology lesson that delved into the difference between scalds and the different classes of burn, but perhaps I shouldn't have. I guess it didn't matter in the short term or, looking at the numbers facing us, the long.

I stepped over Rosalind into the wet ground beyond. Thankfully, my boots didn't dissolve.

Ahead, Eanna was in a bit of a pickle. Surrounded by six false knights in a simplified clock, she pointed one arm outward as if to threaten and kept one back as if in defence. Both hands held knives. Each blade I knew would be sharp and their delivery deadly. It didn't seem to matter as the six closed in as one.

Kitten, to my right, leapt off the throne and ran towards Eanna. The boy was disciplined enough to ensure his two charges were secure, but that was as far as common sense went. He never reached her. Before he could find a toe to nip or a heel to tag, Izdubar stepped forward and scooped him up. Kitten screamed and kicked. I watched with fleeting pleasure as one blow connected with Izdubar's nethers. My father grimaced but then pulled the boy closer, denying him any future angle of attack.

Kitten didn't fade. Even if it was safe to do so, held in his father's arms as he was, I doubted he could.

Dumuz was also engaged. Hammu towered over him like... like Izdubar over Kitten. Even so, it was Dumuz that attacked. The swipe with his staff was short and, at first glance, ineffective. It surprised me that Dumuz could be so incompetent.

He wasn't.

The blow had hit its target, smashing its glass top – and the orbs attached to Hammu's bandolier. The big man screamed and countered. Dumuz wasn't incompetent, but he had overextended.

The mistake was almost fatal.

Dumuz couldn't recover his centre before Hammu's glass-channel sword scythed down. And hit. If human, I imagine the blade would have bit deeper into Dumuz's right shoulder, following the path of least resistance between the ball and joint. Instead, the blade pursued the stroke's natural arc through the wholly uniform material that makes up our kind.

A slice of incorporeal ham feathered onto the floor.

Dumuz grimaced as the hand on his staff lost its grip. He looked frustrated, even annoyed, as the weapon's weighted top fell to the ground. Although Dumuz's other hand dragged the staff back and out of range, it was clear any respite would be short.

Suddenly, a wall of white blocked my view. There were four of them. Taller than me, wider than me, and stinking of testosterone. Oh, and they wielded glass-channel swords against a knife that looked, in comparison, like a proverbial toothpick. I stepped back over Rosalind in an artless retreat and slid away – literally. The liquid coating the entire base of my right boot acted like oil. I threw my right arm forward and my left arm back for balance. The immediate downside was that my knife slipped out of my fingers. I heard rather than saw it clatter and skate backwards across the water-soaked floor. But I didn't tumble, though, which had to be an up. I felt almost joyous. The liquid would have dissolved any descending hand like acid.

I was even more pleased when four blades clattered against each other where that pretty little neck of mine had once been.

Nicolò swept in on their line like a skittle-ball. His axe bit into my rightmost opponent, separating his ribs with a crack and a sucking puff of air. The man went down screaming and sideways, smashing into the next, who hit the next, who hit the next. The resultant clump of humanity lay tangled and ruddy on the ground as blood from the man on top splattered and soaked. I regained my footing and pulled Nicolò away. Come wash-day, these guys would need an extra order of bleach.

Nicolò shook me off and attacked again.

Well, perhaps not these guys.

It seemed my darling woodsmith had some anger issues. After what their kind had done, I struggled to blame him.

Idle, for the moment, I looked for Dumuz.

Hammu had driven him back almost to the throne. Dumuz's right arm hung limply from a shoulder, too damaged to be of use. His left hand held his staff vertically, fingers wrapped around its middle. Dumuz deflected each thrust or cut that Hammu made rather than fully block it. If an attack was too strong for such parries, Dumuz avoided it with a backward step. There was no counter. With the throne now at Dumuz's heels, it seemed only seconds before the duel would come to its inevitable end.

Lilith doesn't do inevitable – even as Eanna. It appeared she saw a difference between a lack of choice and the inevitable. She also ignored the memo about the *don't fade* thing. Eanna formed behind Hammu and cut savagely at the tendons behind his right knee. Hammu seemed more confused than in pain as his leg folded on his next step. He went down *hard.* It would have been a mercy if Dumuz had brought down his staff on the back of Hammu's head, but he didn't. Instead, Dumuz merely watched as Eanna leapt onto Hammu's back and stabbed and stabbed and stabbed again.

She was screaming. She was elemental. She was Lilith.

Finally, eventually, Eanna stood. As Hammu's blood slipped from her form, she looked towards the throne and understood the one problem left. She then turned around and screamed again – this time in anguish. The problem wasn't with the six who had attacked her. They lay on the ground, a reconstructed clockface, each with a puncture wound to the back of the neck. The problem was with what was at its centre, the thing that had taken my mother's place.

Izdubar glanced at the corpses at his feet before meeting Eanna's gaze. 'It's been a while,' he said. Izdubar still held Kitten firmly. Alive, the boy would suffocate. This clock had no hands.

Eanna flipped one of the knives she held, caught the blade between her fingers, and *threw*.

Before Izdubar could properly turn and duck, the knife caught him in profile – its point entering his left cheek and exiting the right. He winced briefly, let go of Kitten with one hand and pulled the knife out. As the glass and steel left the wound, it began to heal.

Damn.

Izdubar placed the knife at Kitten's throat. 'You literally didn't miss me then,' he said with a snort. I hate when the teller ruins the pun, but there are worse things. Threatening Kitten was one of them.

Dumuz lifted his staff in one hand like a hammer.

'*Uh-Uh,*' Izdubar said as the blade he now held edged into my brother's neck. I watched, horrified, as the indentation became a cut.

'Let the boy go,' Dumuz said. If the mirrored walls could shake, they would have.

'Seriously?' Izdubar replied. 'You've killed ten of my... well, apparently, not very best. You've killed another who really should have been, and you expect me to let the boy go? I think not.'

'Take me instead,' I said, hardly believing I just had.

Izdubar laughed. 'I don't think so. I can get by with just one of my... mistakes.' He turned the knife slightly. Both Kitten and Eanna gasped. 'This one will be more malleable.'

Steeling myself, I stepped forward. 'You could have left with Kitten when it became obvious your men were losing. I know you're not a coward, but why are you still here? You want something else. I can tell.'

His forearm tensed, but the knife didn't dig deeper into Kitten's neck.

I was right.

'You can leave, or you can stay,' he said. 'If you stay, there will be another 10 and then another. There will always be more.' He smiled. 'You can take your mother when you go.' He looked snidely at Dumuz. 'And him.'

'Why should I leave?' I asked, reaching the edge of the circle. 'What is the point? You're not about to let Nicolò, Rosalind or the infant go. You're only allowing the dead to leave because you can't stop us.'

'True,' he confessed. 'So, you'll stay then? Really? You cannot win, you know. If you stay, you will die.' He smiled again. 'Truly die.'

I shook my head. 'Someone once told me there is no such thing as choice, but I disagree. I could say I have to stay, that I have no choice, but that would be wrong. The lack of choice comes after you decide, not before. In the before, there is always a choice. So, yes, I plan on staying for Nicolò, the children... even Rosalind.'

I bit my bottom lip. What I had to say next, I didn't want to say. 'Aren't you lonely, *Father*?' But I still said it though.

I continued. 'I'm lonely.' It wasn't even true. Not now, not with Nicolò.

I glanced at the mass of bloody crow bait at Dumuz's feet. 'You no longer have Hammu or even Hugo. You might not have been that close to either, but you had history with them. What do you have now?'

I looked over my shoulder at the aisle mother. 'You can do better than someone like her, you know. Don't you need someone to talk to? Even if you've tied them to a chair while you drain them of their vitality. You need an opponent, father. One you can beat every time, but you still need an opponent. We both know my brother cannot be that.'

I took a deep breath, knowing it was false. Rather than shout, though, the words that followed emerged as a *whisper*. 'I may not be as attractive as either of my mothers, but there is a family resemblance… and I'm still quite young.'

Izdubar's pupils spasmed. I didn't care whether it was in lust or revulsion. It was that they did that mattered. At that moment, he was no longer thinking of the present – it was all the time I would need.

I faded.

I moved.

It wasn't a hug. I couldn't hug this man, but I wrapped my arms around him – and didn't stop. When my chest met his, I did not stop. When my head touched his head, when my groin touched his groin, horribly, I did not stop. But that was my intent. At that moment, I was nothing, literally nothing. The moment was brief, fleeting, and it was enough.

Before he could react, before he even understood our bodies were one, I firmed. I solidified. I was no longer nothing.

I was granite.

Being the literal insider, I wasn't best placed to observe the subsequent explosion. At a guess, my companions also struggled to comprehend my first, last and greatest artwork while it was in motion. They were too busy reacting to its consequences. The mirrored walls, theoretically, might have managed a criticism or two before becoming part of the work. But that was only in metaphor. Because, while walls have ears... in this case, now literally two of them... they cannot, as far as I know, talk.

At some point, I must have closed my eyes because I found it difficult to open them again. Some visceral matter had fixed my eyelashes closed. I had to use my hands to prise them apart, which was painful. Not as painful, of course, as seeing and then *feeling* one of Izdubar's ribs sticking out of my chest.

'Fuck! That was spectacular!' Eanna said. The voice, though, was all Lilith. My mother was drenched in offal, but then again, so was everyone and everything else, and, oh, I really didn't feel well.

I staggered backwards before slipping and landing on my backside. The blood-coated surface of the floor might as well have been ice as I slid uncontrollably towards the throne. There must have been remnants of orb water mixed in there somewhere because I was losing ethereal skin from my buttocks, heels and elbows at an alarming rate.

I stopped a few feet from the throne, dazed by the pain. This felt bad. This felt *really* bad. My mouth filled with a semi-solid liquid that tasted of salt and iron. A fluid I knew couldn't be there. I...

The aisle mother stuck something into my back.

Nicolò was on her before she could pull it out again. Grabbing her hair, he dragged the aisle mother away. The resultant tug made me scream, and roll, and turn to see what Nicolò intended to do next. Nicolò held the aisle mother against the throne. I watched as he banged her head against the lip of its seat. I watched as he raised his axe. He…

'Stop!' I glugged.

Nicolò hesitated.

I spat a wad of something out. 'No,' I said.

The axe didn't fall, but neither did he let her go.

'No,' I repeated.

Even now, I couldn't be that cold – or hot, which was a surprise. I looked at the aisle mother's right wrist. It was bloody but free of restraint. Looking closer, I saw some glass remained embedded. It wouldn't make sense to pull it out. Not without the ability to plug the subsequent leak. I reached around and drew the thing that was in my back free. The pain was less than expected – recent events had forced me to recalibrate. I looked at what I held in my hand. It was always going to be a knife.

My knife.

There seemed little point in trying to rise – my peripheral vision was already filling with shadows. Instead, I looked ahead. The two infants writhed on the throne, griping no doubt about the blood and other ickiness. Together, they suddenly decided to roll. Even with her neck twisted, I watched in amazement as the aisle mother raised her left hand to push one…

…and then the other child to safety.

'She killed your sister,' I *whispered* again. This time I couldn't manage anything louder. 'You may not recognise her in this skin, but that woman still standing killed your sister. She butchered Hammu… and she will kill your child.'

I coughed, struggling to keep my throat clear. 'It would be a mercy if she took you first, of course, but know she will kill your child.'

The aisle mother didn't even gasp. Could she hear?

I continued, forcing out whatever breath I had left. 'But you have a choice. There is always a choice. You can help them escape. If you do, she might let your child live... She might even let you live.'

I rolled away from the woman and onto my back. To my dismay, it hurt even more. I would have turned again, but I was out of strength. As my universe closed in, I looked up at the sun. It turned out to be a bloody chandelier.

Wow!

Suddenly, a cloud blocked my view of the star. 'You know I cannot hurt the child,' the cloud hissed. Its voice sounded pleasantly gruff. 'Or the mother,' it added.

'I know,' I said. 'But she doesn't.'

I did not accuse. The thing that was once my heart wouldn't let me.

And then it went quiet.

And then it went dark.

Chapter twenty-five

The Thing That Is Not

I opened my eyes. This time the cold did not freeze, and the light did not blind. I'd become accustomed to both. The sudden weight of a cat was a new thing though. Although the subsequent kneading was pleasant, having a cat perched on my chest while dressed only in my skimpies was… somewhat unsettling.

'So, you're awake?' a voice said.

I ignored it.

The room was the same. Not the one in the house that burnt down. The other one. The bed felt the same, and the curtains just as faded. Even the sun that washed in from the garden entered at the same angle as before.

The bookshelf by the door was now empty, of course.

He tried again. 'There's something different about your hair? It was blue before. Well, a tuft anyway. It's now mauve, I think. Yes, mauve.'

'He's right,' Pollyanna said, extending her claws.

I sat up before she pricked a nipple. Stroking her warmly, I reached for the amulet that hung around her neck. 'Can I borrow this?' I asked.

Her left ear rotated quizzically.

'You can have it back later. I promise.'

Pollyanna stepped off my chest and onto a pillow nearby. Taking her action as permission, I unhooked the amulet. Sadly, my fingers weren't as awake as I thought. Both Pollyanna and the pillow landed in a heap on the floor.

'Sorry,' I said – not quite suppressing a giggle.

Pollyanna hissed briefly, but her heart wasn't in it. 'It's good to have you back,' she chirruped, before licking a paw. Dignity restored, Pollyanna turned and trotted out of the room. As she stepped into the hall, she added, 'Mauve? Isn't that a bit pastel?'

'True,' I replied. 'But it's better than grey.'

'What are you talking about?' the voice said, confused.

Of course. Pollyanna was *my* familiar. Adapa lacked the skills to hear.

He sat by the window.

'You survived then,' I said. 'When I last saw you, you were sinking beneath a wave of black.'

Twitching my nose in my best witchy fashion, I changed into my jacket and skirt. I then twitched again. With the angle Adapa had on the bed, I wanted to make sure I was wearing knickers.

Adapa scratched an arse cheek somewhere in the chair. 'Ah, lass,' he said. 'My poor head. They bashed me in the brainpan, they did. After that, I was dead to the world, or at least to them. They left me be. I only came around when it was all over.'

I said nothing.

Adapa frowned. 'So, what happened?' he asked. 'I missed the shenanigans on the lawn.'

Oh shit, he didn't know about Tiama. 'What did you do when you woke up?'

Adapa puffed, confused that I hadn't answered him. 'Being

I wasn't in any fit state, I kind of crawled away and found a bed to hide under.'

I tried to imagine that mass under a bed frame. 'And when the local watch turned up?' I asked.

Adapa snorted. The resultant mucus was worryingly red. 'They might have scared off the Fedhyow, but they weren't exactly professional. They set up a perimeter and left just one poor girl to guard the place overnight. Even she disappeared the next day. Pity, really. I could have done with the company. That girl was cute. She might have…'

'No,' I interrupted. 'I *really* don't think she would.'

Adapa winced. 'Yeah. You're probably right.' Rubbing his mouth and nose with an arm, he only managed to smear more bloody slime over his face.

'You stayed,' I said. 'You don't seem the sort to hang around and mope.'

He coughed. The resulting liquid that oozed from his mouth was more black than red.

'To be honest,' he said. 'I've not been at my best since my little "tête-à-bâton". So, I thought a day or five of rest might be in order. *What with you lot all disappearing and all!*'

He calmed. 'You know, dearie, with a big slab of gammon, a nice bottle of wine, that sort of thing. For a second home, Dumuz keeps this place well-stocked. Odd, really, what with him being on the dead side of things and all.'

'Dumuz told me they rented it out. I imagine what you found were leftovers.'

He sighed. 'I guess so. We never talked about what he was doing with this place.'

'Didn't you come on their visits? I thought it was a regular thing.'

'No. I stayed back to look after Kitten. Back then, he couldn't leave the island. But now, I…' Adapa's voice trailed off, his eyes full of regret.

'Where did you all go anyway?' he asked. 'Where's Kitten? The others? Um – where's Nicolò?'

I was wondering when he'd ask about his grandson.

'The Fedhyow took Kitten,' I said. 'We went to Guitt to get him back.'

'*What!*'

Spittle again landed on my shins. What was wrong with people? I looked down. It was vermillion.

'You don't seem well,' I said.

'To be honest, I'm not brilliant. In fact, you're looking sort of silvery right now. My legs stopped working a while ago. And my bladder? Unfortunately, that's still working.'

He squinted. 'Em… what happened on Guitt?'

I needed to be sure. 'You're dying?'

'Seems like it,' he said. 'Did Nicolò make it? Did he survive?'

'No,' I lied, or at least I hoped it was a lie. The flat tone of my voice belied the fluttering in my chest. True or not, I needed this conversation to go in a different direction.

'*Oh!*' he said.

'I wasn't there, but I imagine Lilith cut out his heart. With Hugo dead, the Fedhyow are probably having a few "what next" issues. I suspect Lilith, Dumuz and Kitten will return home to Marhasyow – hopefully, with what's left of Nicolò in tow.'

Adapa looked lost. 'Hugo's dead as well?'

'It was on the lawn. Hugo was about to kill Nicolò, so Tiama aerated the sod – and I don't mean the grass. She saved Nicolò, but…'

'But what?' he interrupted. From the slackness in his jaw, he already knew.

I let some emotion reach my mouth. 'The Fedhyow killed her... properly this time. Nicolò told me she was your daughter. I'm sorry.'

'Tiama sacrificed herself to save Nicolò – *and he died anyway?*' he said in a voice thick with self-pity.

I stayed quiet. Time would tell, but I hoped he would survive.

Instead, I pursed my lips and looked puzzled. I almost felt sorry for Adapa as he tried to pull himself together and hide what he had just exposed.

Almost.

He coughed again. The droplets came out like a spray of rust. 'It's lucky you woke up now,' he said. 'A few more hours and you'd be looking at a corpse.'

'Most people would be apprehensive about dying.'

'Yeah, well. Of course, it's something I've been putting off. I...'

'*With Nicolò's help,*' I said.

'*Ah...* you know about that.'

'I only worked it out recently. The thing I don't understand is why?'

'Why what?'

'Okay then, I'll try for "where". *Where, in any possible reality, do you think you have the right to drain your grandson of his very self?*'

'It's a cultural thing,' he said defensively. 'Our people...'

'Your people, not mine,' I snapped back. 'For pity's sake, teeth or not, you pretty much sucked out his blood!'

Adapa sniffed again. 'You must understand, I wasn't at my

best. A few months ago, this ominous cramping in my left arm and shoulder started up. I asked Lilith to…'

'*Procure Nicolò?*' I screamed, glad there was someone I could accuse other than her.

Adapa laughed. 'Don't be silly. Lilith would never… Oh dearie, you must know Lilith finds the whole thing abhorrent. We're talking about children here.'

'She didn't…' I couldn't finish. Something in my chest had just… *twitched.*

'No,' he said, squirming. 'All I asked her to do was sit on my face when my time came.'

'And cut out your heart?'

Adapa nodded his head… and farted.

'To be honest,' he said, wrinkling his nose, 'Lilith didn't really commit to the face thing, what with Dumuz being on the scene and all.'

The overwhelming smell brought back memories of the dungeon.

'Anyway,' he continued. 'Then, of course, Tiama and Nicolò arrived in Marhasyow. Even then, I only asked Lilith to watch over them.'

'And after she brought Nicolò to the castle?'

'Lass. I didn't know I'd be tempted. But when push came to shove, I found myself wanting to live a bit longer.'

'You said you were ready to die.'

'Then I had no choice.'

Git.

He continued. 'In my defence, I didn't try to stop Nicolò when he left with Frederick.' He screwed up his face. 'Of course, that was more to do with Tiama's browbeating than anything else.'

I squinted. The sun had shifted its angle slightly, no longer falling as before. 'I don't get it. Lilith was your wife, but that was a literal lifetime ago. There was at least one other woman. You've had at least one other child. Why did she rescue you from that jail in Aberfal?'

The sun was now behind his head. I tilted away. The man had lost his right to a halo a long time ago.

I added, still not sure I wanted an answer, 'And if Lilith loathed the idea, why did she let you take Nicolò's blood?'

'She didn't know what we were doing, at least initially. It was just between Nicolò and me. In the end... Well, Lilith cares for me.'

'Not good enough.'

He grimaced. 'Have it your own way then. Guilt... and the need for forgiveness.'

'Guilt?'

I watched in horror as Adapa bit down on his lower lip. When he opened his mouth, his teeth were a ruddy pink. He then clenched his right hand into a fist, his knuckles turning corpse white.

'Do you have a knife?' he hissed.

I stared at him.

Adapa shut his eyes tightly before opening them again. In between large gulps of air, he repeated, 'Dearie. Do you have a sharp knife?'

I reached into my jacket. It seems I did.

I drew it out and showed it to him. Lilith must have stuck it in there when I died... again. No doubt she thought she was being helpful.

Perhaps she was.

The puffing receded. 'Quid pro quo,' Adapa said. 'I'm

dying. It'll be fast or slow, but I'm dying. Fast, and there's a chance I might make it to the beyond. I'll tell you about Lilith and why she feels guilty… but only if you promise to use the knife afterwards.'

'*You want me to kill you and take your heart?*' Was this really where I had wanted the conversation to go?

Adapa pulled open his shirt. Hanging between two massive man-breasts was an amulet.

'It's my only option left,' he said. 'Of course, it would be helpful if it came as a surprise.'

I imagine anyone would be squeamish.

Could I?

'One more thing,' he said.

'Yes?' I asked, making sure it sounded like a question. Could I do it? I honestly didn't know.

He smiled, still probably misinterpreting the "yes". 'Will you sit on my lap while I tell you the story?'

I snorted. 'Not a chance, but I will come closer.'

Pushing myself off the bed, I walked over to where he sat and lowered myself onto my knees in front of him.

Adapa raised an eyebrow whimsically. The man still had strength enough to daydream. 'Anyway,' he said. 'I think it's about time you knew the real story about the miller and his wife. Em… Did you ever ask Lilith how she wound up in Marhasyow?'

I shook my head.

'Ah… I was hoping… Oh well, never mind. Anyway, I was born on the island where Marhasyow Castle now stands… stood. My family owned a grain mill there, which was also our home. I inherited that mill and another on the mouth of the Koner – a wool mill. Next to the wool mill was a small dock, a warehouse and a riverbank's worth of sheep pens.

'*Two mills,*' he added. 'History does so like to conflate.'

'I already know,' I said.

'Do you?' He looked lost.

Oh, for crying out loud. 'But I don't know how Lilith got there.'

Adapa recovered, grinning bloodily. 'Oh, okay then. You see, there was this cargo boat heading along the coast to Marhasyow. It had a brush with some rocks... I think you can guess where. Despite that, it still almost reached the harbour. Almost. Unfortunately, the boat sank just as it rounded the island. Everyone drowned. Very sad.'

He arched an eyebrow. 'Did you know most sailors can't swim?'

'What on earth are you drooling on about?' He really was. Pink foam slid down his chin, peppered with bits of black.

'But Lilith could,' he continued, ignoring me. 'So, I guess not everyone drowned after all. Of course, she wasn't a sailor, which probably explains it.'

I gave up. 'You're saying Lilith was a passenger?'

'More like a stowaway.'

'Okay. Why was Lilith a stowaway on the cargo ship?'

'She always refused to say.'

'*Seriously?*'

'Seriously. Now, where was I? Oh yes. I pulled her the last few feet out of the water, got her home, and gave her some dry clothes. I did get the idea she was on the run, though.'

'Why?'

'She didn't want anyone to know how she'd ended up in Marhasyow.'

I stared in disbelief.

'We all have our secrets,' he said. 'Actually, perhaps she'll tell you when she visits in the spring.'

Perhaps. Hopefully, we'd got past the need for half-truths and lies.

'Anyway,' he continued. 'Lilith wore an amulet, which made her almost kin back in the day. She also had a certain book with her, which made her most definitely not.'

'The book of the Wycche?'

'Never thought much of the title, but yes. I'd never seen the like before – and before you ask, she wouldn't say where she got it. To be honest, it wasn't the sort of thing the Wycche wrote down – we were too embarrassed.'

'*Embarrassed!* The Wycche abused their own children. Killed them, even. Embarrassed can't be the right word.'

'Deaths were always rare and even rarer by my time. Believe it or not, we were becoming civilised. In another generation, it would likely have stopped altogether.'

'*You said it was cultural!*'

'Yeah… I fibbed a bit there. I guess it comes down to perspective. When the opportunity with Nicolò came about, my perspective was that I wanted to live.'

Adapa paused to look out the window. In profile, his chubby face looked peculiarly white.

He turned back. 'Nicolò was willing, you know. At least at the time. Do you really think I shouldn't have done it?'

'You're quite the piece of work. *No!* And Lilith shouldn't have let you.'

He smiled in reflection. 'The Lilith who washed up on the beach that morning wouldn't have. The guilt thing only came later.'

'*When?*'

He looked down at the knife. 'We can cut to the chase if you want? In fact, I'd prefer it that way. It's not a story I want to tell. If I must, though, and these are my last living words, it's going to be done proper.'

I said nothing.

He nodded his head – and winced. 'Okay then. So, I offered her a job. Cook, clean, polish, whatever came to mind. I expected her to move on eventually. But to my surprise, she stayed.'

I raised an eyebrow. 'By *polish*, do you mean… candlesticks?'

Adapa looked disappointed. 'It wasn't like that. Lilith wasn't obligated or indentured. In fact, I was the captivated one, not her. Unusually, at least for me, I didn't even try to feel her up. You could almost say I courted her. Did she return my affection? Well, to my amazement, she did – although I suspect her commitment was never total. Indeed, it was a surprise when she agreed to marry me.'

'She wanted a child,' I summarised.

He sniffed. 'That's what got me into Lilith's nightdress. Yes.'

'*Nightdress?*'

'Lilith wasn't the ballsy tomboy you know now. A proper lady she was – elegant. Well… at least until she opened her mouth.' Adapa glanced at the material more or less covering my thighs. 'She never did like skirts though.'

He grimaced. 'Anyway, and far too quickly, Lilith became pregnant. After that, she wasn't in the mood for anything filthy… apart from the occasional candlestick.'

I tried not to think of Eanna and Dumuz on Izdubar's bed.

Adapa didn't help. 'Speaking of hand-jobs,' he said. 'Just after our boy, Dara, was born, those wankers turned up at my door, offering to buy the wool mill. Unfortunately, I didn't realise how uppity they'd get when I refused to sell until it was too late. Far too late. They dragged me outside and beat me shitless.'

He sniffed, distracted. 'Which, given what I'm sitting in…' His voice trailed off, and he shook his head. A shower of semi-congealed blood splattered onto the floorboards.

And my face.

'Where was I?' he said. 'Oh yes. They beat me senseless as well.'

'But…'

Adapa interrupted. 'There was no negotiation, just the kicking and the robbery.'

'Robbery?'

'I only found out later, but while I was out cold, they broke into the house and took anything interesting they could find… including Lilith's book… and her body.'

'They raped her?' I asked, my eyes wet with tears.

So were his. 'Multiple times. When I woke up, my house, the grain mill, was on fire. Lilith was inside screaming… Dara was silent.'

I couldn't speak.

Adapa lifted his left arm into the air. Discoloured ridges ran down the back of his forearm and hand. 'I tried to get in,' he said. 'But I couldn't break down the door. I smashed the window, but I was far too big to get through the frame.'

He looked down at his belly. 'Even then.'

Adapa grimaced. 'It was the last time I saw Lilith alive. I remember her lying there, her legs trapped under the millstone. Dara was in his cot on the other side of the room. Lilith… Lilith was trying to pick up a piece of glass, but she couldn't grip it. I… I knew what she wanted to do. I wish I didn't, but I did.'

He took a breath and continued, 'Hanging from the belt of my fat-arse trousers was, of all things, a set of sheep-shears. I forced one edge of the shears into the window frame and broke the other edge free. I threw it to her, and I... I pulled away.'

His face resembled wallpaper paste. 'Lilith stopped screaming.'

Adapa sniffed huffily, reclaiming some crimson gunge. 'I thought Lilith was dead, proper dead, with no chance of an encore. *I couldn't imagine anyone cutting out their own heart.*'

He puffed. 'But Lilith did. Although I didn't find out until years later.'

I found my voice. 'Did you kill the miners... in revenge?'

'No. Much to my shame.' He eyed me guiltily. 'If I had, the results might have been more proportionate, but I didn't, and the mostly innocent died just as quickly as the bad.'

He snorted. 'Of course, the reaction of those in power was predictable. They didn't touch my wool mill. They just turned it into the harbour master's office for their newly-purloined, dredged, and expanded port. Bastards.'

'So, it was the farmers that killed them?' I asked. 'For what? A loss of revenue? Revenge? They couldn't have been that desperate – and I can't believe you were exactly well-loved.'

Adapa didn't take offence. 'Dearie, you're missing the bigger picture. Haven't you figured it out yet? No one killed them. Well, no one living.'

'*Lilith?*'

'Who else? Lilith manifested. She killed and kept on killing. It wasn't the Lilith I knew or even the Lilith you know now. There wasn't much of her left, not really. But what there was knew how to use a blade.'

'She went mad?'

'Is a storm mad? She killed the miners. She killed many more afterwards. Then, years later, she killed someone who had particularly profited. The one who'd now had her book.'

Dumuz's father.

'Why did she stop the first time?' I asked… and then I realised. *'Oh shit, it was you!'*

He pulled a disgusted face. 'Yeah. Well. I suspect that'll be my line in a moment. The numbness in my legs appears to have reached my hips.'

He refocused. 'I never told you about Tiama's mother, Kaya.'

'Your one-night stand has a name? I'm surprised you remember it.' The man's mind was wandering.

'Another fib, I'm afraid,' he said. 'Kaya and I grew up together in Marhasyow. We even dated for a while.'

Adapa sighed. 'It could have become something, but it didn't. Not then. Kaya moved to Aberfal before things got serious.'

'So, you know what it feels like to be ditched?' I sniped.

He eyed me sharply. The skin beneath them had turned blue.

A bit like my mood.

'I couldn't face a search for Lilith's remains,' he said. 'In fact, I didn't even wait for the building to cool. I left Marhasyow – or ran away if you prefer.'

I did.

He smiled sadly. 'Still, it proved to be one of my better decisions, given what happened to the Wycche.'

'And after that?'

'I travelled. I even passed through Sulis. It would be nice to think I did it for cultural enlightenment, but I'm afraid

Sulis was just another stop on my "drink to forget" tour. I reinvented myself as an itinerant bouncer – a tavern guard who took his pay in liquid currency.'

'You were a doorman?' I asked, thinking of Hammu.

He looked down at himself. 'Back then, I could pass myself off as a muscular thug with anger issues. Of course, in the beginning, when push turned to shove turned to a glassing, I had the crap kicked out of me.'

He shuddered. 'Not a prerequisite I require now.'

Sniffing again, he added, 'But eventually, after the first few beatings, I learnt a few tricks.'

Adapa pursed his lips. 'My travels finally took me to Aberfal, where I met Kaya again. We weren't in love, not really, but we were both alone, and the result that was Tiama was inevitable.'

He paused. 'You know,' he said. 'All pretence aside. I haven't had an erection for years. My winkle really is a winkle. I don't suppose… well… new friends as we are, you might give me one last…'

I interrupted. 'Too much information. And again, *No!*'

Adapa took a deep breath. 'Okay then,' he said. 'No more delays. We decided to return to Marhasyow. Although I don't really mean "we". Kaya was against the idea. We travelled by road. Describing it as arduous doesn't, er, describe it.'

Another breath.

'It was just unfortunate that we met Lilith in the black of night just outside Marhasyow.'

Oh.

'Of course,' he continued. 'It wasn't Lilith. Not really. She didn't even remember me, at least not then. Lilith had no idea who I was when she gutted Kaya with a knife – the same makeshift one she'd used to cut out her own heart.'

'*No!*' I hissed.

'Yes,' he replied. Adapa sucked in more air. 'I didn't try to defend myself when Lilith came at me. I… What stopped her was Tiama. Tiama cried. She bawled, she screamed, and Lilith stopped.'

'And then?'

He sighed. 'Lilith vanished – dissipated. There were no more killings after that. You asked why she owed me? Why, when years later, Lilith finally understood what she had done, she felt guilty. Killing Kaya without cause is why.'

Shit.

Still, there was one last thing. 'Why did she stop? Why did she give up and disappear?' I asked, feeling drained.

His eyes remained on mine. 'Lilith would deny it now, but you already know the answer.'

The Lilith from before, the one who was not also Eanna, made a choice. After killing the mother of a child and seeing the consequence, Lilith chose to stop. She chose to be different from what she once was.

And now, so had I.

My left hand, the one that held the knife, twitched. 'Why did you abandon Tiama?' I asked.

Adapa tried not to look. 'I am not a good man, just not a worse one. I was a drunk, well on the career path to maudlin. Back then, the orphanage seemed the better option.'

'An option that didn't work out.'

'Not for her.' Adapa turned his head to face the sun. 'But if Tiama hadn't followed that path, Nicolò wouldn't exist. Can you honestly say your life would have been anywhere near as complete without him?'

'No.'

347

Adapa snickered wickedly. 'Mine certainly wouldn't have been as long.'

'You truly are a despicable example of humanity,' I said, but there was no anger in it.

'Dearie, the universe can be infinitely variable if you allow it.' He smiled. 'Lilith told me that many years ago.'

I felt numb and sat up, lifting my, well, apparently still-tender buttocks from my heels. The numbness, though, wasn't just physical.

'If I just let you die,' I said. 'What would be the loss?'

Adapa remained fixated on the sun. 'Then I would be a failed possibility – although not a significant one, I grant you.'

I rose and moved closer, placing the knife's tip just below the amulet on his chest. Adapa didn't flinch, but it wasn't a complete surprise when I felt a hand slide between my thighs. 'The Geas that Lilith cast when I was a little girl. She used that phrase.'

'Ah, yes, the letter. There was more in it, of course. It talked about hope. Back then, although Lilith thought she had no choice, she still had hope.' He hesitated before speaking again. 'Of course, Eanna…'

It wasn't my left hand that drove the knife deep and hard and fast.

It was me.

'You can tell me in the spring,' I said, offering a kind of forgiveness.

I might even be ready to hear.

Adapa turned his head in spasm… or perhaps he just wanted me to see. There was pain, of course, as the irises flared to black. But beyond that darkness, I think I saw amusement.

And then I saw nothing.

Chapter twenty-six

Ash

I dreamt of a fire. I did! There were flames, I remember, and ash, and finally dust. But now I am awake, now that I am truly awake, I remember nothing else.

I rubbed the box in my jacket pocket, a box with one less match. The view of the bedroom window from the garden wasn't as impressive as the one looking out – but I did not care. It might have been because of the smashed glass and seared window frame, but I believe it was more than that. I was a queen who no longer needed her castle.

Or boots.

The sandals I now wore felt fine – a compromise between risk and reward.

The local watch arrived swiftly and put the fire in the bedroom quickly out. Too late for Adapa, of course, but the house survived. Hopefully, it was still too late to identify how the old goat had died. I imagine the resultant heap of fat and bone was pretty gross, but I didn't think Adapa would mind. If Adapa still had a mind, if I hadn't completely messed it up.

The watch left almost as quickly as they arrived. This time, they didn't bother to post a guard. I'd soaked Adapa's corpse in Dumuz's best brandy before setting it alight. When the watch noticed the empty bottles, they'd reached the only logical conclusion. Adapa was just a vagrant who'd set himself on fire by accident. He was also, likely, the same pitiful soul who caused the previous incident.

At least there's much less paperwork if you write it that way.

Pollyanna curled around my left leg, giving my exposed toes a wet nose of approval. I liked Pollyanna. She told it as it was. She certainly did after seeing what fire had done to her bed. Still, I needed that right now. Pollyanna would keep me grounded. If I ever got up my own arse again, my new best friend would tell me to go lick it.

Suddenly, I heard a voice behind me, from the ha-ha of all places, but I didn't feel scared. I would never be afraid again. I turned and saw Nicolò dusting himself off, walking towards me. Next to him strode Rosalind with an infant in a papoose around her gut. Nicolò looked happy, Rosalind less so. Dumuz, it seemed, had found a new tenant.

Nicolò carried a book under his right arm. Despite his distance, I could see the book's binding was worn. I fingered the box of matches in my pocket and imagined the book in flames. Lilith, and it could only be her, had given me a choice.

Bitch… But my non-heart felt swelled with hope at what that might imply.

Still, that was for later. Spring, even. For now, though, I raised a hand and waved. In response, my Nikka broke into a run.

I watched as Nicolò drew near. It seemed Dumuz was right. There was at least one chapter I should read.

Acknowledgments

Siduri may have taken a long time to write, but it always featured the same cat, Pollyanna. Pollyanna wasn't the only reason I kept going, or even the main reason, but I so wanted to get some of her personality onto the page.

So, thank you Polly – you mad little minx!

Once I'd finished the novel, I sought some expert advice before trying to publish it. Every author hopes to be showered with plaudits and acclaim. When Bryony Pearce (a wonderful writer) didn't exactly do that, she did the hard part – she told me precisely and kindly where I'd gone wrong and how to fix it. If haven't followed all her advice, that's my bad, not hers.

So, thank you Bryony.

Of course, then there's my partner K. K was there each time I gave up. K was there to say, 'I don't understand'. K read *Siduri* on at least three occasions and each time offered encouragement – before following it up with page after page of comments.

So, finally, and although I now suffer from RSI, I'd like to thank my K.

J J

AUTHOR BIOGRAPHY

J J Vason was born and educated in Edinburgh, Scotland, before relocating to England's New Forest with JJ's partner and forever-hungry cat.

To discover more about Siduri's world,
check out https://jjvason.com.